PREY

BY THE SAME AUTHOR

How the Dice Fell
Walking Alone
Trial Balance

JOHN ROBERTS

PREY

Copyright © 2018 John Roberts

The moral right of the author has been asserted.

Apart from any fair dealing for the purposes of research or private study, or criticism or review, as permitted under the Copyright, Designs and Patents Act 1988, this publication may only be reproduced, stored or transmitted, in any form or by any means, with the prior permission in writing of the publishers, or in the case of reprographic reproduction in accordance with the terms of licences issued by the Copyright Licensing Agency. Enquiries concerning reproduction outside those terms should be sent to the publishers.

This is a work of fiction. Names, characters, businesses, places, events and incidents are either the products of the author's imagination or used in a fictitious manner. Any resemblance to actual persons, living or dead, or actual events is purely coincidental.

Matador
9 Priory Business Park,
Wistow Road, Kibworth Beauchamp,
Leicestershire. LE8 0RX
Tel: 0116 279 2299
Email: books@troubador.co.uk
Web: www.troubador.co.uk/matador
Twitter: @matadorbooks

ISBN 978 1789013 689

British Library Cataloguing in Publication Data.
A catalogue record for this book is available from the British Library.

Printed and bound in the UK by TJ International, Padstow, Cornwall
Typeset in 11pt Aldine401 BT by Troubador Publishing Ltd, Leicester, UK

Matador is an imprint of Troubador Publishing Ltd

*To Jan,
my helpmate and first reader*

PART ONE

HATCHING

1.
1st June

Faysal Samara shoved the fifth heavy wooden tray of bread onto the racks in his van. Slowly he straightened up, his hands at the small of his back, flexing his spine, pushing his shoulders back. He took deep breaths of the cool pre-dawn air. Any exertion these days and he was breathless, panting. He waited for his heart to slow, leaning against the side of his rusty Toyota van with *Faysal Samara, Amman, Jordan, Baker* in English and Arabic, in faded yellow paint over the red bodywork.

At times like this he wondered if his wife, Baheera, was right. She pleaded with him to stop work at the bakery he had set up fifty years ago. But he was the boss; he had to carry on, be around, make sure standards didn't drop even if, for the last two years, he had only done the deliveries. He could now start at five in the morning instead of four and, though he would never admit it, he relished that extra hour in bed. And he liked to chat with his customers.

But he loved this time when the smells of thyme and his own warm bread swaddled him against the dawn chill, before the city was loud and full of petrol fumes, before the spice stall next door opened, before the camel bags were put on display for the tourists, before the streets were crowded.

Stooping, he stepped back into his bakery where his elder son Latif and his nephew now did the sweaty work, shaping the flatbreads and baking them in the traditional fashion on hot ceramic stones. Latif was placing dough loaves into the oven with the long-handled round paddle. Faysal carried out the final tray: a selection of breads, sesame seed buns, *ka'ek* loaves and *mamoul* filled with dates, walnuts and pistachios. This was his first delivery on his regular daily route to the British Embassy. It was a long time since the slight, polite, dark-skinned, Arabic-speaking Englishman in a linen suit, wandering through the souk, had stopped at his bakery to drink mint tea and eat *ka'ek* with eggs, cheese and *zaatar*. It was too dangerous for him to come now. Faysal had to deliver so the British could eat safely behind their high walls topped with razor wire, beyond the armed guards at the iron gates. Everything had changed. For the worse.

With an effort he slid the van door shut and was about to get into the driver's seat when hard steel rammed against his temple and a soft voice said, "Do as I say, old man, and no harm will come to you."

Faysal turned his head a little and saw a balaclavaed head, dark eyes blazing at him through the eyeholes, and a finger over the mouth.

"We need to borrow you and your van for fifteen minutes. Stay quiet and get in."

Terrified, Faysal got in. The man went round the front and got into the passenger seat. Faysal felt the hard pistol barrel held just below his fevered heart, saw his hands trembling on the steering wheel.

"Third left," said the man. "Normal speed."

Faysal switched on the ignition, drove forward, then turned into the narrow unpaved road.

"Pull up next to that car on the right, with your sliding door next to the boot. Keep the engine running."

Faysal obeyed, put on the handbrake and looked straight ahead. There was no one about, just a dog nosing among the rubbish.

"Your first delivery is to the British Embassy," said the man in the passenger seat. "Listen carefully. You will drive there now and stop outside the gates as usual. But you will not be delivering bread. We will be delivering our gift to them."

In his wing mirror, out of the corner of his eye, Faysal saw two men, also wearing balaclavas, get out of the estate car. Beneath a covering of sand and dust, the car was dark green. One opened the sliding door of Faysal's van, the other the boot of the car. Then together they lifted a shape wrapped in cloth – the wrong shape for a bomb, too long and sagging in the middle, registered a horrified Faysal – and laid it on the floor of the van. The men climbed in and slammed the door shut.

"When you stop," said the passenger, "my friends in the back will open the door and roll out our gift. As soon as I say, you will drive off, fast."

In a cold sweat, Faysal forced himself to concentrate.

"If all goes well, five minutes later you will drop us off where I tell you and you will be free. Perhaps to go back and deliver your breads and tell the Embassy men of the green car. And to tell your friends." The man laughed. "Now drive, as normal."

There was no traffic, only a donkey cart. Faysal turned into Ar Radwan. His heart had slowed, his hands were almost steady. A drop of salty sweat dripped into his left eye. He drove past the curved, high white walls of the embassy. It was his usual time, maybe two minutes late. He stopped at the gate and saw one of the two armed guards come to unlock it. A kitchen boy was waiting behind him to receive the tray of bread. Then the van door slid open, the shape was pushed out and Faysal saw in his wing mirror that it rolled over on the tarmac. With a shock, he saw an unwrapped bearded head at one end hit the kerb.

"Go!" said the passenger, the sliding door still open.

Faysal accelerated away.

"Slow down. No need to race."

Five instructions later, cornering to left and right in the old town, el-Balad, he was told to stop.

"Thank you, old man, praise be to Allah. You will never forget you were in at the beginning."

The passenger thrust a small purse onto Faysal's lap, the three men got out and Faysal watched them run away and disappear around a corner. That was when he started to tremble. He closed his eyes and thanked Allah he was still alive. He thought suddenly of his second son Rafeeq, who had left to fight jihad in Syria against Bashar al-Assad. Was this anything to do with that stupid, hot-headed, misguided son of his who had broken Baheera's heart?

Six hours later there was a small plate of dates with four date stones on the low table in front of Faysal. His wife was pouring him another cup of mint tea and repeating that this was a sign from Allah that he must finally retire. Faysal just nodded and chewed.

Two kilometres away across the city, another plate of dates, untouched, no stones, lay on the scuffed top of a desk in the safe room in the basement of the British Embassy. This was a room built within a room, a bubble isolated from any listening devices that the host country, Jordan, might have installed. Its plastered breeze-block walls were bare.

By the door stood SAS Sergeant Craig Bradshaw, at ease but alert, hands clasped behind his back, sunburnt muscular arms revealed by his rolled-up shirtsleeves, a Browning semi-automatic pistol in its unbuttoned black holster. He was not looking at the other two men in the room but he could see them, feel the tension between them. Beneath the bright light in its white plastic shade, they sat, silent as if in a vacuum, air sucked out. On the desk was a tape recorder, its red recording light on, the black flex snaking across the concrete floor to the socket in the wall.

Also on the desk was a brass hornbill-spouted coffee pot

and two small handleless cups. The cup in front of the man whose hands were manacled was still full of coffee. He sat, upright in his straight-backed wooden chair, his hands in his lap. On the opposite side of the desk, in a captain's chair, sat the MI6 head of station, Davoud Nariman. His chair had rounded arms on which he was resting his elbows, his hands in front of him steepled, the tips of his fingers touching his lips. He was a slightly built man, his small head narrowing towards his chin so that it was almost triangular. His fine black hair fell over his forehead, but his neatly trimmed beard and moustache were flecked with grey. Over his half-moon rimless reading glasses, his brown eyes were looking across and slightly upwards at the manacled man's face.

"You are Suleiman al-Hariri," said Davoud quietly in Arabic.

The man looked back at him and said nothing. The clothes in which he arrived had been washed and returned to him. He sat now in his white kurta, embroidered with a thin strip of gold thread each side of the four black wooden buttons down his chest; black wooden cufflinks held his sleeves neatly in place above his manacles. His trousers were loose-fitting white salwars, and his bare feet were in sandals.

The guards had hurriedly carried him in from the gate. Davoud, one of the MI6 analysts and the ambassador had identified him. They had been jubilant – a gift from God, they had laughed. Immediate encrypted messages to Thames House. When he came out of his drugged state, they had given him water to wash, food to eat. Through the peephole in the embassy's only cell, they had watched him kneel and pray. He had said nothing, not even asked for the Qur'an.

From a beige folder Davoud took four A4 photographs and placed them in front of the man. They were photographs of the man, but he didn't even glance at them. Davoud leaned back in his chair and took a sip of his coffee. He tasted the cardamom. In the bare room the smell of coffee was sharp.

"We know you are one of the leaders of Al-Qaeda," continued Davoud.

Was there a momentary trace of a smile on the man's face? He had dark skin, a full beard and a moustache, ebony eyes. Davoud recognised the type: the man had exactly the same sense of entitlement and superiority as the Eton alumni who were Davoud's bosses back in Whitehall, the same self-confidence as Her Majesty's ambassadors he had met in his various postings.

"What we are interested in is: who brought you here. Who betrayed you?"

A pause.

"Perhaps you don't know."

Craig Bradshaw, listening but impassive, knew who was controlling this interview. Two Arabs, both Muslims: one of ours and one of theirs. And ours was getting nowhere. He looked at both their hands: neither had ever done a proper day's work. Nails trimmed and uncracked, half-moon cuticles visible; their soft-skinned fingers had turned pages and tapped at keyboards, never dug earth or shifted stones.

Davoud took off his glasses and stroked the corner of his eye. "This evening you will begin your journey to London," he said. "There you will be charged with acts of terrorism against British citizens and conspiracy to murder: the bombings in Mumbai, the attacks on the Ritz-Carlton hotels in Jakarta, the Marriott hotel in Islamabad. Two hundred and twenty-nine innocent people killed."

The man looked steadily at him, impassive.

"And that you planned the suicide attack on the Shia Jamia Mosque in Zahedan in the Baluchistan province of Iran last year in which nine people were killed."

He paused again, cleared his throat. "Including my mother and sister, who were visiting our family."

Davoud thought he heard a single clink of the manacles. He saw the man's head tip slightly to one side, his eyelids hooded but his eyes still drilling into him, a twitch of the lips. Not totally impervious, then.

I have no faith any more, Davoud wanted to tell the man. *When my mother and sister were murdered, my father became even more devout, accepting the will of Allah. But I have become what you hate: an apostate.*

In that poised moment, Davoud knew the man acknowledged a balance: an equal hatred and contempt for each other. But nothing visible. Belief matched unbelief.

Davoud selected a date and chewed it, licked his sticky fingers.

Decisions had been made quickly. Someone knew Suleiman was here, and that someone was not peaceable. It had all been agreed with the Jordanian authorities: the embassy had a very sick man who must return to the UK. The man would be taken back to his cell and drugged. Then he would be lifted onto a hospital trolley. Doubtless there would be foreign eyes, friend as well as foe, watching from rooftops and windows as two soldiers in medical uniforms wheeled the trolley, complete with drips, through the embassy gardens to the football pitch next to it. A helicopter would land, a stretcher would be loaded in. In less than two hours the helicopter would land at RAF Akrotiri in Cyprus. From there this gold-standard windfall would be flown by military transport to RAF Northolt near Uxbridge in West London and then taken across London to Belmarsh high-security prison at Thamesmead.

Davoud switched off the useless tape recorder. "Take him away," he said to the soldier.

Craig took his pistol from his black holster and went to hold the man's arm. But the man shook him off and stood up in his own time. Davoud heard his sandals slap across the concrete floor, the tread of the soldier's boots, and watched the door close behind them. He thought of his mother and sister, whose bodies had been blown to pieces; of the woman suicide bomber who had been sent to kill the worshippers; of how man's apparent need for something spiritual, beyond this world, could be exploited by the cruel lunacy of religion; of his old father praying in his Kensington apartment to the same God Suleiman prayed to.

Davoud gathered up the photographs.

Where had Suleiman come from? Who had captured him and delivered him to them? And why?

Davoud drew in a deep breath and let it out in a long sigh. He stood up and pushed back the chair. Questions to answer. He must investigate Suleiman; he would be summoned to London to report.

He took two dates from the plate, tasted their tacky sweetness and left the basement safe room. Upstairs, beyond the air-conditioned corridors, he entered the embassy gardens. He needed the sun's warmth, the scent of the bougainvillaea.

Soon he would no longer live with his daughter. Every moment with her was now acutely painful: her laughter, her curiosity and her hugs cut through him like a knife. And of his mother and sister, he had only photographs. He closed his eyes and lifted his face to the sun.

Upstairs in the silent apartment, his guitar lay on his bed. Missing his daughter's voice, he could find solace in his music, even hope – and sometimes answers.

2.
9TH JUNE

The huge steel gates in the outer security wall of the US Embassy in Sana'a were electronically bolted shut. But the small pedestrian gate was open, a Yemeni policeman beside it, uniformed and helmeted, cradling an automatic rifle. Six women, all dressed in black niqabs, were queuing there, one holding the hand of a little boy. Yusuf had not anticipated the queue. He was lying on the roof of a house opposite, his elbows on the dusty concrete, the butt of his AK-47 snugly at his shoulder, his left hand steadying the barrel, the forefinger of his right hand curled by the trigger but not on it. His watch, propped on a stone in front of him, showed 0914. One minute to go. The queue did not move. The child had let go his mother's hand and was kicking small stones against the wall with his sandaled foot.

Sweat trickled into Yusuf's left eye. His right was focusing through the rifle's sights on the policeman. "Get away from the women, for fuck's sake," muttered Yusuf. From a flagpole above an inner building, the Stars and Stripes was stirring in the breeze, red and white twisting in the blue sky. An emaciated tabby cat slunk along his rooftop, looked at him with yellow eyes and disappeared behind some broken mud bricks.

From the left, as planned, a white car shot round the corner and screeched to a halt outside the gates. Yusuf saw the six men, all dressed in policemen's blue camouflage-style uniforms, leap out, their guns already firing as they raced, crouched, to the steel gates. Five women turned and ran, black clothes billowing against the cream stone walls, their screams rising up to Yusuf. But the sixth ran to the boy, who was transfixed as he watched the attack. She grabbed his hand and pulled him away, then fell, sprawling, her niqab spread like a cape, a splodge of red on the ground by her head, the little boy kneeling over her.

Yusuf forced himself to look away, at the gates. Behind them, other policemen had rushed out from the guardhouse, some in dark and pale blue uniforms like the attackers, some in yellow and black, firing at the attackers by the gates. He followed one through his sights as he ran, squeezed the trigger and fired. The man ran on. Yusuf targeted another and fired again. The man ran on. And then Yusuf was firing blind and automatically, the wooden butt jabbing repeatedly into his shoulder, ranging his rifle over the heads of his comrades spraying the embassy courtyard, spent rounds spurting out and tinkling on the roof rubble.

Yusuf's body was trembling, his arms aching, the heat of the sun hammering down on him, his hands greasy with sweat. He wiped his eyes with his sleeve. Bodies of police lay inside and bodies of his comrades outside the gates. The little boy had disappeared. The gunfire had quietened a little; he could hear shouts from below. And then a second car appeared. It raced at full speed to crash into the white-and-yellow concrete security blocks and explode in a ball of fire. Yusuf jumped up and ran, bent double, across the roof, down the wooden ladder and along the street at the back of the house. There was a car waiting for him, as arranged, at the corner, door open.

Four hours later he was back at the Dammaj Institute, curled like a foetus on his blanket, exhausted but unable to sleep, his mind racing. All his comrades had been killed, including the suicide bomber in the second car. The shot woman was dead; no one knew anything about the little boy. At least a dozen people inside the embassy compound had been killed. There had been celebrations at the institute, rifles fired into the air, the operation deemed a success. But he had killed no one, he was convinced of it, though he did not admit this to his comrades. His first active service, all his weapon training, the exercises and practice out in the desert – and he had not killed a single enemy.

On the same day, the Felix Airways plane from Sana'a to Djibouti bumped along its one-hour flight. Shalima stared down at the desert mountains beneath her, then the blue sea of the Gulf of Aden. She saw tankers in the Mandeb Strait making their way north to Suez. As the plane lost height it passed over Perim Island and she saw the reed huts of the fishermen and pearl divers in the bay. Her progress through customs at Djibouti International Airport was smooth: her British passport only glanced at and no official was interested in looking into her wheeled holdall. She had not needed to produce the false paperwork supporting her cover story of being an aid worker.

The most worrying stage of this, her first mission, was over, Shalima thought, as her taxi sped the five kilometres into the city centre. Now was the exciting part: the drop. This was her first test: if she returned to Sana'a successful, there would be further missions – not just for her but for other women. She was a pioneer. In her holdall was equipment for Al-Shabaab, an Al-Qaeda affiliate winning territory in Somalia and recently designated as a terrorist organisation by the US State Department.

The taxi dropped her off at the Auberge Sable Blanc, tucked away behind the main Boulevard de République. There were only eight rooms and hers was small and bare, but clean. The air conditioning, the receptionist apologised, only came on between 7pm and 7am.

Shalima unpacked her few things, placed the holdall in the

wardrobe, and adjusted the burka she had to wear. How could women bear this? Peering through the narrow, lace-meshed eye opening must be like being one of those police horses at a demonstration wearing blinkers. She immediately felt imprisoned and, at the same time, dangerous, as if she were a bomb that could explode at any moment.

Locking the triple-locked door behind her, Shalima stepped out into the narrow street. She had taken no more than half a dozen paces when a siren screamed, unseen, along a nearby street. Her heart hammered. She shivered with a sudden chill. And then, across the end of the street, an ambulance sped past, blue light flashing. She breathed again and walked on.

It was only two hundred metres to the internet café, the main reason for the choice of hotel. Relieved to see three other women sitting at computers – fingers on twenty-first-century keyboards, eyes made medieval – as well as half a dozen men, she sat down at one of the three vacant machines and logged on to the shared email account she had set up. There, as arranged, she found the Djibouti phone number she must ring to arrange the drop.

Back in her room, sitting on her bed, she inserted a local SIM card she had bought at the café into her phone and called the number.

"Yes," said an African-sounding voice.

"I have the medicines you need," said Shalima, keeping her voice calm while her heart beat fast.

"I was expecting your call."

"Tomorrow morning, 0930, in the car park of the Acacias Hotel. My black holdall will have a red strap round it."

"I'll be there."

The phone clicked off and Shalima breathed a sigh of relief. Her organisers had selected the time and the location for the drop. She had watched the holdall being packed: a camcorder, portable filtration equipment, a PowerMonkey solar mobile phone charger, a GPS watch, two pairs of night-vision goggles. She now placed four hundred US dollars from her wallet into a zipped pocket.

Less than two and a half hours ago she had left the Yemen and, so far, her first field operation had gone as planned.

She sat in her room and drank some bottled water, too excited to be hungry. During the evening she watched television, a French sitcom she couldn't understand, and heard doors slam and voices in the corridor. She slept fitfully, but at least the air conditioning worked.

At 0910 the taxi the receptionist had ordered for her arrived. Following instructions, Shalima had the taxi drop her on the main road so she had a short walk to the entrance of the hotel grounds. Already hot in her black burka, penned in behind the lace eye-covering, conscious that the rattling holdall wheels on the pavement slabs drew attention to her, she nevertheless concentrated on maintaining a casual pace. But there were few other pedestrians. She turned into the hotel gates and walked along the driveway towards the entrance lobby. Two uniformed attendants were opening the doors of a black limousine. Then she noticed the police guards standing either side of the entrance: pale khaki uniforms, black boots, blue berets and holding black AK-47s. She had to be unconcerned, continue, not turn her head to look at them. She waited for a shout, a challenge. But none came. She could almost feel the rifle barrel hard between her shoulders. But there was nothing. Another deep breath as she walked to the car park. She chose as inconspicuous a place as she could, next to a line of parked cars, and looked at her watch: 0928. Perfect. Her fingers were clutched tight on the holdall handle.

People came and went from the hotel doors, Arabs and Africans, a couple of Westerners. Then she saw an African in a Western suit come down the steps, look around, then walk purposefully towards the parked cars. It was him, she knew. He strode up to her, bent his head in greeting, smiled and said just one word: "Cornucopia."

That was the code.

He took the holdall with its bright red strap from her, bowed slightly again and wheeled the holdall away. Lights flashed on a car as he unlocked it. He put the holdall into the boot; the car drove away past Shalima, with no acknowledging wave. It was done. Over. She turned and walked out along the driveway, half-expecting to hear the sound of running footsteps and feel the hand of a security official on her shoulder. But nothing happened. Though her heart was thudding, it was almost an anticlimax. But she had succeeded. What would be the next test?

Five thousand, eight hundred and ninety-nine kilometres north-west of Djibouti, Davoud Nariman stood at the window, fierce eyes staring unseeing at Lambeth Bridge and the River Thames below. His lips thinned, brows contracted into a frown. He held himself still, in control, hands in pockets.

Dunia, his ex-wife, had phoned him yesterday evening, as he was eating dinner with his father. She had chosen a school for Sara, she said, a private day school with high academic standards and excellent facilities – the Malsis School in Kensington. He'd checked it immediately on the internet. He'd no objection to the choice, just that he had not been involved, his opinion never sought. That high-handed bloody woman had shut him out; deliberately limiting his role again, keeping him at a distance, already marginalising him.

"Bitch!" he muttered to himself, then blinked and took a deep breath. He focused for a moment on a barge approaching the bridge, saw sunlight flashing on the windscreens of cars crossing the Thames, then turned away to face the table in the room.

There were ten upright, hard-backed chairs with green leather seats around the polished, rectangular mahogany table; at each place was a glass and a carafe of water. He switched his mind to the meeting. Compartmentalising was a strength, but Sara would sorely try it.

He looked at his watch: ten minutes before they would come in, prompt to the minute, he was sure – except maybe for one. It was the first meeting he had called for the group, primarily an information-sharing update so that everyone had a complete overview. He turned back to the window and its view of the river from the sixth floor. Less than two weeks after the gift of Suleiman, here he was at Thames House, MI5 headquarters, in charge of Section G3A, International Terrorism, but also responsible for monitoring fundamentalist Muslim groups in the UK. It was a key appointment in this new world of Islamic terrorism. His job was to ensure that the different sections and agencies collaborated – not easy, because some liked to keep their empires and contacts to themselves, a result of Secret Intelligence Service history. There was competitiveness, too, between some of the department representatives jostling on the same career ladder, slithering on the same greasy pole.

His boss, Sir Charles Mottram, had been as good as his word. Two days after Suleiman was locked in his solitary cell in Belmarsh, Davoud had flown in to report, and to seek a transfer to London.

"Sad news about your marriage," Sir Charles had said. "Difficult times for you. I'll set the wheels in motion. There's a position which I think will suit you down to the ground. Bit of red tape to sort out but you should be stationed here within the month."

Davoud had thanked him.

"Not charity, Davoud. Can't afford charity. You're a good man, excellent record, and we need you here, your experience, your strategic thinking. We think you're the man to put a team together. There's a battle that has to be won, here on the streets of London."

For once, the wheels had turned swiftly.

There was a knock on the door. Tim Bennett entered, carrying a takeout cup of coffee. The others began to drift in, greeting each other or already in conversation, taking their seats and opening their tablets, immediately swiping and tapping on the screens. Talking to departmental bosses, reading professional profiles through the night, balancing operational relevance with Service politics, interviewing his choices, Davoud had swiftly selected his team. He was aware that he was the only non-white in the room, an unfamiliar situation for him after his years in the Middle East. This meeting was vital. Davoud's role was to feed its prognoses and predictions to the Counterterrorism Committee, set up after the Twin Towers attack, which in turn fed into COBRA (Cabinet Office Briefing Room A), which met on the first floor of the Cabinet building in Whitehall when there was a sudden imminent threat to the country. The process was complex and his purpose was to cut through smothering bureaucracy – but then the whole situation was necessarily complex with so many agencies involved.

Davoud deliberately did not sit at the head of the table, but chose a chair two thirds of the way down one side. He disapproved of unnecessary hierarchies: cooperation between equals was the name of the game. Polly Beale sat down next to him. She was head of A1A in Operational Support, a formidably capable organiser of technical operations such as electronic eavesdropping, covert entry and CCTV coverage. She knew every subsection and codicil of the relevant privacy laws and ways round every one of them. She was a great team member, lively, bustling, primed to see the funny side of everything including herself, but clinical when defining priorities. She was slightly overweight, rounded, never wore trousers, always a skirt, and currently spent weekends with a hammer drill removing old mortar from the porch of an old stone house she and her partner had bought. She was the one non-Oxbridge member of the group, with a degree from Nottingham.

At nine o'clock prompt, with one empty chair, Davoud opened the meeting.

"Welcome to you all. It's good to have everyone together for the first time. We will be meeting when I consider the situation demands. And, as you know, the situation is fluid. All of you have been highly recommended and carefully selected."

He paused and looked round the group.

"It is easy to overdramatise," he continued, "but our nation's security is at risk. You all know that well. Our duty is to minimise that risk as far as we can. It is therefore essential we all know what each other is doing. You all know the immediate warning bell: Suleiman al-Hariri is in Belmarsh. He's a top Al-Qaeda leader and it's a distinct possibility that his imprisonment will lead to some kind of reprisal."

He let the word sink in.

"Now, I'm aware we're one short but we won't wait. Polly, can you kick us off, please, with any new operations?"

"At this very moment," began Polly, "a couple of fundamentalist Islamic shops should be opening their doors, one in Birmingham, one in Finsbury. Our team is watching and listening via microphones and cameras we installed over the weekend. A returnee from Syria has been having regular meetings there and we want to know who with and what about. We're also liaising closely with the police in Yorkshire who are investigating a grooming network which might include a couple of characters we're interested in. We're also poring over the contents of computers from three mosques which our covert entry teams have copied."

She continued for a few minutes longer, all clear and factual, no gloss. Just as she finished, the door opened, no knock, and the tall figure of Sir Bartholomew Saunders strode in, gave his usual ironic smile and took the empty chair.

"Apologies, business south of the river."

Davoud knew the others were irritated by this habitual lateness. He should have a word with him afterwards, though he knew he would be met with a condescending half-smile and iceberg-blue eyes. This tardiness was disrespectful; implied his time was more important than theirs, which Sir Bartholomew had no doubts about: the typical view of old-school MI6 officers resenting the compulsion to cooperate with their parochial intelligence colleagues at Thames House, eager to return to the Vauxhall ziggurat with its more exotic work across the world. His lateness was a conceit. Davoud assumed it was not caused by the time he took to shower and dress in the morning, preparing his appearance. His morning routine would be timed to the minute. He was renowned for his surface polish: his pink shaved skin, pure as a nun's, dabbed and scented with aftershave; hair neatly brushed with a parting, but carefully overlapping his collar a touch as a calculated hint of raffishness beneath the controlled front. There were rumours about the nature of this raffishness: from swingers' parties in Ibiza, to S&M in a luxury Buenos Aires mansion, to gay encounters in Morocco. A club tie perfectly knotted at a starched collar, the triangle of a pale primrose handkerchief in his breast pocket, jacket always buttoned, trousers with creases like razors, black shoes polished like mirrors: he gave a simultaneous impression of correctness, propriety and the potential violence of a godfather. Davoud and many others were wary of him. Mercifully, he was the odd one out.

A sudden image of Sara: Dunia was taking her to buy her school uniform today. Sara would want to show it off to him. Davoud switched back.

3.
12th June

In darkness, but with the heat of the desert day still in the air, her army camouflage fatigues clammy, Shalima wrenched an ex-Iraqi army jeep round a corner between shattered buildings in the outskirts of Mogadishu. There was no front line, she knew: buildings could just as easily be controlled by Somali Federal Government or AMISON troops as by her own Al-Shabaab fighters. There was no no man's land either. Somewhere near here were two seriously wounded jihadists. She'd been called in urgently by radio.

As she swerved round piles of rubble and raced down narrow streets, tracer arced into the sky, and bursts of assault-rifle fire came from balconies or roofs or wall corners. She saw the flash of gunshots. Pedal to the floor, engine screaming, tyres squealing, she hurled the jeep forward. At last she saw torches signalling from a doorway and she pulled over, grabbed her medical kit and ran into the remains of a house.

One man lay on the ground, moaning, blood seeping from bullet wounds in his chest; another crouched in the corner clutching his arm, his left foot shattered into a mess of blood, flesh and bone. There was a smell of cordite, sweat and sewers. Quickly she retied the emergency tourniquets, cleaned the wounds and injected morphine. She radioed the crude field hospital that was five miles behind the current fighting zone. Three fighters helped carry the men to the jeep and one stayed with them in the back.

Adrenaline pumping, Shalima began the mazy run back through black streets lit only by burning buildings. She knew each bump and swerve would jolt the injured men, would jab them with new pain in spite of the morphine. She ground the pedal to the floor, desperate for acceleration, tyres clipping random kerbs, messages on her radio blaring out into the night, the screech of static. Bullets shot past with high-pitched hissing sounds, hit stone and spun off into the air. She hunched down as low as she could, making herself a smaller target, elbows tucked tightly into her body, head shrunk into her shoulders.

And then she was out of the city and into scrubland, on the rough track to base. Only then, as the cooler night air whipped around her and the engine noise evened out and the gunfire grew more distant, did she begin to realise what she had done. She had not been afraid – her concentration on driving, and the need to administer rapid medical aid had been too intense for that. A sense of achievement surged through her: her second mission had been successful. Now these two wounded men had to survive to make it worthwhile – but that was in the doctors' hands, not hers.

"Second up, Jamie."

Jamie Lockhart was from the GCHQ 'doughnut' in Cheltenham, a swarthy, dark-haired man, built like a prop forward – which he still was for the fourth team of his club – broad and squat but with a natural charm. He was obsessed with his work because he had, so he'd told Davoud, always been like this from a child: fascinated by puzzles, disguises, codes, cryptic crosswords, and then later by all the technical electronic equipment and connections that GCHQ employed – hundreds of miles of fibre-optic cabling, radomes, satellite dishes and over six thousand employees. He was an intriguing mixture: delicate, intricate brainwork all week, the dark arts of the front row on a Saturday afternoon, and a family man.

Jamie coordinated and directed the intelligence analysts, those boffins who, once the SIGINT was gathered and processed, composed the results into summaries sent to Cabinet ministers, defence chiefs and senior policymakers. It was also Jamie's responsibility to ensure these summaries were whisked away in 'burn bags' to the incinerators to protect their secrecy. He was a liaison man with the USA's National Security Agency in an international network known as Echelon, a vast information vacuum cleaner that sucked in five million intercepts a day, every electronic bleep and fart. Like all the other agencies, GCHQ now dealt with domestic as well as foreign threats, and with organised crime which was often part of the money-laundering, people-smuggling, arms-trading web. Only three years ago twelve billion pounds had been earmarked for a project to master the internet and modernise the interception of emails and phone calls. Jamie was the leading advocate in GCHQ's move from 'the need to know' to the equally vital 'need to share'.

Davoud and Jamie had met years ago when both were stationed in Northern Ireland. Professional cooperation and mutual respect had developed into friendship. Jamie had persuaded Davoud to join him on his rugby-training runs, and since then running had become part of Davoud's life. He loved its repetition, its solitariness.

"OK," said Jamie, "let's start with high-frequency radio equipment sold to Iran which we've subtly adapted so we can monitor transmission. We hope this will inform us about troop movements into Syria and Iraq. Then there are four container ships operating out of the Horn of Africa and Karachi, in the bowels of which we have installed remote collection equipment which beam their 'take' to overhead satellites for more rapid analysis. We're already listening in to Somali pirates and, far more important, to any Al-Qaeda and other terrorist organisations in this highly volatile area. But of course these people know we are listening, and know our computers are programmed to sniff out keywords from all the electronic chatter. So they've begun to disguise the keywords, spelling 'America' as 'Amreeka', for instance, or using alternative words – 'birthday present' for 'bomb'. And now they are using more obscure languages like Farsi and Pashtu. But we're hard on their heels with extra staff and more sophisticated programmes. Because terrorists constantly change their mobiles and SIM cards we're developing voiceprints which allow us to search huge volumes of traffic for people who sound like suspected terrorists or conspirators. Finally, we're beginning to analyse patterns of calls, using neural network computers, which can alert us to terrorist cells or impending attacks."

As always with Jamie's contribution, there was an awed silence around the table. Like the others, he assumed, Davoud had an image of wires like a spider's web or a multitude of tentacles cast across the globe. But there weren't wires, just charged particles dancing in cyberspace, innocent themselves and without any purpose, but manipulated and exploited, transformed into harbingers of slaughter and catastrophe. Or something like that. Davoud was hazy on the science of electronics. What they were all certain of was that it was far easier to deal with state-organised terrorism, say by Gaddafi's Libya, than it was now with non-state organisations like Al-Qaeda and ISIS. Strategy had to be flexible, responsive, able to think on its feet.

"Thank you, Jamie, portentous as usual. Max, can you give some examples of progress before we sink under the complexity and enormity of it all?"

Max ran Section G3W, countering terrorism from parts of the world not covered by other sections.

"Picking up Jamie's last point, as you know, that's my bag: the floaters, the travellers, the shifting cells and lone operatives."

Max Cox was, according to rumours among the female office staff, just that – their curiosity answered with degrees of desirability or revulsion. But the impressiveness of his organ had not apparently animated him, but rather subdued him. He was a shy man, his stature only recognised beneath the sheets. Perhaps he knew that when people looked at him, as now, the image they had of him was nothing to do with his work. What a burden to carry! No wonder he sat, shoulders hunched, voice quiet so they had, as it were, to prick up their ears to listen. He was always succinct, glad to finish his report.

"We're concentrating on two movements at the moment: what appears to be the most proactive branch, franchise, call it what you will, of Al-Qaeda – in Yemen, AQAP, Al-Qaeda in the Arabian Peninsula. You will have heard of the recent attack on the American Embassy in the capital, Sana'a. We also think they're involved, or some of their individuals are, in this morning's bombing in Dar es Salaam. Secondly, there's Al-Shabaab in Somalia, losing ground there against what government there is, but plotting revenge against Kenya. Kenya is opposed to Al-Shabaab because they're afraid they will spread over the border into their territory, bringing their brand of terror and exacerbating religious and tribal strife."

As ever with Max, there would be details he deemed irrelevant to this meeting; the bare bones all that were necessary. His section was held in high regard and no one doubted that the details were there.

There was a knock on the door and a woman's blonde head appeared round it.

"I've been instructed to interrupt the meeting. I'm sorry but, Mr Nariman, there's an urgent call for you."

Davoud shook his head in frustration and apologised. Heads watched him as he left the room. In the outer office, the secretary handed him the phone. A very brief conversation.

"I'll be there immediately," said Davoud.

He stood for a moment, then re-entered the meeting. The chattering stopped. Heads looked up at him.

"I'm so sorry, but that was the Defence Minister demanding my presence now. A new development. We'll have to end the meeting. We will reconvene in two days' time. I'll send details of the time this afternoon. So sorry."

Davoud fumed as he made his way to the Ministry. His initial meeting broken; this better be important.

Yusuf sat with Abdul the Muscle in the cab of a battered tan-coloured Toyota pickup truck in a backstreet at 0930 on a Friday morning in Dar es Salaam, Tanzania.

"*Fight and slay the pagans wherever ye find them and seize them, beleaguer them and lie in wait for them.*" Yusuf quoted the 'sword verses' from the Qu'ran.

His hands on the steering wheel, Abdul turned to look at Yusuf. His eyes were blank, his face set.

"In an hour you will be in Paradise," said Yusuf. Abdul's broad chest was bulked out further with his 'shahid belt': eight cylinders cut from metal water piping, packed with explosives and ball bearings and connected by wire to a red button taped to his chest – the trigger.

He nodded.

Yusuf had expected Abdul to be elated, high as if on a drug trip. But it was more as if he was in the zone, focusing his own determination, rehearsing the action ahead. He had switched out, not switched on.

Four days ago the plan had been changed: instructions had come down that Yusuf was no longer going to accompany Abdul in the truck. They wanted Yusuf for another mission. Up till then Yusuf and Abdul, as comrades and room-mates, had envisaged the mission as a joint action. Now Abdul would be on his own. There would be no comradely death. Yusuf was angry. He felt he had betrayed Abdul and wondered if Abdul felt the same. Neither said anything.

Nor had words been spoken during the night, as they had loaded the truck with wooden crates containing TNT, aluminium nitrate and aluminium powder. With careful fingers Yusuf had wired a detonator to four large vehicle batteries which were connected to a button on the dashboard, aware that he was no longer fashioning his own death, but only his friend's. Then they had washed themselves ritually and prayed together. Lying in the darkness, knowing that Abdul, though lying still, was not asleep, Yusuf could not bring himself to celebrate Abdul's imminent martyrdom. This was the dream of the jihadist – to die in battle and be welcomed into Heaven by Allah. Why could he not be happy for his friend? Even though the high command had singled out Abdul for imminent glory, Yusuf felt guilty. But along with guilt he felt relief. Yusuf's own entry to Paradise had been postponed and he was not disappointed, as a jihadist should be. For his own martyrdom, he wanted his own spectacular mission.

As he watched Abdul's last dawn filter through the window, Yusuf wondered if Abdul felt any regret. Paradise was certain, but even so...

They rose from their blankets and washed again: the ritual of hands and feet and ears, Abdul cleansing himself of his earthly sins. They ate nothing: Abdul needed to be pure at his death.

Now they sat together, waiting for Faraji whose jeep would guide the way to the American Embassy, like a pilot fish, and then speed off, leaving Abdul to smash his truck through the gates of the embassy. Faraji was fifteen minutes late already. Yusuf saw sweat glistening on Abdul's brow. His fingers rapped the steering wheel and he shifted in his thick vest, the heat building already in the cab though both windows were wound down.

And then the jeep drew up beside them, an old army jeep. Faraji gave the thumbs-up. "We will stay off the main roads," he said. "Follow me closely."

Yusuf grabbed Abdul's arm and shook his hand. "The blessings of Allah be upon you. I will meet with you soon in Paradise."

Abdul was silent, turned his head slightly. There was the smallest hint of a smile, but Yusuf could not tell if he felt blessed or rueful.

Faraji was already moving off. Abdul put the truck into first gear, Yusuf jumped out of the cab and the truck pulled away. He could not wave. He was imagining Abdul's black finger resting on and then pressing the red button on his chest. Yusuf knew what he'd been instructed to do. He jogged back to the main road into the city centre, Bagamoya Road, hailed a taxi and jumped in.

"Oyster Bay Police Station, quick as you can."

Studying the map last night, he'd noticed the station was only two blocks away from the embassy. Now he needed to witness the outcome. His taxi had only been travelling a few minutes when he heard the huge blast of an explosion and the taxi seemed to shudder. The driver pulled over, and Yusuf thrust some coins into his hand and ran to the next corner. Down the street, a massive pall of black smoke was billowing over the tops of the buildings, balls of flame bursting out beneath it. He ran on past the police station, where cars and vans were racing out with sirens screaming. People were pouring out of building entrances all along the road. A fire engine and two ambulances sped past him. Yusuf slowed to a walk. The smoke was spreading, he could smell it.

The first hotel he came to was the Peninsula. A crowd of people stood outside the entrance by the tubs of evergreens; a few stood on the ornate balconies of their rooms, hands shading their eyes as they looked towards the fire. Above the entrance hung the flags of Tanzania, the EU and the US. Yusuf scowled; Abdul was dead. He recognised American accents in the group of guests standing outside. Many of them – businessmen and NGO workers – must know their embassy was over there. Slowly they drifted back into the hotel and Yusuf joined them, the first time for a long time that he wasn't the lone pale face. The television was on in the bar, and air-conditioning fans whirred overhead.

"News channel," shouted an American voice.

The black barman switched over. A reporter, in a shop doorway, was speaking rapidly to camera. Then the screen switched to a shot of the burning building. There were gasps among the watchers: smoke and flames still poured out; the front of the building had completely collapsed, the remains of concrete floors tipping, twisted metal rods protruding. The fire still crackled, though fire engines sprayed water into the black smoke, and first-aid teams were running with loaded stretchers. Yusuf saw the few twisted remains of the burned-out truck. Three black women shuffled past, blood streaming down their faces.

"Oh my God!" cried a woman guest.

Oh my God! thought Yusuf, alone exultant among this horrified crowd. Abdul was in Heaven and had earned his martyrdom.

This second mission had been successful but he, Yusuf, must find a more spectacular exploit. Not just a greater bang, but something that would reverberate around the world.

4.
14TH JUNE

"Thank you all for coming at such short notice to this reconvened meeting. I do understand how busy you all are. Let's waste no time. First of all, I better explain why I was called away last time we met."

Davoud cleared his throat. Expectant heads looked towards him.

"Two hours before the minister called me, we received a notification from ISIS, claiming responsibility for delivering Suleiman al-Hariri to us and hoping we're grateful. A certain arrogance."

There were nods and shakes of heads, subdued noises of surprise.

"Do we know it's genuine?" asked Polly Beale.

"My feeling is yes. They attached a photo of Suleiman, drugged, on the back seat of a car. We had forensics do a close examination of the bindings and clothes. It's definitely him."

Davoud saw that there were one or two sceptical faces. "And there's a report from the CIA. They were tipped off about a house where Suleiman was staying and sent in a drone to smash it – which would have killed him if the tip-off was accurate. So how did Suleiman avoid it? The favourite theory at the moment is that ISIS sent the tip-off to the CIA, then warned Suleiman and then, when he left the house, captured him."

"Sounds very convoluted," said Tim Bennett.

"It does. But he's here. Proof of the pudding. Who else but ISIS could have brought him to us?"

"But why?" asked Tamsin. Tamsin Crawford-Holmes represented the CPNI – Centre for the Protection of National Infrastructure – which was interdepartmental, directly accountable to the director general of the Security Service. "Why not kill him gruesomely themselves and put it out on YouTube? They've had plenty of practice. It would be a propaganda coup for them."

"Indeed. We know there's a turf war on between ISIS and Al-Qaeda, competing for jihadis and for leadership of the jihadi movement."

"But why send him to us?" persisted Tamsin. "What's in it for them?"

"Good question. Maybe because it's more humiliating for Al-Qaeda to have their man festering in a British prison. He's less of a martyr for their cause. Maybe, also, because it puts us in a tricky situation. If we bring him to trial and give him a life sentence, we're simultaneously inflicting a defeat on Al-Qaeda and raising the profile of ISIS; the last thing we want to do."

The group pondered this.

"In the meantime," continued Davoud, "we detained him for as long as we could; only fourteen days now because of these civil liberties vigilantes. But then we charged him and of course he was denied bail. So he's still in Belmarsh while we compile the evidence. We're happy to work with our cousins across the pond in this case. The CIA want to extradite him; they can put him away more easily than we can. Remember that Abu Hamza, Captain Hook? Played us for years with his appeals, but once they got him to New York it was life imprisonment with no possibility of parole. We'd be very happy if Suleiman got the same treatment."

Nods of agreement round the table.

"But" – and Davoud paused a moment – "we must bear in mind that Al-Qaeda might try to rescue him."

He let that sink in.

"Now to more information sharing. Tamsin."

Tall, with short dark hair which always looked expensively cut, and always in a trouser suit, the jacket set off by a brooch which obviously came from one of those small exclusive Bond Street jewellers, a complexity of rings on her fingers but none on her wedding finger, Tamsin was old money, moving smoothly up through Cheltenham Ladies' College and then Oxford and straight into the Service. Through her father, a peer of the realm, she had connections at the highest levels of government. None of which altered the fact that she was highly competent – and always gave the impression she had a more urgent meeting to attend. Her role here, she implied, was not to give information but to receive and pass it on.

"The same priorities as last week," she said crisply, "with the additional scare of a possible attack on Heathrow Terminal 5, heightened security for the Pakistan Test match in Birmingham and our continuing pressure on government to increase funding for border security."

She looked around the table, as if challenging anyone to question her.

Davoud noticed the mouth of Sir Bartholomew Saunders begin its preparatory routine: a half-smile, the corners of his mouth starting to twitch, his lips pursing, his head tilted slightly upwards.

"Tim," said Davoud quickly.

Tim was the reluctant acting leader of G9C, the section responsible for countering Islamic extremists. He had two young children, a passion for rowing and an avowal to keep a proper work-life balance, totally committed to the work he did but determined to keep it within limits. He'd stepped into the acting role to cover the long-term sickness of Sir Seb Tansley, rumoured to be being gently pushed into early retirement. Tim was a broad, short man with powerful shoulders and a generous shock of fair hair that was not civil-servant neat. He believed firmly that over the years London had become the epicentre of Islamic militancy, with groups flourishing here that were outlawed even in Muslim countries. London had become Londonistan.

"A busy time," he said. "We're mindful of any follow-up here in London to the attack on the Danish cartoonist in Copenhagen, but no one here, not even *Private Eye*, has reprinted the cartoons. The attacks on the rabbis in Marseille and Toulon mean extra vigilance on the main London synagogues. The Islamic Foundation in Leicestershire now seems to us genuine, not a cover organisation for terror, but we've still got a watching brief. The Committee for the Defence of Legitimate Rights (CDLR), set up by a Saudi who had to flee Saudi Arabia, has close connections with Al-Qaeda. Hizb ut-Tahrir (HuT) is becoming more active – they want to resurrect an Islamic caliphate so there's obvious connections with ISIS. We're upping our surveillance on the Tablighi Jamaat Mosque in Dewsbury and the Finsbury Mosque, where we're convinced there is jihadist recruitment taking place."

He paused and then continued. "As usual, the British perception of terrorism is being warped by so many politicians and liberal leaders demonising the USA and preferring to attack Islamophobia rather than violent Islamism."

"I think that's my cue," said Sir Bartholomew, obviously annoyed that he had not yet been invited to speak. Davoud had noted before how he seemed to address his words primarily to Tamsin, as if appropriating her into membership of his own club, confidently assuming she was intrigued by the edgier, riskier elements of his pleasures. "Across the river, our priority is very much young British jihadis: those planning to go – and that now includes young women as well as men – and those returning from training camps in the Yemen and elsewhere and, of course, from Syria. My personal belief is that these people, now versed in warfare, should not be allowed to return, but that's a matter for... politicians."

He said the word as if it was a piece of rancid food in his mouth. Davoud saw his tongue moving under his lip, as if it were cleansing his teeth. Sir Bartholomew was one of the reasons he ran: running wasn't just about fitness; it dissipated his frustrations, freed him from the shackles of endless words and discussions, gave him tangible achievements, refreshed him with a physical fatigue.

"The police have all the information we have gathered," Sir Bartholomew finished.

There were nods from the police representatives. Gary Wallace from Special Branch was an ex-army officer gone to physical seed: a huge stomach and heavy jowls, his fleshy face emphasised by his close-cropped crew cut. He spoke about investigations into grooming networks being made aware of possible links with jihadi recruitment, and about the difficulties and extreme danger of trying to infiltrate fundamentalist study groups. Training and bomb-making videos were freely available on the internet and impossible to restrict. There were inflammatory lectures available online in box sets, for God's sake, which preached the duty of every Muslim to rise up against the corrupted values of the West.

Next to him sat Claire Luscombe from the Metropolitan Police. Her slight, neat figure and quiet voice contrasted with Gary's passion and paunch. She detailed the surveillance operations currently in force. Claire had a reputation for her grasp of detail as well as a wider strategic sense, and for her highly efficient consensual management of teams.

"Two men who were on our radar two years ago have flown into East Midlands Airport from Amsterdam and Cologne – well done to the border police for spotting them –

and we're currently trailing them with foot teams and cars. We know where they're living in Dewsbury and Leeds."

She continued with details of other operations. Hers was the final report. Tablets around the table were closed.

"Thank you, ladies and gentlemen. As usual, a lot to absorb and process. It's business as usual: lots of intel, ears to the ground, keep your eyes skinned etc., etc. Especially for anything that might be related to Suleiman. But so far, nothing."

"So far as we know," said Jamie. "But we can't know everything – and there are always invisibles."

"Quite correct, Jamie," said Davoud. He looked at his watch. "We must end there. A lot to absorb. Thank you again."

Davoud left them, conversations already beginning, noting that Sir Bartholomew was still sitting, silent, watching, eyes flickering towards Tamsin, who ignored him. Any discussion of these points would take place after the formal meeting, as relevant people got together to trade more detailed information or ask further questions. It was a far more productive and cost-effective use of time than having whole-table discussions.

He gave himself an hour and a half to write a summary report for the top floor: drawing connections, giving pointers to priorities. He liked working under time pressures and he had other things to fit in: a 5K run in Hyde Park and, after that, a reunion in The White Horse with his three fellow musicians from university. It was Matthew, the lawyer and keyboard player, who'd found out Davoud was back in London and phoned him. He, Jacob the drummer, and Roger the social worker bass guitarist wanted to set up a gig – if Davoud was up to it. Like the old days, somewhere a bit artsy, a bit off-centre. This was a side of himself that Davoud had been surprised to discover, that he loved but was nervous about. Creating together, they had developed a style and sound of music he was happy with. He loved making music with them, emerging into solo spots and then eliding back into the group. But he was not a natural public performer: there was always an initial diffidence before the music absorbed him. He had learned to love the few gigs they had done: that heady combination of being lost in the privacy of the sounds he made; yet playing them in public view and with his friends.

Somehow he had to find the time to get some serious practice in. And there was tomorrow to think about: three important meetings, with his boss, Suleiman and Sara.

Back at the Al-Qaeda in the Arab Peninsula (AQAP) base in Yemen, the leaders had praised Shalima's courage, nerve and effectiveness under fire: two missions safely accomplished as courier, nurse and driver. Which was why, on her third mission, Shalima was dressed again in a black burka. She sat on cushions against the wall, away from the window, in a first-floor room up a wooden ladder in a shabby, nondescript house in the outskirts of Mombasa in Kenya.

Tense, impatient and thirsty, she was waiting. In the room below an old woman and a young girl were shuffling about, cooking food. Shalima smelt spices and coffee, growing restless with the heat and expectancy. Guards hidden in surrounding buildings would have checked her arrival. There were rumours of a suicide squad of fifteen, constantly protecting the woman she was about to meet, a woman who never slept twice in the same place, was constantly on the run, wanted for terrorism and conspiracy charges in two hundred countries, the subject of an Interpol Red Notice: an Englishwoman, the White Widow.

Shalima heard a car draw up, doors slam, low voices, the car driving away, running footsteps across the gravelled road. Then a woman's voice in the room below, and the quiet voices of men. The wooden ladder creaked. Shalima watched its top steps bend and strain, and stood up. A guard with an AK-47 climbed in. Then two black-gloved hands appeared on the rough steps, and a black-robed head. Shalima stepped forward and took the woman's hand to help her up. She wore the full burka, her eyes hidden behind black mesh. Two more men quickly followed her, each with an AK-47 slung over his shoulders, one with a rucksack.

"My white skin," said the woman, peeling off her gloves. "It's sunburnt but it's still white. I have to hide it. And my eyes." She laughed.

Shalima saw a faint trace of blue eyes behind the shadows of the mesh.

"Sherafiya," said the woman. "From Buckingham, the Home Counties." She laughed again.

"Shalima." She wanted to add how honoured she felt, how grateful for this meeting. But her throat was dry and she felt herself shrink, tongue-tied, as she stood beside her heroine: such a slight woman with such a huge history.

They arranged themselves on cushions and the man drew out of his rucksack a set of papers. The young girl climbed up the ladder with coffee and Shalima poured it into the small cups, glad of something to do. There were small pieces of honey cake to go with it.

"We must hurry," said Sherafiya. "It's not safe for me to stay here for more than an hour. AQAP told us they wanted you to understand how we planned our activities, that you have ambition. Al-Shabaab is happy to cooperate with our jihadi brothers, and sisters. We are still finalising the details of our next attack, in Mombasa city centre. There's no time to give you a tutorial," she laughed again, "just watch and listen."

Shalima saw a street map with yellow highlights and red routes marked on roads. There were computer printouts of lists of armaments and amounts of explosives, timings, locations.

"The key thing," said Sherafiya, "is to have the actions

happen simultaneously. This really challenges the security services but, even more important, it's so much more dramatic: explosions and gunfire whichever way people turn. It's more terrifying."

Her voice was soft behind her veil as she spoke of the targets: the hotels full of Westerners, businessmen and aid workers; the churches full of Christian infidels; the shopping mall full of Western goods. "We will have fighters, of course, but also suicide bombers."

Shalima watched: the woman's passion was controlled, her hatred channelled, her considerations so meticulous, her calculation calm.

The men spoke with the woman, adding items to the lists, altering a red route, crossing out a timing. Calm, efficient, ruthless; no bravado or celebration, no high fives or pumping of hands. Murder was being planned as if it were a school outing.

Shalima heard a whistle from outside, and a man's voice called from below. One man, with a scar on his cheek, went to the window, his rifle cradled in his arm. The other neatly rolled the papers up, packed them into his rucksack and went down the ladder. Sherafiya pulled on her gloves. They drank the last of the coffee and stood up. The third man, older and with a grey beard, descended the ladder.

Sherafiya said, "Take risks, sister! I will look forward to hearing of your exploits, inshallah."

She descended the ladder followed by the scarred man. A car screeched to a halt outside the house, and there were shouts and the slamming of doors. The car drove off, and dust floated in through the open window.

Was it really no different from planning a shopping expedition? The process had shocked her, the methodology and calculation. Like the Final Solution she'd learned about at school, with its engineers and bookkeepers and railway timetablers.

Shalima ate a piece of honey cake, which the others had not tasted.

And this woman was a mother with four children. Samantha Lewthwaite from Aylesbury, widow of Jermaine Lindsay, the London bomber who had blown himself up between Kings Cross and Russell Street Stations on 7/7. Rising fast through the ranks of Al-Shabaab after drone attacks killed several of its leaders, she was now at the right hand of its leader, Ahman Umar. She was reputed to have planned car bombings in Kenya and Somalia, the bus ambush in which all passengers who could not recite the Qu'ran were slaughtered, the attack on the shopping mall in Nairobi, the attack on the Moi University campus. As the leading logistician of Al-Shabaab, she must be responsible for hundreds of deaths. There were rumours she recruited her teenage suicide bombers by paying desperate families three hundred pounds and then sending off the bombers pumped up with cocaine. It was a long way from reading politics and religion at London University.

The young girl brought Shalima a plate of rice and vegetables, spiced with chillies. But she was not in the mood to eat. She thought of the other Western women who were fighting for Islam: Nicole Lynne Mansfield who died fighting Syrian rebels, Jihadi Jane who plotted to murder the Swedish cartoonist and was now serving a ten-year jail sentence, Amanda Korody who attacked the British Columbia legislature. Across the world it was happening. Shalima wanted to be the Asian woman who joined that all-white list, to add her own part of shock and awe. She was ready. All she needed was an idea. She wanted to do something different, something unique, something which would always be remembered. And she wanted to prove that women, too, could face danger, be clear-headed and decisive under pressure.

5.
15TH JUNE

Next day Davoud Nariman stared out of a window high above Vauxhall Cross. He'd grown up in London and now he was back. His loss of faith had been the final blow for his wife of fourteen years. Dunia had decided to bring their seven-year-old daughter Sara from Muslim Jordan to godless London – to bring her up as a proper Muslim, she said, not realising the irony. They now lived in an apartment in Kensington, largely at Davoud's expense. This afternoon he was spending with Sara, the joy and pain of it excruciating. And then back to his father's. Davoud was living with him, at least for the moment. His father, occasionally confused by forgetfulness, was grateful for his company.

Davoud looked down at the constant traffic crossing Vauxhall Bridge, silent beyond the triple-glazed seventh-floor window. A lone sculler stroked elegantly upstream, a barge chugged steadily downstream. Pleasure craft, leaving cheerful white wakes – some west for Hampton Court Palace, some east for Greenwich. Those places of erstwhile British greatness.

The people who worked here in the headquarters of the Secret Intelligence Service (SIS) spent their days looking down on their world like this. It was in their upbringing, thought Davoud – *My upbringing, must remember that* – the self-congratulatory sense of entitlement absorbed, in his case, from Colet Court Preparatory School, then St Paul's School, then Downing College, Cambridge. Public servants they might be, but they surveyed the lower orders from positions of power – in this tower that was a mongrel cross between Battersea

Power Station and a Babylonian ziggurat, or a pile of egg boxes, or Legoland, depending on your cultural references.

He respected his boss, Sir Charles Mottram. Punctilious, he was renowned for his timekeeping. Davoud looked at his watch: 0845 precisely. The phone rang.

"Sir Charles will see you now."

The door clicked shut quietly behind him as he approached the desk across the gleaming parquet floor. Sir Charles stood and extended his hand. Always the stiff collar, college tie, triangle of white silk handkerchief in his breast pocket, silver cufflinks. But his face was sagging: cheeks slightly puffy, bags beginning under eyes with a hint of yellow in them, a network of broken capillaries round the nose. Not just good wine and good living, but tensions, contradictions, conflicts in the man beneath the chalk-stripe suit. It was why Davoud liked him: supreme at his job, but with demons. His large desk was empty except for the phone and a single buff-coloured folder. An untidy desk was an untidy mind; a favourite Sir Charles dictum. Davoud knew there would be no preliminaries.

"Good to see you, Davoud. Coffee?"

"No thank you, I'm fine."

"Have a seat. You're going to see Suleiman this morning?"

"Yes."

Sir Charles raised an eyebrow. "Still a vow of silence. He hasn't spoken a word except, presumably, to his lawyer. Why the visit, may I ask?"

"I just want to see him in a cell. Remind myself."

Sir Charles looked at Davoud. The whites of his eyes might be jaundiced but the steel-grey irises scrutinised him. Davoud resisted the challenge to explain further. Sir Charles opened the folder.

"A bloody nightmare, the Middle East. Arab Spring, for God's sake. They could do with some beneficent colonial powers." He laughed and turned the pages, skimming the report: lines highlighted in yellow, words scribbled down the sides. Davoud knew Sir Charles rubbed shoulders with the most powerful, listened to speeches about the need for austerity at luxury banquets in the Guildhall, discussed terrorism over fine lunches at his Pall Mall club. His advice was sought on invasions and regime changes. He saw himself as a strategist strutting the world stage. Davoud, by comparison, saw himself more as a humble tactician, almost a policeman, more concerned with protecting the small than hobnobbing with the power-mongers.

"Failed states," said Sir Charles, closing the folder. "Libya, Egypt, Iraq. Ancient tribalism, Sunni and Shia hatred, Israelis colonising the East Bank, Hamas firing rockets into the Jews, refugees everywhere. Unsolvable chaos. Disturbing, what you say about Al-Qaeda."

His pause was an invitation for a response.

"Well before Osama bin Laden's death, Al-Qaeda had changed," said Davoud. "It was never a pyramid corporation with him as CEO, as the Americans conceived. There was a wide-ranging network, but more what we would call independent franchises or affiliates which share a way of thinking about the world. It is still very much about political grievances against the West, articulated in religious terms. Yes, it still has resources and training facilities, now in the Yemen having been forced out of Afghanistan. And it still funds terrorist activities. But Al-Qaeda has for some time been more a coherent ideology than a strict organisation."

"And ISIS, that's the new player on the block."

"Yes," said Davoud. "Islamic State grew in Iraq after the American invasion in 2003. It combines effective military organisation with an extreme interpretation of Islam, based on Wahhabism."

"As in our great ally, Saudi Arabia!"

"Exactly. ISIS aims to restore the great days of the Islamic caliphate, based on fundamentalist sharia law. It is now in competition with Al-Qaeda affiliates – hence the abduction of Suleiman – even fighting against them, we think, in some areas."

Sir Charles nodded. "Good work, Davoud. This report has already been seen at the highest levels. And your coordination meetings are going well, I hear."

Davoud nodded. "We have very good people in there."

"Nothing on the radar about a Suleiman rescue?"

"Nothing we can identify."

"Well, good luck when you see him. But I doubt he'll see you."

An hour later, Davoud strode across Vauxhall Bridge, passing cars and buses edging forward, breathing in petrol fumes, and walked up to Pimlico Tube Station. He switched to the Circle Line at Victoria but, though the rush hour was over, there was still no seat for him to Cannon Street Station. He swayed with the other passengers as the Tube rounded curves, halted and surged off again. Sara seemed happy in her new school, and with a new benevolence to all men he looked around him. What a hotchpotch of races and faces London was! Going about their business, coexisting. He felt a certain pride that, unbeknown to them and just another anonymous strap-hanger with a scuffed briefcase, he was responsible for protecting them. He was glad to be here in London, amongst them. The more he had travelled, the more he loved his homeland: the Britain of fudge and compromise, of cash in hand to window cleaners and plumbers, of accelerating between speed cameras, of self-deprecation, irony and civility, of queuing and complaining, of eccentrics and gardeners and birdwatchers. Yes, there was an elite – and he was of it – and there was corruption beneath the gentlemanliness. But it was a centre-left or centre-right way of life, a comparative tolerance, live and let live. Most of all, a lack of extremes.

Twenty years ago he had gone to Cambridge to read Middle Eastern studies. Then he had prospered as a Middle East analyst in an investment bank in the City. After two years he tired of the endless data and the 'virtuality' of the money transactions he advised on. He sought some reality, making his career switch to the SIS. Defying the extremists, that was his personal mission. His public-school predecessors had ruthlessly built an empire; he was now dealing with the equally ruthless retaliatory consequences of that failed empire. In Northern Ireland he handled IRA informers, liaised with paramilitary groups like the UDA to ease the elimination of IRA volunteers. In the Lebanon he had investigated Al-Qaeda infiltration into refugee camps, in Tunisia he had worked with the CIA to fund pro-democratic rebel groups. All covert stuff, most with the thrill of danger. And now the threat to the UK was even greater.

At Cannon Street he left the Tube, feeling at one with the surge of fellow passengers. Within half an hour, he was clutching a takeaway double-shot espresso as the South Eastern Railways train rattled across the Thames and made for Plumstead. His carriage was almost empty. The reality of the city lay in the mean streets of Bermondsey and Deptford he passed – the tenements with their narrow balconies full of washing, the satellite dishes, back gardens full of rubbish. Yes, there was violence here, abuse, drugs and benefit fraud. He wasn't a fool. But most people tried to live decent lives, wanted the best for their kids, scraped a living. They wouldn't know it, but having Suleiman al-Hariri behind bars meant they had a better chance of getting on with their lives.

The only reason Davoud was going to Belmarsh was to give thanks, to relish the man's loss of freedom.

He got off the train at Plumstead and decided to walk

the two miles to the prison, the busy traffic on Western Way roaring past, the air full of fumes. Though they knew who he was, he was subjected to the strict security checks.

"The prisoner will not see you," he was told.

Not a surprise, but Suleiman could not prevent Davoud from seeing him. A warder led him through a series of clanging metal gates to a cream-painted corridor with steel cell doors on either side.

"That one." He pointed.

Davoud looked at the door for a moment. It was heavy, the grey metal polished and scratched; a keyhole and an eyehole. He moved to the door, gently slid the brass eyehole cover to one side and peered in with his right eye. The cell had a small barred window above head height, a narrow bed and a lavatory with no seat. The man was kneeling on a small sacking mat, facing towards a corner, his arms stretched out in front of him on the floor. The pale yellowy soles of his feet were bare, a shocking innocence about them. Davoud was transfixed by their ordinariness. Anger brimmed up in him, a resentment that Suleiman found consolation in his faith. He wanted him robbed of this, to be truly alone and abandoned.

The man straightened his back and prostrated himself again, muttering Arabic all the time, the intonations and rhythm of a chant. Islam – peace and submission, wrenched by men like this into a vicious creed. He was looking at a ruthless murderer paying homage, the murderer of Davoud's mother and sister and many others.

Davoud let go of the eyehole cover and watched it swing closed. He had come to rejoice, even gloat, to feel the satisfaction of justice and – he couldn't help it – of revenge. He wanted this man in prison for the rest of his life. But it wasn't enough. The man was untouched, still whole.

★

Nearly two hours later, he waited, as arranged, at the northern end of the Millennium Bridge. Of course he was early: how could he possibly be late? There they were, walking down among the crowd – his ex-wife Dunia in a smart beige coat with a pale blue silk scarf around her neck, and Sara holding her hand, looking up to her mother and chattering. It would be Sara's eighth birthday in a couple of weeks. Surprised to find he felt nothing towards Dunia except a general regret, Davoud's heart leap at the sight of his daughter. Then Sara saw him and ran forward.

"Daddy!"

He opened his arms and she jumped into them. Twirling her round, he loved her arms and legs tight around him, burying his head in the warm smell of her hair. He put her down and she smiled up at him, that cheeky smile he adored. How much he had missed her.

"You're looking tired," said Dunia. "Work pressure, I suppose."

He saw her disapproval of him in her tight mouth.

"Enjoy your afternoon," she said to Sara, bending to kiss the top of her head. She straightened up. "Look after her," she added to Davoud. "Back at the apartment at 5.30 prompt, or I shall start to worry."

There was suspicion in her scrutiny of him. Anger surged up inside him. The insult, the restriction. Control. But he held back. For the sake of Sara, they were both hiding their feelings.

Dunia turned and walked away.

"We've been in St Paul's Cathedral, Daddy. It was huge."

"And cold, I'll bet." He held her hand tightly. "We're going on that." He pointed across the river. "The London Eye."

"It's so high. But I won't be frightened. Look, it's moving round."

They looked at the gleaming white wheel with its pods.

"We'll be able to see all of London. But first we have to cross this bridge. It's called the wobbly bridge because when people first walked over it, it swayed and lurched and some people even felt sick."

"Well, I won't. That's silly."

They stopped in the middle of the bridge, watching the Thames flow past, a couple of planks and a plastic container floating on the surface.

"It's dirty," said Sara. "It shouldn't be dirty."

A pleasure boat cruised beneath them and the passengers waved up at them. Davoud and Sara waved back.

"It didn't wobble a bit," said Sara when they stepped off the bridge on the south side. "You were joking me, Daddy."

"So, to make up for your disappointment, I'm taking you for a smoothie – if you like them."

"I love them. Mango and banana is best."

He found a juice bar and they took their smoothies to a bench in the Jubilee Gardens and sat in the sunshine.

"How's school?" he asked.

She chattered away about her project on islands, about her new friends. "My best friend is Amy. She's really good at skipping."

Davoud was glad that she was happy in her new life, but stricken, too, that this new life did not include him.

"Can we go and see Grandad? We haven't seen him once since we came to live in London."

"Yes, next time. He wants to see you."

"I'm glad you've come to live in London, Daddy. I missed you."

He hugged her. He wanted to tell her that he would see her regularly, take her to the zoo and on the river, do normal things like take her to the playground and back to his place for her favourite spaghetti. But for some reason he dared not.

They queued for the Eye, then at last they were on it. It

circled slowly up and Davoud watched his daughter's face as she looked down at the river and across the wide expanse of London. He loved to see her excitement, her eyes shining, her laughter, her quick movements as she pointed out St Paul's and Big Ben. He pointed towards Kensington.

"That's where you live."

So far away from her he was, so separate.

Promptly at 5.30 he knocked on the door of his wife's apartment. He lifted up his daughter and kissed her, holding her tight. Then the door opened. He put her down.

"Amy's coming for tea," said Dunia. Sara ran inside. Dunia did not invite him in and he did not want to enter. He did not want to know any more about a world he was no longer part of. Then Sara came back.

"I did this picture of you, Daddy, for a present."

She gave him a picture, done in colourful fibre pens, of a man with a beard and a briefcase, walking towards a house.

He didn't want to leave her, but he wanted it over, this leave-taking on the threshold.

"See you soon," he said and gave her another kiss.

"Goodbye, Daddy." And she ran inside. Was she hiding her tears or excited that Amy was coming?

"Goodbye, Davoud. I hope things are working out for you."

Dunia closed the door, and after a moment he stepped away. His loss of faith had been an excuse. Long before that they had become irritated, then bored and finally come to dislike each other. They had both tried hard, but this was one arranged marriage that hadn't worked. That word, Daddy, was the most important word in the world. What he didn't consider, at this point, was that other men were fathers, too.

6.
18TH JUNE

Yusuf was lying on his bunk in the cheap backpackers' hostel in Dar es Salaam. Eleven had been killed in the attack on the embassy, including two CIA men and a US Marine sergeant. Eighty-five had been wounded. Most of the victims were local Africans. It was a disappointing tally, but it would scare Americans the world over: nowhere was safe. They would need to be always on the alert, never relaxed, never secure.

Yusuf was waiting for his next coded instructions. He knew it was necessary, but he still resented the fact that he was forbidden to have any communication with England. He had wanted to take selfies as a sniper on the roof in Sana'a, and at the Peninsula Hotel among the group of Americans with the TV news on in the background. He wanted Imran to know the part he played in news items that flashed across the world. Most of all he wanted his father and brother to know. He wanted to see their faces when they knew, to hear their disgust and incomprehension, their self-righteous rejection of him. He smiled to himself: it was they, after all, who had impelled him on the road which led to the sniper's rifle and the truckload of explosives, the journey from Ryan Hudson to Yusuf Javeed.

Before any thoughts of Islam entered his head, his journey towards this purer life began when he rebelled against his father, a prosperous importer of white goods. He remembered watching containers of fridges, freezers and washing machines arriving from China twice weekly at the warehouse before being redistributed to retail outlets. His father wanted him to follow his elder brother Phillip into the family firm. But Ryan despised the business. It bought cheap and sold at a profit. Much of this profit was based on the fact that the warehouse workers and many other staff were paid the minimum wage or were on zero-hours contracts. His father, of course, extracted a generous income – more in dividends than salary in order to avoid paying income tax. The firm existed solely to make money; it created nothing.

With a sneer, Ryan observed his father parading his prosperity, proud of his home on The Boulevard, the most prestigious address in town, a tree-lined avenue of large detached houses with paved driveways and gardener-maintained lawns and borders. His luxury car displayed his success: a gleaming silver Jaguar S-Type with full leather interior, walnut veneer fascia, electric wing mirrors and even what was termed 'climate control'. Sometimes he gave cash to individuals in trouble, but always conspicuously. He was deemed a generous man. A Methodist? He was a hypocrite.

Or maybe it began with Ryan's reaction against his brother. Older by two years, successful at school – reports crammed with bloody As, opening bat for the cricket first XI, captain of the rugby first XV – Phillip was held up by his father (and teachers) as an example to follow. After A Levels, Phillip joined the family firm, starting at the bottom so he would be familiar with all its workings. Nevertheless, his joining present from his father had been a beautifully restored red MG Roadster. Roaring around town, the long blonde hair of his current girlfriend flowing out behind her, Phillip was imitating his father, flaunting himself. Like father, like son; all image.

He, Ryan, decided he would go a different way.

And, by the grace of Allah, he had.

★

Which was why, later that evening, he had left the hostel and was sipping iced fresh orange juice in another bar. He watched the TV, a programme about Suleiman al-Hariri. Yusuf knew he was a top Al-Qaeda man, renowned for his planning of bombing 'spectaculars' in Mumbai, Indonesia and Baghdad. He had apparently been captured a fortnight ago, in mysterious circumstances, somewhere in the Middle East. But, unusually, no one had claimed responsibility for his capture: not the CIA, nor the Navy SEALs who had found bin Laden, not MI6 or the British Special Forces, nor ISIS or other rebel or criminal gangs. Or, at least, that's what the programme reported. Now the UK government had been forced to admit he was in Belmarsh Prison, but the charge had not been made public.

Strolling past Yacht Club Beach, noticing the increased presence of armed soldiers and police on the city streets, remembering the news programme's denunciation of terror and the killing of innocents, the seed of an idea began to germinate in Yusuf's mind. So far he had taken part in two actions but played only supporting roles. With Suleiman's capture, Al-Qaeda needed a spectacular reprisal and he, Yusuf, would plan it and lead it – at home, in England: his own mission. His work would glorify Allah; he would be a famous martyr or a feted hero.

Using his smartphone to access the internet, and three credit cards from bank accounts back in Leeds and Bradford (savings augmented by regular inputs from his mother – and unknown to his father), he booked flight tickets to Johannesburg, then on to Addis Ababa and Frankfurt and finally to Heathrow. He needed to cover his tracks as much as possible. Only when that was arranged did he contact the Dammaj Institute to tell them he had to return home, that he had an idea for an action which he needed to research. They would be angry at his insubordination now, but they would praise his initiative later.

Three days after arriving back in the UK, early in the morning, Yusuf sat in the Eric Morecambe Hide in the Leighton Moss bird reserve on Morecambe Bay, unable to rid his mind of a tune that kept repeating itself: *Bring me sunshine*. He chuckled to himself. Smile, laughter, happiness. Those Christmas Day Morecambe and Wise Christmas special repeats, his father laughing and spluttering, fat and whiskied in his armchair. But Yusuf wasn't chuckling out of fond nostalgia; it was the irony that appealed to him, the black comedy he was about to script – he, the interloper, the cuckoo in the nest.

He smiled to himself and raised his binoculars to his eyes, focusing on a snipe that a fellow birder had pointed out to him. It had taken him a long time to distinguish it from the reeds among which it hid, its camouflage plumage brilliant. He was a beginner, he'd said, and he'd been shown shelducks and redshanks, godwits and black-headed gulls, a cormorant on a rock, with wings outspread.

"They have no protective oil and have to dry their wings."

To his surprise, Yusuf found himself interested. But what he was really waiting for was the sound of a train: the 0837 freight from Crewe to Sellafield.

Ten minutes before it was due at the nearby Silverdale Station, Yusuf thanked the helpful birders and went outside. A path led below the railway embankment to another hide. Little birds fluttered across in front of him, a robin on a branch so unafraid he could almost touch it. He heard the diesel engine approaching from the south. Unhurriedly, unremarked, it thundered slowly past: an engine at the front, two freight trucks, another engine at the back, the reserve.

Later in The Posh Sardine café at Arnside overlooking

Morecambe Bay, he watched the tide come flooding in, just as his idea rose to the full. It was preposterous, unthinkable – but once thought, feasible and viable. Obstacles were surmountable. He would work it out, down to the last detail, then he would take it to the Al-Qaeda high command or executive or whatever it called itself. That would be scary. What he needed was a co-leader: someone to sort the logistics back in the Yemen while he organised things here. A two-coach passenger train trundled across the Kent Viaduct, Lakeland fells in the background.

At high tide, he watched a small boat with an outboard motor set off, its puttering engine scaring some gulls. A man and a boy raised the sail on a yacht and a memory surfaced of another boat that people had watched: their family speedboat on the French Riviera bay where they had holidayed for a month every year, renting a large house with a tennis court. Out in the bay Yusuf and his brother Phillip waterskied behind the boat driven by their father. People on the promenade and beach watched as they did their ostentatious turns, swinging across the swell at great speed, bouncing over the waves, monoskiing. It was exhilarating. Only later had he cringed with shame at his own vanity. What a preening, sweating, overweight, pathetic self-made braggart his father had been!

There was a photograph his mother had taken from the beach. The boat was close in shore, engine idling, his father at the wheel, he and his brother standing up in the back, holding their skis: a pose for the less fortunate spectators paddling their lilos. A growing realisation had sickened Yusuf, made him loathe himself for his enjoyment of it all, for his own bragging. The swanky speedboat summed up everything that was wrong.

He must, he now understood, have had some innate need for an ideal – and that ideal he had found in Islam.

Well, the speedboat had led him to this – the speedboat, his father, his brother. And now a different kind of bay, another very different display to captivate not just a few holidaymakers but a worldwide audience.

He finished his cup of tea. Other customers were buttering their fruit scones, stirring sugar into their coffee, gossiping. Outside, people strolled, paused, looked across the bay. Cars manoeuvred into parking spaces. Normal life ambled on.

He had the big idea, now he needed to do a full reconnaissance. By the time he returned to the Yemen, he must have a tide timetable, a landing place, a hideout, and a plan and location for the attack. Only then could he prepare a proposal to put to the Al-Qaeda executive. What a miraculous series of coincidences and chance meetings had led him here, from Ryan the Methodist to Yusuf the Islamist.

7.
25th June

Shalima didn't register him at first, the warrior who met her off the plane from Mombasa at Sana'a. He was white, lanky with sloping shoulders, fair-haired, with a fifth-rate beard and bulging eyes she found slightly repellent. He was the spitting image of the librarian at Hounslow College.

"*Salaam alaikum,*" he said.

"*Walaikum salaam,*" she replied.

"My name is Yusuf." An English voice with northern vowels.

"Shalima," she said.

"A Brummie?"

She laughed.

He wore jeans and a once-white T-shirt with the faded slogan *It wasn't me*. He offered to carry her bag.

"It's OK," she said.

They stepped out of the airport into the searing heat and Yusuf plonked a floppy, white, very English sunhat on his head. But, as he drove her into the city, his voice was rich and intense, and his blue eyes flashed when he spoke about his teacher Anwar al-Awlaki and his time in the Yemen. He said nothing about himself and she felt it was not right to ask.

He dropped her off at the entrance of the *makar*, the hostel for women, wished her the blessings of Allah and said farewell.

"Back to my training camp," he said. AQAP had told him to meet her, but without explanation other than they were both British. But Yusuf had heard about Shalima's exploits.

He wanted to learn more about her: she might be the very person he needed for his plan.

She'd been here for three months now. At first sight the *makar* had seemed crude: a two-storey building made of mud bricks baked by the sun, with small windows. On the top floor were four 'dormitories', each with four bunks; on the ground floor was a simple kitchen, two bare meeting rooms and a 'bathroom' with a squat-style lavatory to be cleaned with a yellow hosepipe from a large barrel of water. But Shalima soon learned the building was efficient: the metre-thick walls kept the rooms cool, the small windows were located to avoid the direct sun. The house had once been grander: the remains of ornate wooden lattices hung by two windows, and the cracked remains of a lime mortar bordered the door, still with a trace of painted patterns.

The first few weeks in the *makar* had tied Shalima in knots of frustration and self-control. The regime was strict. Prayer was five times a day: near dawn, just after midday, in the afternoon, at sunset, and at nightfall. She expected and accepted the routine, felt at peace in the bowing, the homage and prostration before Allah. But she was impatient with the rituals – the different number of *rak'ahs* to be chanted at different prayer times, the different required positions of the feet, whether the hands needed to be positioned by the thighs or between the navel and chest. She saw the point in ritual cleansing before prayer, but not the strict sequence of washing hands, mouth, nose, face, arms, hair, ears and feet – and each one three times (except the hair, praise to be to Allah for that!). These were specified in Hadiths, suppositions or anecdotes passed down the ages by male clerics, not mentioned in the Qu'ran.

There were regular lessons, too, in Arabic, which she

found difficult. And cooking. Shalima could just about scramble eggs, and before had lived on fast-food takeaways and microwaved meals. But an army marched on its stomach and the way to a man's heart was through his stomach – so her Yemeni teacher said. It seemed a global sentiment. Please a man in the kitchen and pleasure him in bed (much giggling here among her fellow students, and much self-conscious adjustments of veils): the essentials for a happy marriage. And in return? Male protection, the strong arm around her shoulders. She'd heard that before, too, thousands of miles away. But there was more to it than that – and she didn't mean children. She would demand more from her fighter husband.

"In the beginning, your husbands will tell you they will eat any food, the food from your own countries, if need be. But they will not mean it," said the teacher, smiling.

So Shalima learned how to use a round clay oven, how to bake flatbread. She learned to cook the Yemeni national dish, *saltah* – a stew of goat, chicken and lamb, flavoured with fenugreek and a salsa of ground chilli peppers, tomatoes, garlic and herbs. She served it with rice and, yes, scrambled eggs. She learned to like tea flavoured with cloves or cardamom; made sweet honey cake and *masoob* – a mixture of bananas, cream, cheese, dates and honey. And she enjoyed it – it was a welcome break from prayers, Arabic and the Qu'ran.

The final element of her training had been first aid. Her pre-nursing course back home made this much easier for her, and she could even help her fellow students. She learned how to give injections, make stretchers, perform cardiac massage, apply a tourniquet, deal with broken bones and treat gunshot wounds. This was what she had come for. She had used those skills in Mogadishu.

★

Shalima had made friends with a Bosnian girl, Hana, who had learned excellent English before she dropped out of her European literature course at Sarajevo University. As Shalima stepped back into the *makar* with her hand luggage from the Mombasa plane, Hana rushed to her and invited her to a party.

"What sort of party?" asked Shalima.

"A funeral party."

"Whose funeral?"

"My friend's husband, a jihadist fighter."

Shalima wanted to tell Hana about the White Widow, but it must wait.

Together they went to the house of a Belgian *mujahida*, Ghadir. They heard laughter even before they entered. Inside, people sat on the floor around a central carpet loaded with dishes of delicious-smelling food. Ghadir got up to welcome them, all smiles.

"This is a day of joy," she announced. "No one should cry. My husband is with Allah. He won the race. We are celebrating his martyrdom. I am honoured to be a widow."

Shalima looked for signs that Ghadir was kidding herself or forcing herself into this false joviality. But it seemed genuine.

"I have told my children," continued Ghadir, "that their father has bought a house in Paradise and is waiting for them in Heaven, in Jannah."

It was a wake, thought Shalima, that celebrated not a man's life but his death. This man had been killed in battle in Syria. The chatter in the room continued, friends coming and going, food replenished, children playing. Shalima too believed that martyrs were fast-tracked to Paradise and knew that, at times like this, faith was strengthened because the alternative was too distressing. But did these people, on their own at night, with all the uncertainties that lay ahead, never have any doubts? What did Ghadir think about her husband's enjoyment of the seventy-two full-breasted virgins promised to him?

★

Only a week later Shalima, Hana and another friend of Hana's, a Yemeni girl called Yasmin, were drinking coffee in the dining room of the *makar*.

"I have announcement to make," said Hana. Yasmin giggled behind her niqab. "I know a man who want to marry you, Shalima."

Shalima laughed. "Has he seen me?"

"No, but he know about you."

"Have I seen him?"

"Maybe, in a distance. He is Iraqi."

"So you're the matchmaker now, Hana. Well, you need to know that I have some conditions that have to be met before I marry anyone."

Yasmin shook her head.

"Conditions?!" said Hana. "Women don't set conditions, *mujahida* or not. This is Yemen, not England."

"Nevertheless, tell him the conditions. He must allow me to continue on jihadi missions and he must accept that I will wear only the scarf and not the niqab."

"But it is impossible. You will never get husband."

"But not all married women here wear the niqab. I've been looking out for that. This is not the ISIS caliphate, that's why I chose to come here. You don't wear the niqab yourself," she said to Hana.

"But I will when I marry."

Shalima turned to Yasmin. "I've been watching you. It looks really awkward drinking coffee and wearing that veil."

"You get used to it," said Yasmin.

"Can I ask why you wear it and not just a headscarf?"

"It is part of my politics."

"I don't know whether you're smiling when you say that," said Shalima.

"No, I'm not smiling. I'm serious. I'm expressing my faith and my identity."

"But I see it as an affront," replied Shalima.

"Why?" asked Yasmin.

"Because it implies subservience, it's oppressive. It denies that you're a woman, and you should be proud of being a woman."

"I am proud of being a woman. But I feel just the opposite. The niqab liberates me from the way men objectify and sexualise us."

"But doesn't having to conceal our bodies imply we are sinners and temptresses? It actually defines us as sexual because it conceals us," put in Hana.

"No. It's a return," Yasmin said, "to the golden age of Islam and its simple certainties."

"Well, I see it as backward, medieval. In Saudi Arabia and Pakistan and plenty of other places, in the ISIS caliphate, women are flogged if they don't wear a niqab. Do you approve of that?" asked Shalima.

"Of course not, but I wear a niqab because I want to, not because I'm instructed to. This is my everyday protest against Western imperialism." Yasmin laughed. "I know that sounds pretentious."

"Many Muslim men wear Western clothes, even here. Why can't we?"

"To maintain our own culture."

"In an Asian shop back home I once saw hijabs for babies, and they had Calvin Klein logos. What kind of hypocrisy is that?" asked Shalima.

"That's stupid, I agree."

"I found it difficult, Yasmin, back at home: what to keep from our culture, what to bin. I'm British and I'm Muslim. I don't approve of forced marriage, of honour killings, of female subjugation like my mother experienced. My nan's a devout woman but she accepts her place. It's wrong."

"We all have to make our choices. I agree, it's not easy."

"Sometimes I felt too Western, sometimes too foreign. I didn't know who I was."

Hana agreed. And that had been the crux of it for both of them.

Now I do know who I am, thought Shalima: *a Muslim woman who wants some of the freedoms of a Muslim man, who does not play the role that men want me to. I am joining the jihad, but not simply to look after the men, and certainly not to have babies.* She had proved herself in Djibouti and Mogadishu.

"So," said Shalima, "you tell this Iraqi my conditions. If he's still interested, he might be the husband I want."

Not only was the Iraqi not interested in her, the story of Shalima's conditions reverberated like shock waves through the jihadist community. Gently but firmly, an imam lectured her. Most of the other young women shunned her, would not work with her at cooking lessons. If she was out with Hana, who remained loyal, young men passing by would point her out and laugh. Some would shout and threaten her, shaking their fists, a few even swiping a finger across their throats. Shalima said nothing but didn't change her mind. She knew, too, that she was valued: there were young men here whose wounds she had tended in the makeshift hospital, whose pain she had eased. Her care and knowledge had been noted, and also her initiative.

And then one day, Hana said that a fellow Bosnian jihadist wanted to meet Shalima. The conditions that appalled the other young fighters intrigued him, said Hana. His Bosnian name was Petar, his Muslim name Rafiq. He had very little English.

Shalima waited in the small room Hana had found. It was bare except for cushions on the floor where she sat, watching a spider in a corner descend on a thread to examine its web freighted with dead insects. The room was warm, dusty and bright with sunlight. A door slammed somewhere and distant voices tailed away. In spite of herself – *I have a choice*, she kept repeating to herself – her heart was beating fast. She knew there was a limit to Awlaki's toleration. They would not force her to marry but they could expel her back to England to strengthen her faith. Naz would have said waiting here was a ludicrous mistake, perpetuating the miseries Shalima's own mother had suffered. Yet there was something exciting about the very bizarreness of the situation, something that urged her forward into her holy adventure.

There was a knock on the half-open door. She looked up. *This is it.*

"Come in," she said, standing up.

The door was pushed open, and bright light haloed the figure of a man as he stooped in the low doorway. She could distinguish nothing of him, backlit by the sun. He was a slender silhouette, dressed in jeans and a short-sleeved shirt.

He closed the door, turned and said, "*Salaam alaikum.*"

"*Walaikum salaam*," she replied.

She saw his dark curly hair and full black beard; he smiled – no bad teeth, and maybe too young to have five wives. He was lean and dark-skinned, but not an Arab, with hair on his forearms and at the open neck of his shirt.

"Rafiq," he said, his voice soft but nervous.

"Shalima."

Hana would be hovering outside, as chaperone; she would have prepared Rafiq for the conditions. He was studying the oval of Shalima's face, framed by her headscarf. And Shalima was taking in the fact that his eyes were lined with kohl, like black eyeliner. She'd heard that fighters often did this to prevent their eyes from watering in the smoke of battle. But it still looked odd. She smiled and nodded to the cushions. They sat at a corner of the room, she by one wall, he by the other.

He took out his phone, tapped at the touchscreen, then showed it to her.

Serbo-Croat/English dictionary, it said.

Shalima laughed. She saw mischief in his eyes.

"No problem," he said, and laughed.

He was handsome and she liked his awkwardness, so different from the arrogance of some of the men she had seen. Nevertheless, she had to get things straight. She mimed to him, held two fingers out, like a gun pointing at him, and with her thumb indicated him and then herself.

He shrugged. "No problem." He went to his phone and pointed to the word *dowry*.

She was nonplussed, but later Hana told her that part of the group's respect for women was expressed by the man giving a dowry rather than receiving one. He meant shooting lessons would be his dowry.

And now the big one. Shalima circled her face with her hand and then cupped her chin in her palm, looking directly at him.

"It is good," he said. "No problem." With a shy smile he nodded his approval.

He may be a fighter, she thought, *but he is gentle, too.*

He tapped his phone and scrolled through the dictionary.

"You are boutiful," he said. "Boughtiful?"

She grinned at him. "Beautiful, you mean."

"Beautiful," he repeated. "Beautiful. That is right?"

"If you say so."

He frowned; he didn't understand.

For the next hour they swapped the phone, found one-word questions and answers, laughed and relaxed.

"I go," he said eventually, pointing at the words on the screen. They stood up, looked at each other for a long moment, then he salaamed, turned and left. Shalima smiled to herself. Allah had blessed her. This would be fine.

Then Hana came back. "Did it go well?" Her face was expectant.

"Good. No problem," Shalima laughed, and the girls hugged each other. "He's fun."

Shalima and Rafiq met several times over the next week. Rafiq called Hana in as interpreter.

"This is serious," she told Shalima. "Are you ready?"

Shalima nodded, her eyes flashing to Rafiq, who looked at the ground.

"This is what Rafiq wishes to say to you," said Hana. "We know only some things about each other, but when you love someone for the sake of Allah, he will tie a knot between your hearts and make the attachment strong, despite the differences between you."

She stopped. Rafiq lifted his head and his blue eyes were soft. He was asking.

She made him wait, savouring the moment. Then she smiled at him and nodded.

"Yes," she said. "I think that, too."

Rafiq looked questioningly at Hana. She translated, and he laughed out loud with joy and looked upwards. "Inshallah."

"But there is something else," said Hana. "Rafiq says you have to know."

Shalima was suddenly frightened. Another wife? Some other revelation that would destroy everything before it had really started?

He was looking directly into her eyes as Hana translated: "Jihad is my first wife, you will be my second."

Shalima was, for a moment, caught off balance, taken aback. But his eyes were not pleading; he was stating a conviction. Then she understood he was an honourable man, a man she could trust. He was being honest: that was the truth for all of them.

"I know," she said, "I accept that. It is right. Jihad is my first husband."

Hana translated. Rafiq nodded and his face softened; he took in a deep breath and with his finger, softly touched her cheek. Shalima closed her eyes to better feel his touch on her. While her eyes were closed, she said quietly to Hana, "Tell him I am not a virgin. I had one boyfriend four years ago. I was young."

Hana frowned. "Are you sure you want to tell him that?"

Shalima nodded. "He must know."

In the silence Hana seemed to rehearse the words in her head. Shalima felt Rafiq take his finger away from her cheek. She opened her eyes and looked directly into his, now full of questions. Hana whispered the words to him.

He did not avert his gaze. Shalima saw his mouth relax. He looked at her and said something.

"Neither am I," Hana translated. Then added, "We are from Europe. It is normal."

And then Shalima really did want to fling her arms round him. But it would not be seemly. The pill she dared not mention.

Hana and Yasmin arranged the wedding, the nikah. There were few guests as so many disapproved of Shalima's conditions for marriage. She would probably have been stoned, thought Shalima, if they knew she was not a virgin – certainly this marriage could not have taken place in the ISIS caliphate. Because she and Rafiq knew so little of each other, this could not yet be love, but she was confident it was heading that way.

Their wedding night was one of desire and tenderness, the shared wonder at each other's nakedness. In the early hours Shalima awoke and curled up against Rafiq's back. She put her arm gently around him and entwined their fingers. He stirred but did not wake. Shalima had not expected this. The nights were icy, the days burning; they were both here to learn to kill, and the culture they were living in was severe and unforgiving. Yet they had created this haven of softness and understanding. It was a miracle, Allah's will.

In the morning, they prayed together for their future happiness. Afterwards, with Hana translating, Shalima told Rafiq that she had not been a devout Muslim in her youth and went only infrequently to the mosque. Now, she said, her jihad had returned her to the faith, more committed than she had ever been. Hana translated his reply: "It is usually the other way round. But you are different, we know."

When he went on training, she prepared his bag of food and gave a final polish to his Kalashnikov. He told her he was a strong fighter, popular, and his companions would not condemn him for his marriage. He was a good man, she thought. He would not, as most men did, eat his food before her; they would eat together, and he was as gentle with her as she had imagined. He helped her recite the Qu'ran correctly. She downloaded the Serbo-Croat/English dictionary app to her phone and, among laughs and kisses, they learned to speak more to each other. Rafiq taught her to shoot and she discovered she had a good eye as they practised with pistol and AK-47, out in the desert with cans for targets.

Then after fifteen days of marriage, increasing happiness and real love, he was sent on his next operation. The night before he left, through Hana, he said, "We are small in number but great in spirit."

He showed her his contact list on his phone and Hana translated: "Six of my comrades are now martyrs, shahid.

They have joined the caravan of green birds. I have always wanted to be invited but now I want the invitation postponed, inshallah."

He kissed her.

They were committed to the cause, but now they had new feelings.

Rafiq left the next morning, not knowing where the action was to take place. "If I don't make it, I will see you in Jannah, our Heaven."

She wondered if it was the last time she would see him, and when she read the latest lists of martyrs pinned up on the noticeboard the following two mornings, she knew she had inappropriate feelings of fear. She remembered the celebratory funeral Hana had taken her to. Could she react like that widow had?

She soon found out. Five days after Rafiq left, she was informed he had been killed in action at an isolated, derelict village up in the mountains of Southern Yemen. He had been part of the guard of an Al-Qaeda leader. An American drone had destroyed the place, and almost everyone in it, including three children and two women, had been killed.

Shalima was heartbroken. She hurried out of town, desperate to avoid commiserations and congratulations. Out in the searing sun, huddled among bleached rocks in a disused quarry, she watched the heat shimmering across the sand-and-gravel plain. How was it possible to celebrate her beautiful husband's death? She had loved and been loved back. And after just two weeks it had all been snatched away from her.

If this too was the will of Allah, it was also the murderous intention of the USA. She vowed she would not marry again. She would not celebrate Rafiq's death, she would avenge it. Her faith had driven her so far; she had travelled here with an ideal. Now her heart, too, would inspire her. She felt a new fierceness in her, a fierceness that demanded an outlet.

Two days later, that rather odd-looking Englishman came to see her. He had much to tell her.

8.
27th June

While Yusuf and Shalima talked, Davoud, in T-shirt and running shorts, lay on his stomach on the treatment table, head resting on his arms, eyes closed. The thin sheet of bedroll paper beneath him rustled with the slight movement of his leg, and after ten minutes or so of manipulation Jenny's breathing was audible, even, but deeper. Her thumbs worked on his tendons from heel to calf, pressing, easing, loosening. Warmth and friction had dissipated the soreness. He felt her fingers holding his ankle steady while she worked. He had no thoughts: for this brief interval there was only the sensation of healing, a comfort, a timeout.

"OK, Davoud, that's enough for today." Her voice was professional but warm.

He turned over and sat up, legs dangling over the bench. She'd washed her hands and was sitting at her desk tapping the keyboard, her gleaming coppered auburn hair in a ponytail.

"I think we've finished," she said. "You don't need another visit. You've obviously been doing the exercises."

"Yes, religiously."

"You'd be surprised how many people, especially men" – *and especially well-to-do Middle Eastern men*, she thought – "come to me to find out what I can do to make them well, and believe they need make no effort themselves."

"I've even increased the repetitions."

She looked up and smiled. He enjoyed her approval.

"Very good, Mr Nariman," she said in a mock-schoolmarm tone. "A gold star is called for." She was studying her laptop screen, head bent, dangly silver earring resting on her neck, the thin wire looped through her lobe.

He hopped off the bench and crouched to put his socks and trainers back on. He did a series of calf stretches and heel raises.

"Excellent," she said. "Make sure you carry on regularly with the exercises. Your hamstrings should be OK."

It had to be now; this was his last visit.

"Ms Morgan," he said, happy to take refuge in the mock formality, "may I take you for a drink one evening? Just so I can show you my appreciation. You've put me back on track again."

He was putting his sweater on, one arm in a sleeve, and looked at her. He knew what to expect: an amused smile, a quizzical look in those hazel eyes.

"Can you check with reception when I'm free?" She hadn't looked up. "And don't up your mileage again so abruptly. Remember that's what did for your Achilles."

Had he heard correctly? Had she heard correctly?

Then she did look up. "Never mix the professional with the private, that's what the management gurus say, I'm afraid." A serious face. She was wearing her red Welsh rugby shirt again, the three white feathers of the badge over her left breast. "But now your course of treatment is over, there's no dilemma." Her smile flashed, and her eyes were laughing. "That would be really nice, Davoud." She had a scattering of freckles around her nose.

Rueful, wrong-footed, relieved, he half-smiled and raised his eyebrows. "Can we agree a time, then?"

"Next patient's waiting, I'm afraid. Ring me after nine tonight." She scribbled her mobile number on a Post-it note and gave it to him. She liked him: he was neither arrogant nor patronising like so many men, however well educated, from patriarchal cultures.

*

Four days later they sat in a brasserie in Covent Garden, each with a glass of red wine. A thin rain was falling in the courtyard.

"Five miles, twice," he said in answer to her opening question. "Taking it easy – Hyde Park, the Serpentine. Felt good, no twinges."

They talked about fitting running round work schedules.

"You've never really spoken about your work," said Jenny.

"Foreign Office," he said.

"A diplomat, then."

"Sort of, not so grand." He felt awkward about not being open with her. "I've put in for a transfer, another department. Staying in London, though."

He was grateful she didn't probe further, aware she had sensed his reticence. He had needed to say that about London. Had she picked up on that?

They'd touched on things while chatting during his treatment sessions. Now they developed those: her having to dovetail appointments with her son Harry's school commitments and his sailing at weekends; his time with his daughter Sara; how Harry's father had no interest in him, only contributing cash spasmodically; how Sara's mother was wary and possessive. They talked of the contrast between a single mother living with her son and an absent father not living with his daughter: the benefits – and there were some, they both admitted – and the problems.

Then, just as Davoud began to worry he was becoming too introspective and dark, Jenny asked, "What's your most treasured possession?"

It seemed to Davoud like a deliberate conversational switch. So she had felt it too. He wanted to make an impression, give a smart answer, make her laugh. But he couldn't think of anything.

"Apart from family photos and one or two books, it has to be my guitar."

She laughed. "I hadn't imagined you as a wannabe pop star."

So he told her about his group and the sort of music they liked. And that continued on to more talk about spare time. Jenny and Harry attended every Welsh Rugby Union match in the Six Nations Championship. Davoud was fascinated by cryptic crosswords. She'd begun coasteering.

"Never heard of it."

"On a rocky coast – sea-level traversing, scrambling, diving, canyoning, adventure swimming. I've done it in Dorset and North Wales. Fantastic!"

He was becoming obsessive about Sudoku and kakuro – needed to do one a day, at least. She walked and ran with friends. He always ran alone.

The evening passed quickly and she refused his offer to escort her back to her Bayswater flat on the Tube.

"It's not the Middle East," she said.

"Not as different as you'd like to think," he said cryptically.

On their next evening out they had a meal. Davoud talked about his father's worrying loss of memory; Jenny told of her mother's death from cancer and her house in the Cotswolds which Jenny now owned. They shared their backgrounds and childhoods, Davoud anxious to play down his privileged upbringing, Jenny gently mocking it, playing the artisan to his aristocrat. She made him laugh, and he wondered what on earth she might find interesting in him.

Then, over dessert, she announced, "I need to tell you, I've been in an on/off relationship for a couple of years. It's off at the moment."

Why had she told him? To warn him off? To show she was – that horrible word – available if…

They went their separate ways after the meal, but she sent him a text just as he was getting into bed. *Enjoyed the evening. How about Saturday? I've a late-night babysitter.*

So perhaps there was something reciprocal. Davoud was so bad at signals. He sat up in bed with a brandy, buoyant, determined to finish his fiendish Sudoku but unable to concentrate.

Occasionally they snatched a brief meeting during the day, sitting on a bench on the Embankment or in a coffee bar, or strolling in a park. They began to build up pictures of each other. She admired him for living with his father, making him feel safer.

"I love him," he said, "but it's frightening, seeing his memory go. But he never forgets his prayers."

He talked of his father's deep Islamic faith, and of his own loss of faith at the murder of his mother and sister by Islamic terrorists.

Jenny admired him, too, she told him, for insisting on seeing his daughter regularly and never breaking promises to see her, whatever the pressures of his work; for how he managed his life, balancing the personal (including keeping fit) and the professional. Though it frustrated her, she admired too the quiet discretion about his work. He was obviously successful and competent. What also impressed her was how he had a social conscience, a deep drive to help society – in spite of his very privileged upbringing and education.

The nearest he got to saying what his job entailed was that it concerned the protection of ordinary people, protecting what he called "this lovely, easy-going, middle-of-the-road way of life" in Britain. But he never spoke about his marriage and separation. Was this a natural discretion or an inability to articulate confused feelings?

He was good-looking, too. She liked his neat beard; the flecks of grey were more prominent there than in his hair but they added a touch of gravity. His body, she knew very well, was in good shape, remembering her white fingers on the caramel skin of his feet.

There were parallels in what Davoud saw in Jenny: the single parent bringing up her son without help from her ex-husband; the way she had progressed her career – leaving the NHS because its bureaucracy stifled initiative, then moving to a private hospital with more opportunities but worse terms and conditions, taking extra training to expand her professional worth, and finally leaving the private hospital to set up her own physiotherapy practice in a private sports medicine clinic. Her hours were therefore flexible and she could plan her work around Harry's commitments. He admired her boldness in doing this, abandoning a safety net and relying completely on herself. He was certain he would not have the nerve to do that. He knew she was an excellent physio and knew her subject backwards.

She seemed to live life at a pace but was organised so never flustered. She had friends, was sociable and he knew she had an instinctive rapport with a wide range of people. She was a listener and he was confident her friends would confide in her, look for and accept her support in times of crisis. She was warm and outgoing where he was cool and reserved. Above all, she was fun and adventurous, light-hearted and sometimes frivolous. Her face was animated and expressive, and she moved briskly. In spite of working in private practice, she had a strong sense of social justice, railing against government policies that hurt the most vulnerable. She was practical, too, able to repair stuff, understand how things worked.

One day in Regent's Park as they walked – they only had forty minutes together – she put her arm through his. She felt him tuck her hand in the crook of his arm and was silent. They walked on a few paces, then he stopped and turned to her, looked her in the eye. She tilted her head up to him and they kissed. His kissing was soft and gentle, prolonged. She felt him erect against her.

"Well, well!" She laughed.

He shifted back, but still held her.

"Don't be embarrassed, I like compliments." She smiled.

She pulled him to her and kissed him, her hands on the back of his neck.

9.
28th July

They halted. The guiding hand let go his arm and Yusuf rocked a little, standing unsupported. Unsteady, he heard other footsteps shuffling on the stony ground. His blindfold was taken off. He opened his eyes and saw the silhouettes of moving figures. Ahead, a single torchlight wobbled; above them loomed a mountain crest. There was a gentle push on his back and he stepped forward. The narrow path continued to climb; a rock face on his left, a sense of space on his right. The path zigzagged upwards and now the space was on his left, his right hand groping for the roughness of the rock, his sandaled feet stumbling. Shalima was somewhere behind him.

They scrambled across a steep stony lip and the path levelled out, the rock face retreating, the darkness less intense, an arc of mountains around him with the sky lighter behind it. It was like an amphitheatre high up in the hills. Another halt, a hand on his shoulder, pressing down gently.

"Sit."

Yusuf found a rock and sat down. Now they weren't climbing, he felt the cold mountain air and the sweat in his T-shirt cooling. He wrapped his keffiyeh round him. Two of the men were moving deeper into the cirque of rock. Behind him he heard stones shifting on the ground, the faint clack of sticks; saw one bobbing torchlight and four people slowly emerging over the lip. The second figure was led over to him and sat next to him.

"Wherever it is, we've arrived," she whispered. It was Shalima's voice muffled behind her niqab.

"Are you ready?"

"Yes." Certainty in her voice.

Yusuf was reassured, strengthened. Soon, everything would be to play for: in this remote mountain hideaway, an executive meeting in which they would pitch their plan together. The men who had escorted them were some distance away. He could hear their muttering, see their rifles gleam for a moment as they turned to each other, cigarette ends glowing red.

Yusuf was weary: the flight to King Abdulaziz Airport in Jeddah after transfers across Europe to hide his tracks; the nine-hour, thousand-kilometre drive down the Red Sea coast, crossing from Saudi Arabia into Yemen with only two brief stops for figs and water. Then Shalima getting out of another car at a dusty crossroads in the desert, both of them leaving their cars for a truck, being blindfolded for the long, slow, bumpy drive into the hills. Then the long climb up to here. His whole body was aching, and yet he must keep a clear mind for his presentation. He passed a bottle of water to Shalima and she drank greedily.

A month ago he had arranged a meeting with her in Sana'a. He'd been back to the training camp there and been intrigued by the scandalised gossip about this English girl who had laid down conditions for marriage, been married, then widowed. Personal revenge would make her even more devoted to the cause. More important to him, she had gained a reputation for her work as a courier, then in the Mogadishu fighting, and the AQ leadership had invited her to witness the planning of the Mombasa attack with the legendary White Widow. She must be highly thought of. He had not realised at first that she was the girl he'd met off the plane.

Over meetings and many coffees, he had explained the outline – for that was all it was at the moment, not much more than an idea – of his plan. She had been immediately impressed by its audacity and magnitude. The implications were breathtaking. Her enthusiasm had fuelled his and they had developed the idea, working out the information they needed to create a proper plan. It was quickly decided – and Yusuf never knew whether it was his suggestion or hers – that she would be his second in command, another unprecedented move. Because of her experience with the White Widow, she would be responsible for all the preparation in the Yemen, and he would do the reconnaissance and planning back in England.

So here they were, nothing on paper for security reasons, but with every detail in their heads. Now they waited for the summons to the executive. All they knew was that a group of high-level Al-Qaeda leaders had convened to hear their plans; the men who could resource or reject the mission. It was an all-or-nothing opportunity. If they failed to convince, that was the end of it.

A torchlight bobbed towards them, a hand beckoned. Shalima and Yusuf got up. They were led deeper into the amphitheatre towards a deep black patch in the rock wall, which became a cave. A rough tarpaulin curtain was pulled aside. They were hurried into a lamplit space where five men, their faces alternately shadowed and illuminated by the shifting flames of a wood fire, sat on cushions facing them. Two empty cushions were on the cave floor.

"Sit, please," said a voice. The men who had brought them left.

They were given two small bowls of coffee – thick, black and sweet. The bowls were warm in their palms, the coffee scalding, the sugar reviving. The men sat upright still, watching them: black beards, Arab robes, steel barrels of rifles glinting by their sides. Two were older, faces furrowed; of the three younger men, two wore spectacles. Yusuf refused to be intimidated, sensed Shalima looking back directly at them, took heart and felt his mind clear. He wondered how they felt about a woman being there.

"Your plan," said one of the older men. "We understand English."

Yusuf began, his voice echoing slightly in the cave, firewood spitting and settling. "The aim is to rescue Suleiman al-Hariri, at present in a prison in England."

He paused to let that sink in, to see if there was a response, but in the shadowy firelight it was impossible to see any change of expression in the men's faces.

"Why him?"

"In our training," said Yusuf, "we have heard about his work: his thinking and planning, his courage. He is a great man, a great servant of Allah."

"He has accomplished great things," added Shalima. "We cannot let him rot in a British prison."

A silence.

"And to do so, we will break the last taboo," said Yusuf.

Again, no response.

Yusuf described the coded message by which he would give the go-ahead, why the specific location had been chosen, why the timing was essential, how transport would be arranged, how the attack would be made.

"Shall I show you?"

The older man nodded his head.

Yusuf spread out the OS map he had brought hidden in a folder of brochures about Red Sea diving, his cover story for the flight to Saudi Arabia. One of the men held a lamp close and they all bent forward to see better. Yusuf described the landscape, pointed out the locations highlighted in yellow. He left the map open and sat back to outline the bargaining, the leverage they would have with the UK government and, finally, how they would return Suleiman to Al-Qaeda here in the Yemen.

"Shalima will be my second in command." He turned to her, knowing that the men would have had full background checks done on both of them.

In a clear, steady voice, Shalima described the manpower involved, training requirements, research required, the equipment needed – explosives and detonators, weaponry – and transport to the attack site.

She finished and, after a moment's silence, Yusuf concluded by describing in detail the scene as it would be the day after the attack, what the English media would be saying and how the population would be reacting.

He began to fold up the map, but the leader wanted to keep it. There were five questions, one from each of the men, which he and Shalima were able to answer.

"Thank you," said the leader. "We are impressed with your planning."

Yusuf felt that these battle-hardened men, men who had approved violent actions in many parts of the world, were genuinely stirred.

"We will now decide. There is food for you outside."

They were led out, given blankets to wrap themselves in, water and a dish of spicy lamb and rice. So they waited, the waning moon edging across the sky, stars clear. They had both agreed that their presentation would stick to the practicalities: the wider picture, they had assumed, the committee would articulate for themselves, given their experience and intelligence, and so be more likely to agree. ISIS was now outshining Al-Qaeda. It was a long time since Al-Qaeda had carried out a 'spectacular'. An attack by a home-grown English-born team would undermine confidence in the UK security services and divide communities even more, raising mistrust and suspicion. A woman co-leading would boost the image of female jihadists, attracting stronger, more enterprising women who wanted to be more than brides and mothers.

Sleep was impossible. As they waited, they wondered if this had been a mistake. Perhaps they assumed too much. Perhaps the leaders in the cave would just think the whole idea too preposterous, too outlandish, too difficult to implement. They realised again the magnitude of what they were proposing, the possible international implications. Would Al-Qaeda draw back from this ultimate challenge? Was Suleiman still so important to them?

Shalima pondered the two very different routes she and Yusuf had taken to arrive here. For her, a half-hearted Muslim when younger, a chance meeting had led to her jihad, and her jihad had brought her fully back to her faith. Yusuf had converted to Islam and his faith had led him directly to his jihad. Now their futures depended on this meeting.

A man approached, rifle slung over his shoulder. He stretched out his arm and beckoned them. "Come."

They shook off their blankets and stood up, the sky lightening, dawn not far away. The man drew back the tarpaulin and they stepped inside. The committee were standing up. The fire had been renewed and the flames danced, the men's shadows cavorting around the cave walls. Yusuf's heart was beating hard. He touched Shalima's hand, and she oh-so briefly squeezed his fingers.

"Your plan is bold," said the leader. "It will require nerve and total commitment. You will be attacking your own countrymen."

But it was that double betrayal that made it all the more fulfilling to Yusuf.

"You are prepared to die, to be shahid?"

"Of course. Inshallah," said Yusuf.

"And you?" asked the leader.

"Inshallah," said Shalima.

"We accept your plan. We will help you."

He stepped forward and shook Yusuf's hand. The other

men followed. Shalima took a short step backwards and watched. They would not shake her hand, but that did not matter. She was exultant.

Arrangements were made for further meetings with key men. They would be allowed to choose their attack team, but their choices must be approved at higher levels. Now they must leave quickly before it was full light.

So they left, escorted back down the track, needing to be silent, back to the truck and then the cars to Sana'a. Each wanted to hug the other, but that was impossible. The first part was over. Now the hard work started.

The world will know I existed, thought Yusuf.

I will have made my mark in the world, thought Shalima.

Inshallah, each added, almost as an afterthought, guilty at their vanity.

PART 2

FLEDGING

10.
Friday 25th September

Two months later, their plan already being activated, neither Yusuf nor Shalima knew anything about a scene taking place in Rotherdyke's central police station in West Yorkshire.

It was too warm in this small office, thought Detective Sergeant Hannah Walker, too warm for the girl in her bulky brown woollen jumper and her tight black leggings, struggling to confront bad memories and find words to describe them to a stranger in a police station. The window wouldn't open, its frame solid with paint.

The girl's social worker was there, of course: Jane, a saint, worked to the bone by her caseload of lost causes, but never giving up. The girl, Kelly, was taking a gulp of hot sugared tea, her mouth already full of a custard cream from a plateful provided by Hannah, not the police budget. Kelly was overweight, face pale and podgy as dough, dyed blonde hair in a mess, a stud in the corner of her lip.

"You've told us the taxi driver gave you a small bottle of vodka in the taxi and told you to swallow three pills."

"I was glad, I wanted to be out of my head. I knew what was coming."

Hannah glanced across at Jane, and Jane nodded slightly.

"What happened, Kelly, when he took you into the house?"

Kelly bit her lip, her eyes darted everywhere except to look at either of the two women. She chewed her thumbnail. In a low voice which the others had to crane forward to hear, she said, "He led me upstairs and into a room. The curtains were drawn and there was a double bed in it. Lying on it was Leanne. I knew her because we had been together at other places. Two men were holding her arms above her head. She looked at me. She was terrified. Her skirt was around her waist. She still had her black boots on."

She took a deep breath like a sob and covered her face with her hands. Jane leaned forward to hold her hand, but she shook it off.

"Take your time," said Hannah. "But it's really important we know what happened."

Kelly closed her eyes, her hands together on her lap, the fingers of one scratching insistently at the palm of the other. She said softly, "There was three other men, all Asians; I hadn't seen any of 'em before. They unbelted their jeans and pushed 'em down. They all had hard-ons. Then one of them spread Leanne's legs and fucked her. He were really rough with her, smacking her face an' shouting. It were 'orrible. Leanne were screaming but one of the men put 'is hand over 'er mouth. I could see she could hardly breathe. She were struggling but they held her."

Then Kelly shook her head and gave a long, low moan, a keening sound that made Hannah shiver. Kelly curled up on her chair, her thumb in her mouth. Jane went to comfort her but as soon as her arm touched Kelly's shoulder, Kelly winced and retracted even more into herself.

"Just tell us the last part," said Jane. "I know it's hard, but we have to know so we can put them in prison."

Kelly looked at her and then at Hannah, her face set, eyes as cold as stone. Slowly she uncurled herself, sat upright and, staring down at the table, said in a flat tone, as if wearied beyond anything, "The second man made her give him a blow job. Then the third fucked 'er. They changed places with the two men who were 'olding 'er hands and then those two men fucked her. Hard and rough and nasty, calling her a slut, shouting, 'Slut, slut, white slut bitch.'"

She paused, and her eyes focused again. She took a custard cream and nibbled at it, took a bite and crunched it.

"When he finished, he spat at her. Leanne curled up on the bed, crying. The men were all laughing."

"And the taxi man?" asked Hannah quietly.

Kelly licked some crumbs off her lips. "'E said if I didn't suck him off in his taxi, what happened to Leanne would happen to me. 'E took me away and 'e parked 'is taxi in the yard of an empty factory. So I did. Then I got out and was sick. 'E laughed and drove off, just left me there. That's when it started to rain."

Kelly gave a weird smile, her mouth twisted. "I loved that rain, washing my face."

Hannah turned the recorder off. "I want to thank you, Kelly, you've been very brave. We've talked to other girls and they've given similar accounts. We've almost finished our investigations. These men, and others, will be in court and I'm confident they'll be sent to prison. Jane will take you home now. Thank you again."

When they'd gone, Hannah leaned back in the chair. How was she supposed to keep detached, emotionally uninvolved when she felt such pity and such rage? After the shocking failures in Birmingham, Rochdale, Oxford and all those other places, and the reports into them, grooming was a top priority. Resources had been given, IT systems made compatible, agencies now cooperated, councillors and senior officers no longer afraid of accusations of racism.

But the job was also harder now. Grooming was becoming professionalised: no longer just personal sexual gratification, but a career path with good financial opportunities for young Asian males. And she knew it wasn't just Asians. White gangs operated too, British and Eastern European. But in her Rotherdyke patch it was mostly Asians. The abusers, too, had learned from Rochdale and the rest. They were cannier and more cautious, more brutal. A few had become overconfident, though, and made mistakes.

Giving evidence in court would provide Hannah with a lot of satisfaction. For some of the girls at least, the abduction, humiliation, beatings, abuse, rape, trafficking and even torture would be over, if the victims could ever get over experiences like that. She doubted it. They were scarred for life. And the abusers? In prison they would be in safe wings, with other paedophiles, kept apart from other prisoners for their own safety. Hannah wished it were otherwise. They needed to suffer. A bit of revenge would not go amiss.

Many of these men had been respectable members of the community; they were fathers, one was a religious studies teacher in a mosque. Their shame, too, would be a punishment.

The door opened and Detective Inspector Alan Sewell walked in. He was in charge of the whole investigation, Operation Raptor.

"Progress?" he asked.

"Yes, another piece in the jigsaw. Kelly's one of our best witnesses."

"Good. It's all beginning to fit together. That's what I wanted to tell you. We've decided: on Sunday, we'll be raiding five properties. I want you to be in charge of the raid on the Opal Street house."

"That's where Kelly was taken."

"We'll nail these bastards, Hannah. And it won't do your career any harm either."

He smiled at her and left the room. He was a decent copper, a good boss. Career? It had never entered her head. That would be a by-product. What she wanted was a result for the sake of the girls. Taxi man? He was a delivery man – delivering bodies, for that's all they were to the men, flesh. How she hoped he would be at Opal Street, that she would be the one who arrested and cuffed him, saw fear at last in his eyes. She would deliver him.

She hadn't led a raid before. They needed the men in custody, but they also needed evidence. They would have phones and laptops which would incriminate them.

11.

Her hand, hot and electric, rested on his thigh. She was so casual about it, natural. She had got into the car, kissed him briefly, fastened her seat belt and then placed her hand there, fingers curved and occasionally caressing.

Davoud accelerated into the outside lane. It was Friday lunchtime and London's weekend getaway traffic was already thickening up. It would be a two-hour drive along the M4 and then up through the Cotswolds to Uley where Jenny's mother had lived. After her death, Jenny had kept the cottage on, coming for holidays and weekends. This would be their first weekend together, two nights when they could sleep and wake together in the morning.

They had made love only five times – he'd counted: three times at her flat when her son Harry was out with friends, twice in a bijou room he had booked at an expensive small hotel in Bloomsbury when they had both abandoned work for the afternoon. When Jenny had to leave to be at home for Harry arriving back from school, Davoud lay there in the rumpled sheets, the scent of her in the bed, her hot moistness drying on him, hearing her dressing in the bathroom. He had never felt such peace. Dressed and demure again, she kissed him on the forehead, and as he reached for her hand she moved away, jaunty and smiling, blew him a kiss and left. The last time she had ordered champagne from reception, the bottle in its nest of ice cubes on the bedside table.

The fast lane was making progress. He concentrated on keeping his distance.

"Your vastus medialis," she said, stroking his thigh. "Well honed by running."

He glanced at her, saw her eyes mischievous, a half-smile.

"And this is your sartorius," she continued, tracing her fingers along his inner thigh.

He felt his penis stiffen. *Don't stray, don't touch it.* But he wanted her to, in the fast lane, passing Maidenhead, overtaking a lorry and the driver looking down from his cab, grinning and giving the thumbs-up. But she didn't, and he was disappointed, wanting that lorry driver to witness his new, unfamiliar sensual self, wanting that crude male congratulation, even envy.

Jenny was so frank, so direct. And he was so… well, zipped up, buttoned up, made diffident by Dunia, the only other woman he had slept with. It was more than that: learning at prep school how to hide his true feelings, learning that any sign of sensitivity would be mocked, any weakness perpetually exploited by the other boys. Any hint of tenderness or delicacy led to a taunting ritual humiliation. Flippancy, cynicism and banter created a shell with which he protected himself. In its time, it had served him well, but now he wanted to emerge, escape. There was a promise in Jenny's hand, a joyfulness.

The words came unexpectedly: "Dunia told me she has another man," he said. "It's serious, as it would have to be, with her. He's met Sara."

Had she heard the tremble in his voice? Did she understand he already felt his fatherhood threatened, his daughter being brought up by another man? Different values, different interests. His part-time parenting more marginalised.

"I don't want to meet him when I take Sara back," continued Davoud. "Or shake his hand politely, see Sara turn into the house with him and watch the door close on the three of them."

He could too easily see the new family unit forming: the new man buying Sara an ice cream, sharing a joke, being sharp with her, imposing his own discipline, reading her a bedtime story, taking her hand on a walk.

Davoud eased back into the middle lane, slowing to a steady seventy-five miles an hour.

"That must be hard for you," said Jenny. "I don't envy you that." She paused. "Harry's dad doesn't care about him. Makes it easier for me, in a way, but harder for Harry."

Davoud wondered when he would meet Harry, how easily Jenny would share her son with him. Immediately he knew he was way ahead, and that his eagerness to commit might put Jenny off. He was afraid to wonder how serious she was, wanted to just enjoy it for what it was, but knew he found it difficult, just living in the present.

"It's good for Harry," she said. "This weekend away. It's his first time, at the regatta with his club. He's one of the youngest."

Davoud was selfishly glad of it.

"They have a rule, a good rule, but I didn't think that when they first told us," said Jenny. "No contacts allowed between parents and children, except of course in emergency. So I can't phone him or email him."

"What's the reason?"

"It can unsettle the younger ones, make them homesick maybe. Best that they deal with that themselves."

"Sounds a bit harsh."

"Exactly what I thought. But I've changed my mind. He'll be fine. It'll give him confidence, the start of independence."

The traffic was thinning now they were past Swindon.

"Parenting isn't easy, is it?" said Jenny.

Davoud sighed. Life wasn't easy: his father's behaviour was causing more concern, his job was becoming surprisingly frustrating, the prospect of Dunia's man was looming. Jenny was the only haven: a haven he sought but mustn't reach for.

Jenny directed him off the M4 and north up the A46. They

drove into the village of Uley and down a short, gravelled track. Jenny's cottage was on its own, set back behind a crowded garden, warm yellow Cotswold stone, deep-set windows, a porch with a climbing rose, the last browning blooms. There were trees behind it, a small wood, but it overlooked fields.

"They lead to the escarpment," she said. "Beyond that, the Severn and then Wales, the Black Mountains."

"It's beautiful," he said and leaned across to kiss her.

They quickly unloaded the boot – food, bed linen, walking gear. Inside, the cottage smelt slightly damp.

"I always leave the fire laid. You light it and I'll turn on the central heating."

Davoud had never lit a real fire. He took matches from the mantlepiece and knelt, registered the coal piled on a neat lattice of wood and the rolled newspaper beneath. He tentatively lit the paper and watched the flames spread upwards. He was hopeless, practically. What if the wood didn't take? If the paper just collapsed, half-burnt, to ash, and there was just a dreary tail of smoke? If the whole weekend would turn out like that? A damp squib. He felt foolish, unmanned somehow. He stood and watched the fire, heard the first crackle of wood burning and felt better.

"Now we're going to get this meal ready – together," she said, "then we'll leave it to simmer and go down to The Old Crown for a drink. A different rhythm. And take your tie off!"

She freed him. He was glad to comply. He'd never done this before: light a fire, share the making of a meal with a woman, have a romantic weekend away. Were there protocols?

"Fine," he said. "What do you want me to do?"

"Chop onions. They're in that bag. Cutlery drawer's there."

Kitchen work had been Dunia's domain, and even chopping onions was a challenge. Nevertheless they made a chilli con carne, left it on a low light, and walked, her arm in his, through the increasing darkness along the track and into the pub. It was beamed, and warm with a log fire blazing, noisy with chatter. They knew Jenny, of course, the barman and the locals, and greeted her warmly, then looked at Davoud. He felt measured up, appraised, the only non-white face. He wondered with a shock whether he was one of several men she had brought here. He felt her hug him closer, as if to reassure him.

"Try the Hogshead," she said, "it's the local brewery. I'll have a half."

They found a quieter corner.

"It's a long time since I had a pint. I'm usually a wine or gin man."

"So, another new experience for you. Take it slowly, there's no rush."

And she smiled at him, intertwined their fingers on the table.

"No need to be wary."

12.

Around the time that Davoud and Jenny entered The Old Crown, Yusuf stood on the deck of the overnight Northlink Ferry from Lerwick to Aberdeen. At the stern, sheltered from the wind, he watched the lights of Fair Isle passing to the west.

Everything had gone to plan. From Yemen to Rome he had flown with his Yusuf Javeed passport, but from Rome he had travelled on Ryan Hudson's passport beginning with the one-way train ticket to Oslo, paid for in cash. Al-Qaeda had provided the money, but the planning had been his own, the aim being to make any tracing of him difficult. He had an overnight sleeper berth from Rome to Munich, then a twelve-hour journey via a change of trains in Hamburg to Copenhagen. Another train took him from there to Gothenburg, arriving late at night. Spending a fortune of what he supposed was rich Saudi Arabian sponsor money on sandwiches and coffee, he dozed the small hours away until the 0430 to Oslo, passing through endless fir forests. His last train had been from Oslo to Bergen, the carriage full of noisy young Norwegians heading out to the wilds for the weekend.

Never, even in his time training in the Yemeni desert, had he enjoyed flopping down onto a bed so much as he did on the Smyril Line ferry from Bergen to Lerwick. He slept the night away, awaking just in time to go on deck and watch the ship nosing into Lerwick harbour, gulls screeching all around. It was the last ferry sailing from Norway of the season. A desultory look at his passport – his straggly beard probably suggesting he was a folk musician or a birder – and he was back in Britain, carrying a small rucksack and a big idea.

He had three hours to kill in Lerwick, wandering the curved main street, sheltered from the harbour winds, passing the telescope shop and the Ghurka Nepalese restaurant, eating porridge in the co-op café and watching oil and fishing boats. He imagined a mosque here, with its slender minaret above the stocky, crouched stone buildings, the call of the muezzin fighting the cold North Sea wind: the northernmost outpost of Islam. Sharia law among the Wee Frees. He laughed to himself. A crazy world.

It was cold on deck and a thin rain slapped his face in the wind, the last lights of Fair Isle now behind them. He stepped inside, into the warmth, and found the bar where he ordered a fresh orange juice with ice and sat at an empty side table. The ship was pleasantly only half full: laughing young people with beers, going back to a new term at Aberdeen University, maybe; a group of birders still with binos slung round their necks, checking bird books, compiling a group list of birds spotted; a group of crop-headed, muscular men with tattooed biceps, drinking beer, joking and tying delicate flies for the fishing competition they were talking about. None of them had an inkling about the truth of their fellow passenger and his secret. They were so complacent, so naive.

Islam had once flourished as far north as Spain. Now Yusuf was at the beginning of a second surge, a second revolution, gathering momentum. There would be a price to pay – their northern air, with its smells of fish and flares of oil, might soon carry a deadlier threat. Yusuf took another drink of his orange, finished his packet of salt-'n'-vinegar crisps. He felt so superior, so strong with his plan and his faith. In a couple of weeks, when they saw his photo on TV or in the papers, would these passengers – and those on the continental trains – remember him being among them, that they were once within touching distance of history? Would they have a chilling notoriety, as if they had been touched but unharmed by the plague?

He smiled to himself – inshallah, it would all happen.

2010

My father is angry – what a total hypocrite he is – when I refuse to join the family import/export firm when I leave school. It pleases me that he feels rejected by me. Instead, I go to study civil engineering, wanting to learn the skills necessary to construct real things of practical use to the community. There, in my final year, playing for the local cricket team, the Seacroft Artisans, I become friends with the wicketkeeper, Imran. Imran is fanatical about cricket but also quiet, serious and hard-working at his computer studies. He is a devout Muslim, and late one afternoon, in the sunshine on the boundary after both of us have batted, our conversation turns to Imran's religious faith and my lack of it.

"Why don't you come to the mosque and see Friday prayers for yourself?"

So I go – not to the grand, newly built mosque with its golden dome, arched windows and minaret, but to a disused primary school. In the old assembly hall, dust dancing in the sunlight from the high windows, I watch rows of men kneel, bow their backs, prostrate themselves and recite the Qur'an. I think it is amusing that not many years ago, rows of children in here sung out:

Onward, Christian soldiers, marching as to war.
With the cross of Jesus marching on before.

I begin to attend the mosque regularly.

In my sessions at the mosque an old, white-bearded man with a soft voice, a gentle smile and a humble faith tutors me. After a few months I am certain about what I want to do. Islam gives me a code for living.

One Friday evening, in the room which still has **Head Teacher** on the door, where the bookshelves are empty and dusty and there is still an old green filing cabinet, the old man asks me if I accept the Five Pillars of Islam: the shahada (there is no God but God, and Muhammad is his messenger), salat (performing prayer five times a day), paying zakat (charity for the poor), sawm (fasting in the month of Ramadan), and performing hajj (the pilgrimage to Mecca).

"I do," I say, thinking it is like a marriage ceremony.

"Do you accept that Jesus was not the son of God?"

"I do." Then I recite the shahada, the declaration of faith. "There is no God but God, and Muhammad is his messenger."

The old man smiles. "You are now a Muslim."

Imran, observing me nearby, embraces me with tears in his eyes. "You are now truly my brother."

I feel pure, purged and — if I am honest — a sort of vain virtue. Imran takes both of my hands in his.

"Now you must have a Muslim name."

And I am given the name Yusuf.

"It means 'God gives'," says the old man.

I choose Javeed for my second name; it means 'Eternal'.

"Now," says Imran, "Allah will record for you, Yusuf, every good deed you ever performed before you were a Muslim and will erase every bad deed you performed."

"Sounds a good deal," I say. I feel full of the zeal of a new beginning.

"I am so happy I must text some of my friends," says Imran, his eyes bright with enthusiasm. "But remember: you are Yusuf only with us. You must still be Ryan with everyone else, your family and friends. It is important."

I do not understand why but accept it.

After my conversion, Imran invites me to join a study group of young men from another mosque. There I first come across Anwar al-Awlaki, and listen to a series of his lectures on video: ***The Constants on the Path of Jihad***. I learn that jihad is not restricted to a specific land, nor dependent on a specific battle or an individual leader; that going on jihad is a victory over Satan; that the interpretation, spread about in the West, of jihad as a personal, internal, non-violent struggle with oneself is a conscious attempt to undermine Islam.

I watch other videos that fill me full of anger: of Iraqi and Afghan children mutilated by American drones and bombs, of the slaughter of Muslims in the Balkan Wars, of Syrian women and children burned to death or left with hideous scars by the American/British coalition.

2011

The traffic lights change to red and Imran draws the car to a halt. Asian Spice FM is playing on the radio. We are driving back from the Test match, both of us with beards and white skullcaps.

"That six that made his century, fantastic! What a captain!" I say.

"Two-nil, we can't lose the series now," says Imran.

"We? You mean Pakistan. I'm English, remember."

Imran laughs.

A sudden loud thumping on my side window, fists

pummelling the glass. Two faces, white faces, press up, mouths open, lips drawn thin, eyes burning, yelling, "Fucking Paki bastards, fuck off home!"

The lad at my window leans back and swings his arm, there's a blur of something dark – a baseball bat? – and then the windscreen shatters. Then another smash on Imran's side. The lads run off, laughing and jeering. Hearts beating fast, shocked at the suddenness of the action, we look at each other and then at the windscreen: two holes, a shock zone of whitened glass around them and the rest of the screen crazed. Car horns peep behind them. My fear turns to anger.

An autumn evening back in Leeds, getting dark. My head is full of videos I have watched in the room at the back of the mosque – the broken bodies of my Muslim brothers, killed by drones and bombs from the USA and UK. My own country. Last week the mosque walls were spray-painted with ***We don't want you here.***

I walk down a side street to my digs. I turn my new name round in my mouth like a new sweet. Yusuf, meaning 'God gives'. Then I hear footsteps behind me, turn and see three youths. They are on me before I can run. Hands grip my arms, fingers digging into my muscles like a vice, my arms wrenched back and twisted up behind my back. Then a fist, knuckles hard as stone, smashes into my nose. Another punch slams into my mouth; the taste of blood. Then a boot into my stomach. I double up, coughing and spluttering. They hurl me to the ground and I hold my arms instinctively around my head, but daggers of pain stab my knees as they hit the paving stones. I curl up. Kicks to the side of my head, a boot into my groin that make me scream and want to vomit.

Then my head is yanked up by my beard. I open my eyes, smell beer on the face thrust into mine, feel something sharp at my throat.

"Fucking Paki lover!" is snarled through shining teeth. "Next time it's this!"

The gleam of a knife blade below my eyes, the point pricking my cheekbone. Then a gob of spit shoots into my face. A few more kicks and they run off.

★

He would never forget. There was a scar now, below his right eye. A memento as clear as his memory of his terror, his pain, his being alone. He would answer those youths who had attacked him, and with interest. He would help purify the world of godlessness, of his father's corrupting values. He had joined jihad – travelling from Manchester to Amsterdam, then Vienna, then Istanbul and finally to Sana'a – all paid for by some unknown Muslim group behind the mosque. He had his new name of Yusuf Javeed.

Now his mission: to return to England and play his own part. If necessary, to become a martyr. Not just to reach Paradise, but to prove to Allah the strength of his faith and his courage.

He turned his attention to the bar. A slim young woman stood facing him, looking at him, a glass of red wine in her hand. Bright red lipstick and short blonde hair, touched with purple highlights; a tight red top. But it was her legs that drew him: red stiletto heels and pale blue jeans as tight as if they had been painted on her, every contour of her legs visible. She shifted her weight from hip to hip, creating a different alignment of curves, then turned to speak to a man next to her, her back to Yusuf now, a thin band of tanned flesh visible between her jeans and top. She dropped something and bent to pick it up – a coin maybe, or a note. It was as if she was offering her arse to Yusuf, the tight curves of it. She straightened up and continued her conversation.

Yusuf loathed his fascination and the erection he felt rising, was almost nauseous with disgust at himself. In desperation, he looked across to the birders, tried to concentrate on their conversation, heard red-throated divers mentioned, noticed a man in a wheelchair with a pint and the *Daily Record*. Closed his eyes. But the image would not go away: the curves in the denim. He wanted to recite the Qu'ran, chant it to himself, but it felt blasphemous with that image still in his mind.

And then he looked at her again. She was facing him now, standing with her feet apart, the shaped space that began at her ankles aimed upwards like an arrow towards her crotch where the space between her legs was narrow but wide enough, a crease visible there. Now he was hard, hating the power of her, the brazenness, unable to take his eyes off her. Where now was his God? And when he looked at her face, he knew she knew. Her knowing smile mocked him before she turned away, as if she had flicked her fingers at him and forgotten him. He was her puppet. He loathed her power and her scorn. And then the image of Debbie slid into his mind out of nowhere, eclipsing the girl in the jeans and red stilettos. It was far worse – because he had loved Debbie.

He waited for his stiffness to subside. Then he pushed the heavy door open and went out on deck to the front of the boat, clinging to the rail, wind and rain lashing at him, white wave tops creaming by, the ship's prow dipping and rising in the darkness. Slowly he calmed himself, regained control. It was all a test, a temptation. Satan in woman's form.

An hour later, shriven by the cold and dark and wildness, he returned to his cabin. Lying in his bunk, soothed by the rhythmic vibrations of the ship's engines, he congratulated himself. His mind was strong again, and undiverted. He rehearsed the last pieces of the jigsaw: the van in Aberdeen, Imran's lock-up, the message to Shalima, the drive west, meeting the team, meeting Shalima. There was real beauty in her, inner beauty; they had shared minds, shared faith, a joint mission. He turned on his side and before long was asleep.

13.

While Yusuf wandered along Lerwick's Commercial Street under a louring grey sky in the far north, Shalima was crouched on her bunk looking out of her grimy porthole at a passing small blue boat with *Amourata BI 677* on its stern. Her ship – a small tramp steamer with one container in its hold – was moored in the port of Bizerte in Tunisia.

Tomorrow Yusuf's message would come. Must come. Ships and time moved so slowly.

She took a sip from her bottle of water. Her head ached from the heat and the constant humming vibration of the ship's generator. While in port she was a prisoner in her tiny cabin, the door closed, the air stale and oppressive: a woman on a boat would instantly have attracted attention and questions. Her team too were confined below deck; only the captain and his crew of three could be visible. Extra men might again have aroused suspicion.

She longed for English rain, for a shower and cool air. This was still Africa. For seven days they had steamed away from Yemen, and now they were just over halfway. Soon they would leave the protection of the secret Al-Qaeda networks. Soon they would be in Europe, not Africa; more familiar but more dangerous.

She pictured the container in the hold: crates or pallets of televisions from China, spare parts for oil rigs and Japanese cars, agricultural equipment, plastic toys, laptops and iPads, coffee and dates, hides and bleaching clay. All were genuine, correctly documented with a bill of lading, incoterm, packing list, insurance. All were on the ship's manifest. The container number on the paperwork matched the number painted on its side. But there were also her team's crates. These too were documented with all the official paperwork. The only difference was that the contents detailed on the paper did not match the contents in the crates. The whole light container load, as it was designated, was ready for checking by customs at the port of delivery: Fleetwood, England, UK.

Except that it would not arrive there undisturbed.

The container had not been sealed and locked, as it should have been when loaded on board at the port of Hodeida on the Red Sea in North Yemen. The green bolt that would seal the container, with its unique number also stated on all the documentation, was secure in Shalima's cabin. Only when her team's crates had been removed would this bolt be welded on, ready for the official bolt cutters in Fleetwood. She and her Al-Qaeda supervisor had worked efficiently together. He was a Wahhabi from Saudi Arabia. Working with a woman must have been anathema to him but he had controlled his prejudices – presumably under strict instructions from the top – to further the cause. His hooded eyes sometimes glanced at her condescendingly, but he approved her organising skills. It was he who had worked with the local placeman at Hodeida port to get all the correct documentation.

Shalima was confident in her team of five. She and Yusuf had wanted seven, but Al-Qaeda had decided five: a tighter unit, more efficient, more dependent on each other and therefore more cohesive. Al-Qaeda had found the team but given Shalima the right to veto someone – a right she had not exercised. She had read AQ's reports on them: their fighting experience, their skills, some personal background. She had met each of them formally in a small, hot room at the training camp near Sana'a. AQ had told them that for the first part of the mission this woman was their leader. It was vital to get more women involved in action, like the famous White Widow. Women could exploit situations men couldn't and could therefore expand the range of action.

Only Bargo, she felt, had some misgivings, but these had been overridden by his zeal for the mission. He was a natural loner, she had seen, a gaunt-faced man who never smiled, skin pockmarked, a Belgian-born Muslim who had fought in Iraq. He always wore khaki trousers, a black T-shirt and a black skullcap. She knew he would never confide in her. He was not a talker. The AQ report on him had described the discrimination he had experienced as a teenager, the fruitless job interviews. A mosque network had eventually got him employment as a delivery man for a halal food distributor. But he'd been savagely beaten by a gang of neo-Nazis and now kaffirs were to him what Jews had been to the Nazis. He was a hard man, full of anger – seeking to bloody the enemies of Islam, a disciple of sharia law with its clear rules and strict punishments. She knew he would be more at ease when Yusuf took control after they landed. She couldn't warm to him but wanted him on the team. There was something pitiless about him which they might need.

Refuelling was supposed to take about six hours, but they had been moored at this Bizerte wharf since just after dawn. What passed as her cabin curtain had been drawn as soon as the pilot boat set out from the port to escort them in. Shalima looked at her watch: 1430. They were now in the same time zone as Yusuf in England: only six days until their rendezvous in the early hours at the full moon. She wondered what he was doing. It was easier for him: he had things to do, final arrangements to make, she didn't know the details. Tomorrow his message would come: to confirm the mission or abort it. Until then she was in limbo. Everything hung on that message.

Through a tiny gap in the curtain, she saw the wharf

opposite. A grey cargo boat was moored with tight hawsers, rust spreading down from the anchor holes. She watched its on-board cranes swivel, hoisting crates from the dockside. A lorry was parked on the quayside and behind it stood a line of grey goods wagons. A man was gesticulating and shouting up at someone on board, but she couldn't hear his voice. There were muffled sounds of metal clanging on metal, footsteps above her head on deck. There was a smell of diesel. Perhaps at last the refuelling had started.

It was a comparatively small port, she knew, and chosen for that reason. More of a marina. To her right she could just see a line of small boats, many with metal canopies. They had bobbed a little in the wake of the *Amourata*, then settled again on the placid, oil-stained harbour water. Further along were the honey-coloured walls of an old fort with its battlements and tiny windows.

Shalima looked out to a sort of esplanade, men strolling under lamp posts, sitting on benches. Across the promenade was a line of white houses and two multi-storey blocks and, behind them, the green-topped tower of a mosque. All along the route she had seen normal life taking place: men meeting and shaking hands, lorries unloading, cars passing, even donkeys and camels, fishing boats, buying and selling, bartering, men carrying loads of firewood on their backs or pulling carts loaded with bales. Labour and friendship, cheating and dealing, struggling for a living. It was a world away from Doha Airport in Qatar, where she arrived from Heathrow and waited for the next flight to Yemen.

2013

These are the homelands of Islam and I am here to help the struggle for its simple faith. Holy Mecca is just a two-hour flight away but the counters of the coffee bars here are gold-plated, the floors of marble inlaid with mosaics of Moorish designs. The lighting sheds a golden hue over everything, the atrium's soaring roof arched like shallow waves, dotted with lights. In this desert land, fountains of pumped water play extravagantly. At the entrance a monstrous, grotesque yellow teddy bear – how Western is that! – acts as a lamp. Restaurants offer every nationality of food, including McDonald's.

I'd thought Heathrow was posh, but this is something different. I am dazzled and repulsed by it.

Sunk in my deep, cream leather chair on the plush carpet of the departure lounge, I watch the people. There are jeans and T-shirts, Arab men in suits or Arab dress. Only a few women wear headscarves, the rest a niqab or burka – which doesn't prevent them from languidly wandering through the boutiques of Chanel and Georgio Armani and the rest of the luxury shops with the few Western women there. I am still the odd one out.

And I am still the odd one out, here on the last stage of my journey. When my flight to the Yemen is called and I see my fellow passengers, I hastily cover more of my face with my headscarf. I am, I notice, the only unaccompanied woman on the flight. This plane is smaller, the engines noisier and the seat next to me unoccupied. Male passengers, whether in Arab dress or Western suits, look at me disapprovingly, even angrily. The women, in niqabs or burkas, whisper to their husbands or their *mahram*, their covered heads nodding in my direction. In less than two hours I will land in Sana'a where someone, presumably a man, will be waiting to collect me. I am going to live in a new culture which I have yearned for and planned for, but

I feel tension building, my fingers curled tightly, nails digging into my palms. An outsider. Alone. I close my eyes to shut out the censure, but also to reaffirm to myself why I am here: my decision, against Naz's advice and then against Fatima's, to choose this mission and to journey on my own.

So here I sit, next to an empty seat, wearing a black trouser suit, ostracised by the other passengers and ignored by the stewards, trying to restore my resolution. Pushing my face lower down into my scarf, I stare out into the blue sky. I feel the plane beginning its descent. My new life is about to begin, but I feel no elation. I have made my choice. But will I be able to make it work?

*

In all of these ports, she now knew, Al-Qaeda had its placemen – in the customs houses, on the waterfront – smoothing their passage, protecting their cargo, and not for bribes but for belief and principle. Underneath the surface ordinariness was this purifying pulse of an idea, surging, unstoppable, crusading. For years now Al-Qaeda had built up a network that moved arms and medicines and supplies to their fighters across the Middle East and into Africa: people who could forge or sign documents, wave through cargoes, bribe and intimidate. And now she, little Shalima, was part of it all.

The ship's intercom system crackled into life. The announcement in a foreign language was followed by a heavily accented translation into English: "Prepare for sailing in one hour."

Her heart beat faster. They would be moving again, getting ever closer. She could be on deck, breathing in the sea air under the blue Mediterranean sky, her iPhone on charge, waiting for Yusuf's message. If all went well, only six days to go.

14.
SATURDAY 26TH SEPTEMBER

The bedroom curtains were not fully drawn, and from the bed Davoud was watching rain on the window. Leaves on the tree outside were perfectly still. Gentle rain, soundless in the grey early-morning light, a bird call – he didn't know what it was. His phone on the bedside table had remained silent – luck or fate, he didn't care.

Jenny was still asleep, one bare shoulder poking out of the duvet. He leaned over and lightly kissed it, her skin so smooth. He looked at her long coppery hair, tousled and spread, glinting even in this dull light. He wanted to stroke it but not disturb her. He lay back.

Last night a new world had opened for him. To think he might have lived his life without those sensations.

"No need to be wary," Jenny had said. He wondered now if that been a premeditated comment, mischievously made in the knowledge of what she specifically intended? That would be like her. Or was it just a general comment on what she perceived as his cautious approach to life, which she was gently mocking?

Naked in bed, they had been kissing, her tongue encouraging his, when she had slid her head down, kissing his chest, her tongue now flicking his nipples. She had pushed back the duvet, uncovering his body. Then she had gone lower, kissing his navel. He had flinched, felt some kind of objection, some resistance, surfacing in his mind – a resistance that ceased as his mind disappeared.

She sat over him and slid him into her. She stretched

up and backwards, her arms above her head, her breasts rising, moonlight and shadows sculpting her. He had never experienced anything so beautiful. As she rose and fell on him, he came in her, released from all tension and restrictions.

Then she came too, stiffened and shuddering, with a long moan. She collapsed on him, breathless. Then they turned on their sides, he still in her, both relishing the closeness. He touched her face. Awed, spent.

She stroked his lips with her fingers, his teeth with her nail. He kissed her eyelids, caressed the length of her back, her hips. He didn't have the right words for things.

"We need to tell each other what we like."

Casually said, that startled him, too. "I've always been a good learner," he said, "but I'm not very good with my hands."

He laughed. Already he was thinking differently.

She laughed, too. "Tomorrow," she said sleepily, "we're going to a tump."

"What's that?"

But she was already asleep.

Now, in the morning as he remembered, all he could think of was his unpreparedness, his ignorance, his awkwardness. The limitations of his life with Dunia. It was embarrassing.

A thought stabbed him: how had Jenny learned her skills, her self-confidence, her forthrightness? She was an experienced woman and it was as if he was a virgin, an ingénue.

Jenny was stirring now. Could he put all that anxiety aside, and just enjoy? She had accepted his inexperience; he wanted her to tutor him so that he could pleasure her – even if at first it would be following her instructions, like colouring in. He wanted to make discoveries: a new lexicon, a new topography, some – what was the word? – speleology.

He smiled to himself and put his arms around her, curling into her curved back. It hadn't been only the physical sensation last night. It had meant her acceptance of all of him. For the first time in his life he felt all reservations and limitations removed.

Perhaps Jenny only felt so free when she was out of London, away from her son. Just herself. They had made love in London, but not like this.

He cupped his hand around her breast. She snuggled into him.

"Tump?" he asked. "Even if it's raining?"

'Tump' sounded vaguely crude.

Later, he coaxed flames from the damped-down fire with kindling. He showered and, while Jenny followed, he made toast and coffee. They sat on cushions on the floor in front of the fire and ate the toast with butter and greengage jam. The rain was thinning, and pale gleams of sunlight filtered into the room.

"I want to take you to my favourite place: the escarpment that overlooks the Severn Valley. Some good fresh air, but we'll start at Hetty Pegler's Tump," she said. "Five thousand years old, a Neolithic long barrow. It scared me stiff as a kid."

They made a small picnic and filled a flask with coffee, took two apples and two dark chocolate Kit Kats. They spoke little; there was almost a polite formality between them rather than the easy casualness he realised he had expected. He wondered if Jenny was withdrawing, taking stock, perhaps nervous she had been too forward, too indiscreet. But that was projecting himself onto her.

It was only a short drive to the tump and the rain had stopped when they parked. The site overlooked the wide Severn Valley, mist below them along the river. A narrow path led across the grass to the entrance: a black patch in the green mound. To their left, crows called viciously over ploughed furrows of dark, reddish soil. Jenny went in first, bending below the huge stone above the entrance, shining her torch. Davoud followed. The passage was dark, cold and musty, but dry. Brown leaves crinkled underfoot. They crouched at what seemed to be the centre of the cruciform structure. Jenny stopped and shone her torch into the chambers on either side.

"They found about twenty skeletons here," she said.

The torchlight swept across drystone walls, neatly built between huge slabs of rock, curved inwards towards the roof. At the entrances to the chambers stood more huge, vertical slabs, and above their heads a huge weight of stone.

"I feel like I'm trespassing into a secret," Davoud whispered.

Jenny turned off the torch. The black was intense. They turned to the light of the entrance. He imagined a stone being rolled across, being imprisoned in the dark, in the tomb that it had been.

Still crouching, they made their way out and stood upright in the pale sunlight and air, as if something oppressive had been lifted off them. Crows were still calling.

Jenny took his hand. "In the tunnel, a sort of *petite mort*," she said, smiling and looking at him quizzically.

But the weight of the earth was still upon him. He did not respond.

"And now the tower," she said. "Where we'll have our picnic." She squeezed his hand.

It was a five-mile drive along the escarpment, the mist below them dissipating in the sun.

"What is it?" he asked.

"William Tyndale's monument," she said. "He was born near here and died for his faith, in 1536. Betrayed in Flanders, he was strangled at the stake and then burned."

Why had she brought him to these places of death?

"What was his crime?" he asked.

"He translated the New Testament into English so ordinary people could read it."

"And that was a crime?!" he snapped. "Religion, it poisons everyone. Nowadays it's just a different religion that persecutes and demands obedience. Five hundred years ago it was yours, now it's mine – or what was mine. I've renounced it."

"The Catholic church confiscated his Bibles, which had been smuggled in from the Netherlands. He was condemned as a heretic."

"I suppose that's what I am," said Davoud. "An apostate!" And he remembered Suleiman in Jordan and in Belmarsh. His voice was bitter.

At the tower they parked and read the plaque on the wall about Tyndale. The tower was topped by a large enamel mosaic cross which flashed in the sun.

"Come on, misery guts," said Jenny. "Let's climb to the top."

There was a staircase to a gallery and a window space. They looked out over the Severn: fields, farms, pastures, the motorway busy.

"It's lovely, but I'm hungry," said Davoud. He put his arm around her and kissed her. She held her body close to his, and they were fine together, again.

"Tump and tower, you see," she said.

He stroked her hair, and she kissed his eyelids and then his mouth. So tender now.

15.

While Davoud watched the Gloucestershire rain, Yusuf had only one question on his mind: would the van and its key be in position? He stood on the deck as the Shetland ferry nosed into Aberdeen harbour, edging between oil platform service boats, past warehouses and petrol storage tanks, on time for its seven o'clock arrival. He watched the mooring ropes flung to the quay and caught. Men shouted, lorries reversed, metal clanged, derricks whirred over ships with pallets of stuff. He noticed a few fishing boats; a smell of fish and salt mingled with fuel fumes.

It had been a smooth crossing, a grey line of cloud on the horizon merging into mist and then the flat sea as dawn broke. In the cafeteria he'd drunk two strong coffees, watching the girls from last night drinking coffee and putting on make-up, tarting themselves up even at six in the morning. He looked away; he must stay focused. He had a long drive ahead to Leeds, lots to put in place and check. This was the real beginning. But if the van wasn't there, if Imran and the AQ network had failed, it was the end.

With his rucksack on his back he walked down the gangway onto mainland tarmac. Rendezvous was at 0815. If all was well, by 0830 he should be on the A90, speeding south. He had memorised this walk: past Trinity, Regent and Waterloo Quays, then left up Wellington Street and on to the esplanade. To his right he saw the small, low cottages of Footdee, now miniaturised beneath the massive cranes and storage tanks. East over the North Sea was a silver haze where the sun was behind the mist, but it was soon obscured. Three oil rig supply ships were moored outside the harbour entrance.

He passed the amusement park with its big wheel, all garish reds and yellows, the Beach Ballroom, the floodlight towers of Pittodrie Stadium, the golf course. Down two flights of steps from the road, he descended to the lower level of the promenade. On the beach, a couple of dogs ran into the almost still sea, their owners strolling on the pebbles stacked by winter tides against the wooden groynes. A runner passed him, plugged into earphones. Yusuf had to deliberately slow his walk. Mustn't be early, mustn't loiter. He could be noticed.

Every hundred metres or so there was a concrete shelter. He was heading for the furthest one. He could feel the dampness on his face, the air unnaturally still. He strolled on along the curving, empty promenade, shoulders tight, jaw clenched. Two shelters to go. He looked at his watch: 0815, dead on time.

A runner jogged down the steps at the end of the promenade, just beyond the last shelter. His hood was up; he nodded as he ran past. Yusuf turned and watched him lope away, then continued past the last-but-one shelter. He stopped, blew his nose for something to do, looked in at the rubbish under the slatted wooden seat. His watch showed 0816. Damn him! Where was he?

Then a man emerged from the last shelter, tracksuit, no hood up, Asian. Yusuf stopped and scrutinised him as he stood for a moment, looking out to sea. Then the man turned and began to jog towards Yusuf. Yusuf held his breath, fists involuntarily clenched at his sides.

"Rare day the day," the jogger said, stopping. "Do you have the time?"

Dark, expressionless eyes.

"Grand morning for it," answered Yusuf.

The eyes stared hard at him. "The time?"

Yusuf looked at his watch. "Exactly right. Enjoy your day!"

"Thank you. And you yours."

The man started to run. The exchange had been accurate in every word. Yusuf let himself relax and took a deep breath. He turned into the last shelter, looking for an orange Sainsbury's bag. There it was under the seat, in the corner, shoved in among fag packets and lager cans. Yusuf peered out of the shelter; no one about. He pulled the bag out, quickly unwrapped it. There in a smaller, transparent self-seal bag was a key ring with two keys attached. Yes! He took it out, threw the bags back under the seat and walked out of the shelter, up the steps to the road and saw the parked van. Everything as promised. A red Ford Transit, long wheelbase, high top, registration '13. Fucking ace! Allahu Akbar!

Yusuf unlocked it, got in, and threw his rucksack onto the passenger seat. He slammed the door shut, settled into his seat and looked around: clean, in good nick, empty, no seats. Ample space for the team and their gear. On the dashboard was the V5 registration document, in the name of Khaled Khan. It wouldn't be the jogger's real name, but it would match the driving licence he would have had to show as proof of identification. The van would have been paid for in cash, Yusuf knew; usually a suspicious transaction, but not from Asians. Businesses accepted that they dealt in cash.

He turned on the ignition: a full tank. Khaled had done his stuff. The engine ticked over. To his right, the first golfers were out on the course: one swung his club, but Yusuf couldn't see the ball. To his left, the expanse of the grey North Sea. Ahead of him, around five hundred kilometres of driving.

It was happening! He was the leader in action! From now on, it was down to him. Shalima would be in Algiers, waiting for his message, the container secure with its secret cargo. In only five days he would meet her and her team. What a spectacle they would create.

He familiarised himself with the gears, lights, wipers, then put the van into gear and moved slowly off along the esplanade. Union Street was already busy. Stopped at frequent traffic lights he watched the early shoppers: young women going to work, most of them in leggings that showed the shape of their legs, accentuated by the heels they wore. Advertising themselves, displaying.

Two hours later Yusuf pulled into the service station near Perth. In the car park, football fans with green-and-white scarves and cans of lager chanted their inanities and obscenities. Going to pay for his petrol, he glanced at the newspaper stand and saw the *Daily Star* headline: *Snatched for sex, chopped up with power saw and left in shed.* He opened the paper: on Page 3 was a topless, shameless Lana. Inside was a double-page spread on the front-page murder story: there were pictures of the sixteen-year-old victim and headlines – *Murdered in grotesque sex plot. Warped lust for threesome romp with young girl.* Another story: *Paedo priest axed.* And another: *Pregnant aged 12.* On the sports pages he found adverts: *Horny granny sex relief; Proper filthy girls, mobiles 36p a minute; Dirty housewife, I'm at home and wanna make u cum.* This was the West, this was what he was cleansing.

"It's not a library, mate," said the attendant.

"Sorry!"

He put it back. No, better buy it. Mustn't be remembered. Stupid. He added a bottle of water, paid and left.

He fumed at his mistake as he continued on the long motorway drive past Stirling, round Glasgow, through the borders and stopped at Gretna services. His last stop, and just before he entered England.

He queued for his Costa coffee, not impatient; he was on time, casually wondering why coffee-making had become so complicated and time-consuming. As he glanced to his left, he noticed a woman hurry past. His heart lurched. He could see only the side and then back of her. That same hairstyle, blonde, something about the way she held herself as walked. And then she had gone, into the back of the shop, WH Smith's. It couldn't be her. Debbie. His queue edged forward. He kept looking at the shop entrance. If she came out, if it was her, what would he do? There were three in front of him. Still no sign of her. Customers going in and out of the shop. Only two in front of him now in the queue.

And then she appeared, plastic bag in her right hand. He saw her face as she glanced in his direction, registering nothing. Then she strode away, angling out of the shop and straight to the exit to the car park. He was still not sure.

"Yes, sir?" asked the barista.

"Er, Americano, extra shot," he managed to stammer. He looked behind him. No sign of her. She was gone.

"Anything to eat?"

Yusuf shook his head.

He took his coffee to a table for two at the window. Looked out, scanning across the car park. No sign of her. If it was her, she was gone. If it was her she had not recognised him. If it was her, he was no longer in her head. Not a memory. Not a trace, nothing.

But she was in his head. He could not forget her. Debbie.

2012

Watching her at college as she drinks coffee with her friends, laughing, chatting in the refectory. Following her blonde hair down a corridor as she goes to a lecture. In the library, where she does not notice me. But the second time she looks up, she smiles at me. She is always with others. Once I see her on the other side of the street, at a bus stop, and I wave at her, nervously. She waves back and smiles.

I begin to think of her a lot, feel that somehow we would like each other, have things in common. I am confident of that. I work out what course she is on and when her lectures are. I wait, when I can, to see her leave the college, then follow her at a distance. I am shocked when I see her smoking on the street, disappointed, hurt. And once I see her meet a man and put her arms around him. I watch them kiss. It is like being hit in the stomach. She is meant to be mine. But still I dare not talk to her alone or ask her for a coffee.

And then I go to the party. I know she is going, too. It is at a student lodging house. I deliberately arrive late, the house pounding with music, only lamps and candles, milling people all with drink, loud and shouting. The smell of alcohol and pot. I look for her in the semi-darkness, in the kitchen where the booze is, in the downstairs rooms. Nothing. I go up the stairs, past snogging couples. The bathroom door is open and a girl is retching into the lavatory bowl, a friend with her. Scared now, I look at the open bedroom doors, beds covered with bodies. I dread seeing her there. But there is no sign of her.

The music pounds louder. There is one closed door. The last room. If she is at the party, she must be in here. I open it, having to push hard as someone is standing against it. I go in: dark, just the light of a low bedside lamp. People are standing around the bed, male and female, but silent as if at a ritual. I can't see through. I push between them.

There is a woman, naked, kneeling on the bed, angled across a corner. Her back horizontal, her weight on her hands. In the lamplight I see a blonde head moving backwards and forwards. A man is standing in front of her and she has his penis in her mouth. He is thrusting into her. Horrified, I see there is another man, still wearing a T-shirt, at the back of her. Her thighs are spread, and he too is thrusting into her.

"Spit-roast." I hear a whisper in my ear. "Good, eh?" As if he is complimenting a demonstration.

I cannot take my eyes away from the tableau on the bed. Then I see the woman take the man's penis out of her mouth and hold it in one hand, moving her hand up and down. The man groans. Then the woman turns her head, looks across, directly at me, and smiles. The same smile: Debbie. Then she turns away and sucks the penis again.

I want to vomit, feel it surge up inside me. I rush out of the room, down the stairs, and on the pavement I am sick, great retching heaves.

★

Now, at Gretna, he stared stonily out of the window at the parked cars. She had been friendly, he had liked her, he could have fallen in love with her. She was beautiful and popular. Why had she performed like that? Had she been drunk? Drugged? But she had recognised him, had smiled at him as if inviting him to join them. He shuddered. She had so filled his mind, and he had hardly registered in hers. Today, if she had recognised him, if she had come over and greeted him and suggested they have a coffee together – what would he have done? This beautiful girl who was a whore. Never would he forget that final sight of Debbie. As the Hadith says, *Never is a man alone with a woman except that Satan is the third party with them.*

The hot coffee burned his throat, scoured it. He stood up. The future counted, not the past. Time to go.

After filling up with petrol, he continued south, passing

the Solway Firth, following the West Coast railway line. Not far from Leighton Moss he turned off the M6 and headed east, steadily passing Kirkby Lonsdale, Ingleton, Settle and Skipton. He was approaching home territory and his next vital meeting.

It was just after 4pm, only a few minutes later than the arranged time, when he turned into the car park of Rotherdyke Leisure Centre. The car park was almost full, but he found a space, reversed into it, switched off the engine and closed his eyes. It had been a long drive. He got out and stretched his legs, walked around the van, felt his joints begin to work again. Young kids carrying armbands were going into the centre with their parents, older kids with towels under their arms, adults with squash rackets. He heard a car door close, and then saw Imran threading his way towards him.

"Great to see you, bruv," said Imran, grasping Yusuf's hand.

"And you, I'm knackered."

"Good trip?"

"Fine, no problems. Traffic was heavy round Glasgow but otherwise OK."

"Van OK?"

"Great." Yusuf yawned and stretched his arms. "So tell me, why here?"

"In the van."

They climbed in and shut the doors.

"There's an Arabic keyboard at the Leeds mosque but I thought it was too dangerous to use it. It was too public and if it was traced, it would be too easy for the old imam to mention our names, innocently or under pressure."

"Good thinking."

"I have a cousin here who lives in a house with some guys, all Pakistanis, no women. It's a kind of dormitory. Some of them work shifts in the factory, one or two are taxi drivers, some work in family shops and restaurants. He told me one of them has a laptop with an Arabic keyboard. He's on the day shift this week, not due back until six o'clock."

"Some of the others may be there, though," said Yusuf.

"Yes, but no problem. We're not sneaking about. They know me, I've been once or twice to see my cousin. We talk about cricket. The point is, they won't be suspicious if I turn up with a friend who plays in the same cricket team as me."

"Even if I'm white?"

"If you play cricket with us, you're OK. The Rotherdyke Artisans are cool. Champions last season."

"I know, got the medal." Yusuf laughed. "Let's go, then. Get it done. I need my bed. It's been a long drive."

"It's not far."

They locked the van and walked past the leisure centre and across the park, the playground full of Asian kids. Opal Street was a street of stone terraced houses, their doors opening straight onto the pavement. Two old men in traditional dress and white prayer caps were walking slowly along, deep in conversation. The whole street was lined with cars, some with taxi plates.

Imran stopped and knocked on a door. It opened a little and a male face peered round.

"Oh, it's you, Imran, come in," said the face, and the security chain was released.

There were handshakes in the narrow hall and Yusuf was introduced.

"Come into the kitchen and I'll make you a cup of tea."

"No, it's OK. We're only here for a minute. My cousin told me someone here has an Arabic keyboard and I wonder if Yusuf could use it to send a brief message," said Imran.

"No problem. It's in Sanchi's room. I'll show you."

They went upstairs and the man left Yusuf and Imran in a small back bedroom.

"Thanks," Yusuf said. "I won't be long."

The curtains were closed and Yusuf switched on the bare, low-wattage light bulb. There was room only for an unmade double bed, a hard-backed chair and a small table. He opened the curtains a little. Small backyards: wheelie bins, washing draped over a wooden fence and gate, paint peeling on windowsills. Would he be a hero here, in five days' time? He doubted it. Minds here were small, if in a different way. He closed the curtain.

On the table was the laptop. Imran switched it on, sat on the chair and moved a half-full mug of cold coffee to a corner of the table. Yusuf sat on the bed and listened to the laptop humming, warming up. His tiredness had disappeared. This place was perfect: a shabby room in a shabby house in a shabby street. So ordinary, so totally without significance. And from here he would send out a signal that would shock the world. Was this how the 9/11 pilots felt as they boarded their planes – unnoticed, tickets in their pockets, hand luggage in the overhead lockers, fastening their seat belts, waiting for take-off – but with their huge secret intention and detailed plan of action? It was hard to imagine being like them. And yet he was. The idea had been his alone, even though the planning had been shared with Shalima.

"OK," said Imran. "It's all set up for you. All you need to do is enter the email address you're sending to, and then the message. I'll leave you to it and go and talk cricket downstairs."

"Thanks."

Imran left, closing the door behind him, and Yusuf sat on the chair. From his buttoned shirt pocket he took the piece of paper on which he had written in Arabic all the information he needed. He placed it next to the laptop, having to peer because the light was dim. First, he typed in the two addresses – to Shalima and to their Al-Qaeda supervisor in Sana'a. Twice he checked for accuracy. He didn't want *address unknown* to appear.

He paused, looked at the empty message screen, took a deep breath, smiled and tapped in the Arabic for *Four birds, 2-260.*

He sat back and looked at it.

Shalima would be waiting, somewhere off the coast of Algeria. His message would soar up through Britain's grey clouds to a satellite – probably American, which gave an added frisson of satisfaction – and then be reflected down to a phone, cradled by an impatient Shalima, on the deck in bright Mediterranean sunshine. How would she react? Elated, nervous? She was a cool woman. He could rely on her. She would keep her head; it was still not time to tell her team exactly what the target was.

He hovered the cursor over *Send*.

From somewhere came into his mind the phrase *Let slip the dogs of war*. He pressed the key. It was on its way. He didn't know how – electrical charges, binary neutrinos, it was all a mystery to him. He waited for his heartbeat to steady. Then he went to *Sent Items*, highlighted the message and deleted it. Then he went to *Deleted Items*. There were forty-three. He right-clicked. *Empty Deleted Items folder*. He left-clicked. *Are you sure you want to permanently delete all the items and sub-folders in the Deleted Items folder?* He clicked *Yes*. He watched the green line crossing. *Two seconds left*. Then there was a blank screen. He turned off the laptop.

It was done. What he needed now was sleep. Much had to be done tomorrow.

Downstairs there were brief farewells and thanks.

"All done, bruv?" asked Imran as they walked back to the car park.

"All done."

"Tomorrow we sort the van."

Yusuf nodded. "See you at your place, fam."

They shook hands and Imran drove off. Yusuf climbed

wearily into his van. Forty minutes to Leeds and the day was over. He had made his way across Africa and Europe undetected. No one could suspect anything. All going to plan. Five days to go, five days for nothing to go wrong.

16.

Sixteen thirty. Where was Yusuf's message? Her phone, in her shoulder bag and switched to Arabic keyboard, was stubbornly silent. No one else on the ship, not even the skipper, knew about the message that would give the go-ahead or abort the mission.

All day Shalima had watched the African coastline creep slowly by at a steady rate of ten knots, first Tunisia and then Algeria, a line of low, mostly yellow hills. What a strong team she had with her. She'd insisted from the start that the jihadists must all be Europeans, English speakers and born Muslims. She didn't want converts and she didn't want men to whom Northern European weather would be a shock. Yusuf was different. She knew and trusted him, but she feared converts in general could be brittle – all fired up until a crisis came, whereupon they cracked. With a small team, living in compact circumstances, enduring stress, making hard decisions fast, a similarity of cultural background would be a strength. Deep fundamental differences in lifestyles, ingrained from childhood, could be dangerously diversionary. Also, them being European would mean less opposition to a female leader.

Izzy and Ibra, her navigators, were asleep on deckchairs at the prow of the ship. She wished she could sleep, time passing, and then be awakened by her phone alarm with the confirmation she was waiting for.

Izzy the Dutchman had been a keen sailor on the Waddenzee. The AQ report on him stated that he had sailed small yachts along the coast and out to the islands of Vlieland

and Terschelling, that he had loved the challenge of solo sailing in rough North Sea weather. The key was that he knew how to read sea charts. As instructed by Yusuf, on his iPad he had downloaded the app from Nautical Charts and studied *Marine Chart 2010: Morecambe Bay and its Approaches*. With Ibra, his fellow Dutchman, who had sailed along the Aegean, he had studied the position of the deep, narrow, winding channel that led to the landing place, the location of sandbanks, and the speeds of the tidal streams.

It was like Eid al-Fitr when they opened the huge reinforced cardboard box in the warehouse at the Yemeni port of Hodeida. Inside was a massive holdall, and inside the holdall was a black, deflated, folded twelve-man FC530 Futura Commando Zodiac complete with slatted aluminium deck. They'd quickly assembled the boat and inflated it: strong, shallow draught, plenty of room for six with their weapons and crates of explosives. In a separate box was a Yamaha F80 HP BETL outboard motor. AQ had done them proud: Ibra reckoned there was twenty-five thousand pounds' worth of gear, and so theirs must be a high-priority mission. They'd put the boat and engine through their paces out on the bay, screaming round in tight curves, all of the team hooting and yelling like kids, even Bargo. It would be very different on the real trip: there would be only one hour, when the tide was at its full, to reach their landing place from the ship, and stealth would be essential. No alarm.

Afterwards on the quayside, Izzy had chatted to Shalima. He was the most talkative in the team, cigarette teetering in his mouth, the acrid smoke of a strange tobacco, always wearing his Feyenoord baseball cap back to front. He had lovely dark eyes with thick black lashes, razor-sharp cheekbones.

"I do this for my children," he said, "back home with my wife in Harlingen."

Shalima smiled as he threw away the cigarette butt.

"I look up at night and see the same moon as my children. I want to make a better world for them, a cleaner society, not godless like it is now in the Netherlands and the rest of Europe."

He lit another cigarette. "And, if I'm truthful, I'm a mid-life crisis man." He laughed. "Bored with managing a superstore, marriage too – what shall I say? – routine."

He smiled shyly, as if he had confided too much.

"You're a good man," said Shalima. "And a strong member of the team. I'm glad you're here."

"Me, too," he said, and laughed again.

Sometimes she was afraid to remind herself she was only twenty-one years old, yet responsible for this team of fighting men – at least until they landed and Yusuf took over.

2003

I cower in the kitchen doorway, hands over my face, peering through my fingers. My father yanks my mum's long black hair, pulls her across the floor, kicking her shins. I flinch at each blow. He grabs her face with both hands and forces her to look at him. Mum is moaning, blood on her lips. My father, flecks of his spit landing on my mum's cheeks, yells, "Don't complain about how bad you have it – no one else could love you."

"No, no!" I yell. "Stop it!"

But he carries on.

I can't stand it. I leap forward and thump him on his head, thumping and thumping, scratching, biting his hand. He turns, snarling, and slaps me hard across my face, knocking me to the floor. The side of my face is hot and stinging. I hate him. I hate him.

"To your room," he yells, and comes towards me with his fist clenched. His blazing eyes terrify me.

I scramble away. At the doorway I turn and see my mother's face looking up at me from the corner where my father has flung her, such helplessness and fear, her face streaked with tears. I cannot fight him. I have to leave her. I have seen it before so many times.

Up in my room, curled up on my bed, I hear Mum sobbing. Then my father's shout: "I'll send her away to Pakistan."

I hear him stomp out of the house, slamming the door behind him. I hear the key turn, locking us in. I lie there waiting for Mum's crying to go quiet. I cannot go down: she will be wiping the blood and tears from her face.

Slowly she climbs the stairs. I open my eyes. Her face looks round my door and then she comes in and sits on my bed. She puts her arm around my shoulder. She is still trembling. I snuggle into her. I know there will be bruises.

"Did he hurt you?" she asks, stroking my hair.

"Only a bit," I lie.

"It's all my fault," she says. "I can't do anything right for him." She wipes the tears from her face. "You shouldn't see things like that. He has such a temper."

"We must leave him, *Ammijan*," I say. "I'm frightened of him."

"But he's my husband. He's your father."

★

Shalima opened her eyes again. She could never forget. The scene still horrified her but, though she was even now reluctant to admit it, also fascinated her: a child seeing the uncontrolled anger and violence of an adult man, his blazing eyes, witnessing his power to humiliate and hurt.

Her mother had never been allowed out of the house alone. When she went out with her husband she was forced to wear the full burka, even the eye slits covered with black lace. Her mother had been allowed no friends, no phone, no money, was a prisoner and yet her father had been so insanely jealous and possessive.

Shalima breathed a heavy sigh. Her dead mother's face, brave but sad and defeated; the photograph in her bag. What would she have thought about her daughter being here? About where she was going and what she was going to do? First, she would not have believed it, then she would have been horrified. And ashamed. She would not understand.

2010

I sit by my mother's hospital bed, holding her hand. A brain tumour diagnosed too late, my father only reluctantly taking her to the doctor. Her face is wan and still, exhausted. She is unconscious, tubes in her mouth and nose, lights bleeping and a graph juddering along on a machine above her head. I know I am watching her give in; I understand that death for her will be a relief. I don't feel abandoned or betrayed. I am sad for me, but not for her. I am glad she will suffer no more from illness or from my father's beatings.

After the funeral, I live with my father in sullen hostility: he demands I look after him and skivvy for him. He treats me as his property just as he did my mother. He shows no sign of guilt. It was my fault. Why could I not do more to protect her from such humiliation and shame? It's too late now, but still the guilt gnaws into my brain. I will not live like my mother. I have to escape, and the only way is to work hard at school and pass exams.

But after six months my father remarries. I pity his new wife. All she thinks about is my father. I do not exist for her. He makes it clear he wants me gone. Pakistan is mentioned, so I have to move fast. I leave Birmingham and the tentacles of my father's family and go to London to stay at my *Naneejan*'s, my mother's mother whom I have visited occasionally at weekends.

I have to leave my best friend Fiona, who has shared the bad times with me. We have been inseparable. Leaving her is the hardest part of leaving. It is a hard time for me: a big new city, a new school, guilt about my mother. In the following months I binge on burgers and chips and sugary drinks, then starve myself. I stay in bed all weekend, despising myself, drinking whole bottles of wine which I then vomit up.

But somehow I work hard at my new school; I must make myself independent and have a career. I avoid friendships, I trust no one. My *Naneejan* is long-suffering, accepting everything as the will of Allah, even my excesses, silently disapproving but not rejecting. I sometimes watch her from the doorway as she prays five times a day, kneeling on a prayer mat in the small living room of her flat. How can someone to whom life has given so little be so grateful to Allah? How can Allah accept the prayers of this good, simple woman as well as the prayers of my evil, mosque-attending father?

*

Shalima imagined her *Naneejan*: endlessly cleaning her neat little flat or cooking a simple meal for herself, or maybe napping. Now she looked across at Bargo, sweating in the extended exercise routine he stuck to every day. He was the most experienced fighter, a bodybuilder. He'd fought in Somalia for al-Shabaab around the same time as Shalima, in Syria for al-Nusra against Assad, and even in skirmishes against ISIS. He had trained the whole team in the use of their weaponry.

The team had gelled, efficient but joking, taking the piss but respectful of each other. Bargo was always on the margins of the group, not part of the banter. That Shalima was a woman and young had been no problem once they realised she had the whole operation firmly under control and was well organised. They saw she could take a joke but had a sense of authority, that she was a leader. They all knew the matrix of skills they had brought, but none knew the final purpose of the sea charts, the Zodiac, the weapons and the explosives. Only when and if the messages were received would she brief the team fully, as they passed out of the Mediterranean into the Atlantic.

Shalima leaned on the rail, feeling the slight breeze on her face. Now she would have to go below to hide herself in her fetid cabin. They were entering the port of Algiers, past three container ships moored in the roadstead, piled with multicoloured containers like Lego bricks. Beyond the mass of boats, white and cream houses crammed up the low hill, lights coming on. Eighteen hundred, her watch showed; Sa 26.

At last her phone buzzed. Fingers fumbling, she unzipped her bag and took it out. She moved back to sit on a steel hatchway cover. Her hands were trembling. *One message received.* She touched the screen.

Two Arabic words. And the number 2-260.

The words she recognised, etched on her brain since Yusuf had left for England: *Four birds.*

The numbers referred to a verse in the Qur'an. She had memorised the story: *When Ibrahim said unto his Lord, "My*

Lord, show me how thou givest life unto the dead", Allah said, "Dost thou not believe?" Ibrahim said, "Yes, I believe, but I ask that my heart may be at ease." Allah said, "Take four birds, tame them to incline to thee, then cut them into pieces and place portions of them on every mountaintop. Then call them to thee. They will come whole to thee in haste. Know that Allah is Mighty and Wise."

Yusuf was summoning them.

From many lands, they were now gathering together. Educated in the faith, trained in the skills needed, inspired by the cause. Their mission was on.

But Shalima could say nothing to anyone. Izzy and Ibra still slept, Bargo was now on squat-thrusts and stomach crunches, the skipper was at the wheel.

On Monday a final message would confirm all details were in place, that there were no last-minute hitches. Two days to wait, five days before landing. She hurried below to pray.

The ship nosed into the harbour with its secret as dusk was falling.

17.

Sunday 27th September

While Davoud and Jenny had slept in each other's arms in the Cotswolds village, Detective Sergeant Hannah Walker sat in the passenger seat of an unmarked police car, parked on Ruby Street in Rotherdyke. It was still dark, sunrise not due for two hours. The only lights were the street lights: not a room lit, not a soul about, not a car moving.

"Five minutes to go," muttered Detective Constable Tom Bakewell in the driver's seat, looking at his watch. "And all's well."

The target house was a hundred metres in front of them, just left at a T-junction, on Opal Street. Their backup car with three uniformed constables and a steel enforcer ram was parked just round the corner. Hannah hoped they wouldn't need the ram. She was tense: it was her first operation in charge. Elsewhere in the town four other houses were being raided, all at the same time in case any of the suspects had early shifts. There had to be a result. A team of eighty officers had worked for over eighteen months. Now they were almost there: all the interviews, the denials, the protestations of innocence, the cross-referencing, the surveillance, the CCTV footage, the stake-outs, the hours listening to the girls' sickening stories, the evidence gathered. It was arrest time. She looked up at the target house, all in darkness. The suspects just had to be in there, and the technology, the incriminating messages that would send them to prison for a long time.

"Four twenty-seven," said Tom.

"In position," Hannah radioed the other car. The three

constables would move quietly along the backstreet behind the house and into the back yard to prevent any escape and, if necessary, force an entry.

"Four twenty-nine, let's go," said Hannah. Now the adrenaline was running, the waiting was over.

Tom drove the car in first gear up to the T-junction and parked outside the target house. There must be no drama, no alarm. They closed the car doors quietly, walked across the pavement and Hannah rapped on the door with her knuckles; there was no door knocker. The rapping cracked the silence. They looked around at the neighbouring houses: no reaction. No reaction in the house either. She knocked again, louder, the wood sharp on her knuckles. Stepping back, she saw an upstairs light go on. Tom nudged her and pointed. A light was on downstairs in a house opposite.

"Come on, you bastards," Hannah muttered between clenched teeth. At least someone was in.

Then a light came on in the hall. She heard a bolt drawn back at the top of the door, then another at the bottom, the click of a Yale lock. The door opened a couple of inches and a face peered out.

Quickly Tom shoved his foot in the threshold and pushed the door back.

"What? Who are you?"

"Police." Tom flashed his warrant card and shoved past him.

Hannah followed and locked the door behind them. There were no other sounds in the house. She recognised the man's face: a key suspect, one of the main taxi drivers involved. He was wearing a grubby T-shirt and underpants, cowering a little, hands instinctively covering his privates, thin legs naked in the shabby hall with the bare, low-wattage light bulb above his head showing his frightened eyes. *At last, now you're the scared one. I want you scared, I want you fucking terrified and snivelling when I force you to listen to me, to look at me when I describe to you every detail of what you've done in the rooms upstairs.*

She turned away. Was he the only one here? The only one they would take? Tom hurried through to the kitchen and unlocked the back door. The other three policemen came in. A rapid look into the two small downstairs rooms: empty.

Then there were footsteps above, and two of the police rushed upstairs with Tom. Hannah heard shouts and protests, a scuffle. The taxi man was looking up the stairs. The first Asian man came down, arms behind his back, cuffed. Behind him came Tom, his hand gripping the man's shoulder. The man fired a torrent of what she assumed was abuse, in Urdu, at the taxi man. Hannah heard the word 'fucking' several times. Then two more Asian men were led downstairs, already cuffed, by the policemen. Hannah recognised all of them. All had figured in the investigation, all had been incriminated.

"Good work, lads. Door keys?" she asked the men.

No response.

"It's up to you. The less you cooperate, the harder it will be for you."

The taxi man nodded his head towards a jug on a small table. The other three stabbed him with their eyes. She radioed in for a police van that was ready and waiting.

She turned the taxi man round, twisting his arms up his back more than was necessary. He winced. She jammed the cuffs hard on him and locked them. She'd got him: the delivery man – the wholesale butcher. That's all those poor girls were to the men: meat, easy meat. Treats. Now they'd got the slimy sods. It was up to the lawyers and the jury now. She could already hear their not-guilty pleas, their hard-working decency proclaimed, their lawyers' worming questions, the insinuations of racism.

Hannah walked three steps up the staircase so she was slightly above them. She looked at them, huddled in the small hallway, faces sullen, some defiant.

"You're all under arrest for offences connected with child abuse," she said, enunciating her words carefully, savouring the satisfaction. "You do not have to say anything, but it may harm your defence if you do not mention when questioned something you later rely on in court. Anything you say may be given in evidence."

One of them, Kabeer Sajd, smirked.

"Better get some trousers on them and something on their feet," she said. Human bloody rights, even for the lowest of the low. "But don't uncuff them."

They were sullen, more humiliated – she supposed – because it was a woman in charge.

"Where's your search warrant?" asked Kabeer. Smart-arse.

"Here you are, Mr Sajd. Issued by the court yesterday." She took it out and pushed it in front of his face. "Satisfied?"

The van arrived five minutes later. When she led the men out, there were lights on along the street, men peering out of doors. News travelled fast.

"Congratulations, Hannah," said Tom. "Good work."

Hannah felt triumphant, but knew she had to suppress it.

"Thank you," she said. "A team effort. I just want those bastards in cells for a long time, and for the message to go out that this will not happen in this town again. I want those girls to feel safe."

The men were escorted into the van and it drove off. Hannah and Tom returned to the house. This bit was just as vital as the arrests: collecting all the technology they could find. They'd already taken mobiles from two of the men and checked the SIM cards were in them. Now, waiting for the SOCOs, with gloves on they combed the house, searching cupboards and shelves, moving furniture, looking under beds and in the cheap wardrobes. They found three more phones, an iPad, and three laptops.

"This one's different," said Tom, picking it up.

"I think it's an Arabic keyboard," said Hannah. "Probably a job for Special Branch."

They put the equipment into self-seal evidence bags and labelled them.

Then her mobile rang again.

"Hannah?"

"Yes. Alan?" She recognised the voice of Alan Sewell, the detective inspector in charge of Operation Raptor.

"Good news. All five houses produced the goods. Congratulations! See you back at the station."

She thumped the air in exhilaration.

The same afternoon, Hannah and the social worker talked to Kelly again in the police station interview room.

"Do you recognise any of these men?" asked Hannah, arranging a dozen photographs on the low table in front of Kelly. They included photographs of the men arrested that morning.

Kelly was munching a new supply of her favourite custard creams. "He's one of the taxi drivers." She pointed. "We call 'im the delivery man. He takes us round to all the 'ouses and 'otel rooms, even to Manchester and Leeds."

Hannah had interviewed him four days ago. He'd denied everything: driving Kelly from one house to another, assaulting her in his taxi, he and four other men having sex with her. When she'd shown him photographs of him leading Kelly up the steps into a house, he'd simply shaken his head. But there were other girls who'd made statements and identified him. The stories of the other suspects were contradictory. Repeatedly listening to the tapes, Hannah had listed five important inconsistencies.

She waited a moment. "Do you recognise any of the men who were in the room?"

Kelly tapped four photographs. "They were there."

"For the benefit of the video," said Hannah, "the men Kelly has identified are the taxi driver Hamid Aziz, Adil Rauf, Kabeer Sajd and Abdul Hassan." She sat back with a sigh of satisfaction. The case was a solid one.

*

That evening, in their pleasant, tidy semi on a small estate, Hannah waited for her husband Tony to come home. She sat watching a programme about a comprehensive school in West Yorkshire. It wasn't so much about teaching as about what they called 'pastoral care' – all those teenagers with problems. She'd once wanted to be a teacher but knew she didn't have the patience. She preferred dealing with bad adults to problem teenagers. So it was ironic that her past two years had been concentrated on some very troubled young people.

Then the phone rang. It was Jane. "Kelly won't allow the recording to be used as evidence."

Hannah slumped, closed her eyes, took a deep breath. "Why on earth not?"

"When she got home her mother told her there'd been two cars parked outside the house all afternoon, the windows down and the men inside shouting abuse. They made phone calls threatening what they'd do to the house and Kelly's younger sister if Kelly told the police anything. Then they smashed a window and drove off. Her mother and sister were scared out of their wits."

Bastards! It had happened before; even a story of a girl being doused with petrol and threatened with being set on fire if she ever told anyone anything.

"I'm sorry, Hannah. She won't change her mind. I've tried."

"Thanks, Jane. Right, tomorrow we start again. We might still have enough."

Hannah put the phone down and turned off the TV. She had never been as scared in her whole life as Kelly and the other girls had been, and she was nearly twice as old as them. No wonder they were terrified. Somehow, no matter what, she would nail those bastards.

18.

At about the same time as Hannah and Tom were completing their successful house raid, Davoud and Jenny were driving back to London. Jenny had to pick up her son from a friend's after the weekend's regatta.

"I've missed Harry," she said. "It's the first time we've been apart for a weekend."

Davoud felt guilty: he had hardly given Sara a thought. He felt relieved: did that mean Jenny hadn't taken any other man to the cottage? He felt diminished: the weekend's experiences had fulfilled him completely, but that was obviously not so for Jenny.

"I wonder what he's been doing," mused Jenny.

Already they were going their separate ways; the weekend was fading, put into perspective.

"Sara's been at the seaside, hasn't she?"

"Yes, with her mum and the new man. At Aldeburgh with other friends and their families."

He didn't expand. Possessiveness over Sara was futile. A part-time dad was all he could ever be now. He could only continue with her in his own way, give her experiences. Sara, as she grew up, would select her own values and interests.

"Your father will be glad to see you back."

He knew she was making conversation, trying to dispel the subdued atmosphere in the car.

"Yes, he will. But I don't think he'll register that I've been away for longer than usual. He'll assume I'm just back from work."

"Is he getting worse?"

"Slowly but surely, I'm afraid."

"It must be heartbreaking."

"Yes, it's hard." He was looking in the rear-view mirror.

"Tell me – if you want."

Davoud had never been a great believer in 'a trouble shared is a trouble halved'. You could talk all you wanted, but in the end it was your own brain and heart that had to cope, and any decision came down to you. But something in Jenny encouraged him, a genuineness. Or perhaps it was the closeness of the weekend, the lack of restraint that he wanted to maintain by any means.

"I see him in his chair, sometimes, in the evening, just staring. Not focusing on anything. Not with me; somewhere else, maybe. But I think it's often a void: no thoughts. Just an absence."

"It doesn't mean he's unhappy."

"I know. But he's nothing at those times. He still prays, though. I watch him and it makes me angry. Last week when there were all those people crushed to death at the hajj in Mecca, he prayed to his God – the all-powerful, all-merciful, beneficent Allah. Why can he not see the irony, the cruel mockery of it all? Faith excuses and permits the most terrible things. The end justifies the means, but the end is a fantasy. And yet, at prayer, he is keeping faith with himself. That part of him is still fully alive. I am glad for him, but still angry. Does that make sense?"

"Of course."

"He forgets words. 'Don't tell me,' he says, 'don't tell me.' He rummages in his mind, desperate to know he can still retrieve it. Then he gives in. 'Tell me.' Each time it's a defeat for him."

Davoud stopped. He'd been running on. He hadn't said any of this to anyone else before.

"It's very difficult for you to deal with: watching a parent who was once competent and intelligent decline into senility. I'm grateful I didn't have that with my mother."

"He's like a leaf, turning brown. Once he was vivid, enthusiastic, part of life. Now life is preparing to reject him. I know it's natural, the wheel turning and all that, but it still comes as a shock."

Jenny was silent.

"Anyway, enough of that, it's depressing." A pause. "I haven't told you: I've started a new job. I can't tell you more than that it's all secret government stuff."

"Don't tell me anything I shouldn't know. That way, if I get captured by the enemy, I'll have nothing to confess."

He laughed. "I got fed up with just coordinating. It was important stuff, I know, reporting to the high-ups, making recommendations. Perhaps it's being with my dad. I needed more action. I can't tell you what it is, but I'll actually be in charge of running operations, making decisions on the ground – real stuff, not paperwork. Not a promotion, a sideways step. I'm amazed I haven't had any phone calls this weekend."

"Still in London, though?" she asked.

"Oh yes."

They stopped at traffic lights. He glanced at her.

"Can you see me as decisive, clear-headed, even ruthless?"

Jenny laughed. "I like what I see, Davoud. And, yes, I can. It's part of what intrigues me about you."

She touched his hand. He remembered her hand on his thigh on the journey out, imagining a lorry driver looking down and grinning.

"Can I ask you something else?" she said.

"Go ahead."

"Did I shock you in bed?"

He looked at her. "You're shocking me now."

She was so direct, left no room for the nuances behind

which he himself often sheltered. What should he say? Yes, was the honest answer. Did his lack of sensual adventurousness bore her? If he made too big a deal of it now, did this just emphasise his gaucheness?

"Did I?"

No evasion allowed.

"You thrilled me. You were devastating."

"That's not what I asked."

Why did she want to know?

"I think a woman generally expects a man to know the score," she continued.

"Well, that marks me down," he laughed bravely.

"Wait a moment. Let me finish. But I think a woman knowing the score can be threatening to a man. All that competitive stuff, as you've just demonstrated. So a woman has to be more discreet in showing her hand, so to speak. Especially if it matters to her how the man reacts. And you do matter to me. But I decided against discretion. I decided to trust you. It's all about trust."

"Don't get me wrong," replied Davoud, "I like that kind of trusting."

They both laughed.

"You can trust me any time," he added.

She slid her hand from his thigh to caress his penis.

He groaned and smiled. "I might have to make an emergency stop."

"I won't change up a gear in that case," she said.

"Getting back to your question, yes, I was taken aback." Another moment. "As it were."

They both laughed again.

"Don't be anxious, Davoud. Whatever your imagination is building, I can assure you it will be much exaggerated. No need to be nervous. It's that public school you went to; not the best grounding for being confident with women." She leaned over and kissed him on his cheek. "I think I know the solution."

"What's that, then?"

"You redefine me as one of your assignments or operations or whatever you call them. Then you'll be able to be determined. I'll look forward to your being ruthless."

He grinned and held her hand close on his stiffening penis.

"You see," she said, "it's not hard, is it?"

"No, but it's getting there."

Later, when they reached Central London, he said, "I'll drop you off. You'll be picking up Harry, and I'm going for a run in Hyde Park. Scour out the gremlins. Relish the pain."

"Is that what a weekend with me does to you? Watch your hamstrings. And I'll see you at the jazz club tomorrow evening."

"Must you?"

"Yes, I must."

He smiled. He wanted her to be there. And that was unprecedented: sharing that part of his life.

19.

While Hannah sat at home, angry but determined, Yusuf was admiring the red van which was no longer red. He'd left it last night in the double lock-up Imran had rented and then gone back to Imran's flat. He'd slept till noon, then eaten a microwaved chicken jalfrezi. In the afternoon he had checked, yet again, the tide timetables for Morecambe Bay and the rail freight timetables from Freightmaster. He hadn't made mistakes. The moon was full and it would be a ten-metre tide on Thursday night, the highest of the year. He'd prayed, read the Qu'ran and made a list of what he needed to buy and transport in the van to the meeting place.

He'd laughed to himself. So simple: for a twenty-nine-pound subscription to Freightmaster he'd been able to access timetables. There, among the iron ore tipplers, empty box wagons, loaded cement tanks and coal hoppers, he'd seen the DRS designation. Direct Rail Services, he learned, was a publicly owned subsidiary of the Nuclear Decommissioning Authority. The Greenpeace site, too, had been informative.

Then, in the still, mild early evening, he strolled round to the lock-up.

As soon as he entered the fumes caught his throat and he coughed. "A professional job, eh, bruv?" laughed Imran, who was wearing a baseball cap. The van was now white, with new number plates.

They shook hands.

"Do you want this face mask? Health and safety, you know."

Yusuf shook his head. "Nah, but what a stink!"

"It's supposed to smell like pears, some of this two-pack paint," said Imran.

"Bloody funny pears! I could get high on that. Have you been working in that all day?"

"The fan's been on," said Imran, pointing to the corner, where the fan was still whirring. "And I did have a face mask, and it only took three hours."

"I thought it would take all day."

"Well, we're just covering the red, no preparation, no putting right. That's what takes the time. You'll be abandoning it before the end of the week."

"Will it be dry by tomorrow?"

"Give it a couple of hours and it will be hard, finger-touch hard. Then all I've got to do is peel the edge masking and brown masking paper off the windows and the lights. You've got a different van."

Yusuf walked round it.

"Satisfied?"

"Great job," said Yusuf. He nodded with satisfaction. "Set up the Facebook page, bruv?"

"Aye, man. It's been up for a couple of weeks," replied Imran.

"What did you finally call it?"

"The Morecambe Bay Amphitheatre."

Yusuf laughed. "I like it, dramatic. Gladiators and that. So what did you post?"

"All the guff. Heritage open days and guided walks around a castle, and a hill fort and the old salt industry."

Yusuf laughed again. "Perfect."

"A charity walk across the bay, beach-cleaning sessions, paragliding, parachuting, windsurfing, ballooning, cycling."

"Man, that should get some likes: all those eco keep-fit punters. And Leighton Moss?"

"I added a link to the reserve, like you said."

"That's where it all started," said Yusuf. "Seems a long time ago but it's only about three months."

"And you'll like this. I also put on the North Lancashire Soul Music Festival."

"Hey, didn't know you did irony, Imran."

"So it's all perfectly innocent. Anyone wanting to know about Morecambe Bay can visit it. All my friends are liking it and sharing it, saying they think I've gone crazy: Imran doing beach cleaning. I'm already getting some grief."

"Brilliant, fam. It's lying there, dormant. Then – pow! – it will suddenly rise up and the world will not believe it. That's after I've sent you the vital message and you've put it on the page. That message will go viral. Don't know when it will be, all depends on the negotiations. Don't know what it will be – could be *Armageddon for Morecambe Bay and Paradise for me*. Or could be *Suleiman is free and we're heroes back in Yemen*."

"I'll be waiting."

"Both phones, remember, both charged up. I'll send to both just in case." Yusuf clenched his fists.

He suddenly turned and hugged Imran. "It's going to happen, fam, we're going to do it."

"I still don't know what *it* is."

"You soon will. Your last part is tomorrow. We drive over to Rotherdyke and send the final message on that laptop. On the way back we'll drive up some tracks to get the van a bit muddy. It's too shiny-new. People might remember it."

"Good thinking. Who'd have thought it, Yusuf? That quiet, well-mannered young man I introduced to the mosque will soon be top of the wanted list of terrorists."

"A journey, as they say," laughed Yusuf. "Inshallah."

2014

I sit cross-legged on the cushions by the wall. Born in Keighley in West Yorkshire in May 1992, christened Ryan Hudson in Slaymaker Lane Methodist Church. I am Yusuf Javeed. It is a miracle to be born again. I sit absolutely still, hands on my thighs, fingers tightly interlocked. Eyes on the door, I must keep my face composed, conceal the excitement I feel. The man I am waiting for is my hero, the tutor whose speeches I have pored over on video and debated with my friends back in Leeds. Anwar al-Awlaki is the reason I am here. I shift my weight, lift my shoulders to take a deep breath, feel my heart beating fast.

The room is in a whitewashed brick, two-storey house in the compound of the Dammaj Institute, one hundred miles north of Sana'a, the capital of Yemen. Twenty other full-bearded young men sit with me, round three of the walls. I know most of them well now, including two from Birmingham and London, an Afro-American, and English speakers from Mexico, Indonesia and Tunisia. I am the only Caucasian. Fair-skinned and fair-haired, I am known as the Pale One, *Al-waahid ash-aahib*. My beard embarrasses me: thin and straggly as well as fair. In fact, I am all thin and straggly – long-legged, narrow-shouldered, bony-faced. I do not look like an Islamic warrior, in spite of the Yemeni dagger in my belt, but I am accepted by all as an equal comrade.

The door is pushed open and the muttering among the young men ceases. A wedge of bright sunlight slices across the floor, and a man in Arab robes enters and closes the door. He is slighter than I expected but carries with him a quiet dignity. Without a word, the tutor strides to a cupboard by the back wall, opens it and takes out two flags.

"Yusuf," he says, and beckons me out.

I am startled, hardly believing my name has been spoken. I stand up, legs weak, throat dry, conscious all eyes are upon me. Uncertain, I join Awlaki in the centre of the room. He hands me the corners of both flags. I hold them, afraid to drop them. Awlaki steps back a stride and the flags open out: the Stars and Stripes and the Union Jack. Awlaki hands me a cigarette lighter and nods to me. I flick the lighter. No flame. Desperately, I flick again. This time it sparks and I hold the flame to the flags.

They take a moment or two to catch alight. Then a yellow flame shoots upwards and spreads across the flags. We drop them to the floor and watch them burn, bright flames dancing in the shaded room. I feel a pulse of heat, smell the acrid smoke. In a few minutes all that is left is a smouldering handful of smoking ash.

The tutor gestures to me to return to my place. Dazed, elated, feeling chosen, I stumble back.

*

"I'll leave you to it, then," said Yusuf.

Outside he leant against the wall, catching the sun. Shining on Shalima too, but higher in the sky, hotter. They'd still be in the Mediterranean, somewhere between Suez and Gibraltar. It would be harder for her. Just waiting, the freighter making its slow, steady way. And the team: a week was a long time to be doing nothing. Would he have a team to work with, or just a set of individuals? Would they be united? Would Shalima have been strong enough? And how would they react to him – a new leader – and having to go straight into action within hours of landing? There would be no time for tensions and disagreements. For a moment he felt daunted, not up to it. Now that he had others to work with, it was much more complex. So much easier to be a solitary suicide bomber, or Abdul alone in that pickup truck in Dar es Salaam.

But this was so much bigger: his idea, his initiative. He stood up straight, gritted his teeth. *It. Will. Work.* He would make it work. Soon now he would reach his next destination. Maybe his last – in this world.

Inshallah.

20

Shalima could not believe how easy it had been. No problems, no arguments within the team – they even prayed together, not five times every day but at least three. They were fervent jihadist believers but, without discussing anything, the group had come to an understanding about a flexible approach to certain rituals. No rows with the skipper, an easy-going, overweight, heavily moustached man who had never before skippered an AQ-sponsored voyage beyond the Mediterranean; no tensions with his mate and engineer. They had sailed together for a long time, knew each other's idiosyncrasies and worked around them.

Sitting under an awning on deck in thirty-five degrees of heat, she watched Kal the Frenchman and Bargo the Belgian fishing at the stern. Their plan required two men able to drive diesel railway engines, two able to navigate by sea, and one explosives expert. The Al-Qaeda network had found them. Yusuf had specified the driver expertise required. Kal had once worked as a mechanic with the French company which ran Euro Cargo Rail. He had serviced the Class 66 and Class 37 diesels which the British firm, Direct Rail Services, had sold to them. Direct Rail Services were the freight company that ran west coast freight trains using those engines. Kal had trained Bargo as the other train driver.

Kal was a strange mixture of a man, and Shalima liked him. He hated the English. Nothing to do with being a Muslim, but because he was French, he said. How could a man whose parents came from the former French colony of Tunisia have absorbed the age-old French tribal hostility towards the English? He had told her his story of being rescued from heroin addiction by his local mosque, of working in a kebab shop before leaving to follow the path of the Prophet.

She had overheard snippets of conversations Kal had had with Ibra – how he loathed gambling, alcohol and drugs. Typical of the born-again. How he was disgusted by homosexuality. But he was vain, too, rubbing olive oil cream into his beard to moisturise it. It hung down over his chest and smelled pleasantly of vanilla. His eyes were shielded by a shock of curly, wiry hair, and he always wore a red-checked keffiyeh and black military-style boots. Bargo would not have been an easy man to teach train driving, or anything else. But Kal had been patient and clear. Shalima knew she could rely on him totally.

Benny, as usual, was below deck, sleeping. A German, he was the explosives expert. He'd lived in Oberndorf in the Black Forest, working at the vast Heckler & Koch munitions factory whose MP5 sub-machine guns and G36 assault rifles were used around the world. Since his recruitment to the team he'd worked on a mock-up of the target cargo carrier, constructed from dimensions sent by Yusuf. He and Ibra could now attach the explosives in nine minutes.

Shalima was confident they were all as prepared as possible. No one had asked about how she had arrived at this point.

MARCH 2012

The door opens and I get off the bus; it's less than a hundred metres to the college entrance. Ahead of me I see three teenage girls in black burkas, chatting at the bottom of the steps. I hear their laughter and their excited Cockney accents. Always makes me laugh.

Suddenly, from round the corner, four white girls, in jeans and hoodies, faces obscured, race past. They surround the burka girls, pushing their faces up close, yelling, "Paki bitches!"

The three cower. Then the white girls ram eggs onto their face veils, squashing them in with the palms of their hands.

"Fuck off back to your own country!"

They run off down the street, cheering and thumping the air with their fists.

Rooted to the spot, stunned, my fists clenched and gripping my bag, I see the yellow yolks clotting the black mesh screens across the girls' eyes, smearing down the black cloth. It happened so fast.

You fucking ignorant, vicious bitches!

But you asked for it: always in your burkas, you challenge and taunt. You stupid, stupid girls. Always the victims.

And the fucking burka demeans us – you just don't get that, do you? Why do you insult yourselves, submitting to some pathetic male insecurity? Like my mother did, all her life.

I could scream, tear my hair out. *We'll get back at you, somehow.*

I hurry up the steps to see if I can help them.

★

They had sailed steadily north through the Red Sea, passing white beaches and the port of Jeddah. Two swirling dust storms forced them all below deck as they passed between Saudi Arabia and Sudan, and then they headed into the Gulf of Suez. At Port Tewfik they waited to join the northern convoy which set off just after four o'clock. They crossed the Great Bitter Lake, and fourteen hours and 192 kilometres later arrived at Port Said. As at Port Tewfik, there were no cargo or documentation checks and their ship was free to turn west in the Mediterranean.

Now to the south was Morocco, to the north Spain, somewhere ahead the Rock of Gibraltar. In the evenings in her cabin, Shalima pored over the map and plans that Yusuf had sent her. Once they landed, he would be in charge: he knew the topography and the timings. As soon as the second and final message came, she had to brief the team. They knew nothing of the actual target, were ignorant of the purpose of the mission. Her briefing would give them some details, but still not all. So she rehearsed and rehearsed the operation – from landing to ambush. After that, what happened was out of their control. Success was guaranteed, but not the nature of that success. Their own deaths were more than likely, but not inevitable.

At night, as the engine hummed and the ship ploughed on across a gentle sea, she often thought of England. It had been her home, but now she could see only its complacency, its self-righteous trumpetings about toleration. But underneath the surface, in spite of the law, there was intolerance in the towns and streets and workplaces, Islamophobia, prejudice, inequality.

May 2013

Thump! Thump! Thump! From the apartment above me, the bass guitar hammers into my brain. I squash my pillow round my head, but I still hear them.

I curl up in my single bed, knees up to my chest. I have cried myself out. Throat raw, tears dried on my cheeks. Exhausted, empty, alone.

Naneejan is sleeping peacefully in the next room, snoring quietly. She must not know why I'm heartbroken. And I don't want to talk to Naz, my only friend in London. She doesn't know about when I was young in Birmingham, and I don't want her to know.

I crave sleep, but I can't stop my brain whirring round, remembering. Fiona has smashed the last piece of my childhood.

She was my best friend all through secondary school, the only person I could talk to about my mum and dad. All the other girls fell out with their friends, but Fiona and me stuck together. We just got on. Her mum Christine was great – she let us try on her clothes and we danced around the room and posed and had loads of laughs. Of course Dad wouldn't allow me to wear make-up, so in Fiona's bedroom, listening to Black Eyed Peas and Lady Gaga, she let me experiment with hers – eyeshadow and lipstick and mascara. She loved brushing my long hair, and I loved her doing it.

I loved her world, the laughs and the fun we had. Then I felt guilty when I got back home to Mum. Fiona and her mum wanted me to do sleepovers, but my dad refused. We never stopped talking, Fiona and me – walking to school, in the canteen at dinner time, shopping, in cafés, sunbathing in the park in the summer. We were inseparable. She told me things about boys I just couldn't believe. "So immature," she said, but I knew she liked their attention.

Upstairs, he turns off his heavy metal at last. I release the pillow from my ears and check the time: 0130. Lights from the street lamps shine round the edges of the curtain. I can hear traffic on the road. A police car or ambulance races along nearby streets.

The worst part of coming to London was leaving Fiona. But I had no choice because of my dad. At first we texted a lot. I told her about my drinking and binge-eating. She told me about this lad she'd met, Jason, twenty years old. She texted me a photo. I didn't like the look of him. He seemed hard to me, or trying to look hard: shaven head, earring, fierce eyes. But I didn't say anything.

Then she stopped replying to my texts. A couple of weeks ago I said I was coming up to Brum to see her, but she said no.

Then today she sent me this long text. Jason's in the English Defence League, a taxi driver. *All Muslims are terrorists, they run drugs and grooming gangs, carry out honour killing, arrange forced marriages and have their own sharia law. Muslims just can't be English.*

And she didn't want to ever contact me again.

I couldn't believe Fiona was saying these things. She was parroting Jason, I knew, but how could she? Each of those statements was like a kick in the head.

I read it again and again. But Fiona knows me better than anyone, knows I'm not like that, that I detest those things as much as they do.

Muslims just can't be English.

That's when I thumped the table, swept my college papers onto the floor and stamped around the room.

"No," I yelled.

Naneejan came in from the kitchen.

"It's not fair, it isn't right," I shouted.

"Shalima?" she said, her face frightened and anxious.

I managed to say, "It's not you, Naneejan. Just something." Then I charged upstairs and collapsed onto the bed, sobbing and punching the pillow.

Fiona had betrayed me. All those years of friendship gone.

I cried for a long time. Naneejan knocked on the door and brought me a cup of tea. I couldn't look up. She touched my shoulder gently.

"I'm sorry, I'll be OK," I muttered. "Don't worry."

She went downstairs.

So here I am, in the cold early hours: sore nose, aching head, puffed-up eyes, fingers clutching scrunched-up Kleenex, weary. A motorbike roars by, rain begins to tap on the window.

Alone, shunned, no one to talk to. Drifting in the dark, awake. And over and over again, like a chant, **Muslims can't be English.**

★

She shifted restlessly in her bunk. Western aggression and interference everywhere across the Muslim world – in Iraq and Afghanistan and Syria. Bombs, drones, killings, nations broken apart. Yet somehow a sense of innocence prevailed: that nothing was their fault, that they acted for good.

The Twin Towers had shocked the USA out of complacency forever. Very soon England, the UK, Europe would be profoundly changed.

Tomorrow Yusuf's message was due. She needed to sleep. Needed time to quicken up.

Four days to go.

21.
Monday 28th September

Hannah Walker marched into Rotherdyke Police Station, barely acknowledged the desk sergeant on duty with a flick of her hand, strode down the corridor into her office and slammed the door. It was not quite seven o'clock. She stared out of the window at the warehouse opposite. She'd hardly slept – all the excitement of the successful raid on Opal Street, the arrest of the men and their identification by Kelly had been replaced by rage. Not at Kelly for withdrawing her statement, but at the thugs who had terrified her and her family. Hannah was nearly back to square one.

Tony had been cross with her, too. It was obvious from his familiar preliminaries that he'd wanted to make love last night, but she'd not responded.

"That bloody job of yours…"

She'd not explained, angry that he needed an explanation. The stories that Kelly and the other girls had told her whirled around in her head. She could have told Tony one of them and he would have understood, but why should she? Could he not just accept that sometimes she did live the job? Which was why she was good at it.

She turned away from the window, switched on her computer, filled her filter coffee machine – she couldn't stand the rubbish in the corridor machine – and sat at her desk. The computer was so slow getting itself organised. From a file she took the photos of the groomers. Their faces stared impassively at her, resistant. She would get the bastards. Today would be a long day: checking statements for inconsistencies, confirming surveillance evidence and all the rest of it. The seized phones, iPads and laptops would be examined; texts, emails and phone numbers investigated. It would be a tedious process.

There was a knock at her door.

"Come in."

It was young Constable Graham Driscoll.

"You're in early," said Hannah.

"Yes, Sarge, wanted to get to work on this stuff we collected yesterday from Opal Street."

"Well done, me too."

"Any progress on the Arabic keyboard? Could have incriminating stuff on it."

"Certainly could. But no progress yet. Keep going on the other stuff. We need all the evidence we can get."

"Yes, ma'am, we've already done forensics. A mass of fingerprints we haven't had time to match yet."

"Well done again."

He closed the door quietly behind him. A good lad, that.

Why an Arabic keyboard? The phone calls they'd listened to so far had been in Urdu or English. So far as Hannah knew, none were in Arabic. The men all spoke good English; there'd been no hesitations in interviews. It was odd. How common were Arabic keyboards? She'd no idea. Did mosques have them? The more she thought about it, it would be best to send it on fast to someone in authority.

It took an infuriating time to navigate the automatic phone system, tapping keys from the menu and waiting in queues. So much for swift response. When she finally got through to a human being, it took three call transfers before she spoke to someone in Special Branch in London who could make a decision. And he did, immediately: grooming was a top priority – there'd been too many serious mistakes which had put the police under severe pressure – and any Arabic communication had the security forces jumping about.

"Get it to GCHQ immediately. Ask for Jamie Lockhart, he's a top man. I'll alert him you're on your way."

That was decisive. What could be on it? There was more to this than met the eye. If it was so important it wouldn't be fair to entrust it to someone else, someone more junior. She'd have to take it herself.

So much for a day combing through the grooming case details. Rapidly Hannah gave instructions for interviewing Opal Street residents – a long shot, but necessary – and for organising and prioritising anything that was found on mobiles and the other laptops. She phoned Tony but he didn't pick up, probably still sulking, so she left a message saying she was going down to Cheltenham and didn't know what would happen after that. Sometimes he needed to grow up a bit.

*

The laptop lay on the passenger seat as she sped down the M6 and M5. Perhaps it should be chained to her wrist. She laughed to herself. She was excited; this was out of the ordinary: a courier with urgent material, maybe of national importance.

Three hours after leaving Rotherdyke, blues and twos occasionally switched on, she sat in a queue of traffic at a roundabout at a corner of the fence that surrounded GCHQ, the famous doughnut. It was a massive circular five-storey structure of green glass and a grey arched roof. The fence surrounding it, two metres high and topped with coiled razor wire, was also grey. In spite of this, to Hannah the centre seemed deliberately understated, undramatic. Opposite the main entrance was a bus stop, and an ordinary double-decker bus was parked there. She watched the staff walking in, carrying laptop bags and shopping bags. This was the centre of the UK's intelligence-gathering network, probing cyberspace around the earth – and a family strolled past the entrance. The whole place was surrounded by estates of houses; she saw the name Galileo Avenue, and trampolines in gardens.

Her car moved forward. On the fence was a notice: *This is a protected place under Section 128 of the Serious Organised Crime and Police Act 2005.* She loved the word 'protected'; not prohibited or forbidden. Organised crime; not security or military. Was this a particularly British low-key approach? In France or the USA would the public be kept at arm's length, would there be armed guards patrolling? She was suddenly proud of being British. She and Tony had not long ago seen *The Imitation Game*, and she realised she probably knew more about Bletchley Park in the 1940s than its current incarnation as GCHQ.

Now she moved forward to the entrance – a maze of grey-fenced lanes, barriers with sentry-box-type booths and traffic lights. A few men in black uniforms with yellow high-vis jackets and security cards hanging from lanyards round their necks were checking pedestrians with a smile or looking into car windows. She looked up at a CCTV camera: under the casualness, there was an efficient system. She was being watched and checked, carefully processed. She felt as she did driving through customs: guilty, though entirely innocent. It was like being in a film. There was a glamour to it. She looked in the rear-view mirror and tidied her hair. Then stopped – come on! She wasn't going to a casting couch.

She gave her name and that of Jamie Lockhart to the man in the booth. He made a telephone call. She heard a radio crackle a message to an attendant standing beside another car. Then she was given the OK, the traffic light turned green and the barrier rose.

Driving past a large white satellite dish, Hannah followed a *Visitors* sign to a line of concrete bollards preventing vehicles from approaching the entrance. In the car park, CCTV cameras recorded her every move. Her ID was examined by a security man who pointed her to the reception desk where she explained her visit.

She waited only five minutes in a reception area before she was approached by a broad, dark-haired man who held out his hand and said, "Jamie Lockhart. Hannah Walker?"

She stood up and shook his hand.

"You've made good time," he said. "Come with me."

He tapped in the code on the security reader and they went through a door into a long, curving corridor.

"Welcome to The Street," he said.

Everybody here must be super intelligent with weirdly wired brains, thought Hannah. The electronic hub. Secrets from around the world. Signals from everywhere.

He showed her into a small room, like a cleanly decorated interview room. A strong smell of coffee, and on the desk a plate of sandwiches, a couple of plates with paper serviettes, a carafe of water with ice cubes still in it, a couple of mugs, a small jug of milk, and a bowl of sugar.

"Help yourself," said Jamie. "You know best how you like it."

The window looked down onto a grassed central area with trees and benches, the centre of the doughnut.

Hannah poured herself some coffee.

"Now, fill me in."

She placed the laptop on the desk.

"An Arabic keyboard. We found it in a raid on a house as part of our investigation into grooming. We need the stuff on it translating; there could be vital information on it. We need all the help we can get."

She heard herself talking in a clipped, efficient, businesslike way – as if she'd absorbed something already from the surroundings and Jamie's brisk manner. There was a half-eaten chicken sandwich on his desk. She took a salad one herself.

Jamie picked up the phone and tapped in some numbers. "Sandra? Jamie here. I'm in Room 043. I've a laptop here that needs taking down to the Arabic desk. Many thanks. We'll sort the paperwork later, signing for stuff and all that."

He took a bite of his sandwich. Hannah took a drink of coffee, hot and strong. He didn't waste words.

A knock at the door. Sandra, presumably, came in and smiled at Hannah. Jamie nodded at the laptop.

"Tell them I've said top priority."

"I will."

The door closed behind her and Jamie said, "I don't envy you working on grooming. Must be emotionally draining. I've read what's going on. I have two girls of my own. It's horrific."

"Yes, it is hard. Hard to keep that professional distance when, to be frank, I'd like to spit in their faces. Oh, sorry, I shouldn't have said that. Lots of time to think about it all the way down here."

Jamie smiled at her. "No, you shouldn't have said that. But it's good to meet a human being. We're all geeks here."

"It's the usual problem: we know they're guilty. But we need the evidence."

"That's what we're defending," said Jamie. "All of us here, and all the kit we've got. British justice! The right to a fair trial."

Hannah gave him a rueful smile. "I know. But sometimes I think people have forgone their rights."

"And so do I. But that's a dangerous road to go down. We end with ISIS and Mugabe and Karimov."

Hannah had vaguely heard of Mugabe, but not of Karimov. She tried to look intelligent.

"And I shouldn't have said that," continued Jamie.

He looked at his watch. "Sorry, I have to go. Top-level security meeting – I have to say that, but it's actually true. It's been good meeting you. No point in my trying to make the country safe if things like grooming happen in it."

"And vice versa," said Hannah.

"And vice versa indeed. I guarantee I'll send you the translations ASAP. You have my word."

They shook hands.

From the corridor he pointed her the way to reception and turned to stride in the opposite direction.

Quite an experience. The laptop was in the best possible hands. The evidence on it, she hoped, would compensate for Kelly's withdrawn statement. She had confidence in Jamie. You couldn't go higher than GCHQ.

Hannah drove back at a more leisurely speed. She must Google... Karimov, was it? And be nice to Tony. He was a good man, she loved him and mustn't take him for granted. But with grooming she was on a mission. Surely he understood that.

22.

That same evening around 8.30 Jenny turned in between massive stone gateposts and went down a flight of worn stone steps to the red iron doors that led to the Catacomb Arts Centre just off the Euston Road in London. She showed her ticket to the girl in the tiny ticket office and went in.

An arched tunnel, built with dirty yellow bricks, the flagstone floor uneven; table lamps on the floor by brick pillars casting low glows and Jenny's giant shadow curving ahead of her on the walls. The air was surprisingly dry and warm. Off the main tunnel were shadowy alcoves. Several other people were wandering about, but not a crowd.

It had taken four meetings before Davoud confided in her about his music. He'd started guitar at St Paul's School, teaching himself slowly and putting in hours of practice. His father was a conservative Muslim, suspicious of music inflaming the passions and 'the lower self'. Later in life, Davoud couldn't decide whether his guitar playing had been a conscious form of rebellion. Initially, he played only for himself, never joining one of the groups that flourished in the school. At Cambridge he met three other students who eventually formed a group. They played together for sheer enjoyment and then occasionally at gigs in small venues as part of an arts festival, and once in London at the Central College of Art union. They called themselves The Riders. Davoud's hero, he told Jenny, was John McLaughlin and his Mahavishnu Orchestra, playing a combination of rock, jazz and Indian music.

"It was labelled jazz rock or jazz fusion or prog rock," Davoud told her. "And we loved it. Off the mainstream. That appealed to us. We had to be a bit different."

Jenny was intrigued at this other side of him. He refused to play for her, for reasons he never explained, but gave demonstrations of the whammy bar, the hammer-ons and pull-offs, the two-handed tapping he had just mastered. The guitar was more technical than she thought. Since leaving university, the four men had met up infrequently, usually just to play together in one of their homes. Now that Davoud had returned to London they had been able to practise together.

"Would you like to listen to us play?" he'd asked as they lay together after making love. Softly he'd whispered the question into her hair, hesitant. She sensed he was risking inviting her across the threshold into his personal haven.

Davoud had told her of the upcoming gig at the Catacomb, their set starting at nine o'clock. So here she was, ignorant of John McLaughlin, not knowing what music to expect. In some of the alcoves were installations, all in low coloured light and looking eerie: a paper forest with giant paper moths hanging from the ceiling, slowly gyrating in the moving air; in a refrigerated glass case were frozen white plants, delicate as corals, which had, said the notice she bent to read, *been dipped in liquid nitrogen*. All highly symbolic of something. Trying too hard, easy to mock. Trendy, very underground. Subterranean.

The only sounds were footsteps, heels tapping on stone, hushed conversations and occasional suppressed giggling among the visitors, and the intermittent distant, dull rumble and vibration of underground trains. Along the tunnel and in the alcoves were solitary wooden slatted chairs. A larger alcove, almost a room, was obviously the performance area: on a low stage were music stands, a drum kit, keyboard and amplifiers. Old pews were placed along the walls and there was a scattering of chairs. Lamps on the floor threw weak cones of light up the curved walls of brick and across the arched ceiling; a spotlight shone on the stage. Jenny took a seat at the end of one of the pews. This place, she had read, had been used for crypt burials, a coffin repository, an air-raid shelter and an operating theatre. Ghostly, unsettled spirits. She shivered.

Slowly the chairs and pews filled up. Looking behind her into the tunnel she saw people taking their places on the chairs there. At quarter past nine, the four musicians filed in: Davoud, shorter and more slightly built than the others, with the gleaming, treasured black-and-white Fender Stratocaster guitar he had shown her.

They were all dressed differently and casually. Jenny smiled at Davoud's self-conscious red necktie below his neatly trimmed greying beard, loose grey fisherman's sweater and worn navy cords. As if he had disguised himself. He had an effects pedal plugged into his amplifier – later, in bed, he told her this produced what was known as the 'woman tone': deliberate feedback which created an elongated note, a kind of crooning sound which could be shrill and smooth like a flute, even creamy and syrupy, or mean and bluesy. "Quite a chat-up line," she laughed.

A few introductory notes, nods between them, and then they started to play. Jenny watched and listened, concentrating on Davoud. There were no dramatic postures with his guitar, no exaggerated facial expressions, only occasional passages when he closed his eyes, and just the barely visible rhythmic tapping of his shoe. And as he created the sensual curves of sound, as the notes sprayed out, as the music switched from soulful and tender, the bass dancing, the studious, reserved Davoud she knew faded out and he became the music: ethereal, strange, haunting, abstract, musing, experimental, improvising. His fingers (this man who said he was no good with his hands) flicked at a dazzling yet controlled speed, plucking, stroking, tapping, strumming, creating softness then drama, sadness then exhilaration. Very sensual. And then he played his solo. The audience watched him closely, aficionados who could appreciate the technique. This was music to listen to, not dance to, music that was somehow cerebral and sensual at the same time. It reminded her of Bach. And when Davoud merged back into the group the players smiled and nodded at each other. There was a knowledgeable applause.

Jenny began to realise that in bed she had contacted something in him that had expressed itself before only in his guitar playing. Which was why he had been able, at last, to let go: parts of himself were fitting together for the first time, dovetailing.

At the end of the third number she left the room, moved back along the tunnel and leaned against the curved wall out of sight of the group. The music eddied and swirled down the tunnel, rising and falling as if following its contours. Disembodied from its players, it became even more haunting, insinuating itself into her. Davoud the man had morphed into a sound, beautiful and questioning, knowing but at the edge of not knowing, pushing out into something hinted at but not defined – and she was with him. Drifting, swirling, tingling, salved.

He had told her not to wait for him after their set. He, with orange juice, and his friends, with a bottle of Jack Daniel's, would talk, slowly reorientate themselves back into the world of jobs and homes and decision-making. So when the music ended and clapping echoed through the Catacomb, Jenny left. She only had a babysitter until eleven. Something magical had happened, some alchemy, an enchantment. Neither she nor Davoud would look at the other in the same way again: he because he had invited her to see into him, offered her something from deep within him; she because she had responded to the invitation and accepted the gift. They had both been unsure, uncertain of what to expect. But the daring of surrender had been humbling and honest and unprecedented.

What would it be like when they next met? An awkwardness, a slight recoil from this new knowledge?

23.

At three o'clock that same afternoon, Yusuf parked his white van on The Boulevard in the outskirts of Keighley, three doors down and on the opposite side of the road from the house he had been brought up in.

Fuck you, I'm all right, Jack was the message of The Boulevard's houses: the double garages with BMWs and Mercedes parked in the driveway; tall, clipped, protective hedges; manicured lawns and neatly planted borders. They were all large houses – like his parents' – with two bathrooms, as well as en-suite bedrooms, a breakfast room and a dining room, elaborate drapes at the windows, electrically operated gates and CCTV cameras.

Yusuf snorted. All was right with the world. Anyone who could afford to live here had exploited other people or done something wrong or illegal. They made their pile and then often graciously decided to 'give something back', working unpaid for a charity a few hours a week. As if that evened the score, was some kind of redemption.

He had lived here for seventeen years but now he had nothing in common with the place. He looked up at his bedroom window from where, at this time of the year, he had watched landscape gardeners lopping trees and weeding flower beds. The workers had accepted their place and he had never questioned the system.

Godless getting and spending – his father and brother were still doing it, increasing the profit margins, expanding the business so they could consume more, upgrade their HD curved-screen TV or their iPad, buy designer clothes, show off their success to the world in their exclusive cars. Godless, materialist. Replacing and accumulating possessions. He spat out of the van window, felt that burning in his brain.

Their self-assurance and self-delusion. Yet when they saw on TV in three days' time what he – their son and brother – was doing, they would take the moral high ground. They would disown him, oblivious that they had spurred him on to the very action that appalled them.

His home stood now for all he despised; he had rejected it all. He burned with a different zeal, Allah be praised.

"It is the love of death in the path of Allah that is the weapon that will annihilate this evil empire of the West, by the permission of Allah."

He drove off with no backward glance and in less than an hour was parking on Opal Street in Rotherdyke. He turned the ignition off. This was a different world from The Boulevard. Several front doors of the small, terraced houses were covered with metal grilles. Last time he had not noticed the corner shop: *Atta's Food Stores, General Grocers, Sweets, Tobacco, News and Booze, Lottery.* This was an Asian area, Imran had said. So why the booze and lottery? The West was corrupting even Islam. Al-Qaeda was cleansing Islam as well as the West. He noticed several satellite dishes: porn and sport, game shows and Hollywood films. Western wickedness corrupted everyone, exploiting human weakness. What he was doing was right. Allah had guided him.

His satellite phone rang. Before he could say anything, an agitated voice said, "It's Imran."

"What is it?"

"Yusuf, I've only just been told: there was a police raid on the Opal Street house on Sunday."

It took a moment for the information to sink in. Yusuf forced himself to stay calm. "That's the day after I sent the Four Birds message."

"I know. But I don't think it was connected. They raided it because they suspect grooming has been going on there."

"Grooming?"

"Yes, grooming young girls."

"Those Asian men?"

"So they say. But the point is, they took the Arabic laptop along with a lot of other electronic stuff, mobiles and iPads."

Shit! He found he was gripping the steering wheel hard. Bastards! The first bloody thing to go wrong. He couldn't have foreseen that.

"I'm sitting outside the bloody house now, just about to send the last message."

"Well, get out, quick."

Yusuf scanned the street ahead and looked in his wing mirrors. No sign of police. In fact, the only person he could see was an old white woman with a shopping bag, shuffling along with her stick, eyes focused on the pavement. He drove off, careful not to accelerate too suddenly and draw attention to himself.

Once out of Rotherdyke, he pulled into a lay-by. His heartbeat was almost back to normal. He took stock. The laptop find was an unfortunate accident, but it didn't mean the authorities were on his trail. But sooner or later – probably later, given the inefficiency and reduced resources of the police – his message would be found. It was only four days to the attack – was that too short a time for anyone to discover what was going on? It had to be. But it was vital he send the last message, the final confirmation, and he had to do that immediately: Shalima would be waiting. He'd use voicemail – it would surely be harder to trace than text or email.

More determined than ever, spurred on by the confiscation of the laptop, he took out a piece of paper with Arabic writing on it and dialled Shalima. She would not pick up, that had been the clear instruction from the Al-Qaeda man: no telephone conversations after leaving Hodeida. The phone rang and rang. Then a male voice, in English: *I am not able to take your call, please leave your message after the beep.*

Yusuf was startled: the voice was so ordinary, so normal, no accent. The beep. He carefully spoke the Arabic: "*The birds are gathering. 67.19, 105.3.*"

No going back now.

Shalima should be in the Atlantic now, turning north towards England.

He repeated the call to the Al-Qaeda man.

It was done. He breathed a sigh of relief, realised his fingers were trembling, pressed them onto the steering wheel.

So be it. He bent his head. *May Allah be with me.*

2014

The wooden shutters of the room are almost closed, to keep out the heat of the sun. But bars of light shine through gaps, quivering with dust, highlighting the tutor's white gown. With a neat beard and brown eyes that can suddenly blaze behind his wire-rimmed glasses, with the smell of smoke still hanging in the air, Anwar al-Awlaki begins to speak softly, gesturing elegantly with his hands.

"You are nearing the end of your novitiate here and I want to name for you three men," he says.

But I am finding it hard to concentrate; my heart is still hammering, and I can feel the flag material on my fingers, smell its burning in my nostrils. I see Awlaki's face smiling at me, so near, his eyes warm.

I force myself to listen.

"The second is Abul A'la Maududi."

I have missed the first name. Awlaki's eyes range across us all as he speaks.

"He was born in India and died only thirty years ago. He taught that Islam was not just a religion, but an ideology of political struggle.

"I will quote to you what he wrote after he had been in prison, concerning the Prophet Muhammad, peace be upon him: *The moment the Qur'an began to be sent down it impelled this quiet and pious man to pit himself in a grim struggle against the lords of disbelief, evil and iniquity. Muhammad drew every pure and noble soul and gathered them under the banner of truth.*"

Awlaki holds out his arms towards us. "Maududi founded a movement, Jamaat-e-Islami, to train cadres of young men who would be the vanguard for the Islamic revolution." Another pause. He smiles. "Like you."

I feel warm tears well up in my eyes. I am called to jihad; mine is a divine mission. There is a shuffling among the group and we sit straighter.

Awlaki's sandals slap across the floor as he returns to the cupboard at the back of the room. He takes out a book and faces us.

"The third man is Sayyid Qutb. He lived for two years in the USA in the 1950s where he witnessed what he called a return to *jahillyya*: barbarism, ignorance and unbelief. Imprisoned by the infidels, Allah inspired him to write a book. He wrote: *Behold this individual freedom, devoid of human sympathy and responsibility for relatives except under force of law; this materialistic attitude which deadens the spirit; this behaviour, like animals, which is called free mixing of the sexes; this vulgarity which is called emancipation of women; this evil and fanatic racial discrimination.*"

It is exactly how I think of the England I have left. That sickening final image of Debbie flies into my mind, but I shut it away as if it were blasphemy and concentrate on Awlaki's voice.

"The deaths of three thousand civilians are legitimate in the global struggle between Muslims and unbelievers." Pause. "The use of suicide bombers in the West is right." Pause. "We are not against Americans just for being American, we are against evil. And America as a whole has become a nation of evil." Pause. "Jihad against America is binding upon myself, just as it is binding on every other able Muslim, on you."

His eyes seem to focus on me alone. And America includes the UK. Our military have fought with them in Afghanistan and Iraq, brothers in arms, criminals together.

There is a silence, then Awlaki bows slightly to us.

He says, "Allahu Akbar, Allah is most great."

It is repeated, and more join in until the whole group of us are chanting. Awlaki bows again, turns. He opens the door to leave the room and light floods in.

Hardly exchanging a word, we file out into the glaring heat of the desert day. There are two hours to ponder the lecture before the next call to prayers.

I love the austerity and purity of this life. I share a bare breeze-block room with an American convert from Delaware, a bodybuilder once known as Memphis Reed, now Abdul A-dha-la. Food is frugal – rice, beans and the occasional egg, ginger tea – and laid out on a plastic sheet on the floor. We sleep on blankets on the concrete floor, our toilet a hole in the ground in the washroom. I have learned to clean myself with water with my left hand.

I love the rules: the call from the muezzin five times a day for compulsory prayers, the call of the loudspeakers to classes and lectures. I love the single-mindedness, the fervour. I love my brotherhood.

Lying on my blanket that night, hearing the dogs bark in the street and the wind in the date palms, feeling the cold, pure desert air through the open window on my face, I see my journey as following a tradition from the very start of Islam: hijra, the flight from oppression, and then jihad, the struggle. I am part of this continuous movement.

24.

The Atlantic was different. The whole team swallowed seasickness pills and drowsed below deck, joining Benny who had already spent many hours asleep, or reading, as Shalima suspected. From his AQ report she knew he was the most educated of the team, doing two years of an electronics degree before dropping out when his father – a local government bureaucrat – died from a heart attack. His mother had withdrawn into herself and his elder brother had bullied him. Benny had rebelled, become involved in petty crime, taken to drink. Then he had found an alternative supportive family in the mosque.

"Like a bean plant growing up a wigwam of bamboo poles," he'd laughed.

The mosque had instructed him to get work in the huge explosives factory nearby. He'd been diligent, won promotion, taken on responsibility, learned so much.

"And now is my time," he said. "Now it is harvest time. It is our Muslim duty to make war on the infidels."

But he had spoken this calmly, matter-of-fact, no burning passion. Yet Shalima sensed a wistfulness about him when he stared out to sea, a sense of loss, hidden deep. Had there been a woman? But Benny would never say. He had soft brown eyes behind his wire-framed glasses, a black-and-white keffiyeh wrapped round his head, and always a scuffed black leather jacket and jeans.

As the ship pitched into the swell, through her porthole Shalima watched the grey sea rise and fall, flecked with white spray, beneath a grey sky. She was waiting for the final message from Yusuf: the trigger.

With the Rock of Gibraltar astern, ahead now were Land's End, the Bristol Channel and then the showdown. Leaving the Mediterranean had been like leaving a different planet. For twelve months she had lived in a separate sealed world where she had done things she could never have imagined – in Djibouti, Somalia and Kenya. She had seen death, planned and caused death. And she had been praised. She had Allah's approval. Hot sun, blinding light, intense prayers, raw battle, fierce belief, camaraderie, training – all in an alien desert land, to a set of different values. She had become a different person.

SEPTEMBER 2013

It was Naz's idea – Naz, my friend on the pre-nursing training course. She had been asked to come by a friend of hers and she wanted me with her because she was a bit nervous.

So here we are, on the pavement outside the Danish Embassy on Sloane Street, Chelsea. I've counted just seventeen of us; five women – two in niqabs, one in a burka and Naz and me in headscarves. The rest are young men, all bar two in black balaclavas.

We stand at the back of the group; it's the first demonstration we've been to. There's a line of policemen in front of us in those yellow high-vis jackets and beyond them is another group, protesting against us. They are chanting, "Freedom of speech, freedom of speech." Some wave Union Jacks.

The young man next to me waves his placard: *Freedom go to Hell*. Behind the police another waves his: *Freedom to insult*.

I can see their placards with magnified copies of the Danish cartoons. I can see the one with a picture of Muhammad with a bomb in his turban, the fuse lit, and the shahada written on the bomb: *There is no God but Allah and Muhammad is his messenger*. Another shows Muhammad dressed like a mullah, standing on a cloud as if in Heaven. He is greeting freshly arrived dead suicide bombers with: *"Sorry, we have run out of virgins."*

Of course they offended me when I first saw them. Naneejan would have cried out in horror and knelt to pray, terrified that Allah would punish us all.

But the virgins one makes me laugh.

Now we have started to chant. At first I feel self-conscious as well as nervous, my voice barely heard. But somehow I am drawn into the group so that I begin to shout with them, thumping the air with my right arm: "Sharia law, sharia law." The group opposite reply with their chants. We chant, they chant. It is hypnotic. But I see some of the other group are laughing and chatting. One couple are kissing as he waves his placard.

The police watch us, silent and stony-faced. I can see their hostility. Waving in their faces are our placards: *Kill those who insult the Prophet Muhammad* and *Butcher those who mock Islam*. Ordered to protect us, they despise us. I can see it in their mouths and eyes. And that provokes me, thrills me. I chant louder.

But I gasped when I first saw our placards – so vicious and violent. I wanted to turn back, but I couldn't abandon Naz. I don't even believe in sharia law. But here I am now, chanting it, throat sore, caught up in the group, no thoughts in my brain. The words I chant have lost their meaning. They're just sounds that bind us together, that defy the police and the others. We are a band of brothers and sisters.

November 2013

This time it is me who asks Naz to come to the protest: Remembrance Day in Croydon, South London. She's reluctant but Khalid, one of the 'Danish' protesters, has asked us to come.

This is different – a large crowd, servicemen on parade, regimental flags, speeches. I'm nervous, heart beating fast, looking round at all the serious, respectful faces – all races. I don't know what our group has planned but our men are excited, tense, eyes flashing as they glance at each other. No balaclavas. This time there are only a dozen of us, standing at the front of the crowd. We came early.

After a prayer, a woman and two men, one in uniform, walk forwards and place wreaths of poppies on the war memorial. An old man, medals across his chest, reads the poem:

They shall not grow old, as we that are left grow old:
Age shall not weary them, nor the years condemn.
At the going down of the sun, and in the morning,
We shall remember them.

There is a minute's silence. Then a trumpeter blows the last post, mournful notes floating over the bowed heads of the crowd. The last notes fade away. I know that this is the signal. I hold my breath, clutch Naz's hand.

Then three of our Muslim men bend and reach into the small rucksack at their feet. They unfurl three large red cotton poppies. The crowd have noticed nothing. With a cigarette lighter each lights his poppy, waits for it to catch and then flings it over the metal barrier. There they lie on the grey pavement, yellow flames surging up from the red poppies.

I am shocked into stillness. Naz's hand is gripping mine hard. Now I hear angry shouts from those nearby in the crowd. I see four policemen running towards us. Our young men hold up posters: *Our dead in Paradise, your dead in Hell.*

So... stark. So aggressive.

"Let's go," Naz whispers to me. She sounds scared.

Heads bent, we begin to shuffle our way back through the crowd. An old woman shouts at us, "You should be ashamed of yourselves." I look up. She has tears in her eyes.

I hear chants behind us: "Sharia law for the UK."

My shoulders bump into people; I tread on feet. "Sorry, sorry," I mutter. I'm terrified we'll be grabbed and held while police are called.

People here at the back are standing on tiptoe, straining their necks.

"What's happened?"

"What's that smoke?"

Finally we are free. We hurry away, not looking back. We round a corner and slow down. It's a pedestrian precinct: shoppers, families, a busker with a guitar. We are making for the Underground station.

Naz turns to me and says, "I was ashamed. I wouldn't have gone if I'd known that was going to happen. It's wrong, offensive; it makes people hate us."

Nobody is looking at us, no one accusing. They are browsing the shop windows.

"I didn't know, either."

"But we knew something would happen, didn't we? That's why the group went."

"Yes." I try to clear my head. "I agree it was wrong," I reply. "Because it was pointless. It gains us nothing."

"I want nothing more to do with the group," says Naz. "For me now it's my head in my books, get my qualifications, start a career."

She turns to go down the Underground steps. I pause.

"Are you coming?"

"I need to buy some stuff."

She looks at me quizzically. "OK then. See you at college on Monday." She leaves.

I find a bench and sit down. I need to work things out. I'm still shaking. The protest will achieve nothing, I'm sure. It's just words. But the passion I saw in those young men's eyes, their defiance, their lack of concern about being arrested, being attacked by the crowd. Their courage. The hostility they provoked. The drama...

In the end, it was just a play. A brief performance, talked about for a bit and then forgotten.

But the strength of their belief... I envy them that.

★

Now she was returning to what had been her homeland. To the rain she had often longed for, the cool wet, the temperate. Turning towards the damp north, she feared that her new persona would fall away like a skin sloughed off, that she would revert to the muddled thing she had been before. The decisions that had been so clear and straightforward in the desert light would become hazy and indistinct. Her determination would falter.

The enormity of what they planned ballooned into a looming thing, too big for her. For the first time it was real. She could envisage the shallow bay, the green hills, the small town with its church and promenade, a train in the station, women shopping, young kids in classrooms. Into this she would detonate terror.

Suddenly, she dropped to her knees on the swaying cabin floor and prostrated herself. *Give me the strength, Allah. It is to praise thee, it is in your name, Holy One.* She knelt, arms outstretched, touching the cabin wall, felt the ship pitch up and down, repeated her prayer, and at last felt her breathing calm, her heart beat normally. She sat up on her haunches. It was normal, this nervousness before a challenge. It proved she was herself. It was OK.

She stood up, her hand on the wall for balance. What she needed was fresh cold air to clear her head. She was impatient now: this endless, unhurried voyage. Perhaps the satellite signal could not penetrate down to this cabin. She pulled on a sweater, grabbed her daysack with the satellite phone in it and climbed the narrow iron gangway up to the deck.

The cool breeze hit her, whipping her hair. She had forgotten her scarf. Near the stern, in the shelter of the bridge she wedged herself between a bollard and a hatchway, the white paint chipped and peeling into rust, and watched the ship's wake, the flag flying.

Then her phone vibrated. Fingers fumbling, she unstrapped her sack and took it out. *One voice mail received.* Shalima pressed the key and listened.

The birds are gathering. 67.19, 105.3

Yes! Everything in place. *Do they not see the birds above them, spreading and contracting their wings? Naught upholds them save the Beneficent. He is the Seer of all things.*

He was seeing her now, in the corner of this deck on this ordinary cargo ship in a wide grey sea, her ear clamped to the phone. He would see everything, saw the future already. She closed her eyes in humility and bowed her head.

"Peace be unto thee," she muttered to herself. She opened her eyes, brushed back the hair from her face, saw the ship's white wake with a slight curve in it. Slowly but surely the time was approaching.

The second reference was the one that inspired her most: *And send down to prey upon them, flocks of birds.*

She saw an image of birds: black, ruthless, sharp-beaked. Saw herself as one of them, swooping down with glittering eyes and wild cries. And her doubts were gone. She was on fire again. She had passed the test. Returning to England and the familiar, the familiar she would pierce with a certainty, sharp as a lance.

Their plans were sound, detailed, practical. Yusuf would have done the rest, like a sword of vengeance. Tomorrow she would brief the team.

Three days, seventy-two hours to go.

She walked over to the rail and, as instructed by Yusuf, threw the phone in a looping arc to splash into the sea. She imagined it turning as it fell, finally landing softly on the sandy seabed.

25.

TUESDAY 29TH SEPTEMBER

It was five in the morning. Rocked gently in her bunk, Shalima was dreaming of crows attacking a corpse.

In London, Davoud's mobile rang on his bedside table. Startled from a deep sleep, he leaned over and his fingers fumbled for it. He lay back on his pillow.

"Nariman here."

"Good morning, Davoud, it's Jamie, Jamie Lockhart."

"Jamie, is it a good morning this early?"

"Significant, I think. I'll be knocking on your door in about thirty minutes. Have some coffee on, and croissants in the microwave. And butter, none of your bloody Flora."

"Where are you?"

"Being driven down from Cheltenham. It's been an all-night session."

The call ended. Croissants? He didn't have croissants, multigrain toast would have to do, but butter he did have, and some greengage jam Jenny had given him.

Davoud got out of bed. He'd always had that ability to be instantly alert on waking up. Section G9C was responsible for countering Islamic extremism and Davoud had been in charge for less than two weeks. Tim Bennett, who had been reluctantly heading it up on a temporary basis, had welcomed Davoud's appointment.

When the knock on the door came, a tray with filtered coffee, butter and jam was on the coffee table. Jamie entered, and they shook hands.

"Congratulations on your appointment, Davoud. I don't

think I've had the opportunity to say so before. Well, you might have a job on."

Davoud waved him to a seat. "Won't be a moment."

He returned from the kitchen with a rack of warm toast. "Sorry, no croissants."

"I was only kidding. Hot toast and melting butter on an early autumn morning in England. What could be better?"

Davoud poured coffee. "Poetic thoughts from a fourth-team prop forward."

Jamie smiled. His dark hair was tousled, stubble unshaved on his chin; a long night.

"So, tell me," Davoud said.

"Essentially," said Jamie, buttering his toast, "we've found a message, in Arabic, on a laptop. It said simply, *Four birds 2-260*. The numbers referred to the Qur'an. Do you know the reference?"

"No, I'm afraid not. I've shut it out, different life," replied Davoud.

"The verse says, *Allah said, 'Take four birds, tame them to incline to thee, then cut them into pieces and place portions of them on every mountaintop. Then call them to thee. They will come whole to thee in haste.'*"

"Who was the message sent to?"

Jamie sipped his coffee. "That's where it gets interesting. It went to two mobile phones: one apparently in the port of Alger, the other in the Yemen."

"The Yemen?"

"From previous sigint we have, we're virtually certain that it's an Al-Qaeda contact but we can't specifically identify it. Both phones are registered in the name of Mohammed Khan and there must be tens of thousands of them."

"What's your thinking, then?" asked Davoud.

"It sets off alarm signals. The bird story is about Allah confirming to Ibrahim that he can restore life to the dead, and so affirms Ibrahim's faith in Allah. It's about a coming together of separate parts."

Davoud nodded.

"And, since Al-Qaeda's involved, there's the possibility of a plot, an attack."

"That's certainly plausible. Do we know who sent the messages and where from?" asked Davoud.

"Sent from Rotherdyke. And that's why the attack could be planned for here in the UK."

"Rotherdyke? Never heard of it."

"West Yorkshire. And they've got form up there – remember the Tube bombers were from Leeds and Dewsbury, and several young men from that area have travelled to join ISIS."

"And do we know who sent it?" asked Davoud.

"No, not yet. We're working with the local police and Special Branch. There's a young detective, Hannah Walker, who seems on the ball."

"When was it sent?"

"Last Saturday afternoon. Alger port was packed, that's why it was impossible to pinpoint where the receiver was: could have been a resident, a port official, a docker or someone on a ship."

"Help yourself to coffee. So the message was sent in Arabic, but why wasn't it encrypted in some way?"

"I've been thinking about that on the way down and, frankly, I don't know," said Jamie. "Could just be careless. Officials and officers aren't the only ones to make mistakes. The sender might just have been excited: the message might be giving the go-ahead. Could just be overconfidence, cockiness. Or they believed the laptop was safe."

"In which case, the fact that it was sent from Rotherdyke could be meaningless. The sender just visited there, used the machine and then drove back to his base."

"That would figure, but his base probably isn't that far away. The laptop turned up in a raid on a house during a grooming investigation. It was an accidental bonus."

"Or perhaps," said Davoud, "they don't mind if we spot it. It could be a diversionary tactic. We deploy our resources to solve this riddle while they act somewhere else. Or it could be they believe it's too late for us to do anything about it anyway."

They both sat, silent; the implications were frightening. Jamie stood up.

"Must go," he said. "Anyway, you're in charge now. Best of luck. This is what you wanted, isn't it – action not paper-shuffling?"

"Yes, but perhaps not so soon. I'll get a meeting together and call up that detective, Hannah… what was it?"

"Walker, Hannah Walker. My team have forwarded all the other messages to her. They think they will help her, very incriminating."

"That grooming stuff disgusts me. Makes me feel sharia law might justly apply there. Slice their bollocks off, in public."

"My feelings exactly. We're all cheering her on," said Jamie. He looked across at Davoud, his face suddenly grim. "There's something in the air, I can smell it. We're due a big one, aren't we? Ten years since the Tube bombings. By the way, how's that Suleiman extradition going?"

"Inching along, as you'd expect. He's still down at Belmarsh."

Jamie drained his coffee, took a last bite of buttered toast, muttered something about fine jam, and left.

It was still only 0630 but Davoud phoned his duty officer to set up the meeting at ten. He waited fifteen minutes and then phoned Rotherdyke Police Station. Hannah was there. After brief introductions and support for what she was doing, he said, "I'm involved because there may be something on that laptop that's connected to a possible terrorist attack here in the

UK. If you pick up anything on that front, however vague, let me know."

It was a terse, businesslike conversation, and when Hannah put the phone down, she felt a new excitement as well as responsibility. It would be really great if her team turned up something that averted a terrorist attack. But she found it hard to link any of those sad, inadequate, pathetic groomer bullies with anything as daring and dangerous as a terrorist attack, let alone believe they'd have the brains to plan it. Nevertheless… you never knew what might turn up.

Promptly at ten in his new office on the fifth floor of Thames House, Davoud opened the meeting. There was virtually the same membership as at his previous meetings, but now there was an urgency all could sense. Davoud, they all knew, was in charge of a possible imminent operation, not just collating reports. Tim Bennett, Davoud's second in command, and the others sat drinking coffee from flowered china cups, all avoiding sugar and the plate of biscuits, except for Jamie who began by repeating what he had told Davoud. They listened intently and when he finished there was silence, a few intakes of breath.

"Tamsin," said Davoud, "what might be prime targets for any attack in the next few days?"

Tamsin, from the Centre for the Protection of National Infrastructure, thought for a moment before she spoke. "The usual targets, of course – Parliament, Buckingham Palace – but the Rugby World Cup and the party conferences would top the list. There are matches with sell-out crowds, up to eighty thousand, at Twickenham, Wembley, the Millennium Stadium in Cardiff, Birmingham and Newcastle. Labour are in Brighton, as are the Lib Dems – but I think that's not a big enough target."

There was a ripple of laughter.

"Tories are in Manchester, SNP in Aberdeen but that's in two weeks' time. UKIP have had theirs already, in Doncaster. Tories would be the likeliest target, they're in government."

"Thank you, Tamsin. Max?"

"It's the Yemen reference that troubles me. AQ are very active there. It's the most likely place a big spectacular would be launched from. We'll turn up the surveillance and I'll get the latest analyses over to you."

"Gary?"

"The possible link between terrorism and grooming is a new one," said Gary, the Special Branch representative. "As you know, we're already following that thread and we have no evidence so far. There are very different types of men involved. I'll contact the West Yorkshire branch immediately."

"And Polly?"

"No information about any imminent attack. There's no more activity than usual."

"Which means," broke in Gary, "that we might be looking for an invisible, a lone man with no previous record."

"And that's the toughest nut to crack," said Davoud. "Claire, I need you to check on suspicious arrivals at airports, ports, St Pancras, Ashford, Ebbsfleet."

Claire nodded.

"I've decided not to recommend upping the national security level yet: it's already at severe. We'll put it up to critical if we get any further info. And we're not putting anything out in the media: if we raise alertness, we also raise alarm and the last thing we want is panic. I've alerted MI6 across the river to be even more vigilant about returning jihadists, but they're pretty reliable on that. They just have to tell us and not keep it to themselves. I've already arranged for the other technology found on the grooming raid – phones, iPads – to be couriered down to GCHQ. They should be in Cheltenham about now, Jamie. They'll be top priority. Let's see what your boffins can come up with by midnight."

He paused and looked round at them all. "If indeed we have an invisible, as seems most likely, who is he? Where is he? Where is he going? And when he gets there, what is he going to do?"

"Or she," said Tamsin.

"Quite right, thank you, or she, these days. And we haven't a clue about the answers to any of those questions." He leaned forward, elbows on the table, and frowned. "Thank you, all. We have a job to do. Meeting closed. Make sure you're available at short notice for another. Things might develop quickly."

They filed out purposefully. Davoud was keeping the lid on things but the situation was deadly serious. Responsibility was solely on their shoulders. A mistake, an omission, a lack of concentration, a failure in cooperation – any or all of these could lead to catastrophe.

26

Yusuf packed the van as neatly as he could: he had to leave room for seven people, their rucksacks and weapons. There were cool boxes full of water, milk, sandwiches of halal food; four flasks for coffee; seven new sleeping bags; toilet rolls; phone chargers; changes of clothes for himself; seven hooded waterproof padded jackets; head torches. In a cardboard box were the three rail track detonators, stolen by Imran. Yusuf covered everything with an old tarpaulin.

It was nine o'clock when he left, traffic still heavy on the ring road by Horsforth and on the A65. As he drove through Ilkley he thought of Keighley on the other side of the moor, and it was like thinking of a previous life. Beyond Skipton there were fewer heavy lorries. He could relax a little. He had been so busy with details and timings that now was the first chance he had to think. He was leaving Leeds for the last time. Whatever happened to the mission, he would not be returning – to Leeds or Keighley or Yorkshire. These would be his last days in England; he hadn't quite realised that before.

He began to look about with new eyes. It was a perfect autumn day: in the still air no trees swayed, and straight ahead of him, high up in the cloudless blue sky was the faint image of the full moon – the moon that would pull in tonight's high tide. The sun shone, throwing long shadows of trees across fields. Green fields, soft, rolling, so different from the rocky harshness of the Yemeni desert. He had driven this road before but never looked in this way before – at the bright red berries on trees, the leaves already turning red and brown and yellow, sheep grazing, cows with calves. He didn't know the names of the trees. He knew so little; he was a city boy. This was an England he didn't know: names like Lawkland and Masongill, The Maypole Inn on the village green, drystone walls. There was a calm permanence about things, symbolised by the stone houses.

A tractor with a huge muck trailer passed the other way. An old man in a flat cap walked slowly along the pavement, carrying a shopping bag. An overweight woman in a tracksuit and with earphones jogged by, her face screwed up with the unfamiliar exercise. This was normal life beyond the city. There was no connection between the two. He hadn't seen one non-white face since he'd left Leeds. But was there the same complacency, the same ignorance? Did these people care about what their elected government had done in Iraq and Afghanistan, was doing in Syria? Did they know of the thousands of murdered Muslims? Theirs was a different dreamworld from his father's, but a dreamworld nonetheless. In twenty-four hours they would have a rude awakening.

To his left was the railway, not his line but one that focused him again. Beyond, out west towards the bay, mist still hung low. Ahead now were the Lakeland hills. He passed a sign: *Lancashire welcomes careful drivers*. He smiled: careful he was, but hardly welcome. The day stretched ahead; things to check, but plenty of time. And then he saw the sign: *Hideaway Café*. Time for a leisurely coffee.

He pulled into the lay-by, locked the van and entered. He sat at a table for two by the window. Why not treat himself? When the waitress came over he ordered a cappuccino – "Be generous with the chocolate sprinkles" – and a slice of quintessentially English lemon drizzle cake. Outside, the sun shone on green fields, a heathery fell and the busy M6. Inside, four silent couples, in their seventies probably, sat at separate tables, eating scones and jam, or cake. It was elevenses time, after all. In the far corner sat a younger man, with a laptop open on his table, drinking coffee. One couple exchanged a few words. Yusuf caught 'visit' and 'daughter'. All of the couples wore glasses and had grey hair, except for one bald-headed man. The men were clean-shaven, neatly dressed for a day out. One got up to go to the gents' – back bent, small shuffling steps, with a stick.

Yusuf licked the coarse sugar from the cake off his fingers. A smell of bacon began to emerge from the kitchen. He couldn't put it aside. It should repulse him – he hadn't eaten a bacon butty since he'd converted to Islam. Now he was salivating, he couldn't help it. Then the waitress brought it out and carried it across to the laptop man. Yusuf's eyes followed it. The man was looking at him. It was overwhelming, that smell of bacon. He remembered rainy holiday lunchtimes when they retreated to a warm café for hot tea and bacon sandwiches, joining the hoi polloi, as his father put it, slumming, dumbing down to prole level. That made Yusuf enjoy them even more, opening up the sandwich, ostentatiously squeezing the brown sauce onto the crispy bacon with its edge of browned fat, then letting the sauce ooze out of the corner of his mouth and drip down his chin, horrifying his father: mission accomplished. He smiled: good times.

It was tempting, that sandwich. He was still hungry, and the sweetness of the cake was cloying. But bacon was forbidden: *the flesh of swine is impure.* Yet there was a rider to the words of Allah, something about *if forced by necessity, your Lord is Forgiving and Merciful.* But this wasn't necessity. Or could it be? He remembered a girl at college who'd had a ritual feast before she started a strict diet – it was a form of farewell, she'd said, a final rejection of the unhealthy. These were his last hours of personal freedom before he submitted himself to the Holy Mission, to the struggle of his jihad. Would Allah condemn him for what, in the scale of things, in the context of his imminent mighty work, was a small sin? Allah, the Bountiful and All Merciful, would surely smile indulgently at his puny human weakness.

Yusuf had convinced himself. It would be a ritual. So be it. He went to the counter and ordered a bacon roll with brown sauce. As he returned to his table he was aware the laptop man was again watching him. Yusuf sat down and looked out at the lorries speeding by on the distant motorway, busy, busy.

"Excuse me," a voice said.

He looked up and the laptop man was standing next to him.

"I'm sorry if I've been staring, but are you Ryan Hudson?"

Yusuf felt the blood drain from his face.

"It was the beard that put me off. I'm Chris Holdsworth. In the same year at Greenbank School in Keighley. It is Ryan, isn't it? You were in the cricket team."

Heart thumping. Must act normal.

"I'm sorry, I don't remember you. But yes, I'm Ryan. What a coincidence. It's the first time I've called in here."

Chris Holdsworth put out his hand and Yusuf, after a momentary hesitation, shook it.

"It's a regular stopping-off place for me," said Chris. "Handy for the M6, before I head up north to Scotland on business."

"What line are you in?" managed Yusuf, desperate to appear natural.

"I sell green energy – showing companies how they can save thousands on their fuel bills."

Yusuf forced himself to listen.

"Not exactly thrilling, but I make a decent living. I'm still in Keighley, got a couple of kids. And yourself? In the family business?"

"Er, no, not a chance. Just this and that, not a career like you." He almost said he was a delivery man but realised at the last moment that Chris might then note the white van parked outside. "I start on a building site in Barrow tomorrow, going up to sort some digs. Still single." He gave a forced laugh.

The waitress brought over his bacon roll with two packets of brown sauce.

"Don't let me interrupt your work," said Yusuf, nodding towards Chris' laptop.

"I'll leave you in peace. Tempting, aren't they, those bacon rolls? I should be off them – trying to lose weight, too much time sitting in a car. Anyway, nice to have seen you. Got to be on my way."

They shook hands again.

Yusuf pondered for a moment and then tried to tear open the sauce packets. Fuck it, these never fucking worked. He wrenched at the packet, his fingers feverish. *Calm down, stop a moment.*

The waitress came over. She smiled. "Problems? Try these." She handed him a pair of scissors.

He looked up at her. "Thanks. Need longer nails."

He snipped off the corners of the packets, opened the roll and squeezed on the sauce. The waitress would remember him now, as well as Chris.

Chris, with his laptop bag slung over his shoulder, gave him a wave from the door and left the café.

Yusuf bit into the roll and saw his father's disapproving face on the opposite side of the table. It was like giving him the V-sign. The taste should have repulsed Yusuf, but it was beautiful: hot, salty, tangy, the roll buttery. Yes, Allah would grant him this paltry, fleeting joy. Praise be to him.

His heartbeat was back to normal. He could think straight: what were the implications of this meeting? Was this a second setback, after the police finding the laptop? But first he would enjoy his bacon roll, have another coffee too, an Americano this time, black. Time to move on. Last checks to do. No need to panic.

★

He drove over the M6, took the A6 dual carriageway towards Kendal, took the A590 west on the Barrow road, then almost immediately rejoined the A6 south to Milnthorpe. There he bought shaving gear and scissors. Once through the small, busy town, he soon saw again, through high, trimmed hedges, the Kent Estuary with its sand and channels of water. Now driving down the edge of the bay on a minor road, at Sandside the view opened up: the narrow channel of the River Kent winding among Milnthorpe Sands. He passed The Ship Inn with its red and yellow hanging baskets, and saw the viaduct, as if suspended above the sands. To the north was Grange-over-Sands. And then at last he was at the welcome sign to *Arnside, a Fair Trade village.*

His first check was the landing place. He drove south towards Silverdale, past the screes, and slowed as the road turned sharp left as it met the coast again. There was a pull-in beside the small bay he had chosen, rocks and pebbles visible now as the tide was not yet fully in. He got out. On his last visit he hadn't noticed the small sign. The place was called The Dip. There was a sign warning, among other hazards, *Beware breaking waves. Do not use inflateables.*

Yusuf laughed at that.

A laminated notice was attached to the sign: *European Commission – 3 fish daily limit for sea bass.*

Rules for all the small things, while the big issues were ignored.

He drove on to the Leighton Moss RSPB reserve, walked back to the hide below the railway line where the idea had come to him, then strolled over the reclaimed fields, full of grazing sheep, towards Jenny Brown's Point. So peaceful and still, the sky cloudless.

Back at the reserve visitor centre he had vegetable soup

and a roll; he'd treated himself at the Hideaway Café, and now he had to be disciplined, ascetic. Prepare himself in the proper way. He climbed the new viewing tower and gazed over the reed beds back towards the motorway and fells. Whatever happened to the residents here, it would not be his fault. Responsibility lay with the government who had declared war in Iraq and Afghanistan, with the sick society which had permitted itself to decline into degeneracy. He imagined Chris Holdsworth driving north to Glasgow along the same M74 that Yusuf had driven south on Saturday. Opposite directions.

That evening he drove up the rough, narrow road to Arnside Knott car park. From there he made the short climb to the summit. He watched the sun set in glory over the bay, the reds and oranges reflected in the sea. It seemed a fitting preliminary.

In the darkness he walked back to his van. He would spend the night here. But first he would shave off his beard and hair. Just in case. Not panic, precaution. He would feel more secure.

27.

They were in the hold, the ship still pitching, now rolling a little. The container doors were wedged open and her team sat on crates inside it. A bare bulb, cabled in, shone, accentuating shadows and the ribbed walls of the container. Shalima could see only half of their faces, beards, black eyes glistening as they looked up at her.

"Yusuf sent the final confirmation yesterday," she said. "We're on."

There was a ragged cheer, and faces looked at each other, a few hands thumped shoulders.

"So now the serious business starts. In two days we will land. Today Izzy and Ibra will unpack the Zodiac, take it on deck and assemble it, lashing it firmly to the superstructure. Without it, we've wasted our time. In less than forty-eight hours we'll be on it."

She looked directly at Benny. "Benny – explosives are your department: the Semtex and RDX. Uncrate them and the detonating mechanisms. Repack them in waterproof tarpaulin, absolutely secure. Have them ready for hoisting on deck tomorrow. Kal and Bargo, you're in charge of the weapons. Each man will be responsible for his own weapons: each of you – and me of course – will carry Barrett M82 sniper rifles and the ammunition, courtesy of US forces in Iraq. You're familiar with them, trained with them. Each of us will also have a Glock G43 pistol."

She looked around. "Tonight the skipper will radio in to Fleetwood, and report our position and expected docking time. Of course, we will not be going to Fleetwood. But the skipper and the rest of the cargo will."

Now it had come to it, were they nervous, as she had been? "Any questions?"

"We've seen the sea charts," said Izzy, "and we know the landing point. But what happens after that? What are we attacking?"

Shalima had deliberately kept that information back, knowing the question was inevitable. "A train," she said. "In fact, two trains."

"We guessed that – why else would Kal and Bargo be here? What's on the train?" asked Benny.

"Yusuf will tell you that."

"Must be someone important. Prime Minister, Prince of Wales, an infidel archbishop or two."

There was laughter.

"We will ambush two trains," continued Shalima. "As you say, that's when Kal and Bargo come into their own. It all depends on how cooperative the British drivers are."

"Oh, they'll be cooperative," laughed Kal, pointing two fingers at his temple.

"OK," persisted Izzy. "But what happens after we've ambushed the trains? Why are we doing it? For ransom?"

Shalima smiled. "I read about the Dutch football team. Always arguing with the coach, among themselves, always asking questions. Izzy, you have to trust us. You will be famous after this."

"I'm not interested in that," replied Izzy. There were murmurs of agreement.

"We're doing the work of Allah. Listen. Izzy and Ibra will navigate us to land. They will need all their skill. We can only travel across the bay at full tide. It's a spring tide, the highest tide, but even so we have a maximum of two hours when the water is deep enough. Our Zodiac will be heavily loaded. OK?"

They nodded.

"When we land, Yusuf will meet us. Again, we have to unload fast. There's a full moon but it could be covered with cloud. This is England, remember. Yusuf has a van and he will take us and all our gear to a hideout for the rest of the night. I don't know where that is. Once there, he will give you a full briefing on the attacks – he has detailed plans of the sites and will tell you exactly who does what, where, and in what order. There will be three hours' sleep maximum."

She paused. "And you will learn what is on the train."

There was a silence, the throb of the ship's engines loud down there in the hold.

"What about food?" asked Kal.

They laughed.

"Typical bloody Frenchman," said Benny.

"I'm sure Yusuf will have taken into account your dietary requirements. Did you fill in the form?"

They looked at each other.

"Joke! Don't worry. Yusuf will have everything we need. Any other questions?"

"We still don't know why," said Izzy. "We know the target, we'd worked that out anyway. But we don't know the objective, the reason."

"You will. In around forty-eight hours."

She knew Izzy wasn't satisfied, guessed he resented not being trusted, even out here in the Atlantic.

"To work, gentlemen."

On deck she paused. Nothing on the wide grey sea, not even a smudge of land to the east. They would be passing Vigo and the north-western tip of Spain, heading into the Bay of Biscay. It could be rough out there. Nobody must be ill as they nosed up the Celtic Sea. She would insist on more seasickness pills. After all their planning, after the meeting high in the mountains, after all the requisitioning, the work with the

AQ linkman – now it had come together, the birds were assembling. She felt calm, proud, at ease. She had fulfilled her part of the mission.

2014

After the demonstrations I am alert and aware in a different way. I notice the looks on white people's faces as they pass me on the street, ordinary people going about their business, but flashing me brief glances of suspicion and dislike. Reading the newspapers, I no longer skim over stories of assaults on Muslims; I read them properly. I watch news stories on TV about American drone attacks on Muslims, see pictures of families living in bombed-out cities or being rescued from sinking boats in the Mediterranean.

And I begin to question how I am living – just like the other girls I listen to the latest music, buy the in-fashion accessories, update my phone apps. Making sure I'm 'in', I'm cool. But I am not 'in'; I am Muslim, brown-skinned, different. But nor am I like Naneejan or my mother. I belong nowhere.

So I contact Khalid from the Remembrance Day demo. But he will not see me, just gives me a phone number.

I sit, elbows on the kitchen table, chin in my hands, very still. I stare out of the window, but my eyes flick down to my phone: the blank, black screen. Upstairs Naneejan is vacuuming the landing carpet, stubbing the skirting board; the floorboards creak. My phone's on silent and my ears are tuned to the vibration it will make on the plastic tablecloth.

Khalid gave me your number, said you'd phone me back. Shalima.

That's what Khalid instructed me to text. Fatima, he said you were called.

I try to picture you. How old are you? What were you doing when my text came through? What has Khalid told you about me?

I am so still I can feel my heart beating. My eyes are stinging; I must have been staring hard. I take a deep breath, breathe out in a measured way. I glance again at my phone: still blank. **Ring, ring. Come on**. But I'm scared, too. It's like daring to take a shortcut at night down an unknown, unlit alley between shadowy doorways.

The vacuuming has stopped. Silence. I hear Naneejan coming slowly down the stairs, always left leg first, protecting her arthritic right knee. She opens the door, leans against the door frame.

"Cup of tea?" I ask.

"Er, no thanks, I've not quite finished."

I can't sit here like this, waiting for what might not happen. Shalima gives her *Naneejan* a hug. "I'm just going out. Need some things, you know. Back in a couple of hours."

I take the Tube to Charing Cross, cross the Thames on the Hungerford railway bridge, trains thundering by, wheels screeching. In my pocket, my hand grips my phone. It's sunny and breezy on the Embankment. I pass the queue for the London Eye and turn onto the wobbly bridge. Halfway across I lean on the railings and look up towards Big Ben and the Houses of Parliament.

Then my phone vibrates. My heart lurches. My fingers tense round the phone. This is it. I take out the phone, hesitate, then decide. I touch the green symbol, hold the phone to my ear. A barge hoots as it passes beneath the bridge.

"Shalima?" A soft voice, warm.

"Yes."

"You want me to help you travel?"

It takes a moment for me to understand. I press the phone tighter to my ear, hunch my shoulders.

"Yes," I say, wanting to sound strong.

"Buy a new smartphone. Use it only to ring me. As soon as you can."

And she ends the call. That's all there is. Anticlimax. Disappointment. And why must I have another phone, exclusive to her? Because it must be secret. A sudden thrill, already a double life. People pass me by on the bridge, chatting, laughing or alone. If they notice me, they see only a young woman staring down at the grey water, watching barges and tourist boats. How easy it is to have a secret.

Within the hour I buy a new phone with my credit card. I phone Fatima. She will send me a text which will include a link to download an encrypted app. This must be our only form of communication.

And so the conspiracy begins. I am two people: student and granddaughter – and plotter. I feel like a spy, encrypting and decoding messages. I bloom in this subterfuge. I am joining a brotherhood and a sisterhood. It is an adventure, but blessed by Allah. Our mosque now seems tame, routine, suburban. I look at the bowed backs and see subservience – not just to Allah but to the abuse and injustice we suffer.

I already have a new passport – for holidays on the Continent. I complete my pre-nursing course. It has a different, nobler purpose now – helping fighters in hot, blazing cities and in the desert.

But I have to argue with Fatima. I insist I will not go to Syria and ISIS like the other girls do. I will go only to Yemen, to Al-Qaeda, Al-Qaeda in the Arabian Peninsula (AQAP).

I know what AQAP is. Don't insult me, she messages back. *You must follow my guidance, surrender your wishes to the cause*.

But I will not give in, and I will not explain. She would never agree. ISIS is not for me: the compulsion to wear double-layered veils, loose abayas to hide the shape of my body, gloves in desert temperatures, never to be allowed out of the house except with a male chaperone. I know that in their caliphate ISIS police board buses and stop taxis to ensure women are properly dressed and beat them if they aren't, that even in the sweat and pain of labour, women have to wear niqabs. ISIS are more concerned with killing Muslim heretics, whereas AQAP attack Western infidels.

I have my own vision, and Allah must have guided me to it. This is my private secret within the bigger secret: that the role of jihadi women is to marry jihadi fighters and look after their husbands. But this is only the start. There is a role for women, says Al-Qaeda, on the edge of the battlefield: they can carry messages, reconnoitre and gather intelligence. They are also trained in first aid. And I know about the White Widow and American jihadist women who have risen to be military commanders. This is what I aspire to. But I can tell Fatima none of this. Nor will I bear children – I have already started on the contraceptive pill. I have hidden them in tubs, labelled *Vitamin C tablets*. I must take great care about that; my husband-to-be must not know.

But there is a final test for me. Fatima sends a video to my phone. I watch beheadings of orange-clothed prisoners, see throats slit, and hear the accompanying cheers and celebratory rifle shots of the jihadist fighters. At first it sickens me, but then it becomes an appalled fascination. Somehow the horror is an exorcism and a catharsis which simplifies and purifies me. The unambiguous violence of the men and their embrace of martyrdom dazzle me. The young men I know here are into porn and PlayStations, football and men's toiletries. These men on the videos are real men, not like my bully of a father, men who – as Fatima describes them – are lions whose drink is blood and play is carnage. They fight for a cause. She has sent me a picture of one: chest puffed out, smiling, standing erect, an assault rifle slung across his shoulder, a black bandana embroidered with Islamic State's white insignia covering his forehead. They choose to look like glamorous rock stars, but they are idealists who play on the world stage. These are the men who will teach me to shoot, lead me to a life where I have a real role, where I might even be loved. Underneath the photo is a smiley face, a winking yellow emoticon.

Finally, the date of my departure is set. I must pick up my flight tickets from the Islamic bookshop in Edgware Road. As instructed, I ask at the desk for a copy of *The War Within our Hearts.*

"It's ordered," I say.

I wait until a man comes out of the back office and gives me, not the book, but a white envelope. I walk quickly out and, a hundred metres along the pavement, in a shop doorway, I open it. Single tickets to Kuwait, Doha, Sana'a. I read the names of the places. I am really doing this. And the street in front of me, the noise of traffic, red London buses, the shoppers passing – all seem an illusion, as if I see through a veil. A rush of sadness. A stab of fear. I put the tickets away. Two young women pass by me, in high heels, carrying glossy bronze bags from Next, talking and laughing. And I want to be away from all this, in a purer place. It will be a long five days before I fly.

At home I tell Naneejan I am going travelling in Europe with my girlfriend Naz. I do not want to lie to her, but I must.

She looks long at me, nods. "You are old enough to make your own decisions. Be a good Muslim."

And I wonder if she really knows.

The only person I tell is Naz.

She tells me straight: "You are being groomed for abuse. Fatima is like a cult leader luring the faithful."

Naz mocks me when I tell her a husband – a good man, they said – will be found for me among the Al-Qaeda fighters.

"You think the niqab is medieval," she storms, "but you will accept that kind of marriage? You want a young handsome fighter with curly black hair and burning eyes. You might get an old guy with bad teeth and five wives already. You're crazy."

Those are my last words with Naz. Fatima has given me strict instructions so the authorities will be less likely to question me: pack nothing Islamic, no Qu'ran, throw away this phone and fill your old one with games. Don't wear hijab or niqab, wear make-up. Pack normal things – epilator, cosmetics, socks, underwear. I am just a girl, travelling.

★

And now I am here.

Forty-seven hours to go and, for the first time since leaving Hodeida port, time was speeding up.

28.
Wednesday 30th September, 0630

Detective Sergeant Hannah Walker sat in the interview room. Next to her was Detective Constable Tom Bakewell. On the opposite side of the table sat Adil Rauf and his solicitor, still grumbling about the early hour. This was Hannah's last chance and Rauf, roused from a deep sleep in his cell, might be more vulnerable. They'd got nowhere with the taxi driver or that cocky young Kabeer Sajd yesterday evening. Adil was older, married with a family, a community spokesman. Hannah's line had been that they had all the evidence they needed for conviction – phone messages between the men, texts about arrangements for meeting the girls, testimony from the girls, identification from photographs. She'd exaggerated a bit and the solicitor, raising his eyebrows, had known this.

"You will be convicted, Mr Rauf. You'll be humiliated in your own community. You've brought that upon yourself and I have no sympathy, none at all. You have done appalling things. All that's left for you is to help us and maybe – just maybe, I cannot even guarantee that – your prison sentence will be reduced."

Adil Rauf was staring at the table. She thought he was seeing his whole life unravel.

"Prison will not be easy," she pushed on. "Child abusers get a hard time from other prisoners. They become the victims."

The solicitor objected. "Enough," he said.

There was sweat on Rauf's upper lip.

"But if you help us we can protect you, put you in a special high-security wing."

The solicitor whispered something in Rauf's ear.

Hannah forced herself to look relaxed and confident. She had this urge to shuffle in her chair, to rearrange papers, drum her fingers on the table – any physical movement to release the tension she felt. This was the key moment.

Rauf raised his head and looked at her. She saw moistness in his eyes.

"What you want to know?" he muttered. He lowered his eyes.

"How good is your Arabic?"

Rauf was puzzled. "How do you mean?" he asked.

"Do you speak it?"

"I have few words, but I can read Qu'ran."

Gently, Hannah asked, "Can you write it?"

"No, not at all."

After a pause, Hannah said, "In the Opal Street house where we arrested you, we found an Arabic laptop. Did you know about that?"

Rauf looked up. He was frightened. "No," he said, more forcefully than he intended. "How would I know? I didn't live there." He paused and then said, in a quieter voice, "I only visited."

Hannah realised he was now frightened because he didn't have the information she wanted and so wouldn't have the protection in prison. He knew he was guilty, was certain he would be convicted. And now he couldn't help himself.

She took a decision. "I believe you," she said.

Rauf raised his head quickly. In his eyes was hope.

Hannah continued, in the same soft voice, "Among the people we arrested with you, is there anybody who was likely to use an Arabic keyboard?"

Rauf's face sagged, and she saw panic again.

"I don't know. How would I know? I never used it, I promise you. I didn't know it was there."

"OK. Was there ever anybody there you didn't know? Any other men, who were not involved with the girls? Who maybe were there by chance, or just visiting a friend?"

She saw Rauf was genuinely racking his brains. He was now desperate to help. His lips were twitching. He held his hands together tightly. She saw the paleness at his knuckles. She waited. Silence.

Eventually he said, "There was an Englishman."

"What do you mean, an Englishman? You're an Englishman."

"A white man," said Rauf. "Only once I saw him."

"When?"

Rauf thought. "It was the day before you arrested us."

"Saturday?"

Rauf nodded. "I suppose so."

"Do you know who he was?"

Again, that alarm in his eyes. "I had never seen him before. I promise."

"Was he on his own?"

"No, he was with friend, an Asian."

"Do you know him?"

"No, I don't know their names." Rauf's voice was rising. "They were in kitchen a few minutes." A pause, then he added, "Talking about cricket."

"Cricket?"

Rauf seemed energised. He separated his hands, looked directly at Hannah. "They played in the same team, I think. They were talking about a match."

Hannah saw relief in his eyes, as if he had finally given her something valuable. Something that would help him.

Was it something valuable? Maybe it was a lead. That Secret Intelligence man on the phone yesterday had impressed on her how urgent it was to get some information. If only she could, she might have a key role to play in foiling what could be an international terrorist plot. A surge of excitement, but she had to keep her cool.

"I don't suppose you caught the name of their team?" she asked, as casually as she could.

Rauf looked disappointed. "No," he said dully.

"Do you know where they came from?"

Rauf seemed uninterested, as if he was resigned again to failing. "Maybe Leeds," he said. Then, as an afterthought, "I think they were boasting about winning the league."

Hannah's heart lurched. Was that a clincher? She collected her papers, made the concluding remarks for the tape and turned it off.

"Thank you, Mr Rauf. To be honest, I'm disappointed. I thought you would know more. It's not enough. When you're back in your cell, I'd advise you to think back to that scene in the kitchen. See how much more you can remember. Do you understand?"

0730

Excited and apprehensive, Jamie Lockhart rang Davoud on a secure line.

"Two things, Davoud. And the first makes me very worried."

"Tell me."

"The message about the four birds – we have two satellite phones that received it: one currently in the Yemen with, we believe, an Al-Qaeda man; the second somewhere in the port of Alger. The message was sent from a laptop in Rotherdyke. I've already told you all this. What our techies have discovered now is that throughout August and the first two weeks of September there was a flurry of calls between the two phones and a third one. Most of the calls were made and received in the Yemen, but a couple were in Somalia and Nairobi. They were mostly messages about weddings and presents, i.e. codes for meetings and deliveries, deadlines. Then, suddenly, the calls stopped."

"That's a bad sign," said Davoud.

"Exactly. It's a pattern we've had before in Africa and India and Indonesia: a flurry of calls, then silence, then a terrorist attack. Finally, after the silence, there was one call from Rome to Yemen last week, from the same third phone."

"Do you know who the third phone is registered to?"

"Another Mohammed Khan, so no."

Davoud was silent. At what stage did this information merit an upgrade from severe to critical in the threat level from international terrorism? Hard evidence was negligible. The politicians wouldn't wear it.

"That was the good news," said Jamie. "Want the bad?"

"Hit me."

"Two days ago, Monday, the third satellite phone sent a voicemail to the other two."

"A voicemail? That's unusual."

"Yes, I don't understand it."

"And what was it?"

"Same format as the laptop message. The man's voice says, 'The birds are gathering' in halting Arabic."

"That implies he's not a native speaker."

"Probably. And then there's what turns out to be another reference to a verse of the Qu'ran."

"Which says...?"

"*Do they not see the birds above them, spreading and contracting their wings? Naught upholds them save the Beneficent. He is the Seer of all things.*"

"That's it?" asked Davoud.

"That's it. And the voicemail was sent from Rotherdyke. It went to one phone still in the Yemen, but the other – which was in Alger for the laptop message – is now near Cadiz."

"So, on a ship in the Atlantic. Probably heading our way. That's ominous, Jamie."

"Very."

0750

Back in the grooming operations room, Hannah addressed the morning briefing. She had been sworn to secrecy about the possible terrorist plot. "No point in alarming people... yet," that intelligence man had said.

The white man would be the easiest to find. In this world he was in a minority.

"We've had a lead from Adil Rauf. It could be significant in identifying a wider network of groomers than we had imagined. Now don't laugh, I'm deadly serious: drop everything else. I need to know the name of every adult male cricket team in Leeds containing white and Asian cricketers and which won a league in the season just ended."

She heard a groan. "There'll be dozens of them, there's loads of leagues."

"I know. But there's a lot of segregation, isn't there? Voluntary segregation: all-Asian and all-white teams. I want team names, their home grounds and the name of their managers or captains. And I need that in two hours. There's huge pressure from above and we need to deliver. Hit the phones, the internet, any friends you have who play. The lot."

Hannah realised she was getting carried along. She was being diverted from the investigation she'd been leading for over a year. *I'll do what I can on this*, she said to herself, *then it's back to the main business. Kelly*, she thought, *keep focused on Kelly and the other girls*. This intelligence stuff was exciting but her part would be brief, and was perhaps already over. But she also knew that if Leeds didn't bring a result she'd have to extend the cricket search: to Rotherdyke and Keighley next. She scanned her notepad. Davoud Nariman was his name, the intelligence man. He had been quietly but unmistakenly insistent. She had nothing for him yet, but she didn't want to fail him. Something big was in the air.

0805

Yusuf slept soundly in his sleeping bag in the van. He awoke only when a dog barked outside. He struggled up to peer out of the passenger window: a dog walker was disappearing through the gate into the mist. That was OK. His was just a white van and there was nothing incriminating in it.

He dressed, tidied his bag away and stepped outside. There were no other vehicles parked.

This time tomorrow; twenty-five hours from now.

He stretched his legs and arms, rubbed his hands together, stamped his feet. The air was cool and damp, the mist thick. He rubbed his shaved head and bare chin. They would feel the cold more. He found a baseball cap and put it on; he'd take it off again when he got down to Arnside. If noticed, he needed to be noticed shaven, a skinhead.

0815

Tom Bakewell came over to Hannah's desk. "Just had a call from Susan doing the Opal Street interviews. The usual unwillingness to say anything, but an old lady said she'd seen a white van parked outside the house on Monday."

"Is she sure it was Monday?" asked Hannah. "Old people's memories aren't reliable."

"She's certain it was Monday because she always goes to the greengrocer's for fresh apples on a Monday, every week. And she says she thinks the van was there only for a few minutes."

"Thanks, Tom. File it. Any progress with the cricket teams?"

"We're working flat out."

Hannah felt bad about not letting Tom into the story. She liked to be open; it was the way teams worked.

"Keep 'em going, Tom."

Should she keep Nariman up to date? But there was virtually nothing to report, and the local team was far more able to carry out a local investigation.

0820

Yusuf drove down and parked on a pooled parking place by the viaduct. Probably flooded by the high tide. The mist was thick and low over the bay. The viaduct curved out over the sands and river, past derelict railwaymen's huts at each end. He could just see the white farmhouse on the other side, but not Grange. He threw his cap into the back of the van and walked to the station, crossed over the footbridge and came down to the south platform. Four people sat on metal seats in the small shelter, waiting for the 0851 Northern Rail to Preston. He wondered if they were regular commuters and whether they would be here tomorrow.

Above the timetable board was an electronic sign: *Smile, you're on CCTV*. Attached to the fence was a yellow notice: *Images are being recorded for your safety and to help prevent crime*. An old lady slowly crossed the footbridge, holding the rail as she came down the steps. Yusuf ambled along the platform to where he could see the double track curving away over the estuary. Right on time the 0851 passed the white farmhouse and started approaching along the viaduct. It slowed as it neared the station. Just two carriages in purple and blue, a noisy, smoky diesel. Two men alighted, one wearing a high-vis jacket, the other in a suit and carrying a briefcase. The waiting passengers climbed aboard. As the train set off, Yusuf counted them: fifteen, he thought, distributed evenly in the two carriages, including the newcomers. Were they workers going to Preston, birders going to Silverdale, shoppers going to Lancaster? A couple of young children, he noted: that could be an unnecessary complication. Or, he suddenly thought, perhaps an added opportunity.

Was it only three months ago that he had first reconnoitred this place? He checked the Office and Information Centre was open, looked briefly at some white birds on the green salt marsh beyond the parking area, the river hardly moving in its channel, mudflats glistening. He noticed a female dog walker on the built embankment, black birds scattering as the dog ran ahead; he heard sounds of traffic in the village. It was as he remembered. A faint smell of diesel in the air.

At the foot of the bridge was something he hadn't remembered: a help point with an green emergency button and the instruction: *Push.*

The electronic sign showed the next train due – the 0928 TransPennine to Manchester Airport. All they would have was half an hour. But that was time enough.

0900

Back in the operations room he had set up in Thames House, Davoud could only wait for more information. The committee would meet again at 4.30 that afternoon, and absentees would attend via conference call.

He picked up a bottle of water from his desk and walked to the window. The grey Thames was below, Lambeth Bridge clogged with traffic. So many people getting on with their lives, busy, busy. Oblivious, most of them, to the threats around them. Perhaps that was the only way: just to carry on. A fish is safer in a shoal – some fish will be eaten but the odds on any individual one being safe are high. And if your number's up…

Sara was out there somewhere, Jenny, his father. Was that where real life was? Sara adjusting to life with a part-time father and a full-time stepfather? Davoud's own father confused, memories in fragments with only the rituals of his faith to hold him together?

And Jenny, was she wondering whether to commit to him or was she determined to take it casually, more casually than he was? He needed to hug her, feel her warmth seep into him and deliver him from his isolation. Forbidden from discussing the developing crisis with her, he wanted to rest his head on her shoulder and feel her arms around him. Jenny was his hope. The question was: was he her hope? Or would this, too, dismantle? They hadn't spoken since their return on Sunday from the Cotswolds. Was she already cooling? Had she taken him into a new sensuous world only to abandon him?

And while that real life went on, was he playing games? Fitting jigsaw pieces together, making chess moves, assembling a Lego structure? Yes, what he did or didn't do over the next hours and days might seriously affect people's lives – but was that why he did it, or was it just the thrill of the chase, the intellectual challenge? Was that his real motive? And if it was, as he suspected it was, what did that say about him? A cold fish, detached from real human empathy? Did he have the passion of Suleiman, who was prepared to sacrifice his life to a cause? No, was the blunt answer. Davoud's only consolation was that if it was a game, he was good at it. He had foiled an IRA plot in Northern Ireland, pulled out compromised agents in Tunisia, negotiated hostage rescues in the Lebanon. He was a strong field officer and operation leader. If the current crisis came to anything, he would back himself to deal with it. But he was not martyr material.

The world had always had its share of shahid, martyrs. They were not a new phenomenon. Tyndale had been shahid, giving up his life so people could read the word of his God in their own language. Names Davoud dimly remembered from school history – Cranmer and Ridley, was it? – burnt to death for an interpretation of a few words or for who should be boss of their church. What he considered ridiculous, others thought inspiring.

It was ridiculous, of course it was ridiculous. The difference for the contemporary martyr was that he – or she – killed so many innocents with total impunity. That was more than ridiculous, it was evil. And it was right to try to prevent it. Whatever his motive, it was right. And now he wanted his guitar, to lose himself in his music for an hour, in its sounds and patterns.

0915

Hannah now had a list of nine leagues, nine champions and just three with white and Asian players. The list included their home grounds and captains or managers, with phone numbers.

"Fantastic work," she congratulated her team. "Now for the last lap. I need the names of all the white players in those three teams. And I've ordered up coffees and sandwiches on the house."

There was a ragged cheer.

Thirty minutes later, she had five names: two in one team, two in another, and one in the final one: the Seacroft Artisans.

Pot luck, but something in her gut led her to the lone white man. Why not? She allocated the first four to Tom and the team.

"I'll take this one," she said. She read his name: Ryan Hudson. "Find out where they live, where they work, if they've any criminal record – anything about them."

She grabbed a sandwich and a coffee, closed the door to her office. If she learned anything it couldn't be known to the team.

First she rang the captain.

"I have a few more questions for you, sir. Just routine, won't keep you long."

"What is this about?" An Asian voice with an educated accent. "I've already spoken to one policeman."

"Just an initial investigation. I'd rather do this over the phone but if you prefer to come down to Rotherdyke Police Station…"

"OK, OK, I'm not being awkward. What do you want to know?"

"A Ryan Hudson plays for your team, yes?"

"That's what I told the policeman. Ryan is a middle-order batsman. He's hardly played this season because he's been away, but he did manage the final match. I only played him because we had some injuries. It's not good for team morale when a player suits himself when to turn up. But all was forgiven when he scored fifty-odd not out and we won the league."

Hannah listened impatiently. "Does he have a particular mate in the team?"

There was a silence.

"If I had to say one, it would be Imran Khan. He's a regular for us, top-quality leg-spin bowler. Not many of them about."

"You've been very helpful," said Hannah. "Last thing: do you know where Ryan works?"

"So far as I know, he was at college. But he didn't talk about it, at least not that I heard."

"Do you know which college?"

"One in Leeds, but that's all I know."

"And Imran – do you know if he attended mosque?"

"What is this about?" Hannah heard a new note of anger in his voice.

"He may be able to help us in our enquiries." She sensed she had to put the squeeze on a bit. "I wouldn't want to get back to you in the future and accuse you of refusing to give information and obstructing the course of justice."

Another silence.

"Imran is a good Muslim. He goes without fail to worship at the Ilaahi Mosque here in Leeds."

"Thank you very much; you've been most cooperative."

So was Ryan Hudson the white man who'd been to Opal Street? And whoever that man was, had he been to use the Arabic keyboard, and why? Soon she might be able to give Davoud Nariman some information he wanted. She needed a strong coffee.

1000

Hannah rang the biggest Leeds college, Leeds Central. When she finally got through the protective barrier of receptionists and secretaries to the principal she said that in two hours she would be there to receive and take away all information they had on a student named Ryan Hudson. When the principal duly protested, Hannah assured him this was a matter of national importance – no, she couldn't be more specific – and neither he nor his college would benefit from accusations of withholding information from the police. Feeling satisfied and a little intoxicated with the new power she was savouring,

Hannah left the rest of the team following up the other four names, took a car from the pool and drove to the Ilaahi Mosque in Leeds.

It wasn't like the shiny new red-and-cream stone one in Rotherdyke with arched windows, a green dome, minaret, security lights and a clock set to Mecca time. This place was an old primary school with a battered sign outside, a building of blackened stone with high, narrow windows. There was a light on behind a window blind. The step at the entrance was worn concave, doubtless by the shoes and maybe clogs of generations of kids.

She knocked on the door, saw a shadow move behind the blind and then the door was slowly opened. An old man in a white prayer cap peered out. Hannah showed him her card.

"Detective Sergeant Hannah Walker," she announced.

He smiled. "Come in. I am the imam here."

Hannah bent to take off her shoes, but he said it wasn't necessary, they weren't going to the prayer room. She hoped it had been a gesture he appreciated.

"I'm sorry to disturb you," she said.

"It is no matter. Come in," he said, and opened a door that still had a *Head Teacher* sign on it.

She had imagined cushions and low tables, but it was an ordinary office. The imam pulled a chair up to the desk for her and then sat in his own chair. Hannah felt comfortable with him.

"How can I help?" he asked.

"I'm told an Imran Khan worships here. All I know about him is that he is a devout Muslim and a very keen cricketer."

The old man chuckled. "Imran," he said. "Yes, he is a spin bowler, I believe. He lives for his cricket, but also he is a dutiful and, as you say, a devout young man."

"Can you tell me anything else about him?"

"He is in his final year of computer studies at college. He

is very clever. I do not understand three quarters of what he tells me. I believe he set up a website for his cricket club." He stroked his beard and smiled. "He is perhaps a little too strong sometimes in his profession of our faith. I have tried to calm him; these are difficult times when trouble can be so easily stirred up."

Hannah nodded. "Do you know if has any white friends?"

The old man looked at her a little more guardedly. "Is Imran in some kind of trouble?"

"Not so far as we know."

"It would disappoint but not surprise me," said the imam. "He can be headstrong at times, impressionable."

He paused, as if considering whether saying more was the wise thing to do. Then he said, "Yes. There was a serious young man."

Hannah felt again that she was on the edge of something. But she had to let the old man go at his own pace.

The imam smiled. "Imran brought him here, a young man who wanted to learn about Islam. I should have offered you something to drink. I'm so sorry."

"I'm fine," replied Hannah, wanting to hurry him on.

"I taught him. He was a good student, eager to learn. He always did the studying I gave him."

"And then did he just leave?"

"Oh no, he wanted to convert to Islam. It was I who gave him his Muslim name. It was a great privilege for me."

Go on, go on, urged Hannah silently.

The imam frowned. "I remember, it was Yusuf. It means 'God gives'. Yusuf Javeed was his new name."

"You have been extremely helpful," said Hannah. She had only one more question. She stood up. As casually as she could, she asked, "Do you know what his English name was?"

"Ryan, I think," said the old man. "Ryan something, but I can't remember."

Gotcha! She felt a surge of triumph which she had to hide. So Ryan Hudson, the white man, was a Muslim. That surely was a nugget for the intelligence people.

Hannah thanked the imam again and he courteously showed her out. How could the faith of someone so gentle and gentlemanly lead to beheadings with a serrated knife? It was incomprehensible.

Back in the car she smiled to herself: a job bloody well done. Humble little Rotherdyke had uncovered something of value to the big boys down south. She phoned Davoud and gave him the news.

"That's fantastic work, Hannah, well done. At last, something to work on."

Praise from a London high-up! She basked in it for a moment and then drove off to Leeds Central College.

1040

Davoud rang GCHQ. "Jamie, now I've got something for you. That superb woman in Rotherdyke – the detective sergeant who came to see you – has given us a young man with two names. Ryan Hudson was born in Keighley, not far from there. He converted to Islam in a Leeds mosque and his Muslim name is Yusuf Javeed."

"So that means," said Jamie, "we have a white Muslim from the area where a laptop and a satellite phone were used to send these messages."

"It could be coincidence, or he could be the sender we're looking for," said Davoud. "Can you get your guys to try and trace any flights he's made in the last eighteen months to and from the Yemen?"

"Will do. I've got a nasty feeling about this. Yemen means Al-Qaeda. Al-Qaeda needs a headline operation, our suspect is English, and there's been no big attack in the UK since the Tube bombings in 2005."

"My feeling as well," agreed Davoud. "ISIS is grabbing all the headlines now. Al-Qaeda needs to re-establish its profile. I'll get the Border Agency to follow up Yusuf/Ryan's travels in and out of the UK. I'll convene the Counterterrorism Group – the one I used to chair – to get everyone informed. You don't know how glad I am to be running an operation instead of just talking and passing on reports."

"I think I do."

"Cheers, Jamie."

Davoud rang the Border Agency, then Tamsin Crawford-Jones who had taken over the chairmanship of the group.

"We have a situation, Tamsin. Call the group together, it's urgent."

He needed the pieces to start falling into place. He stared out of the window at the grey Thames below, found he was drumming his fingers on the windowsill. Something big was in the offing. He was sure of it.

1050

Yusuf walked back to the village. Time for breakfast. He chose The Posh Sardine again. He didn't regret the bacon sarnie yesterday, but he didn't want to push Allah's forgiveness too far. So he chose muesli, toast, butter and jam. An old man with trembling hands was spreading jam on a scone. Yusuf checked he could have his flasks filled with coffee that evening.

Afterwards he wandered along the promenade, already filling with visitors' cars. On the railings were several boards: *Warning. Extreme danger. Beware quicksands, deep channels, fast-moving tides, sudden drops.* He remembered watching on TV the story of the Chinese cockle-pickers who had been drowned out there. Victims of gangmasters – his father writ large. He passed a dementia home; in the bay window an old woman in a pink dressing gown sat with a mug, staring out. Over the bay, everything was grey: mist, sea, viaduct, the opposite bank – not a shred of colour.

He continued on the shore path beyond the end of the promenade. It was wet and muddy and would be covered when the tide came in. After the coastguard station the path deviated into a wood – Grubbins Wood, an information board said, a place of orchids, wild flowers and butterflies. An old lady with a small brown dog was coming towards him.

"Lovely morning," she said, smiling, as she passed.

"Aye," he replied.

They had no idea – this woman, the man in the café. His secret exhilarated him: to stroll like a rambler and plan like a general. When the path descended to the shore again the tide was already flooding in. There was no way he could continue to Blackstone Point. But he needed to be active. Irritated, his equilibrium disturbed, he returned to the village. In a gift shop he bought a National Trust leaflet describing a walk round the nearby hill of Arnside Knott. Through the mist he strode along the path that steeply ascended the limestone scree – 'clitterbed' was the local name, according to the pamphlet – and wound between gnarled yew and juniper bushes. He reached a three-sided stone structure, sweating, feeling better for the exertion. There were panels indicating all the Lakeland fells he should be able to see. Nothing but mist.

The path flattened now. On his left he passed the skeletal remains of a knotted tree, all that remained of a pair of larches deliberately twined together years ago as a love token, said the pamphlet. Yusuf stared at it, unmoved. He'd never experienced love, except his love for Allah. That was worth more than the love of all women combined: no deceit, no disillusionment, no humiliation. No Debbie – a fleeting image he banished.

He continued past the bench at the summit and began to descend the other side, through woods and crooked gates. Now the mist was thinning and from a viewpoint through the trees, he saw the railway line beyond the ruins of Arnside Tower where, by tomorrow, Shalima would have led the opening stage of the mission. He sat down on a fallen tree. Meticulously he went through his plan, envisaging everything from the moonlit landing to the end: the timings, the actions, the possible responses should there be problems, the necessary ruthlessness. He had gone over it countless times. It was a good plan.

Energised and confident, Yusuf strode along the path beneath the Shilla Slopes of scree and circled round back to the village. The waiting, the anticipation and the excitement were making him hungry all the time.

1100

At Leeds Central College, the four-storey-high glass-and-steel atrium felt like an airport lounge. The receptionist's desk looked tiny, tucked away at the side next to a huge potted plant, and she was on the phone. Hannah glanced into the refectory with its ugly purple and lime one-piece plastic chairs. Students were chatting in there. A group of Asian girls with headscarves were passing through the security gates, laughing.

"I'm sorry to keep you waiting," said the receptionist, nail varnish bright red, big gold hooped earrings. "And I'm afraid the principal has had to go out."

"But…" began Hannah, annoyed and deflated. She realised she was stupidly expecting a higher level of respect since the London flattery.

"His PA is expecting you. I'll call her."

The PA came straight out – a stern-faced woman with well-cut grey hair, wearing a dark trouser suit.

"The principal told me to assure you that we have researched very thoroughly – he ordered us all to make this a top priority."

Hannah sensed her resentment at having her routine and her own priorities disturbed.

"Here is everything we have: attendance record, reports, tutor comments, drawings and assignments, pastoral tutor comments, even a photograph."

She was carrying two manila folders. She opened one. Paper-clipped to a form was the photograph.

"How recent is that?" asked Hannah.

"It would have been taken at the beginning of his last year. We update the files, so we only keep the most recent one."

A thin face, a straggly beard and fair hair were all that Hannah had time to take in before the photo was slipped back into the folder.

"There's a DVD in this one." The receptionist took it out. "All the students on Ryan's course had to produce a project on an engineering model. His was about a bridge. He had to deliver a spoken commentary on his work. It's all here."

She slipped the DVD back in the folder and handed them both to Hannah.

"I appreciate the work you've done, and so quickly. Please pass on my appreciation to the principal."

"Glad to be of help." The PA smiled, softening a little, or perhaps just being professional.

Back in the car, Hannah made a second phone call to Davoud.

"Tremendous stuff," said Davoud. "We couldn't have asked for more."

They agreed she would upload the DVD's contents to their file-sharing system so Jamie could access it at Cheltenham GCHQ. The photograph she would scan and send to Davoud.

The phone rang again. Davoud, pacing his room, moved back to his desk.

"Davoud? It's Phil Downes from the Border Agency."

"Hi, Phil, that's fast. What's the news?"

"Your man Ryan Hudson, or at least someone with his passport, arrived in Lerwick last Friday, 25th of September."

"Lerwick, is that the Orkneys?"

"No, Shetland. Then he took the overnight ferry to Aberdeen. I got our people to trace his journey back. He came by ship, the Smyril Line ferry, from Bergen, Norway. He'd got to Bergen by train from Oslo. The train companies have been really helpful. He'd booked tickets all the way up from Rome to Munich to Hamburg to Copenhagen to Gothenburg and then to Oslo. Separate tickets for each stage, which is suspicious."

"Nothing before Rome?"

"No, sorry, the trail went dead."

"No flights?"

"None that we could find. He just appears in Rome."

"That's brilliant, Phil. Pass on our appreciation to your team."

Flying direct to the UK could have been problematic, but why had Ryan not flown direct to Bergen or Oslo? He had deliberately complicated his journey to conceal it. He was definitely on a mission.

Davoud rang Jamie to pass on the information. "Here's another nugget: a file on the system containing a video made by Ryan/Yusuf at college, and on it is a commentary."

"His voice?"

"I assume so."

"Another job for the techies," said Jamie, "matching the video voice with the voicemail. I'll get them onto it."

So, Ryan/Yusuf was in the UK, as Davoud had feared. But who was he? What was his background? Was he working alone? There was too much they didn't know.

Davoud thumped the table. Patience: this was the waiting phase. He'd been here before, but that didn't make it any easier.

1210

Shalima stood huddled on the deck of the tramp steamer. So far as she could tell, there had been no change in speed on the whole voyage from Port Said, just different weathers. The skipper had told her the forecast was good: tonight would be calm as they steamed up the Celtic Sea.

She looked past the Zodiac, securely lashed to the deck, seeking a sighting of Land's End to the north-east. Somewhere to her west was Ireland. Then they would pass Wales. All was grey, the horizon indistinct, all ordinary and undramatic. Far away a tanker was travelling in the opposite direction, creeping along.

Everything was as ready as it could be. The equipment was complete, the team good, the timing on schedule. Even the weather was on their side, praise be to Allah. She had complete confidence in Yusuf: arrangements at his end would be equally in place. Here on deck, wrapped against the damp and chill, she admitted to herself that since leaving Hodeida the mission had crowded out her religion. Her faith, which had impelled her from England all the way back to here, had been superseded by the planning and detailed organisation, the need for a successful outcome and, yes, by her own self-satisfaction. The operation must succeed, but for its own sake. Only when the action was over could her religion reappear and the divine purpose reassert itself.

With a shock she realised she had not yet prayed today. How could she forget?

She pulled up her hood and turned to look at the white wake foaming behind them. For now, the fear of something going wrong, something for which she was responsible, was uppermost in her mind. She wondered if the team felt the same, or whether this fear applied only to a leader. How would the team react when they learned the means to the end? It was possible the enormity of it might overwhelm them, the power they would have might paralyse. She could hardly imagine it herself.

She shivered and wrapped her arms around her body. Until the attack, they were taking the initiative, they were in charge. But afterwards it depended on others. The attack was planned, the outcome clear. It was the bit in between that was unknown. There would be questions to be answered, dilemmas to be solved. Yusuf and she were in charge: would they agree? Would the team agree? Seven people united for the same initial objective, caught up in the excitement of the action. But all from different backgrounds, with different personalities and histories. Would they stick together under stress? In those circumstances, would her being a woman complicate things? Would that undermine everything else she had got right?

Somewhere out there beyond the grey, on shores either side of her, were cities, towns and villages. Normal life being lived: routines, habits, chores. But what was happening under the surface? Only she had seen the reality of her mother's misery, her father's viciousness. The outside world had seen only an ordinary couple going about their daily life.

Now she too was part of that secret undercurrent, part of a shocking violence. She had already healed and killed, in Africa and Arabia. For the sake of a greater good. She was radiotherapy attacking the cancer that killed, the cancer of un-Islam. She was in the right.

Spray broke over the rail, and she saw curtains of rain far out over the sea, watched a long-necked black bird fly low over the waves.

A door slammed behind her, and she turned and saw Ibra.

"Fresh air," he said, and, looking around, "not much to see."

"We're somewhere between Wales and Ireland, heading towards the Isle of Man."

"Are you scared?" he asked, his heavily lidded eyes underscored by dark circles, his beard tinted with henna.

She smiled at him. "Not scared. Excited, nervous, maybe."

"As we should be," he said. "Like before a match. I used to play football. I was always nervous in the changing room, wondering if I'd play well, or make a mistake that would let the team down. But once on the pitch it was fine, after I'd made a pass or beaten a defender." He paused. "I enjoyed it. The Arabs aren't too hot on sport. They like cheating too much."

Shalima raised her eyebrows.

He laughed. "I'm going for a walk round the deck. Get blown about a bit. Clear my head."

She watched him grab the rail and shuffle away. He was a good man, quiet, dependable, efficient. She knew his story: wife and child killed by an alcoholic driver, members of his mosque seeing his vulnerability, his anger and grief needing an alternative commitment, giving him a purpose. He had fought in Syria, but as a man in her team she saw him as a soother of ruffled feathers, a peacemaker, affable, liked by all, even Bargo.

The ship lunged and a tail end of spray hit her in the face; she tasted salt. Twenty-four hours from now, where would they be? Going their separate ways, running for their lives? Or notorious? Having the power of life or death, or crouched in hiding? She thought of the White Widow and the other women jihadi leaders. Would she become like them or would she be an anonymous, unremembered failure, martyr but failure? Ibra would have his seventy-two virgins. Women's reward had not been quantified.

Whatever happened, she would need her wits about her. She shivered. In her cabin she would pray. She wouldn't be able to sleep, but she could rest.

1230

When Yusuf arrived back at Arnside promenade the sun was shining, although there were still shreds of mist over the distant hills. He bought a cheese-and-onion pasty, an apple-and-rhubarb pie and a takeaway coffee and took them down to the pier. He chose a bench below a flagpole with a Union Jack, looked up at it fluttering. *You'll see*, he thought. On the other benches sat old people, most eating ice creams, women with grey perms, men with walking sticks leaning against their knees. Four fishermen held rods over the pier railings. Yusuf heard the word 'flounders' as they chatted. Two kids were looking through the telescope.

"Like the Costa del Sol," said an old man.

Yusuf heard shrieks of laughter and turned to see four girls sauntering along the promenade, arm in arm. Short skirts, red and yellow, bright. Heeled sandals with thongs up their legs. Skimpy tops, bare midriffs and arms. Sixteen? Kids. But no modesty, unabashed, inviting attention. The thrill of tantalising. So knowing, they were, of their power over men. They licked their ice-cream cones.

He looked away, his anger controlled. The mission, so soon now. The best way to pass the afternoon was to go for another long walk. Anyway, there was nothing else to do except watch the occasional train trundle over the viaduct. After the exercise and fresh air, he would be more likely to rest for the few hours before his alarm went off. He would pick up the filled flasks at six o'clock, have fish and chips for tea from the shop by the viaduct, then park his van in a small car park he'd found near Waterslack. At 0130 he would be on the move. The beginning.

He drank the last of his coffee, threw his rubbish in a litter bin and set off.

1600

Davoud's phone rang again. He snatched it up.

"Yes?" he snapped.

It was Jamie.

"Yusuf's your man," said Jamie straight away, unable to conceal the triumph in his voice. "We've used the latest voiceprint technology and the voice on the video matches the messages on the phones."

"Any doubt about that?"

"None at all. It's one hundred per cent certain."

At last, things were moving.

"That's good to know, well done. But it's beginning to scare the shit out of me."

"There's more," continued Jamie. "In July last year a Yusuf Javeed flew to the Yemen. In December he flew to Dar es Salaam. In January he flew back to Heathrow, but by a roundabout route via Johannesburg, Addis Ababa and Frankfurt."

"Dar es Salaam last December: wasn't that when there was an attack on the American Embassy?"

"I think you're right."

"I'm sure it was. We can only assume Yusuf was there to be part of it. Too much of a coincidence."

"Things are hotting up. Let me know if there's anything else you need doing."

"Thanks, Jamie."

No sooner had the call ended than there was a knock on the door and Davoud's PA came in.

"A photograph for you, from Rotherdyke Police Station, a Detective Sergeant Hannah Walker."

It had been enlarged from a passport-sized original, the detail a bit fuzzy. An almost adolescent face; long, thin beard; fair hair; pale skin; eyeballs slightly bulging. Davoud scrutinised it, seeking some indication that here was a violent terrorist in the making, or even a leader. The face seemed weak and pallid, unexceptional. Even meek, long-suffering like a saint. But he had learned long ago that appearances can be deceptive.

Enough! He placed the photo on his desk. Two pieces of the jigsaw. He had decisions to make.

1630

Promptly Tamsin Crawford-Holmes called the Counterterrorism Group meeting to order. Voices quietened more quickly than usual.

"I appreciate your being here at such short notice," she said. "Jamie, as you can see, is on a conference call from Cheltenham." On the screen, Jamie nodded to them. "And Sir Bartholomew is abroad."

No one seemed disappointed that the MI6 man was unavailable.

"Of course, I will keep south of the river fully informed," she added. "Now to business. Davoud – your report please."

Davoud stood up. All eyes were on him. They knew virtually nothing, but he could see they sensed the urgency of the meeting: they were all sitting forward, none of them drinking the coffees they had brought in with them.

"I'll be as succinct as I can. I believe a serious situation is developing with the potential for a terrorist attack here in UK.

"A Muslim convert, born Ryan Hudson in the north of England and now known as Yusuf Javeed, spent the last eight months in the Yemen, presumably in one of Al-Qaeda's training camps. His travel records might link him to the bombing of the American Embassy in Dar es Salaam last December.

"He was the prime mover in a flurry of calls in and around the Yemen which appear to be connected with a series of meetings, plans and weapon logistics. This has been followed by a silence, a pattern which in the past has meant that arrangements for an attack have been finalised. The attack then takes place."

He let that sink in. Some of the group glanced quickly at each other; almost imperceptibly, two of them shook their heads.

"He returned to the UK in January this year and then flew back to Yemen in August. Last Friday he returned again via a very roundabout route, landing in the Shetlands and then travelling to Aberdeen. On Saturday he sent a message from an Arabic laptop in the town of Rotherdyke in the West Riding to the Yemen, and also to another satellite phone located in the port of Alger. The message was a reference to the Qu'ran, about reassembling separate parts of a bird. The laptop was found accidentally as part of an investigation into grooming. On Monday he sent another message, voicemail this time, to the same two phones. Again a reference to the Qu'ran, and again to a gathering of birds. I quote: *And send down to prey upon them flocks of birds.* The phone that was in Alger was on Monday off the coast of Cadiz, and I can only assume on a ship heading our way. People are working on that. But there is now no trace of the phone; it was probably dumped at sea once the final message was received.

"We have a photograph of Yusuf/Ryan from his student days in Leeds." He slid copies of the photo across the table. Each of them studied the unassuming face of the young man.

"We know nothing about where an attack might take place or when or how many others might be involved. We have, in fact, no firm evidence that any attack will take place, only circumstantial but very worrying evidence. My gut feeling is that something big is on the way."

He sat down. The very act of explaining had confirmed to him how everything was circumstantial and nothing certain.

Around the table many questions were asked, which Davoud, and Jamie via video link, answered to the best of their ability. Hypotheses and scenarios were suggested. But there was only so much that could be speculated upon.

"I think," said Tamsin after forty minutes' discussion, "it's time to draw some conclusions. Over to you, Davoud."

Davoud stood up again. "Thank you all for your valuable contributions. This is where I believe we are:

"One. All the components of our security systems need to be on heightened alert, and that is the responsibility of all of you: borders watched, returning jihadists identified, electronic eavesdropping intensified, suspects already under surveillance checked even more closely. There'll be moans about reduced resources. We have to ignore them.

"Two. I will speak with the Home Office, and it will be the Home Secretary's decision to call a meeting of COBRA and to decide whether to raise the international terrorism threat level from severe to critical – meaning, as you know, an attack is expected imminently rather than just highly likely. My recommendation is to leave it as it is until we get more concrete information."

There were nods around the table.

"Three. We ask the media to publish this photo, but without any mention of terrorism. The story is that we need to trace this young man urgently; he has not been seen for several days and without his medication he can be violent and therefore dangerous. We ask the public to contact the police if they see him, but certainly not to approach him. We'll ask for it to be on every channel's six o'clock news today. It's less than an hour away but we'll put pressure on if necessary. They'll manage."

Again, nods of assent.

"For the moment, that's it. We can do no more."

Again he felt how impotent they were. Time was rushing by. He was certain that somewhere, something was moving forward, over which they had no control.

"Davoud – it's in your capable hands," said Tamsin.

Smiles and nods. As well there might be, thought Davoud. He was at the sharp end; final accountability was with him. But it was what he had wanted.

"Thank you all again. The safety of the realm etc. in your hands etc.," Tamsin ended.

The meeting dispersed, the screen went blank and Davoud went back to his office.

Now he could only wait – for additional information, for a breakthrough, for a sighting, for them to make a mistake – if there was a 'them'. The technology and electronics might be top of the range, the watchers and listeners totally committed, but all they had was one man's name and the possibility of a ship. They didn't know where either was. There would be many ships on their way across the Bay of Biscay, heading for the English Channel. And why the concentration on birds? Was that significant?

Sooner rather than later he hoped he would be informing ministers. What would they decide? What would they demand of him?

And then he remembered his father. This evening he was

supposed to be visiting a residential home, checking it out. It was inevitable now that his father would end up in a home. Having multiple carers was just too complicated; there were still times when his father was on his own and a danger to himself. And Davoud could not guarantee that he would be at home every night – especially now. He did not know how much his father would understand about leaving the apartment he had lived in with his wife for thirty years and in which he had brought up his children. Would it be heartbreaking, or would it be just another part of the confusion and forgetfulness in which he increasingly lived?

Davoud rang the carers to arrange for forty-eight hours' constant cover starting now. Somehow, even at the last moment, they were able to provide cover – he supposed that was why he paid such premium rates. Then he rang the home to cancel the visit. He knew his PA could have done this for him, but he would have felt guilty.

And Jenny. He couldn't talk to her about any of this but he wanted her company more than ever, the brightness she brought. She hadn't contacted him. Was she deliberately giving him space and time to assess, or giving herself space? They could meet for a meal in a restaurant less than five minutes from his office, and he would be instantly contactable if anything new was discovered. But it would hardly be satisfactory if he had to suddenly leave her without any real explanation.

He couldn't even lose himself in his guitar. It was impossible to play while he was on edge, expectant, responsible.

No, alone, he could only wait. And try not to think of Sara, who he was supposed to meet from school tomorrow to take to McDonald's. Her mother would not approve, but that secretly pleased him. He would probably have to disappoint Sara.

No wonder he liked jigsaws: the pieces were all there, the

spaces into which they would fit ready-made, the whole puzzle made finite by the edge pieces, the final picture known. Not like this situation. He needed to check through it all again, make sure he hadn't missed anything.

1800

As the sun shone low over the bay, Yusuf returned to his van: past a charity shop, a chemist, another gift shop, a bank, two clothes shops, an electrical goods shop and a café. There was a TV on above the counter; a news programme. He stopped to watch and recognised the female newscaster. Pictures of wrecked buildings, dead bodies, a reporter speaking to camera. Yusuf couldn't hear anything, just saw her mouth moving. Then it was the newscaster again. She began to speak. A photograph of a man filled the screen. It took him a moment to realise it was a picture of himself. He couldn't hear what was being said. Then the picture was replaced by another reporter standing outside his college in Leeds, his mouth moving, pointing to the building. Yusuf stood, appalled. The newscaster again, another story, pictures of rugby fans waving scarves.

He dared not turn round. Nobody else was looking in the window. His picture had gone. It must have been his college ID photograph, enlarged. How had they got it? Why had they got it? The authorities knew about him. They wanted him, they'd publicised him, so they must know about the mission. But how was it possible? Had something happened to Shalima's team or the ship? Had there been a leak from Al-Qaeda? Perhaps they suspected something was about to happen but didn't know what. That must be it. If they knew already, he would have seen signs: more police, perhaps armed soldiers, helicopters flying over. He'd had a beard then and a full head of fair hair. Now he was bald and clean-shaven. Would he be recognisable?

Thoughts raced. Should he test it? There was a pub, The Fighting Cock, near where he'd parked the van. They would have TV screens on. He could go in and order an orange juice, just stand at the bar and see if there was any recognition. But if there was, what would he do? No, that was stupid. He would walk calmly back to his van and do what he had planned to do. The van! Had they traced him to a red van purchase? But an Asian had bought it and, in any case, now it was white. They couldn't know about it. *No, stick to the plan. Be innocent, stay natural.*

The worst-case scenario: the plot was discovered and he and his team would die in a gun battle as martyrs, shahid. But there would be fear in every sleepy English backwater, not just in cities. No one would feel safe. A victory anyway. And he would be in Paradise.

Yusuf realised he must have been looking in the boring shop window for minutes. He took a deep breath, turned and walked away. He felt scrutinised, but no one appeared to give him a second glance.

Everyone would assume what was planned would happen in a city, not here, in a place like this. Slowly he began to relax. Shalima and the ship should be in British waters. The mission was still on.

1820

Before the news programme was over, the first call was put through to Hannah Walker.

"It's Ryan Hudson's father," the copper on desk duty told her.

"Hello, Mr Hudson—"

But she was interrupted by an angry voice. "What's going on? I've just seen my son's picture on the news. It gave your number to ring. There must be some mistake. As you can hear, I'm upset, and I can tell you Ryan's mother is sobbing her heart out."

"I'm grateful you've called. Could you tell me what the mistake is?"

"There's two big mistakes. What's this about him also being called Yusuf something? He's not a bloody Muslim, for Christ's sake. And, secondly, he's never been on medication in his whole life, so how can being without it make him violent and dangerous? What's going on? It's crazy. I've already had some very distressing phone calls from friends, and I can't explain anything to them."

Hannah soothed him a bit, told him she'd get back to him when there was more information. She would pass his concerns on to those higher up.

Twenty minutes later came a second call.

"My name's Chris Holdsworth and I'm phoning about that picture on the TV news." His voice was more excited than angry.

"Detective Sergeant Hannah Walker speaking. Please go on."

"Just that I saw him, Ryan, yesterday. Ryan Hudson. We were at school together. We had a chat; it was a chance meeting in a café."

"Where was this, Mr Holdsworth?"

"The Hideaway Café, near the M6 turn-off for Kirkby Lonsdale. It was only yesterday morning. He seemed fine, dead normal."

"What did you chat about?"

"Nothing really. We only spoke a few words. He wasn't that friendly, but nothing dangerous. I told him about my job and he said he was on his way to work on a building site."

"Did he say where?"

"Barrow, I think. What's this about him having a Muslim name? He was eating a bacon sandwich when I saw him. They're not supposed to do that, are they?"

"You've been extremely helpful. Could I have your number in case we have to get back to you?"

Hannah sensed disappointment in Chris Holdsworth's voice. He had wanted more drama, presumably.

She immediately phoned the information through to Davoud, who again thanked her profusely. "Vital news," he said.

Whatever was going on, she was definitely part of it. GCHQ, the Intelligence Service, a Muslim. It all pointed one way. But she had to concentrate on her primary investigation, the groomers. Jamie Lockhart had sent valuable information from the laptop down from GCHQ. There were translations from Urdu and Arabic and some messages in English. All corroborated the network of men, the transport of girls, planned meetings with girls. There was more than enough to justify prosecutions.

1900

Stretched out on a couch, Imran Khan was dozing in his flat after a takeaway chicken tikka makhani. A copy of *The Hacker's Manual 2015* had fallen from his lap onto the floor. Radio 5 Live was on, a commentary on the Chelsea match. He only supported Chelsea because he liked their manager, José Mourinho. Imran dreamed of one day having Mourinho's success, arrogance, charm and shrewdness. The score was nil-nil at half-time. Imran was only half-listening, but suddenly he was wide awake. The news summary had mentioned the names Ryan Hudson and Yusuf Javeed. There was an alert, he was potentially dangerous. But Imran hadn't heard why. He picked up his phone and accessed Sky News. Had something gone wrong? The only thing he knew about Yusuf's mission was that there was a mission and that it was a significant one. He found the picture of Yusuf and read something about medication.

He was scrolling down when there was a knock on the door. That was unusual. When he opened it, two policemen were looking at him, one jamming his foot in the doorway.

"Imran Khan?" the first one asked.

"Yes."

They stepped in.

"I'm arresting you under Section 41 of the Terrorism Act 2000 on suspicion of the commission, preparation or instigation of terrorism," began the first one.

The second policeman pinned his arms behind his back and clipped on the handcuffs as his colleague continued the caution.

1930

Davoud still felt like a provincial newscaster when he addressed his laptop screen. There should be an autocue.

"That's all I have for you, I'm afraid. Two names for a possible terrorist, possibly on his way to Barrow, two messages referring to the Qu'ran, and a feeling in my bones."

In the twin windows of his computer screen were the faces of Chief Superintendent Steve Mack, in charge of the Counterterrorism Unit of Cumbria Police, and Chief Superintendent Jude Livingstone of the Special Branch unit in the Lancashire Constabulary.

"Of course," said Jude Livingstone, "he could have used the M6 to go north to Scotland – Glasgow, Faslane and the hunter-killer nuclear subs – or south to Manchester and Liverpool or the Midlands, the big conurbations. Anywhere, really."

"I know," replied Davoud, trying to hide his growing sense of helplessness.

"If he was really going to Barrow," said Steve Mack, "there's the BAE Systems shipyard there where they are building the *Astute*-class nuclear subs. And, of course, the nuclear power plant at Sellafield."

"Attractive well-known targets. Anything else in your area?"

"There's RAF Spadeadam on the border with Northumberland. You probably haven't heard of it but it's the largest RAF base in the UK."

"What happens there?" asked Davoud.

"They teach electronic warfare to RAF and NATO aircrew. During the Cold War it was a launch site with missile silos. It was ideal because it is so isolated."

"There's Fylingdales," added Jude Livingstone. "Not our areas, it's in North Yorkshire: the Ballistic Missile Early Warning System. He could be on a roundabout route to there. So far as we are concerned in Lancashire, the only military targets are the barracks at Fulwood and Weeton. There's a BAE assembly and testing facility near Preston. There are rumours on YouTube that there's a Tornado Stealth plane being tested in a wind tunnel there."

"There'll be big football matches, I expect," said Davoud, "in Liverpool and Manchester. These guys usually choose soft targets, civilians. No World Cup rugby, though?"

"No," said Steve Mack. "At Cardiff, Milton Keynes and Twickenham over the next few days."

On their screens the three looked at each other in silence.

"I'll obviously contact you if I receive any more info. In the meantime, all we can do is be on high alert. Make sure all your people have seen the photo of the suspect. Sorry I can't be more helpful. Thanks for your time."

The two police chiefs smiled and nodded.

Davoud switched his camera off. Were the two of them convinced? Or did they see him as a twitchy Londoner? Maybe he was bigging it up, making a fool of himself. He couldn't win. The more sure he was that something was in the offing, the more helpless he felt. They needed some kind of breakthrough – another sighting, uncoded messages, suspicious arrivals on a cross-channel ferry, a mistake. Something.

His phone rang. He picked it up, not recognising the number.

"Davoud?"

His heart lurched. It was Jenny.

"Hello, you," he said tentatively, and it was as if he was plugged back into the alternative real world.

"I really need to see you. Do you fancy dinner tomorrow evening?" she asked. "Are you free? I've been so busy, lots to talk about with you."

Relief flooded through him. "Excellent idea. I'll book somewhere quiet."

"Even better!"

"I'll pick you up at 7.30. OK?"

"Fine. I'll put a proper frock on then."

"Just one thing," said Davoud. He hated to appear to put a damper on things.

"Yes?"

"There's just a chance I won't be free after all. I'm sorry."

"Secret work?"

"My job."

"Sealed lips, then?"

"'Fraid so."

"No problem."

He heard disappointment, but understanding too – he hoped.

"I'm sorry, Jenny, I'll have to go. Things are hotting up. I'm waiting for an important phone call."

"Don't worry. I've got my class to go to. See you tomorrow."

The line went dead. Would he be free tomorrow? The trouble was: if he wasn't, he could never give a truthful explanation. And he needed her to be able to trust him.

2005

Davoud's phone rang again. He recognised Hannah Walker's number.

"Hannah. You're working late."

"What's new?" she laughed. "I don't know if this will be any use. We arrested a man called Imran Khan earlier. He was at college with Ryan Hudson and was the person who introduced him to Islam at the Leeds mosque. We put the frighteners on him with the Terrorism Act. I'm sure he knows more than he's told us."

"What has he told you?"

"He confessed that Ryan – Yusuf – had come to him with a red Transit van and asked him to respray it white. Imran saw him drive off in it. Not much, but something. And we haven't finished with him."

"Did he give you the registration number?"

"Said he never noticed."

"Did he know where the red van came from?"

"Said he'd no idea, never asked."

"Did he know where Yusuf was going?"

"Again, never asked. I don't believe him."

"Well, thanks, Hannah. As they say, every little helps."

He put the phone down. A white van! Must be thousands

of them, most unmarked. He couldn't tell the chief supers that. They'd laugh. He growled in frustration, stretched back in his chair and cracked his knuckles. He needed to get out of this office, pound out a run in Hyde Park, get a real sweat up. But he couldn't leave the building.

One decision, anyway: he was staying here at Thames House tonight. They had small bedrooms for emergencies. His father was sorted with the carers.

Would an essential piece of information come in time to forestall whatever horror was planned? Or would it be too late? Davoud had a nasty feeling the hurricane was about to make landfall.

PART 3

FLYING

29.
THURSDAY 1ST OCTOBER, 0030

As the Zodiac swung from the winch wires, its shadow cast onto the sea by the freighter's arc lights looked like a giant turtle. The sea was flat, and a full moon shone spasmodically through gaps in the clouds.

Where the Celtic Sea met Morecambe Bay, the skipper was holding the ship steady over the Lune Deep. East were Yeoman's Wharf and the Shoulder of Lune, great banks of sand not far beneath the surface of the bay. Izzy and Ibra had studied the chart; they knew the sandbanks and channels shifted each year. They had plotted their course. With luck and moonlight, they would see the tall sticks which every year local fishermen stuck in the sand to mark the course of the River Kent across the shallows.

Shalima sat in the prow of the Zodiac which dangled about five metres above the deck. Ibra, wearing night-vision goggles, sat at the stern, his hand resting on the huge outboard motor which was hinged up. Bargo, Izzy, Benny and Kal sat on each side; all wore orange life jackets. Between them, on the aluminium decking, were their weapons and explosives, securely wrapped in tarpaulin and tightly roped, some in rucksacks, some in holdalls.

Ibra was grinning. "All systems go!"

The winch arm creaked as it swung the Zodiac clear of the deck and lowered it. There was a flat thump as the hull hit the water and Shalima clutched the grab ropes slung along the sides. Then she unclipped the two front quick-release fasteners from the winch while Ibra unclipped the rear two.

The arm swung away, and Ibra knocked the outboard's hinge down and lowered it into the sea. He pressed the electric ignition button. The engine started first time and he steered the Zodiac away from the ship's side and flicked the gear into neutral, waiting. Above the freighter's black hull, the bright arc lights cut a sharp-edged cone of light. The outboard idled, the sea slapped the inflatable hull. There were shouts from the freighter and Ibra waved his arm and pointed forwards.

They gave farewell waves to the two crew members watching them at the rail.

"Inshallah!"

Ibra put the outboard in gear and the Zodiac moved off. Shalima looked back at the freighter, saw the arc lights extinguished, the ship a black shape against the dark sea beneath slivers of silver moonlight shifting among the clouds above. Two hours ago, together on the deck, they had said their night *isha'a* prayers – their chanting voices low beneath the occasional shriek of gulls, water lapping at the prow, ship's engine throbbing, a salt breeze freshening their faces.

She had made her peace with her God.

High tide was an hour away. In the shallow bay the tides rose and fell rapidly; they had a maximum of an hour either side of when the tide was at its fullest. The sun would rise in six hours. If Ibra failed to navigate the narrow, winding river channel, dawn would reveal them stranded on the mud with their weaponry. The bay, she knew, was full of quicksands, swirling currents and sudden deep pools. They had little chance if they tried to swim and wade to safety, visible from both sides of the bay as they floundered about. No victory, no martyrdom – just a life sentence in a British jail, full term, no remission. The stakes could not be higher.

Yusuf had forbidden any calls or messages, and for the next hour she was not responsible. They were all in the hands of Ibra. Sitting at the prow, she leaned forward: blessed, uplifted, so alive, on the brink. Wavelets, caught momentarily by moonlight, stretched out into darkness; the lights of Barrow and Carnforth far away and tiny; the black skyline of the Lakeland hills. Through this peace, their Zodiac was ferrying death. Into this place of parishes and pubs, she was implanting Islam – from the harsh, dry, uncompromising desert light into this gloomy, damp and green land. She imagined church bells silenced, the muezzin's call wailing over stone terraced cottages and village greens.

It was crazy, unthinkable.

0130

Yusuf peeled his sleeping bag off. He'd slept badly in the van on the car park. His face on the TV news had rattled him, so he had not risked going into the fish-'n'-chip shop, nor had he got the flasks filled with coffee. The team would be looking forward to a hot drink after a couple of hours on the bay. It would have been a positive welcome. But they'd have to settle for bottles of water. He'd explain why later – he didn't want questions.

The weather was being kind: no wind, flat water, bits of moonlight.

He was impatient to see the results of Shalima's organisation. Everything would be correct, he knew. She was ace. She would have put a good team together. It would have been better if he could have met them beforehand, but his travel and his part of the preparation had made that impossible. He wondered vaguely now if that had been a mistake. Teams had to gel, to trust their leader, obey and follow him. Perhaps Shalima would have to play a bigger part. Anyway, too late now.

He pulled on an extra sweater, started the engine and drove

slowly out of the puddled car park onto the road to Silverdale. He passed beneath the Shilla Slopes, scree polished grey in the moonlight, where he had walked yesterday afternoon. The road came down to the bay and turned sharply left. He parked in the lay-by at the landing place, The Dip, and looked out across the bay. All was grey. Seabirds called, and he strained to hear the sound of an outboard motor, faint from across the water.

0140

"Shalima!" said Izzy, and pointed ahead.

Ibra was changing course. They were almost there. The Zodiac's plotter screen was now blank: there were no charts for this section of the bay. The gaunt sticks in the water, the river's marking poles, were picked out in the moonlight as they turned away from them. Ibra read the log of speed and distance and nodded to himself.

From close to the western shore of the bay by Holme Island, the lights of Grange-over-Sands just behind them, Ibra now headed east. Briefly, in the distance Shalima saw the outline of the Kent Viaduct, where the river estuary narrowed. They were heading for the darkness between the lights of Arnside and Silverdale, Ibra slowing, the engine almost silent. She trailed her hand in the grey water, licked the salt on her lips, felt the breeze in her hair, smelled petrol from the engine, rubber from the hull. The tide at the full. Perfect timing. Yusuf would be waiting.

Ibra now turned slowly south, coasting along, close beneath a wooded hillside. They were looking for a light on shore. Then it was there: three flashes from a torch only two hundred metres away, low down at sea level. Ibra killed and hinged up the outboard. The Zodiac glided in, the silence uncanny.

Did they all feel as she did? Everything was suddenly real again after the grey expanse of the bay: the pebbles the Zodiac nosed gently into; the low, wet branches that brushed past them; the cool land of England after so long away.

Yusuf's soft voice whispered, "Inshallah!"

She had known for certain he would be there, in the right place at the right time. Nonetheless she heaved a sigh of relief, felt the burden of responsibility now shared. Reunited with her co-conspirator.

In some hidden place nearby, soon he would divulge the details of the attack and allot them their tasks. At last the team would know the enormity of the mission. They would pray, eat, and rest for a couple of hours. The game was on. Was it too big for them? The plan she and Yusuf had explained so confidently in that desert mountain cave those months ago seemed a thing of fantasy now she was here on this gentle shore.

"Come," said Yusuf quietly.

Carefully, efficiently, they gathered their loads and stepped ashore.

"The tide is just starting to turn," said Yusuf. "Push the Zodiac out. It will float away. The tide ebbs fast."

"But—" began Izzy.

"That's the order!" hissed Yusuf.

Izzy and Ibra looked at each other; understood this was not the time for an argument with a leader they had never met. They pushed the Zodiac out, nose with the current. Shalima watched it drift slowly away into the night. There had been no way back for some time, but this was the final confirmation.

In single file the group followed Yusuf up a short path to where his van was parked. They took off their life jackets and stuffed them into the van. Two trips were needed to carry and load the gear. When it was all in, Yusuf turned to Shalima.

"Today the world will take note of us," he said, his voice firm.

They climbed in. The van was packed tight.

"Five minutes," said Yusuf.

Shalima noticed he had no beard, and his head was shaven. He looked bonier, tempered, his bulging eyes more prominent.

He drove up the lane away from the shore. Above the fields to her right, Shalima watched clouds slide across the moon. Yusuf slowed, turned left onto a track which led into thick woods, and drove only on sidelights. The track got rougher, the van bounced along and then stopped.

0200

"This ruined tower is where we stay till dawn," said Yusuf.

They all stepped down from the van and Yusuf shook hands with each of them. They gave him their names.

"May the peace, mercy and blessings of Allah be upon you," said Yusuf. "There is no God but Allah and Muhammad is his messenger."

They muttered back the responses.

"First, there is food and drink. All cold, but we are warriors, yes?"

Shalima noticed disgruntled looks, but no one complained. These men were jihadists, but they still had to be managed. Shalima realised how key the relationships between them all would be, but Yusuf seemed unaware of this, as if finalising arrangements was all there was to it. She should have thought of this earlier. There should have been a time to get to know each other. But it was too late now. Welding the team together, she realised, had been her unspoken responsibility. Yusuf, if he'd thought about it at all – and he almost certainly hadn't – had trusted her to do this.

After eating and drinking, they wandered off into the woods to pee. Then Yusuf gathered them round him. He insisted, though there was only torchlight and one Gaz lamp, that they check their rifles. Bolts slid and clicked under the trees. They sat on the low stones of broken walls, their weapons beside them, and Yusuf sat in the centre of the circle, the Gaz lamp on the ground in front of him.

"Switch off your torches," he said.

The light from the lamp shone upwards onto his face, its hissing the only sound as they waited for him to speak.

"We will have no second chance. We must succeed first time." He paused. "Our two targets are trains. One is a passenger train, because we need hostages. The other is a freight train." Pause. "It carries nuclear fuel."

Yusuf let the information sink in.

It was Izzy who spoke first: "Radioactive nuclear fuel?" His voice was disbelieving.

"Yes. It is misleadingly called spent nuclear fuel. But it is still radioactive. That is the point. We are hijacking the train, attaching explosives to the fuel and then demanding the release of Suleiman al-Hariri, who is in an English prison for fighting for Islam."

Feet shuffled among the stones. Shadowed faces looked at each other.

"Who," asked Bargo, "is Suleiman al-Hariri?"

Yusuf stared at him. "You must have heard of him. He is a top Al-Qaeda leader, number two. He is responsible for arranging more attacks on the infidels than any other individual. Allah has given us the task of rescuing him."

"And for him," interrupted Izzy, "we will blow up nuclear fuel and radiate the land, like Hiroshima?"

"It is a fantastic plan," said Kal from the other side of the circle. "If they do not give us Suleiman, it is not us who radiate the land, it is them."

Shalima heard muttered agreements.

"This is the ultimate weapon," said Kal. "Allah has honoured me to be part of it."

"All of us," said Yusuf. "He has honoured all of us. The world will see how strong is our faith, how weak are the infidels. The world will hold its breath as we make our demands. Allah will sustain us."

His voice had such an all-consuming intensity, at the same time intimidating and inspiring. He lifted his face to the sky and in the lamplight Shalima saw that his bony face without its beard was almost triangular, his eyes beneath his shaven skull bulging unnaturally. He held his bent arms in front of him, hands together as if he was making supplication, praying; his long, thin legs hinged at the knee, splayed as he sat on the ground. Like a praying mantis, she thought, but also like a prophet.

"Inshallah," she said softly.

"Inshallah," repeated the others in a ragged refrain around the circle.

"We will do this thing," said Yusuf, turning his head back to them. "And this is how."

What he and Shalima had discussed and agreed before their presentation in the mountain cave he now explained to the team. He took a large-scale map from his pocket and spread it out in the lamplight.

"We will split into two teams, one for each train."

He named the teams: each had one of the trained engine drivers.

"Shalima, Bargo and Ibra will be the nuclear train team."

Using the map, he explained what would happen and where.

"I will lead the passenger train team: Kal the driver, Izzy and Benny."

Then he unfolded a plan of Arnside Station and did the same for the other team.

"The timings are crucial. The whole action must be completed within forty minutes. My team especially must be prepared for the unexpected – we do not know how many passengers will be on the platform, or if and how they will resist. Will the engine drivers comply? Our rifles and pistols are not decorations."

They understood.

"Are there any questions?"

Shalima expected Izzy to raise a point; it was his nature to question. But he remained silent. They seemed impressed by the detail of the planning.

"Fine," said Yusuf. "We will pray together in silence and then there are nearly four hours to try and sleep. We do the work of Allah. We do it as a team."

At last, thought Shalima; after fourteen days aboard ship and the months of preparation before, what they all needed was action. They would sleep little, think a lot, rehearse their individual parts. With the help of Allah.

0740

In the grey early-morning light, they knelt on the broken stones of the ruined tower among the first fallen yellow leaves, prayed and prostrated themselves, their low voices muffled even more by the undergrowth and overhanging trees. They wore jeans, and denim or worn leather jackets, Shalima without her headscarf.

Yusuf drove the van slowly down the track back to the road and turned left towards Arnside. One car passed them, going towards Silverdale. Outside the village, at an old farm gate into a wood at the edge of the cemetery, Yusuf stopped the van. He had feared there might be an early dog walker, but no one was about. The door slid open and Shalima, Bargo and

Ibra jumped down, holding their Barrett M82 rifles, pistols in holsters. They vaulted over the gate and disappeared into the thick brushwood. The white van drove off.

Shalima's team found an old overgrown path through Hagg Wood and came out at the edge of a field. They sprinted across it to a bridge. Once a farmer's access bridge, it was now barred off with a *Danger* sign nailed to a post. The roughly cobbled bridge led over a drainage channel full of green water, and then over the railway line. They stumbled down the steep side of the cutting to the railway track which stretched virtually straight south to another wood.

Just south of the bridge, the two men took up position, sitting on sleepers between the rails, checking their rifles yet again. Shalima walked on for a further fifty metres. She left her stick with a red flag on it and walked a further 450 metres. From her bag she took the three yellow-capped 'banger' detonators Imran had stolen from a Network Rail permanent way van. She fixed them to the rail with their lead strips, ten metres apart. Then she walked back to her flag to wait, where Bargo had calculated the train would come to a halt. She waved to the two men, gave the thumbs-up, and they waved back. The air was still and mild, birds called, and a sheep bleated. She smelled the grass. The sun was rising in an orange glow. Her heart was beating fast, and her palms filmed with sweat.

0806

Keith Walters stood on the empty Platform 1 at Barrow Station, watching the two-coach blue-and-purple-liveried Northern train for Lancaster pull in. On his back was his newish Mulepack telescope and tripod carrier, its pockets containing his notebook, bird identification book and some mint humbugs. It promised to be a warm day but, at his age – seventy-five – he was taking no chances: a woollen beanie covered his ears, and he wore padded trousers, strong boots freshly dubbined last night, and two layers beneath his waterproof jacket. His binos were round his neck. A widower living on his own, this was his fortnightly outing to RSPB Leighton Moss. There was a nice café there where he would have his lunch. He would get the late-afternoon train back.

The southbound 0806, as usual, was empty: too late for workers in Lancaster, too early for the discount rate. He liked it quiet.

0811

Emily Khusar boarded at the next station, Roose. She carried her laptop and a small rucksack, on her way to Lancaster University to meet her supervisor about her PhD in molecular genetics. She was twenty-three years old with a Punjabi father and a Cumbrian mother. After the tutorial and an afternoon in the library she would join a training session for the university netball team.

0820

Yusuf parked the van on waste ground behind Arnside Station. A red and a blue car were already parked next to the Office and Information Centre. He looked out of the window up the narrowing estuary, broad mudflats with the narrow, winding river near the shore. White gulls bickered. Behind him in the van, the rest of his team – Izzy, Benny and Kal – sat quietly, their sniper rifles at their feet. Earlier this morning, before they left their hideaway, Benny had unwrapped the protective tarpaulin and the packages of explosive now stood in the corner of the van.

A silver car drew up and parked near them, Yusuf watching in the wing mirror. A middle-aged man with a laptop case got out, locked his car and walked onto the platform.

Peter Marsden was on his way to work at his estate agent's office in Carnforth. These days he only went into the office three days a week. He was looking forward to another long weekend.

0825

The two men and Shalima, now sitting on the rails, all felt the vibrations at the same time. The men jumped up and flattened themselves into the grass and bracken of the cutting, their rifles by their sides. Shalima stood and raised her red flag.

Train driver Charlie Hopwood always looked forward to this stage of the run – across the two viaducts and along the shore of the bay, heading west and then north to his destination at Sellafield Nuclear Power Station and the reprocessing plant. As his diesel engine trundled steadily past the end of the woodland, he looked across the flat fields of Silverdale Moss with their many parallel drainage channels. He'd often spotted herons there, and marsh harriers quartering overhead. He slowed slightly to have a closer look.

Then, in quick succession, three sudden bangs sounded beneath his engine. He almost jumped out of his skin. It took him a moment to realise that they were warning detonators that work gangs on the line would leave. Odd; he'd had no information about maintenance being carried out today.

"Better drop the lot," he said to himself, knocked the power off and swivelled the brake handle. As the train lost speed, he radioed control in Preston to report what had happened. They were perplexed: no work was being done on the line that day.

"Protect your train," he was instructed, "and wait for further advice."

When he stopped he would need to run back down the line and place more emergency detonators to warn any following train. Then he noticed a figure just ahead of him down the line, waving a red flag on a long stick. Was it a woman?

0827

The passenger train, southbound to Lancaster, pulled into Ulverston Station. After three passengers got off, two elderly women got on. Joan Dawson and Muriel Webb, friends since school, carried handbags and shopping bags. They were off to Lancaster to Marks & Spencer to look for winter coats, and then for lunch in their favourite café near the castle. Sitting down, they resumed their conversation about their grandchildren.

0829

Charlie Hopwood's train was slowing now, drawing nearer to the flag-waving figure. Definitely a woman. His train came to a halt just in front of her. He half-opened the cab window. The woman was just below him.

"There's a blockage on the line by the bridge, a sleeper or something. I was just out for a walk."

While Shalima grabbed the driver's attention, the other two in her team had sprinted the fifty metres down the line to the engine.

With a red flag? wondered Charlie, looking down at her. She was Asian. Alarm bells rang in his head. Then the window on the opposite side of the cab was smashed. Splinters of glass flew in. He put his arm across his eyes and saw the butt of a rifle. There was an Asian man's face at the window and the rifle was now pointing at Charlie's head. The door was already being opened.

"Don't do anything fucking stupid," yelled Bargo, and released the rifle's safety catch.

Charlie was paralysed. For the briefest moment, some instinctive defiance rose in his mind. His cargo: the nuclear waste! But he was terrified.

"I'll fucking kill you if I have to," shouted Bargo.

Immediately the Asian man with the rifle clambered up. At his door, another Asian man jumped up, followed by the woman. The cab was packed tight and the woman held a pistol to his temple, the hard metal barrel pressed into his skull.

"Move over," she said.

Charlie lumbered up, was grabbed and pulled out of his seat.

Bargo replaced him and studied the controls. They were familiar; he remembered them from France and from training.

0832

Yusuf slipped his Glock G43 pistol into his jacket pocket. He looked into the back of the van. "You know when to move," he said to his team.

They nodded.

Yusuf got out, shut the door and walked across to the Office and Information Centre. He went in. The room was warm, a bright fire already burning in the grate. On the walls were posters and display racks of pamphlets, shelves of bird books and local area histories; on the low coffee table were piles of timetables and walk leaflets. The door into the inner office opened and a man appeared, grey-haired and balding, overweight.

"Can I help you?" he asked.

"Yes," said Yusuf. He took his pistol out and pointed it at the man. "Turn around and go back inside."

The man frowned, unable to believe what he was seeing. He had turned pale. He turned. Close behind, Yusuf followed him. There were three desks, and at two of them women sat at computers.

"Stay calm," said the man.

"Good advice," said Yusuf, waving his pistol. He looked around the office. The window which overlooked the platform was made of frosted glass. "Take your chairs," said Yusuf, "and put them in a row in front of that bookcase. Then sit on them."

The women, mascaraed eyes wide, looked at the balding man. He nodded. They did as they were told, manhandling the chairs awkwardly in the confined space. When they sat down, Yusuf noticed there were tears in one woman's eyes and her fleshy arms were trembling. The other was twisting her wedding ring round and round on her finger.

"I do not want to harm you," said Yusuf. "But I will shoot you if I have to. It depends on you."

0836

At Cark Station Laura Dobson and her two children, Noah aged four and Daisy aged nearly three, got on the train for Lancaster. It was on time. Noah and Daisy were looking forward to seeing their grandma in Carnforth. She would, as usual, be cooking their favourite meal: sausage, baked beans and home-made chips, followed by red jelly and ice cream. Laura would put a clean duvet cover on her mother's bed, change the vacuum bag and mow the small front lawn, probably for the last time before winter.

0840

The nuclear cargo train trundled slowly and loudly alongside the northbound platform at Arnside Station. The two passengers waiting in the shelter on the southbound platform watched it and were mildly surprised when it stopped. They had seen it but not regularly: an engine, two flatbed trucks, each with a container lashed to it with steel hawsers, and then the reserve engine behind it.

0845

At Grange, only one passenger boarded: Finlay Mitchell, aged eighteen, with white earbuds plugged in, going for a job interview and then to meet a mate at Lancaster. He wore a jacket for the first time for a long time, chivvied by his mother, a tie rolled up in his pocket.

Paul Robinson, the ticket collector, dawdled down the train. He liked this soft-option journey: no trouble, all passengers usually had tickets, regulars to greet at Arnside and Carnforth. Already he was looking forward to the next episode of *Unforgotten* on the telly that evening. The secrets people had, fascinating. He'd decided he was boring; he had no secrets and no adventures to talk about. And nor did his wife. But how did he know that? Mary? No.

At Arnside, an old lady painfully climbed the footbridge steps from the village side of the station, halted at the top to regain her breath, walked across and descended to the southbound platform, firmly gripping the handrail, wincing as each knee bent.

0847

As the Lancaster-bound train passed the salt marshes on the left and Sunnyside Farm on the right, the radio in Geoff Firth's cab sounded the alarm.

"Geoff, there's been an incident," the voice said. "Down the line, east of Arnside. We don't know quite what has happened. But when you get to Arnside, stop there until you get any further instructions from me. OK?"

"Mysterious," said Geoff. "No problems."

An early coffee from his flask would do fine, he thought.

Then the phone rang in the Office and Information Centre. Yusuf, the balding man and the two women looked at it.

"Leave it," said Yusuf.

It rang and rang, the sound filling the small, taut room. When it stopped, the silence was equally deafening.

0848

The two passengers in the shelter (Peter Marsden had been joined by Nicola Smith, plugged into her earphones and going to meet a friend in Lancaster) saw their train to Lancaster curve round onto the Kent Viaduct right on time. They stood up and joined the old lady by the yellow line on the platform. The freight train was still waiting there on the other line, engine idling. The passengers did not notice the three men, also right on time, sprint from the white van to the platform. The first they were aware of them was when brown hands gripped their shoulders tightly.

With no time to think, Peter and Nicola, pistols stuck into their backs, were marched by Izzy, rifle slung over his shoulder, into the Office and Information Centre and pushed down into chairs, staring down at the walk leaflets.

"Quick, onto the platform," said Yusuf. "The train's on time."

Izzy ran out.

On the platform, the old lady, Marjorie Mather, protested, tried feebly to shrug Benny off. He realised the pistol, jammed into her side, meant nothing to her. She just wasn't frightened. Too old, he thought.

"Get off me, young man!" she said. "My train is coming. I'm going to see a friend in a home. She's got dementia. She sometimes recognises me."

It wasn't that she was unafraid; she just didn't realise what was happening. Hadn't even twigged he was Asian, hadn't noticed his rifle. So Benny left her and ran to join Izzy further back along the platform.

0850

The 0851 southbound train to Lancaster drew into the station alongside the waiting northbound freight train and halted. Ticket collector Paul Robinson pressed the button to open the doors. They slid open and he was about to step down onto the platform when a young man jumped up and bundled him back into the carriage. A forearm pushed his head back and he felt cold steel under his jaw.

"Don't panic, and you'll be OK."

Paul was staring at an Asian face.

That was odd, thought Geoff Firth, the passenger train's driver; usually the freight train passed him as he approached Grange.

Then he noticed there was only one passenger waiting, an old lady. That was odd, too. There were usually two or three regulars. His instructions had been to wait here until further orders. Looking up the line beyond the station he could see nothing untoward. Something strange was happening, but before he could think more, there was a battering at his door into the carriage. Suddenly scared, he picked up the radio. As he did so, there was a deafening shot and the lock on the door behind him was splintered. The door was wrenched open and he saw a rifle barrel aimed at his face. At the same time, he heard screams from back in the train.

"Into the other seat," yelled the man with the gun. "Now!"

Geoff, trembling, moved quickly across.

Kal sat in his seat instead. "I know how to drive this," he said. "Don't interfere. If you do, I will hit you, hard."

Geoff looked at the Asian man's eyes and fierce expression. He knew the man was telling the truth. The realisation: he was a terrorist.

Izzy and Benny had leapt onto the train and, shouting and waving their rifles, now herded the passengers and guard into the first coach, bundling them along the narrow aisle, pushing them down into the seats.

Hanging on to their mother, both children were crying. She tried to calm them while looking with hate and fear at the two Asians. The two elderly women could not be hurried: they shuffled and stumbled along, trying to push away the men impatiently. The old man, protesting, had tried to bring his rucksack with its telescope and tripod, but this had been roughly seized and flung onto a seat. Emily and Finlay seemed in a daze, the lad with his white earphones still dangling from one ear. They ended up occupying three table areas: the family at one, the three women at another, the men at the third.

Izzy and Benny stood in the aisle.

"Do as we say and you will come to no harm," said Izzy.

"You must stay quiet," added Benny.

"But what—?" began the old man.

"Shut up," yelled Benny. "I said shut up."

"I'll tell Yusuf what we've got," said Izzy. He jumped down from the train and ran round to the Information Centre.

"Eight," he said, "including two young kids. Then there'll be the driver and guard as well."

Yusuf looked at him. "OK," he said calmly. "Everything's OK. Now it's the loading up."

Izzy nodded. He joined Shalima and Ibra, who were already at the white van. Quickly they ferried the explosives, boxes of ammunition, sleeping bags and all the other items into the Lancaster train. The next train was not due until 0928, but passengers might arrive for it early. Shalima hoped not: they would add another complexity.

Inside the Information Centre, Yusuf was changing his mind. According to his plan, whatever hostages he had here would be transferred onto the train. But now he was wondering what would be gained from that. They had ten, and the jewels in the crown were the two children – a bonus, the strongest bargaining counters. The three office workers cowering in the chairs in front of him and the two from the shelter with their arms on their heads would just be additional burdens. He made his decision.

"Lie down," he ordered, "on your stomachs."

They hesitated. Yusuf pointed his pistol at the younger woman office worker. Her face wobbled and she began to cry silently. They slid from their chairs onto the floor. The fatter woman's dress rode up above her knees. Yusuf nudged each of the hostages with his foot.

"You, too," he said.

The estate agent and the teenage girl lay down.

"Stay there."

Yusuf disabled the computers and ripped the cords out of the two landline phones. Izzy threw the mobiles into the fire in the other room.

Shalima entered. "All loaded, Yusuf, ready to move."

"Get them going, then."

She ran out and Yusuf returned to his hostages lying on the floor. "You will hear the trains move out," he said, "but my comrade here will wait on the platform with orders to shoot you if you try to leave. Is that understood?"

There were mutterings from the floor.

He closed the door and they hurried out. Exultant, Yusuf shouted, "Inshallah!" to the old lady on the platform. "You are brave."

0900

Ibra joined Bargo in the driver's cabin of the cargo train and looked across at Charlie Hopwood. The elderly man's face, hit by glass splinters, was covered in blood, his eyes were staring and he was gasping for breath. He was in a state of shock. He'd be nothing but a problem, too much trouble. Quickly but gently he helped him out of the cab and lowered him to the platform.

"You're lucky, old man," he said, and leapt back into the cab. Bargo moved the power control lever to forward and the nuclear train moved, with great noise, past the platform's end, out onto the embankment and then onto the Kent Viaduct.

On the passenger train, Kal slid his power control lever to reverse and the 0851 to Lancaster began to move. Yusuf jumped on and slammed the door behind him. The train reversed out of the station, slightly behind the other train, onto the embankment and then the viaduct.

The two came to a halt next to each other: the two-coach

passenger Northern train and the DRS freight train with engines at each end of the two flatbed trucks. They were directly over the main channel of the River Kent.

0904

Almost at the end of their midweek break, Kate and Adam Feather were walking their Yorkshire terrier along the Arnside promenade.

"Look at that," said Adam, pointing at the train reversing onto the viaduct and coming to a halt next to one already there.

"What's happening?" asked Kate.

"No idea."

A small, curious crowd had gathered at the pier.

In the Carlisle HQ of the Cumbrian Police, Chief Superintendent Steve Mack was drinking his first coffee of the morning, strong and black.

"There's a call for you, sir," said his PA. "Won't speak to anyone but you. Arnside Police."

"Put them through. Steve Mack here. What's the problem?"

"We have a situation on the Kent Viaduct, sir."

The chief super listened. "Thank you," he said. "Do nothing. Stay there. I'll get back to you."

He put the phone down. "Jesus!" he said softly to himself.

Davoud Nariman had just decided where he would take Jenny that evening: the Bassoon Bar, hidden away in the Corinthia Hotel on Whitehall Place. He wanted to impress her, spend money, relax a little.

Then his phone rang.

"Chief Superintendent Steve Mack here, from Carlisle."

Davoud listened and the pieces of the jigsaw slotted into

place. So it was happening. His instinct had been right.

A spent nuclear fuel train. Hostages. The invisible had materialised. Their efforts had been in vain; they'd been too slow, the terrorists always one step ahead of them. A potential nuclear bomb, and on his watch. Ryan Hudson, the sleeper, had awoken with a vengeance. What would he be demanding? How could Davoud possibly resolve this?

The duty constable at Arnside seized the phone on its first ring.

"Sir?"

But the voice was a woman's. "Thought you ought to know. I've found a big inflatable dinghy washed up on the shore. A Zodiac, I think it is."

"Where?"

"Holme Island. Outboard still on it, but empty otherwise."

"And could I ask your name, madam?"

0908

Immediately the trains came to a halt, Benny and Ibra carried the explosives out of the passenger train, around the front of the first engine and climbed up onto one of the flatbed trucks. Benny gave the instructions. They had practised the procedure back in the Yemen. He placed the ninety-centimetre-long, thirty-centimetre-diameter section of grey plastic pipe on the top of one of the containers. Ibra then sprayed white expanding foam thickly around the pipe on the surface of the container. It would harden and hold the pipe rigidly in place. Benny pushed the inverted copper cone down the pipe until it touched the container top. It was a snug fit. Ibra unpacked the blocks of orange Semtex and Benny began to pack it into the pipe, pushing it hard so there were no air gaps. He had a fleeting memory of the Play-Doh he helped his young son model. He crammed in three blocks of Semtex. When the pipe was full he pushed a Phillips screwdriver into the centre of it to make a six-centimetre-deep hole. He then inserted the slender silver detonator. Ibra handed him the plastic lid they had cut from an old storage box, a small hole drilled into the centre of it. This Benny fitted over the detonator and pressed firmly down onto the pipe.

He worked expertly, his fingers deftly fitting a pair of white and red wires to the detonator. He led them down the side of the pipe and laid them on the already hardened foam. He attached a second pair of wires to the detonator and led them down the side of the pipe next to the first pair. He wrapped both pairs of wires tightly in black insulating tape right down to the surface of the white foam, and then taped them to the pipe. The second pair of wires he bent so they stuck up almost vertically.

He took the designated mobile phone out of his pocket and flipped off the cover. Ibra, meanwhile, had prepared the miniature soldering iron which he handed to Benny, who soldered the first pair of wires onto the phone's tiny circuit board. Then he clipped back the phone cover and placed the phone on the foam.

"Spray more foam over everything," he instructed Ibra. "We need it covered, out of sight. It's the insurance. Yusuf is a belt-and-braces man."

While Ibra did that, Benny soldered the second pair of wires to the circuit board of another phone.

"Just spray a thin layer of foam so we can bed the phone into it. It must be visible, and the wires that lead to it."

Ibra did as instructed. Benny looked at their handiwork.

"A neat job," he said.

He took out his own phone. The contact list consisted of just one number: the number he would ring to detonate the explosives.

"All set," he said.

They picked up their stuff, clambered down off the flatbed and went back to the passenger train.

Izzy bundled driver Geoff Firth out of the cab and into the first coach with the passengers. Izzy and Shalima guarded them, the old women slightly relieved to see a woman, the mother even more terrified. She'd read about jihadi women suicide bombers.

"I didn't think there would be children," said Izzy.

"I want a wee-wee," cried Daisy.

"See what I mean?" continued Izzy. "Problems."

"I really want a wee-wee."

Laura looked up at Shalima, her eyes questioning her.

"I need to take my medication," said the birder. "It's in my rucksack."

At one end of the trains Yusuf and Bargo stood guard, sniper rifles at the ready. At the other end, Kal did the same.

0923

A green Toyota Auris drove up to Arnside Station and parked behind a big white van. A man got out, locked his car and looked at his watch. Very early. He noticed the van's sliding door was open and looked in – empty except for some orange life jackets. He walked over to the Office and Information Centre, knowing there would be a warm fire in there and ten minutes to start his *Times* crossword.

He opened the outer door, closed it behind him to keep the lovely warmth in, popped his head round the open door into the inner office, and saw five people lying on the floor.

"What on earth…?!"

★

While Shalima kept watch over the hostages in the first coach, the other jihadists in the second were unpacking the provisions. All the stuff Yusuf had brought was scattered on the seats in this coach: cool boxes full of food and drinks, sleeping bags, toilet rolls, extra clothes, padded jackets.

Yusuf was outside, leaning on the iron railing that stretched the length of the viaduct. He was looking upriver over the sandbanks and tapping his mobile: 999. He smiled. Seagulls called and flew overhead.

"Which service do you require: police, ambulance, fire?"

He smiled again.

Softly, he said, "Counterterrorism."

Davoud texted Jenny. *Can't make tonight. Big operation starting. Out of London. Will ring when I can.* He paused for a moment and then tapped in two kisses.

Then he phoned Steve Mack back in Carlisle. The wheels were already turning.

30.
Friday 2nd October

Outside the Arnside Educational Institute on Church Hill, caretaker Colin Naylor tugged down the peak of his flat cap and opened the Perspex doors protecting the noticeboard. He took a last drag of his cigarette, threw it down and ground it into the gravel more forcibly than he needed to. The world had gone mad, even here in sleepy Arnside. He scowled and unrolled a large poster, held it in position on the board with his elbow and from his overalls pocket took a staple gun. He fired in the staples, three down each side, the gun punching them in. *ALL ACTIVITIES CANCELLED UNTIL FURTHER NOTICE* in threatening red ink.

Bloody taken over! With not even a by-your-leave. Bloody southerners mostly. This was his last task before being dismissed from the site 'until further notice'. They'd moved their own team in. Security, they said. "You'll still be paid, don't worry." Madmen, bad men and fools; that's what Colin thought of people in charge, especially politicians. He locked the noticeboard doors, watched some suits entering the institute, gave his left nostril a final pick with his grubby thumb, turned and left. *You reap what you sow*, he thought, without quite knowing what he meant.

Inside, the Joyce Nicholson Hall had been transformed into the Raven operations room. Earlier that afternoon Davoud and Oliver Bilclough, the Home Office representative, had flown in from London by military helicopter. Max Cox had been left instructions to find out anything else he could about Al-Qaeda in the Arab Peninsula, Jamie Lockhart had made top priority for his GCHQ team any communications from or to Arnside. Polly Beale had been left in temporary charge of the Thames House team. Hannah Walker in Rotherdyke was excited and rather overawed about being kept in the loop of the unfolding story; asked to forward any information gleaned from the grooming investigation that she thought might be relevant.

The army were establishing posts in the railwaymen's huts at each end of the Kent Viaduct; an SAS team was assembling at the Arnside yacht club; the Zodiac found on Holme Island had been driven over the bay and was already parked there. A tactical firearms unit would soon be on standby.

Inside the institute three army explosive experts in camouflage kit were getting familiar with the galley kitchen on the ground floor, and an anti-radiation team of four were drinking coffee in the café next to it, their white suits draped casually over chairs. The full-size snooker table was still in the snooker room, but the classroom used for an after-school club was now Davoud's office. The Willowbank Guest House along the promenade had been completely taken over, all previous bookings compulsorily cancelled, with compensation promised.

The floor of the Joyce Nicholson Hall, a gym usually used for badminton, table tennis, and Zumba and Pilates classes, had been covered by temporary sheets of chipboard. Davoud looked around. Trestle tables now filled the hall. Each table carried the initials of a different aspect of the operation: Special Branch manned by the overweight Gary Wallace from London who was already sweating in the overheated room; the Cumbria Counterterrorism Unit under the command of Chief Superintendent Steve Mack, a tall, fair-haired, bearded man with an honest smile and an immaculate black uniform.

The adjacent table was for the local Cumbria and Lancashire Police forces, tasked with finding out who were being held as hostages on the passenger train, all leave for the local forces having been cancelled. MI5 was represented by the unkempt, powerfully built Tim Bennett, and there was a table for Tamsin Crawford-Holmes who answered directly to the director general of the Security Service, with links to the CIA who were also monitoring cyberspace for messages and electronic chatter. At the army table sat Lieutenant Colonel Malcolm McPhail, in charge of the military part of the operation, whose last action had been a stake-out in Afghanistan and who was now overseeing the deployment of troops. He was in what Davoud assumed was shirtsleeved order: shirtsleeves rolled up to the elbow, no tie, collar open but with prominent red badges. The Lieutenant Colonel's khaki trousers vied with the chief superintendent's for sharpness of crease; the shoes of both men competitively polished. There were two empty tables: one labelled *Media Liaison*, a vital responsibility and the Home Office were still vetting people for that role; the other for a trio of experienced hostage negotiators. People were already tapping at keyboards and speaking on landlines or mobiles, some wearing earphones.

At the far end of the hall a large incident board had been erected and on each side computer screens were showing feeds from cameras in the railwaymen's huts – two empty, gleaming railway lines leading to the stationary trains – and from the helicopter out over the estuary: grey, empty water. On one side wall was an electronic map of the region showing where roadblocks might be set up, where military units were stationed and where the two helicopters currently were – one in the air near Sandside and the other on the ground at the decommissioned Cark airfield on the peninsula between the Kent and Leven Rivers; apparently now a skydiving centre with a café serving the local speciality of chilled Snickers.

Between the windows, Blu-Tacked to the wall were photos of Yusuf Javeed/Ryan Hudson looking down at them blankly.

Davoud was pleased that everything had been established so quickly, his instructions carried out to the letter. Back in his ex-classroom office, kiddies' chairs stacked in a corner, was a desk with hotlines to Downing Street and COBRA. He was awaiting a phone call from COBRA and a message from the hijackers. Someone on the train, presumably the leader, had phoned 999 demanding a number to contact. Davoud's operation mobile had been given. The two contacts would define the operation, give him something to work on. From his window he could not see the two parked trains, just a glimpse of the grey bay over the house eaves, where lines of starlings stood, packing the TV aerials.

What were the hijackers after? The silence from them was deliberate: to stoke up the tension, to keep everyone guessing. At least it wasn't happening among the millions in London – Sara, Jenny and his father were not at risk.

One phase of waiting had ended, only for another to begin. Stakes had never been so high, so unprecedented: the possibility of a nuclear wilderness in England's green and pleasant land. A fanatical young man holding the whip hand and thumbing his nose at the Western world; a young man who had kept one step ahead of the game, and so far succeeded with his audacious plan.

Now it was down to him, Davoud.

On the screen he saw the two suburban trains marooned on the viaduct of a provincial line – one carried a potential apocalypse, the other a group of terrified hostages, trapped by pure chance.

31.

In Cabinet Office Briefing Room A, Home Secretary Nicky Mason looked up at the fluorescent light that flickered, ticking and buzzing like a doom-laden Geiger counter. It was her call.

Prime Minister Cambourne was in China bribing the Chinese to take over the British nuclear industry – there must be a deadly irony in that somewhere. The bean counter was in Brussels, in a grotesque parody of charm, trying to persuade the Eurocrats into some face-saving fudge that would keep Britain in Europe, yet mollify the 'Kippers and their ilk. Jaunts and chickenshit – while here, Armageddon was on the doorstep.

Nicky and five other people were grouped at one end of the long table. Brief introductions had been made. She knew only one of them: slippery, eel-tongued, highly ambitious Minister of Defence Julian Pendlebury, in his city suit with a vivid pink-and-purple tie that she supposed was meant to signify a promise of unconventionality. He sat with a slight smile, watching her, relishing the pressure on her. Whatever they decided this evening, she would make sure he signed up for it, signature on the paper. The other four were shuffling paper. She drained her coffee cup.

"Right, let's start. What exactly is on this train?" she asked, looking at Roger from the Nuclear Decommissioning Authority. He was not what she had expected: fair, almost blond hair in a long ponytail, jeans and black leather jacket, low-heeled brown boots.

"There are two flasks of spent nuclear fuel, each on a flatbed wagon. Each flask weighs sixty tonnes and contains a skip of 2.5 tonnes of spent nuclear fuel."

"And what does 'spent' mean?"

"It is irradiated Uranium-235 which no longer produces enough energy to sustain a nuclear reaction in a thermal reactor. The fuel on this particular train comes from Hinckley Point in Somerset."

"So 'spent' means 'dead', does it?" asked the Home Secretary, whose degree from Oxford was a 2.1 in English.

"Unfortunately, no," replied Roger. "Many of the products of nuclear fission are short-lived or non-radioactive or both. But some are medium- or long-term radioactive isotopes. They continue to generate heat and radioactivity, even after being cooled in water for nine months at the reactors. You may have heard of Caesium-137 or Strontium-90, for instance. They were – are – major health risks at Chernobyl and Fukushima. Strontium-90 can cause bone cancer."

"And this stuff is being carted up and down the land along ordinary railway lines, through stations and cities, day and night?" Her anxiety must have shown; she saw the hint of a smirk on Julian's face at her discomfort. "Is there no military protection?" And here she looked at the Defence Secretary, seeing a chance to share the blame.

"There used to be a railway guard on each train, not police or special security, but that practice has been discontinued," said Roger.

"To save money, I suppose," said the Home Secretary.

Roger did not reply. He wasn't a spokesman for DRS who ran the trains.

"So," continued Nicky Mason, "we have two skips – as you called them – of radioactive waste. If those skips or flasks were blown up, what would happen?"

"A lot would depend on atmospheric conditions – the

wind, for instance; high- or low-pressure zones – and on the chemical form, volatility and particle size of the material. But radiation could theoretically spread over two hundred square miles, dispersed via a long-range radioactive plume. And that radiation, depending on its strength and distance from inhabitants, could cause almost immediate death or injury and, as at Hiroshima, produce deformities in foetuses."

She took a deep breath. "Hiroshima, for God's sake!" She'd seen the photographs and newsreels, interviews with survivors.

Very quietly, Roger added, "The Hiroshima atomic bomb released three million curies of radioactivity. Each of the flasks on this train contains about one million curies."

At that, there was silence in the room. The two politicians, who had decisions to make, stared at their closed, black iPads. Nicky felt the steady thump of her heartbeat.

Deborah, the Direct Rail Services representative, cleared her throat nervously. "But I have to say that over thirty-five years, more than fourteen thousand flasks and nine thousand tonnes of spent fuel have been successfully transported with no incidents or radioactive release."

"That's not very comforting at this moment," the Home Secretary snapped.

"We are absolutely confident those flasks cannot be breached," persisted Deborah.

"Well, you would say that!"

Deborah looked down at the table, then continued, "There have been many tests – here, in Europe and the USA. A train has been driven into a flask at a hundred miles per hour; the locomotive was destroyed but the flask sustained only cosmetic damage."

The Home Secretary nodded. "What contingency plans are there for this situation?" she asked, her eyes challenging the Defence Secretary.

Julian Pendlebury held her gaze. Now was not the time to falter. "European Council Directive 96/29/Euroatom does not apply to spent fuel consignments," he said.

"Which means there are no plans?" Exaggerated astonishment in her voice. He'd done his homework, but so had she: she knew the answer to her question.

"As I said, they are not required and therefore the local authorities along the route have no spent-fuel-flask-specific emergency plans." He wasn't giving an inch.

She turned to the fourth person at the table, Warrant Officer Matthew Brodie, sitting in his army camouflage kit, his cap neatly placed on his closed silver laptop. His face was professionally expressionless, but what must he be thinking of these civilians?

"How easy is it, Officer, for these flasks to be blown up?"

"The straight answer is: we don't know. But there is a risk that the flasks are vulnerable to a shaped explosive charge, or to being punctured by armour-piercing explosive rounds. If this was then followed by a fierce fire, the risk would be even higher that the flask would be breached."

"Do we know what weapons they have?"

"We know, Home Secretary, that they have already attached explosives to one of the flasks, most likely to be Semtex or Torpex. These will now be connected to detonators inside the passenger train, or will have been primed to explode when a specific phone number is keyed in. We have helicopter photos of the rifles they have in the train, Barrett M82s—"

"That doesn't mean anything to me," interrupted the Home Secretary.

"The armour-piercing rounds in these rifles comprise two stages: the first pierces the armour; the second fires an explosive designed to obliterate the internals of the target, in this case, the flask."

He was so matter-of-fact, an informed technician, not a

decision maker. A soldier, he did as he was ordered. People like him, all those in the operations room in Arnside, were waiting for orders. Her orders. Her and Julian's orders. The consequences of getting those orders wrong were terrifying.

She turned to Roger. "If the nuclear fuel does explode, what happens next?"

"Sheltering and evacuation countermeasures must have been implemented to prevent people being exposed to radiation higher than the nationally set dose emergency reference levels. For instance, depending on weather conditions, it might take thirty-nine seconds for the radiation plume to travel two kilometres. Evacuation would be necessary to a minimum of six kilometres from the explosion, and sheltering for up to seventy kilometres. Then there would be the clean-up afterwards. Decontamination of beta-gamma radioactivity would be necessary up to a hundred kilometres from the incident. The estimated cost of this is 8.5 billion pounds."

They say fear can be smelled, thought Nicky, taking out a handkerchief and dabbing at the sweat she felt on her upper lip. The room was warm. Money was meaningless. It was about the balance of probabilities.

"Has anyone claimed responsibility?" she asked.

"Not yet," replied Julian.

"Have the terrorists made their demands?"

"Not so far as I know."

"How many hostages are there? How many terrorists?"

"Operations will be finding that out."

Nicky turned to Polly Beale, the fifth member of the group. "You're in charge at the London end of the operation, Polly. No information from Thames House, no insights?"

Polly refused to rise to the bait, the implied blame. What an unpleasant woman the Home Secretary was, the worst kind of woman in power. "Everything we can do, has been done.

We are prepared up there at Arnside. We await the politicians' decisions."

The Home Secretary knew she was avoiding the big questions. She – and Julian – would have to come up with recommendations for the Prime Minister: to negotiate with the terrorists? To evacuate the local population? To inform the public? To raise the security risk from severe to its highest, critical?

She knew the official line: *We never negotiate with terrorists.* But she knew things went on out of sight. And did that line automatically apply to this unprecedented situation, when the stakes were higher than ever before?

"I suppose," she asked Julian, "a snap SAS raid is out of the question?" A swift, dramatic damage-limitation exercise would be the best solution.

All eyes were on Julian. How relieved the other four must be that this responsibility was way above their pay level. There were no right answers to these questions, only varying degrees of wrong.

"I think," said Julian, "we have all the information we need from these good people. The decisions are now political and military."

And confidential, thought Nicky. "Thank you," she said, nodding to Deborah, Roger and Matthew, trying to smile. "Stay in London, we may need to consult with you again. And you, Polly."

They rose and left; the door closed behind them.

"The first thing," said Nicky, "is to get the fucking Prime Minister back here."

Julian nodded. "Indeed, the buck stops with him."

"In the meantime, we have to make some decisions."

"Indeed we do."

She sensed a truce between them, born out of desperation, she knew.

"Just going for a pee," said Julian.

While Julian peed and Nicky waited for more coffee to arrive, each thought basically along the same lines. The responsibility was huge, terrifying: the fate of the hostages was dwarfed by the radiation issue. If they handled this unprecedented crisis successfully, their careers would flourish; if they failed, their political lives were doomed. Being greedy for individual success might double the kudos or the disgrace. More pragmatic to share the victory or the defeat. It was the safest way. Their careers might just survive if they worked together. If they did not cooperate, either or both could fall. When it was all over, whatever the outcome, each would surely be able to outmanoeuvre the other. Both knew the Home Secretary was the senior of the two, which meant she had further to fall.

When Julian returned, Nicky poured the coffee.

"No sugar?"

"No thanks."

They'd never heard of Arnside before. Somehow the figures and statistics they'd just heard had made the scenes up there more real than the TV pictures.

"The first question," said Nicky, "is: do we negotiate?"

"And the answer is no," said Julian.

"I agree. It's the established rule: we do not negotiate with terrorists. It's a sign of weakness, it sets a precedent and encourages the terrorists, especially to kidnap and ransom. That is basically what we have here."

Nicky stirred some milk into her coffee. "The second question is: what about evacuation?"

"Well, there are no grey areas: either we do or we don't."

"If we don't, and the crisis is averted, it will be seen as the right, brave decision. But in a worst-case scenario, we could be responsible for thousands of deaths and appalling injuries. Especially as the world will know we had the information and knew the consequences."

"If we do evacuate," said Julian, "we have to give the public the reasons for it, spell out the extreme nature of the danger. That would cause panic, and not just in the immediate area. There would be a run on banks, investors would turn tail, the FT index would plummet. The whole country would be under siege, not just Morecambe bloody Bay."

Nicky noticed there was a sheen of perspiration above his upper lip. So he was feeling the pace.

"If we told the public anything near to the truth," she said, "it would cause self-evacuation anyway, even if we ordered people to stay and take shelter. They wouldn't believe we were telling the whole story."

"Politicians always lie, you mean?" Julian said, smiling.

"Yes, as you know, that's the general perception. They've long ago ceased to trust us."

"Even if we found some experts to tell them that the fuel was really spent, that the flasks were invincible?"

"Yes," said Nicky. "Because if that were true, why haven't we sent in the SAS?"

"Because the hostages would die."

"A small price to pay for the safety of everyone else. Wouldn't the terrorists shoot them anyway, if we didn't meet their demands? Wouldn't they be killed when the explosives were detonated, even if the flasks remained intact?"

"You mean we sacrifice them?" asked Julian.

"We're talking possible scenarios, not what we'd advocate."

"Most people, Nicky, see radiation as a fate worse than death. That is the terrorists' biggest weapon: fear. They will exploit it by using social media to tell people what will happen if they don't get what they want."

"They've got us by the short and curlies, then."

"Worse than that, aren't Brazilians the fashion?"

"My God, Julian, how can you joke?!"

"Black humour, my dear, always a survival tool."

"I find it amazing that everyone – the military, the government, the nuclear industry – has turned a blind eye to this sort of threat."

"We are the government, Nicky. Sadly, it's happened on our watch. Serendipity."

"So we instruct the people: *Go in, stay in, tune in* and leave it at that? That would be pathetic. Our necks would be on the block. And, as we know, there are willing executioners – among our friends more than our enemies."

They both pondered the truth of that.

"They are in a win-win situation, aren't they?" said Nicky. "They win if we give in to whatever demands they make and they fly back to whatever godforsaken land they've bloody come from. They win if we don't give in and they blow up the fuel and the hostages and take themselves up to Paradise – whether or not the radiation happens."

"If we don't evacuate," mused Julian, "couldn't that be seen as provocative, urge them to be even more reckless? By the way, who's in charge up there?"

Nicky scrolled her iPad. "MI5 man, Davoud Nariman, Muslim by birth but now a non-believer, good track record. Iranian parents."

"Christ, that really adds to the mix."

Nicky drained her coffee. "Right. Here's what I suggest. One, that His Smarminess gets his backside back here from China ASAP. We stress that this is the country's biggest crisis since the Blitz. Two, publicly we stick to no negotiation, but behind the scenes we try to get things moving. Three, the public are told the truth."

"Now, be careful, Nicky, this is untrodden ground."

Nicky ignored him. "They still may not believe us, but afterwards, we can't be accused of deception."

"So, what is this truth?"

"That the fuel is still radioactive; that the flasks are strong, but we cannot guarantee they can't be broken open by the terrorists' weapons; that if they are the radiation could contaminate a specified area, with all the consequences. But we will have experts doing the explaining, not politicians. Experts who will get it right or wrong, not us."

"Sleight of hand, Home Secretary. You haven't lost your touch."

Again, she ignored him. "Four, we order evacuation, set up roadblocks etc. immediately, make sure the military are fully prepared. Five, the security situation is raised from severe to critical."

"We sing from the same songbook."

"Well, that's a change. Crises bring people together."

"Sadly, only for a time."

"So, we're agreed," summed up Nicky. "I'll draft the message now, you countersign it, we send it to the PM. Then it's his pigeon."

Deflect the responsibility as soon as possible: that was the name of the game.

32.

SATURDAY 3RD OCTOBER

After five hours of broken sleep under an overly warm duvet, Davoud had been in his makeshift office at six o'clock. Every desk in the hall had been manned all night, but the only one to produce any additional information was the Cumbria and Lancashire Police desk. There were ten hostages on the train: four men (including a guard and driver), four women, and – worst of all – two young children. The hijackers had the full pack.

What must it be like on the train? The fear and isolation, the mother trying to reassure her children and comfort them. The crazed, rampant fundamentalists, toting guns, shouting, threatening. Were they injured? Did they know the full significance of the cargo on the freight train?

Then at 0645 his mobile buzzed. There was a message: *We have hostages, explosives fixed to one of the nuclear fuel flasks (photo attached). We have sniper rifles with high-explosive, armour-piercing rounds ready to be shot at the flask. We demand the freedom of Suleiman al-Hariri. Allah is great. Yusuf Javeed.*

Davoud looked at the attachment. The photo was a close-up of the explosives on the flask, a rifle propped up.

He strode into the hall. "Lieutenant Colonel, I'm sure they won't be lying but can you check out what they say about these weapons?"

He then forwarded the message to Whitehall, and circulated it and the photo to each of the desks. "Jesus" was the most common response. He returned to his office.

All this for Suleiman? Who was Yusuf working for? ISIS?

Al-Qaeda? Some hitherto obscure group? They'd raised the bar from the London bombings and even from the Twin Towers. How many hijackers were there? Would they really press the trigger – the very first use of a nuclear weapon, headed by a twenty-five-year-old Islamic convert from somewhere called Keighley? Were there people higher up the jihadist organisation Davoud could parley with, people older, wiser, more responsible, with a wider vision?

He could think only of Hiroshima, the only images and information he had about the effects of radioactive fallout. That had been atomic. Things had become even more horrific with nuclear, but he didn't know how. The Twin Towers and London had been devastating but finite, but that mushroom cloud, the fallout, the long-term effects, the deformed births – all of that was immeasurable. It was inconceivable that this last taboo would be broken for the freedom of one man, and in the name of a religion. Davoud's religion, as it once had been, before it slaughtered his mother and sister.

Message received; the problem defined. There were no precedents to work with, but they needed to map out alternative scenarios. And what were COBRA deciding?

His second call came forty-five minutes later.

"The Prime Minister for you."

There was a pause, and Davoud felt his throat go dry. Why did he suddenly feel so small, like a schoolboy waiting outside his headmaster's door? Being face-to-face with power, he supposed.

"Mr Nariman?"

"Yes, Prime Minister."

"Gideon Cambourne here, on the plane back from China. Can you hear me OK?"

"The line is clear, no problem."

"Some decisions for you: we will not storm the train – the stakes are too high. We do not negotiate. Put out a public statement telling the truth about the situation, radiation dangers etc. – get the experts in, no melodrama, but the facts and the differing opinions. Evacuate everyone within twenty kilometres of the incident immediately, yourselves the only exceptions. The Home Secretary is your immediate point of contact. I'll expect a briefing from you when I get back to London. Is all that clear?"

"Absolutely."

"It's a tough situation, the toughest. I know you'll handle it."

The line went dead.

Davoud took a deep breath and walked into the hall. He called for silence and gave them the Prime Minister's decisions. He sensed two responses: an immediate sense of relief – they knew where they were and what jobs they had to do – and also a sense of duty, of their responsibility, which was at once humbling and energising. There was a surge of activity across the room. Davoud assembled the main players in his office and tasks were allocated. Times for the announcement were agreed; the complex operation of evacuation was planned: people prioritised (there were several nursing homes in the small town), transport organised, lists of possible destinations compiled. Many would stay with family and friends, but not all. Businesses would be closed. The army would patrol the empty town to prevent looting. Experienced hostage negotiators were already travelling up from London.

If things went wrong, they would be at the epicentre. And it would be his responsibility.

33.
SUNDAY 4TH OCTOBER

Yesterday Yusuf had decreed that the male passengers be separated into the second coach. Geoff Firth, the elderly engine driver, and Emily began to object, seeing strength in numbers. But Kal grabbed Geoff by the shoulders, hauled him out of his seat and dragged him away.

"Any more problems?" snarled Bargo, brandishing his pistol and ostentatiously clicking off the safety catch.

Ibra and Benny glanced quickly at each other, raised their eyebrows.

"There's no need for that," said Joan quietly, calmly looking up at him.

There were no more objections and the men filed out.

"And you?" challenged Bargo, pointing his pistol at Emily. "You are a Muslim?"

He was so fierce and quick to anger. Emily knew she had to appear calm, but what was the least dangerous reply? "Yes," she said quietly, opting for the truth.

"So why do you dress like a whore?" snapped Bargo, indicating her bare arms. She was wearing a loose white T-shirt with *LUNT* across it in capital letters and, underneath, in smaller letters, *Lancaster University Netball Team*.

"I wear what you wear," she said, nodding towards his black T-shirt.

"You are a woman!" he shouted. "You must not reveal any parts of your body except your face and hands. You will cover yourself."

Emily looked up at his burning eyes, saw flecks of spittle

at the corners of his mouth. She had read how ISIS and Al-Qaeda and even Muslim sects killed fellow Muslims who did not agree with them.

Joan, sitting opposite Emily, had her hands on the table. Emily noticed her fingers moving to indicate *Stay cool*. But she would not simply submit to this crazy man.

"*The best garment is the garment of righteousness*," she quoted.

For a moment Bargo was speechless. Then his eyes blazed and he raised his arm to her. Emily flinched. Then Yusuf appeared and tapped Bargo on the shoulder.

Bargo wheeled round. "She…" he spat.

"I know," said Yusuf. He faced Emily. "Cover yourself up," he said quietly. "It would be better."

Emily raised her eyebrows slightly, half-smiled, then nodded. It wasn't time for a discussion of the semantics of the Q'uran or the Hadith. She pulled on her cardigan.

"And your hair," instructed Yusuf.

Joan passed her a scarf. Emily noted that Shalima had watched but said nothing.

Shalima thought the arrangement better for everyone. A greater sense of support among the hostages there might have been, but also more likelihood of getting on each other's nerves. Noah cuddled up to his mother, who was desperate to pretend that all this was an adventure, fun even. Daisy, leaning into Muriel, had slept. But the women had only dozed. Bleary-eyed and irritable, scared of what might happen, they were restless and thirsty, clothes feeling bulky and grubby. The sun was shining again and the coach was already warm and stale-smelling.

A list of supplies needed had been texted yesterday to the head of the operation, and items had been delivered early this morning: both sides needed the hostages alive. Yusuf and

Shalima watched four unarmed soldiers in camouflage kit carry containers along the railway track from Arnside Station and deposit them fifty yards from the trains. Once they returned to the platform, Kal and Bargo, with their Barrett M82 rifles slung over their shoulders, made two trips to bring the boxes in.

Emily was already wearing the long-sleeved turquoise blouse and the scarf that Yusuf had demanded she wear, as a proper Muslim. Now Shalima checked the contents against the list she had compiled: food and water were first. Yusuf had specified halal food for all the adults: jihadists and hostages would eat the same, that way poisoning was not possible. There were five sets of pills for the old birdwatcher who had heart problems. Shalima had asked Laura what her kids needed. So now Laura was unpacking the toy laptop for Noah and the comfort blanket and teddy for Daisy, brought from their home by their terrified and helpless father, presumably. Was he a good father like Rafiq would have been? Shalima thought of her friend's children back in the Yemen, now fatherless, and of the cruelties of her own father. All chance, the throw of the dice? No, the will of Allah.

There were crayons, fibre pens, activity books – *Fireman Sam* for Noah and *Peppa Pig* for Daisy – and Lego and Playmobil sets. Someone with a sense of humour had chosen the emergency service sets: firemen and helicopters, police, ambulance and rescue boat. Shalima could see that Izzy, bored with the tedium, was tempted to defy Yusuf and join in the play, probably thinking of his own two young children back in Holland.

Late last night she had heard the argument outside the carriage. Izzy gesticulating, insisting, "We cannot keep the children. How can we confine them for days? They will cry and want to run about. They will drive us all crazy."

But Yusuf had stood firm: "These kids are our best

bargaining counters, our aces in the pack. No one out there will want them harmed."

"I don't want them harmed," yelled Izzy. "I did not think this would be a mission to slaughter kids. I am not ISIS."

"I don't want them to die either," replied Yusuf calmly. "If they die, it will be because of the British government's decisions, not ours."

"Bullshit – you may be prepared to kill them, but I am not."

"They stay."

Izzy had stalked off and Shalima had seen Yusuf muttering to Bargo, nodding in Izzy's direction.

If the children were killed, thought Shalima, it would only be because they all would be killed, one way or another. She dismissed the thought: it would be the will of Allah.

She turned to the other items in the delivery. There were packs of cards and dominoes for the adults, magazines and novels, sanitary towels, toilet paper, soap, toothpaste and toothbrushes. It was like running a hotel. But all to ease the tension, to make their own job more manageable. They might be here for days.

Apart from ordering, "No fraternisation", Yusuf had kept away from the details. Shalima saw he was already in love with his role as leader, deliberately keeping a distance, just checking the guard rota in the two carriages and talking tough, his red-and-white-checked keffiyeh now permanently worn.

On their iPhones the jihadists watched the BBC one o'clock news. They heard the announcement of no negotiation.

"This is what we expected," said Yusuf. "But it is only the starting point. They'll change, you'll see."

Then came the news of compulsory evacuation. From the train they soon saw on Arnside promenade lines of cars and coaches drawing up and then leaving. They watched a train pull into the station from the south and, an hour later, pull out again.

Yusuf said nothing. He paced the carriage. Shalima, too, kept her thoughts to herself. She wondered if some of the others were now slightly overawed, as she was, by the situation into which they had put themselves. She'd noted that everyone in the team had performed all five of the daily prayers separately: their prayers had an extra intensity. Now they were actually here, the nuclear fuel with explosives attached almost within arm's reach, *could* she give the order to detonate?

Kal and Bargo were pumped up with power and self-importance, striding through the carriages and out onto the viaduct, their eyes fiery. The others seemed more sunk into themselves: Izzy brooding in a corner seat, Benny with his eyes closed and his earphones in, Ibra self-contained, eyes drooping, and reading a novel he'd brought with him.

Yusuf stood at the open door of the carriage, hardly conscious of the fresh air on his face. He tapped out a text on his iPhone, the next stage, and sent it to the number he'd been given, the top man. He looked across the water towards the small town, envisaged the beep of the top man's phone, the top man snatching it up to read. His face. Yusuf smiled. *What now, top man?*

The afternoon passed as slowly as the tide inching in, then out. Noah and Daisy squabbled. They all needed to move and stretch. Yusuf eventually agreed. He texted Davoud to explain. Davoud answered that he understood. So Noah and Daisy and their mum, accompanied by Shalima, Kal and Bargo, were allowed half an hour out, fifty yards of track to run on, peering over the rails to the sea and sand below, shouting and laughing in the breeze. The men were wary, holding their rifles at the ready. Laura was grateful; ludicrous in this situation. She must not let her children sense her terror.

The carriages heated up and the toilets smelled. In the

men's carriage cards and dominoes grew tiresome. Geoff's hands were trembling; he could not control them. Paul thought about his wife Mary. She would be at church, about the Lord's business and praying for him. It was her turn on the flower rota this week. Finlay dozed restlessly.

Yusuf was aloof but Shalima sensed simmering tensions in the team, their purposefulness stalled, pent-up. She noticed that either Kal or Bargo was always on duty. The tired adult hostages dozed, occasionally glanced at the skip of nuclear fuel, took notice of their guards' rifles and pistols. Muriel read a story to Daisy, who had her thumb in her mouth.

Davoud's face was grim as he replaced the phone on his desk. He knew that when he informed the Home Secretary of this latest development, it would make no difference. The government would not shift. The professional negotiators had arrived, three of them, but the jihadists refused to speak with them. There was nothing he could do. He had sent in all the supplies they had asked for, knowing that cooperation was the only way of keeping possible communication open. The evacuation was proceeding smoothly: alternative accommodation had been readily made available by relatives, friends, hotels and total strangers. Community, solidarity. Even nursing home residents had been found places. Why did it take catastrophe to bring out the best in people? Most of the residents had gone willingly; a few old people had resisted. They had never lived anywhere else. "Gently, gently," Davoud had instructed. "But they have to go."

And now the message from the leader. He had expected it. Of course the jihadists would ramp up the odds. They had only two weapons: the hostages and the nuclear fuel. Their leader had eight adults and two kids as leverage before he moved on to use the fuel. Was there a point at which some of the jihadists would feel a powerful self-disgust? Davoud doubted it. Would the government blink? Unlikely. Very soon the hijackers would post stuff on Twitter or Facebook or YouTube; the world would watch minute by minute. They would watch the first killing live. When would the general population decide they could stand no more 'in their name' and demand that the lives of these innocent passengers were worth more than the freedom of any convicted Islamist bomber? Let alone the threat of nuclear radiation.

And when would he, Davoud, agree with them? His mother and sister had been slaughtered in that suicide bombing masterminded by Suleiman. Was it his turn now to preside over the slaughter of other innocents? Would his crime rival that of Suleiman?

Within fifteen minutes of the terrorist leader's message being forwarded to the Home Office, the reply came through: *No change. Stand firm.*

How much easier it was to make decisions in those imperial rooms in Whitehall, hung with portraits of leaders and battle scenes. Civilised discussion, coffee, maybe even subdued laughter, then closing tablets and moving on to another meeting. Far away from the steady stream of evacuees, from the two trains parked on the viaduct like paralysed grubs, from the lives locked in them, from the fear.

34.
Monday 5th October

At 0830 in the men's carriage, Geoff's nose wrinkled at the sour smell of milk gone off. He and Paul were watching the tide recede, exposing mudflats around the viaduct, populated with gulls. Keith, the old birder, was dozing in the sun which shone in through the train windows. The table was littered with paper cups and plates and a packet of Cheerios. In the women's carriage, Noah and Daisy were colouring in, encouraged by Joan and their mother. Sleeping bags lay untidily on seats. The air outside was still, like a summer's day, no waves on the water. Inside, the air was musty. The four jihadists not on duty were sleeping at the far end of the men's carriage.

Yusuf strode in, pistol in hand, keffiyeh at his neck, and glared down at the men. "Into the other carriage," he barked.

Finlay looked up at him, impassive. The two railwaymen began to rise from their seats. Keith was startled out of his doze by the harsh voice. Laboriously he got out of his seat and stretched his body, slowly straightening his knees.

"Move," shouted Yusuf.

The four men shuffled into the women's carriage.

"Sit there," instructed Yusuf, pointing with his pistol to the table next to the breakfast table.

Laura shushed her children and the adults were silent. Emily and Finlay looked at Yusuf, the others out of the window or at the tabletop. An announcement.

Yusuf stood, tall and gangly, above them. Shalima did not know what he was going to say. She noticed the stubble, fair on his chin and skull, eyes intense and slightly protuberant, shoulders hunched a little, arms thin. The mantis again.

Yusuf bowed his head. "Allahu Akbar," he intoned. "Glory to Allah." He paused, let his eyes roam over each of them. "We have a problem."

Noah started to prod his sister with a crayon. She edged towards her mother. "Shh," said Laura, scared of attracting attention to them.

"You will have seen that the town is being evacuated," continued Yusuf, "because of the fear of a nuclear explosion." He nodded towards the window. "Those crates you see" – all the adults turned to look – "contain nuclear fuel, one of them now with a bomb attached. And our rifles have high-explosive, armour-piercing ammunition which will also explode them."

He heard the indrawn breaths, saw their faces stiffen. A soft, whimpered "Oh no" from Joan. Emily frowned at him with disbelief.

"You two railwaymen will confirm the cargo."

Geoff and Paul nodded, their faces drawn. They had recognised the flatbed truck and its flask, familiar on this line, but said nothing. They hadn't wanted to panic the other hostages any more.

"On Saturday we informed the authorities of our demands. Yesterday, your holy day, we received their reply. We also saw it on the TV news. They will not negotiate with us."

Finlay raised his hand.

Yusuf smiled at him. Finlay was only a few years younger than him, but like a schoolboy.

"Yes?"

"Are we allowed to know your demands?" asked Finlay.

"Of course. Then you will be able to calculate how much your fine democratic government thinks you are worth. In one of your prisons near London is Suleiman al-Hariri, a great man and one of the leaders of Al-Qaeda." Pause. "We are Al-Qaeda."

Yusuf sensed the immediate fear this name produced. His body straightened, his chin thrust out. "The same Al-Qaeda that destroyed the Twin Towers in New York. We demand that Suleiman be freed."

The eyes of the hostages were nervously flickering between each other. Daisy was cuddled up next to her mother. Noah was now scribbling with a bright red crayon, telling a story quietly to himself.

"The question is," continued Yusuf, "how do we convince your government that we are serious? The nuclear fuel is, of course, our last resort." He paused and looked round them again. Shalima saw how he loved playing this game with them. "But before the fuel, we have you."

Again he paused to let the significance of that sink in, saw fear and incomprehension in their eyes, but in Finlay he saw an ironic defiance. Suddenly he heard coughing and spluttering. He turned and saw it was Ibra. He glared at him, furious that his moment had been spoiled.

"Listen carefully," continued Yusuf quietly. "I have sent them a message. If there is no progress by noon tomorrow, if there is still no negotiation… then one of you I will select to be killed. Only that way will they understand."

Muriel crossed herself; Laura gasped and held Daisy closer. The others stared back at Yusuf, stony-faced. Finlay stared out across the estuary.

"I will choose," said Yusuf. "Unless one of you volunteers. Either way, a body will be tipped into the sea" – he looked at his watch – "twenty-seven hours from now, with a bullet in the back of the head."

Yusuf looked behind him and saw that Kal and Bargo were grinning. Shalima looked stern.

"Thousands of Muslim men, women and children,"

said Yusuf to the two tables of hostages, "have been killed by British bombs, bullets, drones and missiles. This will be just one British life, the only one necessary, we hope. It is up to your British government. If one of you has to die, it will be their responsibility."

He looked at Kal and Bargo. "Take the men back to their carriage."

As they filed out he smiled at Shalima. He was intoxicated with power, with a renewed confidence that he was a leader of men. She had no doubt that he would do the killing himself. Yusuf stepped out of the carriage onto the railway line. Ibra was coughing again, groaning. Shalima turned to him and saw that sweat was running down his face, but he was shivering.

"Lay him down and cover him up, Izzy. He's ill with something." She turned to the women hostages and looked at Muriel. "You're a nurse, aren't you?"

Muriel nodded. "A long time ago."

"We may need you," Shalima said, surprised at her own natural politeness.

Back in the men's carriage the four hostages settled round one table. There was a gentle rhythmic snoring from the sleeping jihadists at the far end. Keith the birder sat by the window.

"Look," he said, pointing, "on that river channel buoy: a cormorant drying its wings."

They all looked.

"What did that man say?" asked Keith. "The batteries in my hearing aids ran out and I couldn't hear a thing. By the look on your faces it was something serious."

Finlay leaned towards him and said slowly, enunciating the words carefully, "S-something or other, an Al-Qaeda big cheese, is in a London prison. This lot want him freed, that's what it's all about."

Paul, the ticket collector, said, "The government refuse to negotiate. Skinny miladdo there has given them until noon tomorrow to open negotiations, or else."

"Or else what?" asked Keith, frowning as he concentrated on lip-reading.

"Or else," said the train driver Geoff, mouthing the words exaggeratedly, "he fucking shoots one of us dead. One of us hostages. And drops the body in the sea. He chooses who it is unless someone volunteers."

The four men didn't look at each other.

"It will be low tide at lunchtime tomorrow," muttered Paul.

A low grunt interrupted the snoring at the back, and then it returned to its rhythm.

"Governments can't negotiate with terrorists. They're right," said the old birder. "It would just encourage kidnappings like this, and ransoms."

"That means," said Finlay, touching the old man's hand to draw attention to his lips, "that one of us round this table has to be the volunteer." Finlay was fascinated: he found the situation as exciting as terrifying. As if he was a detached observer.

"Because it's women and children to be saved first, you mean?" said Geoff.

"What? I didn't catch that," said Keith.

Geoff repeated his words, shaping the syllables.

Finlay laughed. "No offence, mate, but this is getting like a pantomime." His mouth working wide and open, his tongue against the backs of his teeth, his lips shaping each consonant.

Keith smiled and shrugged his shoulders. "Sorry, can't be helped."

"It's like that scenario of being in a lifeboat," continued Finlay; "one person has to be thrown out so the others survive. Wasn't there a film?"

Paul looked at his watch. "So one of us has twenty-six hours to live."

They sat in silence. The sun was higher now, the sandbanks gleaming. The men watched the water flow unceasingly beneath the curving viaduct on which stood the two stationary trains, next to each other as if harnessed, coupled. They knew that neither the terrorist leader nor the government would change their minds.

"Look," enthused Keith, pointing, "a heron."

All four watched it flap by, stately, long legs trailing. Oblivious of the drama below.

Paul wondered who the hell this Solomon guy was: what had he done, why was he so important he could not be freed?

Geoff wondered why the government thought his life – and each of the other hostages – was less precious than Solomon's freedom. *If they keep him in prison*, thought Geoff, *I die. But other terrorist conspirators and bomb-makers will replace him, so my death will have achieved nothing.*

Finlay wondered if the other three were doing what he was doing: trying to envisage his world without him. What would be lost to his family and friends, his girlfriend Moira? Who would mourn him? Would the world be less without him? He had no career, no grand plans, so what would be the pleasures he would forgo, or the responsibilities he would avoid? He smiled to himself: perhaps it should be like a game – each of them write on a piece of paper three criteria which should influence the choice. Then collate them and see how much agreement there was. How much would they all try to choose criteria that let them off the hook? For instance: who had the longest life still to live? Or, who had the most dependents? Tricky.

Keith was watching black-headed gulls standing on the sandbanks. Was this what his life had narrowed down to? His wife Annie had died eight years ago, slowly, fighting cancer.

Since then, no one depended on him. Their only daughter Julie had lived near Vancouver for more than twenty years, two children and happily married, so far as he knew. He had visited once. *To be honest,* he thought, *I know neither my daughter nor my grandchildren. I will probably never see them again.* He had a couple of friends he occasionally went crown green bowling with, and he had this, birding. Watching his wife die painfully, his belief in any God or afterlife had disappeared.

Then the flock of gulls flew off. Something had put them up. He scanned the sky for a harrier: no sign. To tell the truth, the effort of filling his days was sometimes tiring and tedious, waiting for the evening telly. He had enjoyed his seventy-five years, had perhaps more than his fair share of life's pleasures and challenges. Mustn't be greedy. These jihadists were evil lunatics, but they called the shots now. What was his own life compared to all the other younger lives corralled on this train? Those young kids: the old made space for the next generation. That was how it was. His sacrifice wouldn't be so big – maybe he had only another two or three years left, anyway. He only survived because of medication. Perhaps we all expected too much, to be kept alive whatever the cost.

He gave a big sigh and looked each of them steadily in the eye. The others looked at him briefly, then glanced away.

"Gentlemen, you can relax," he said. "It has to be me."

After a brief pause, each head turned to him. A fly was buzzing, butting against the window. The air was heating up.

And again Finlay wondered if Geoff and Paul felt the same as he did: a rush of relief, even exultation, then gratitude, then admiration and pity for the old man.

In the women's carriage, Ibra sat hunched in the corner of a seat at the far end. He was shivering but had wrapped himself in his sleeping bag.

"I'm aching all over, every muscle," he told Shalima. "And I've got a blinding headache."

"Probably man flu," she said.

She gave him a couple of Lemsip Max from the medical supplies they'd asked for. She didn't want to involve Muriel the nurse any more than was necessary.

It was four days since any of them had washed properly. Their heads were itching, their clothes felt dirty. The air in the carriage was stale, the water tanks would soon need to be refilled, the toilets would soon be blocked. Fear and panic had turned into a helpless anxiety. Not having slept properly, they were dulled by fatigue. They needed exercise; just standing up and stretching was not enough. They needed fresh air. The still, sunny days outside mocked them.

At one of the tables, Noah was playing with his Fireman Sam figures. Firefighter Penny was driving *Neptune* the rescue boat, Fireman Sam and Elvis were driving *Jupiter* the fire engine, and Tom Thomas was piloting the helicopter. As Noah moved them around he was telling their story to Emily, who encouraged him to develop the story with questions. On the table opposite, Daisy was arranging fences around the duck pond, a sheepdog was herding a flock of sheep and two cows were waiting to be milked at the dairy. She was discussing it all with Joan and her mum. Izzy leaned back in his seat and watched. He had a sudden longing to be with his own kids, about the same age, to play with them, see them laugh, cuddle them, read them stories. He leaned forward and placed Fireman Elvis into the rescue boat. Noah looked up at him, glared at him and removed Elvis. Izzy shrugged and laughed. He loved to provoke the wilfulness of young children, marvelled at how early it developed.

The women had come to their own conclusions about Yusuf's threat. They said nothing to each other, but each decided that Laura would not be chosen as the first victim: her children would be too difficult to manage and they were their ultimate bargaining tool. Muriel the nurse would be kept, too. So only Emily and Joan were left. Emily was a Muslim, so that left Joan the most vulnerable. But Joan knew the male hostages, too, would be making calculations. She was sure the first victim would be chosen from them.

"I'm worried about my husband," she said to Muriel. "Colin can generally fend for himself, cook and so on. But I sometimes have to remind him to take his warfarin tablets."

"He can miss a few and come to no harm," Nurse Muriel reassured her.

"It's a pity my daughter lives so far away. Colin will have phoned her. Maybe she'll get time off to come up and stay with him. But it's difficult with her being a deputy head teacher. And he'll tell her not to. He's due at his bowling club today; the last match of the season. I hope he goes. It'll take his mind off things. He'll be worried sick." She stared out of the window and Muriel held her hand.

"Peter will have no idea," said Muriel.

"Your son. He's out in Singapore, isn't he?"

"Yes. He won't know I'm on this train. At least he won't be worrying, not until he makes his regular call on Wednesday evening and I don't answer it."

Joan knew that Muriel had filled her life since her husband had died seven years ago, working in a charity shop, doing stuff at church, joining a rag-rugging group. She was a brave woman.

Emily looked up and shielded her eyes from the sun. "Where are you from?" she asked Izzy.

"Netherlands," he said quietly, deciding to ignore Yusuf's instructions not to fraternise, as he put it. "A small town on the North Sea coast."

"And you have children?"

"Two," he said, "a girl and a boy."

Noah told her that the helicopter was flying out over the boat to help the rescue. She nodded and smiled at him. Then she said to Izzy, "My Allah is a merciful God."

Izzy's smile disappeared. He straightened up.

"Muhammad himself looked after his children," continued Emily.

Izzy adjusted the rifle strap over his shoulder and stared out of the window.

Later that morning Laura asked Shalima if the children could go outside and run about a little. They had become noisier and cheekier, restless. Chasing along the corridor between the seats had lost its appeal.

"Playing on the railway line," replied Shalima, trying to joke, but she could see the situation was becoming difficult. The children would irritate everyone, heightening the tension in the enclosed space. Again, Yusuf allowed them out. Again, they scampered and laughed. When they returned, the atmosphere had eased a little. Perhaps there was even a little more trust. The children had snacks of raisins and blueberry wheats, as they did at home, because Laura had persuaded Shalima that keeping up their routines was essential.

It was in this peaceful interlude that Joan spoke to Kal as he lounged by her seat, chewing gum.

"I'm an old woman, young man," she said. "And I have learned something from life."

Kal was bored. "What is that, then?" he asked.

"I have heard you talking with Izzy. He has children at home. No loving parent would allow the suffering and unhappiness there is in the world to happen to their children: the famine and disease, the cruelty of men to each other. So there can be no loving God that allows all that to happen. So

I don't believe in God, young man. I was taught to, as a child, but it's all a fairy story."

Kal looked down at her, impassive. Joan sensed Muriel was listening.

"You are young and still have much to live through. How can you be so sure that what you have been told is right? Do you never have doubts? If it was Izzy's two children, taken hostage like these by men with guns, would you think the world was just, that the God in charge was merciful, as your Allah is supposed to be?"

Bargo had been listening. At the word 'Allah', he tensed. Joan saw his knuckles whiten where he held his rifle. His eyes glittered with anger. She thought he might strike her.

He bent his head nearer to her face and said fiercely, "All over the world your government has killed my people – Muslim men, women and children, babies burned with bombs. We have to stop that, make your government think again. That is why we do this, why we point our weapons at that nuclear fuel. We are at war with you."

There was a loud coughing fit from Ibra at the end of the carriage. Moments later, Shalima came up.

"Could you go to him, Muriel?" she asked. "I think he is really ill. He needs a nurse."

Muriel looked up at her and at Bargo. She nodded. "Of course." She shuffled out of her seat, stood up and accompanied Shalima.

"You see," said Joan to Bargo. "That is being merciful. You say we are at war, and yet she will help her enemy."

"She has no choice," said Bargo harshly.

Joan turned to Kal. "But you do," she said. She nodded towards the shore and promenade. "All those people, you would kill them all. Yet probably half would not want our forces in Afghanistan and Iraq. A coachload of us went down to London to the protest march against Blair's war in Iraq.

Mostly, people everywhere want peace, just to get on with their lives – earning a living, having a family, arguing, being happy, breaking up, starting again. It's only leaders who want war. Usually men. Does your mother want war? Does she know you are here, with your guns aimed at two children and two old women? If she saw you, would she be proud of you?"

Joan leaned back in her seat, surprised at herself. Another thought struck her. "Christians did this sort of thing, too, you know – murdering unbelievers, burning witches, torturing people, even other Christians. But that was five hundred years ago. It was wrong then, just as you are wrong now."

Kal closed his eyes for a moment, then turned away. They heard a squawking gull fly past the window.

Then Yusuf climbed into the carriage, summoned by Shalima. He went to the back to see Ibra. The rest of them heard mutterings, saw Yusuf texting, then heard Muriel's voice on the phone. She came back to join them.

"I think he has malaria. It's not infectious, nothing for us to worry about. Nothing extra, anyway."

Joan laughed.

"He's been to Kenya and he must have caught it there," continued Muriel. "It can take a couple of weeks to incubate. They're sending some medication and the medics will talk it through with me."

Back in the operations room, Davoud had immediately responded to the leader's call about probable malaria by calling for medical advice. He couldn't work out whether this was an advantage they could work on or just another complexity. If they were all intent on martyrdom, a case of malaria meant nothing.

There was nothing he could do. The jihadists had made their demand; the government would not accede to it. The jihadists would not talk to the negotiators. It was stalemate. Somebody would be killed tomorrow. Maybe that would change things, but he doubted it. A few lives could be sacrificed for the greater good; that was the bottom line.

But the nuclear fuel was the game-changer: the skip with explosives attached, the sniper rifles able to penetrate it.

Computer screens flickering around him, telephone conversations, people in uniform, instructions quietly given, evacuation figures updated. There was an eerie, efficient calm. And yet amidst it all he saw so vividly Jenny's face, heard her laughter, felt her lips on him, remembered the scent of her skin. It seemed disrespectful, almost irreverent, but he couldn't stop himself from thinking of her. She had no way of knowing he was in charge up here. His appointment had not been made public. But she would, like the rest of the world, follow the story and might easily guess that he was involved. He could do nothing about that.

And Sara? Safe far away in London, going through the routine of her day at school, probably not giving him a thought. Suddenly he hoped she was not giving him a thought. That might make her sad or worry, and that was the last thing he wanted. His not being in her head was best for her. That was a sobering thought.

He turned back, with some relief, to the situation here. He would listen in to the doctor's conversation with Yusuf, the leader, try to glean something about his character. A young man, a convert. Had he been escaping something in his earlier life? Or had he been searching for something to fill a gap, a deficiency? The two of them passing each other by chance, travelling in opposite directions.

35.

TUESDAY 6TH OCTOBER

At ten o'clock Davoud phoned the Home Secretary to ask if there was any change in policy.

"They have refused to negotiate. We have to stand firm." Nicky Mason's voice was brusque, clipped, as if shutting out the reality of – and responsibility for – the imminent death.

Davoud looked at his computer screen: the feed from the helicopter over the bay showed the stationary trains, no activity. The soldiers stationed in the railwaymen's huts at each end of the viaduct also reported no movement. No one was visible: everyone was inside the train, victims and terrorists confined. The river flowed, the tide ebbed, birds flew, the air was still and mild, the Lakeland hills were soft.

In the operations room phones rang, evacuation reports were shared, details checked for any possible SAS raid. Beneath the buzz of conversation among police, army and civilians Davoud sensed the tension of waiting, the expectation of bad news. On the large TV screen, Sky rolling news showed live broadcasts from reporters filling time before noon with interviews, cameras panning across the bay then closing in on the train. All news media had been instructed to stop live coverage from 1130.

All the jihadists were on guard duty. Those who had just completed the night shift were still in position, half of them in each of the carriages. They, too, were waiting, with a subdued excitement: Kal chewing his nails, Benny chewing gum. Shalima was almost certain that Izzy and Benny had not said their prayers during the night. All of them had killed before, but none, she guessed, had been so close to a victim; their killing had all been within the rage of fighting, the noise and fear and elation. This was like being in a dentist's waiting room – a feigned casualness before the drill. Bargo and Kal were even flicking through magazines. This was killing to a deliberate timetable, premeditated, in cold blood.

Yusuf stepped into the women's carriage. The low conversation stopped, the children looked up at him. Muriel was sitting at the far end with Ibra, wiping his brow. Yusuf looked down at his seated hostages.

"You know the deal," he said. "If we have heard nothing from your government by noon, one of you will be shot."

Laura put her arm round Noah, who cuddled into her.

"What does the man mean, Mummy?" he asked.

"It's nothing, he's just saying stuff."

Yusuf continued. "There are now less than two hours to go." He looked at each of them in turn. "The old birdwatcher has volunteered to die. So, for the moment, you are safe."

The hostages slumped. Emily looked up at the jihadists with incomprehension and contempt. Joan thought what a brave man the birdwatcher must be. Was he older than her? Did he have grandchildren like she did? Or was he a lonely widower? Whichever it was, he was dying to save people who were total strangers to him. She wanted to thank him, but it seemed crass. How do you thank someone who is dying for you? And she thought of the story of Jesus, in which she no longer believed.

Izzy turned away from them and stared out of the window; there were patches of sweat on his orange T-shirt. Shalima bowed her head. Kal, sitting straight-backed, grinned back at them, chin up, defying them, both hands balled into fists. Yusuf muttered quietly to Ibra.

Then Yusuf's mobile rang. Immediately everyone was alert, holding their breath. Was this the call from the authorities they needed?

"Hello," said Yusuf. He listened. Then he took the phone down to Muriel. "Instructions about injecting quinine," he said, and handed it over.

Daisy drank from a water bottle; Noah was placing stickers into his activity book. Yusuf leaned forward and placed his iPad on the table next to the activity book. Sky News was on and the women could not resist watching it, hearing the commentary and the interviews. About them. About what would happen if the threat were to be carried out. They were the audience of a play in which they were also the main performers. Then the screen showed a close-up of Big Ben. The reporter explained that nothing else was allowed to be broadcast.

In the men's carriage there was silence. The hostages were dishevelled and worn out, restless and itchy in their sweat-smelling clothes. No one had slept. Keith had said nothing more, and the others did not know what to say. They still sat round the same table, almost but not touching each other. Keith was in his own world and they did not wish to disturb him. Sometime during the night he had written a letter. The others had watched him carefully tear the pages from his birder's notebook, write in neat handwriting, fold them so the message was not visible and write his daughter's address. It lay now on the table in front of him. He had taken his watch off, stuffed it into a pocket. Now he looked through his binos at the birds on the estuary mudbanks. The other men surreptitiously checked the time.

The four jihadists stood in a group, as if protecting and defending themselves. The hostages had shut them out, banished them. They were beyond the pale. Bargo lounged, Benny was defiantly plugged into his music, casting occasional glances at the four men sat round the table. They, too, checked their watches.

At 1155 Yusuf ostentatiously looked at his watch. Daisy complained that Noah had taken her crayons. Yusuf turned to leave the women's carriage, beckoning Kal to come with him. Emily half-stood and reached for his arm.

"Allah is merciful," she cried. "What you do will be an insult to Him. You must not do this."

She could picture her devout father when he saw the news, horrified and ashamed of what was being done in the name of Islam.

Muriel rushed forward from the back of the carriage where she had been with Ibra. "I am saving your friend's life. And in return you will murder that old man. Is that the will of your all-merciful Allah?"

Yusuf brushed past her. His rifle was slung over his shoulder and his hand was on his pistol in its holder. This was his moment, this was when he would prove himself – to the team, the hostages, the British government, Al-Qaeda, but above all to Allah. He was the warrior of his God.

He entered the men's carriage and the other jihadists fell silent, looking at him. Maybe one or two doubted him, he thought. Yusuf stood at the table.

"Come on, old man. It is time."

Keith put his binos down. "Redshank and golden plover out there."

He looked at Yusuf's face, then at his pistol, sighed deeply, then pushed the folded letter towards him. "This is for my daughter," he said. "It is my last wish that you have this posted to her. Can I die knowing you will do this for me?"

"Of course. We are not monsters. It is your government that compels me to do this."

Finlay shook his head.

"Excuse me," said Keith, rising. He was sitting at the window seat and Geoff had to get up to let him out.

"This is inhuman. You can't do this," said Geoff nervously, his face pale.

Paul was slumped in disbelief.

Finlay said, "Surely there is another way." Until this moment he had been convinced it was all a bluff, a game of who blinks first. And someone would blink.

Keith was standing now. He shook the other three hostages' hands. "Goodbye. I hope I am the only one."

He turned to Yusuf. "May your God forgive you."

"This is not God's work," Paul suddenly cried out. Bargo moved to stand over him, thrust his pistol at Paul's temple.

"We don't have to stick with one. You could join him," he snarled.

Yusuf shook his head. "Enough." He was the leader. There must be no hysteria, no loss of control. Everything must be deliberate.

"Start filming," Yusuf instructed Kal.

In his head Keith repeated a line that had come out of nowhere: *Nothing in his life became him like the leaving it.* He had to die with a final dignity that would make his daughter proud. Steadfast, he looked directly at the mobile that was filming him. The world would witness this.

"It is a noble death, old man," said Yusuf quietly. "It is a martyr's death. If your God is merciful, in a few minutes you will be in Heaven. You should be joyful, embracing death as we Muslims do."

Keith nodded almost imperceptibly. "You delude yourself, young man," he said, voice firm. "I have no such delusions. I do not believe in God or in any afterlife. If Hell is anywhere, it is here and now."

Finlay clapped his hands, and after a moment Geoff

and Paul joined in. Bargo slammed a punch into the side of Finlay's face. The clapping continued. Bargo hit Finlay again. Geoff and Paul ceased clapping. Finlay gave three final claps and then stopped. His jaw was in pain, he was in awe of Keith; he had never before been near a death. Horrified with guilt at the thought, he realised it was the most exciting day of his life.

Yusuf grabbed Keith roughly by the arm, but Keith shook himself free.

"I don't need your help. I will walk myself."

"This is what you pay for being an unbeliever," said Yusuf and led the way down the steps, followed by Keith, then Kal with his mobile at the ready, and Benny, carrying a rifle.

The other hostages heard their feet step onto the gravel between the sleepers. Then they all heard the whirr of helicopter blades. Looking out of the grimy windows, they saw the helicopter approaching from the sea.

Joan watched the iPad's close-up of Big Ben, the hands moving to noon. The Sky News reporter was silent, waiting for the first peal of noon.

Davoud, too, watched the screen, with everyone else in the operations room. The room, like the women's carriage and the men's carriage, had fallen silent. On the SAS helicopter's feed they watched the four men step down from the carriage and walk along the track to the end of the trains.

In London, Jenny was one of a crowd watching TV screens in a shop window. Davoud's father was also watching the TV in his living room, but he did not understand what was happening.

In the operations room there was a shout. On a third screen, tuned in to Facebook, another film had appeared.

"It's the fucking terrorists' video," yelled someone. The whole room crowded round this screen.

★

Laura sang to her children, trying to get them to join in: "*The wheels on the bus go round and round...*" She needed to drown out the sound of the shot which she, like Joan and Emily, was listening intently for while wanting to shut it out. Muriel forced herself to concentrate on comforting Ibra, sweating with fever.

The SAS helicopter flew in from across the bay and passed above the train, rotor blades clattering. Keith looked up at its army camouflage, saw faces in the cockpit looking down at him. Yusuf, his hand on the small of Keith's back, stationed him by the viaduct guard rail, above the river channel, looking down the estuary towards the sea. Keith concentrated on the birds on the sand flats. His daughter far away would watch him. He wanted to hold her, his little girl from those years ago. Fiercely he held himself in check, standing tall. He glanced up as a posse of oystercatchers flew across the gleaming sand, their piping cutting the silence.

Davoud looked at his watch. Everyone was silent; there were occasional words from the TV. A mobile jingled in a corner but remained unanswered.

Joan wanted to look away from the iPad screen but couldn't, held by a horrified fascination, still unbelieving. Laura and her children were singing, "*The sun has got his hat on, hip-hip-hip-hooray...*" Shalima was licking her lips nervously. Izzy was sitting at another table, on his own, stroking his lips and the bristles of his beard.

Yusuf looked at his watch, nodded to Kal, who moved round to get a better composition, the sun behind him.

Benny turned away and looked out towards the Lakeland hills.

Yusuf raised his pistol, his arm straight, the barrel against Keith's temple. He saw Keith's lips moving, his eyes staring ahead. Yusuf pulled the trigger and Keith's head exploded. The shot echoed across the bay; the flock of plover took flight and swirled up into the air, their wings flashing golden in the sunlight as they swerved. The women jumped in their seats and moaned; Emily had her hands over her ears. Finlay had images of shootings in films he'd seen: the shock on the faces, collapsing bodies. A sudden image of his grandfather – about the same age as Keith – who would be walking along the promenade at Grange to join the gardening club in the ornamental gardens. Life continued. Only the trains had stopped running.

Keith's body slumped over the railings. Yusuf called to Benny to help him, but Benny had walked a few yards down the track and ignored him. Through their binoculars, the soldiers in the railwayman's hut watched Yusuf grab Keith's legs and lever him over the rail. His body fell into the muddy water of the River Kent. Kal turned to film it as it floated slowly away, nudging the sandbanks on either side of the river channel.

"Bastards!" muttered Davoud, watching it on the Facebook feed. "Fucking bastards!" Then: "Retrieve that body."

Inside, Bargo watched over the men intently. They knew he would shoot another at the slightest excuse.

Bargo shouted, "Allahu Akbar!" and brandished his pistol.

Finlay drew a deep breath and said, "Your God thinks that is noble?"

Bargo lunged forward but stopped himself.

Paul suddenly began to talk, his words tumbling out between quick breaths. It was about his model railway layout: gradients, fiddle yards, the main terminus, a viaduct and a waterfall, his LMS engines from the 1950s, his weathered bogie flat wagons, how he modelled felled trees and a colliery sawmill. All in the spare room because they'd had no children. His wife had turned to the church, but he'd gone into OO gauge.

Geoff, elbows on the table, head resting on his hands, looked up suddenly and yelled at him, "Shut the fuck up about your bleeding railway, you stupid man." Then subsided, hands trembling, shaking his head. Was it all his fault? He was the driver: should he have done something different? Should he volunteer to be the next victim?

Paul stopped, looked at Finlay, then bowed his head. Didn't they realise he was the next oldest man?

Bargo laughed.

In the women's carriage, Joan looked at Shalima. "What cowards you are, you call that holy jihad?"

Shalima could not respond. It had been so cold-blooded, like an ISIS execution. Ibra retched and complained of stomach ache. Muriel opened a packet of doxycycline tablets.

Chief Superintendent Steve Mack, on the empty Arnside promenade, watched the helicopter swing back and hover over where Keith's body had lodged at a bend in the river. A man in a red survival suit was lowered down, looped a rope round the body, signalled and the man and body were drawn up.

Alerted by Davoud, the Home Secretary and Prime Minister had watched the Facebook film, coffee untouched. At the shot the PM turned away, while Nicky Mason covered her eyes. *What now?* she wondered. *How will the public react?* For the first time she felt sympathy for Gideon. *My decision*, thought the PM. *My decision.*

Jenny and the small crowd outside the TV shop had heard the first boom of noon. Then the next eleven slow booms of the bell. Had it happened? Silence. The face of Big Ben. Then a reporter's voice: "We can confirm that one of the hostages has been shot."

The crowd turned away in anger and disgust. An Asian-looking man among them was jostled by two middle-aged white men. "Fucking Muslims!" they snarled. "Fuck off back to Pakistan!" He dared not tell them he was a Buddhist from Nepal.

Davoud's father was channel-hopping, trying to find *Celebrity Big Brother.*

Davoud left the operations room and went to his office, alone. Shoulders slumped, hands in pockets, he stood and stared at the floor. The first death. That innocent old man. Failed; at the first crisis he had failed. He looked across at the stacks of kiddies' chairs in the corner. He set his face, tight-lipped. *The bastards won't talk to us. I'm powerless. Next call, the kids.*

36.
WEDNESDAY 7TH OCTOBER

The fluorescent light was still flickering in Cabinet Office Briefing Room A. But this time, noticed Home Secretary Nicky Mason, there was a plate of the PM's favourite bourbon biscuits on the table and there were flowered china cups and saucers for the coffee. It seemed crass and indelicate.

Gideon, she was pleased to notice, looked tired. There were unmistakable shadows under his eyes instead of the usual placid, smooth, well-rested face. Since his return from China on Sunday, he'd been to Brussels for yet more endless meetings on renegotiating with Europe for this bloody stupid referendum. There'd been other meetings about the migration crisis, where he'd been tested severely as he tried to put a compassionate gloss on his mean-minded response to the human tragedies unfolding in Southern Europe. Both were good examples, Nicky well knew, of how venal domestic politics – the need to satisfy Eurosceptics in their own party and counter the attraction of UKIP – trumped national interest. In the meantime, the image of the body of the dead migrant child on the Mediterranean beach had been replaced by the body of the old man tipped into the river in Morecambe Bay. Now the eyes of the world were on Gideon, iPhones and iPads tuned in for the next Facebook live feed from the terrorists on the train, worldwide anxiety about the nuclear threat.

She looked across at Julian, the Defence Secretary, looking cool as usual with a sky-blue tie – registering loyalty in these tough times? – and wondered if he still really wanted the top job and ultimate responsibility. And did she? Next to him, that dandy Sir Bartholomew Saunders from MI6 was sipping coffee, a pale primrose handkerchief in his breast pocket. Julian was a pale imitation of Sir Bartholomew's fabled raffishness: the poser compared with the real deal. How could a man with so many vulnerabilities to blackmail have risen to the top of the Intelligence Service? Because he was so open, she presumed, didn't give a fig. The final member of the assembled quartet, sitting awkwardly at the corner of the table, was Max Cox, head of G3W, counterterrorism: a formidable brain (and that wasn't all, she'd heard) but shy, sitting with hunched shoulders, staring into his coffee cup, reaching self-consciously for a second bourbon.

A big TV screen at the fourth side of the table showed four men sitting in the operations room at Arnside: Chief Superintendent Steve Mack, bearded, in his police uniform, who ran the Cumbrian Counterterrorism Unit – Nicky was surprised they had one; in his army uniform, Lieutenant Colonel Malcolm McPhail; the man in charge up there, Davoud Nariman, looking very slight and well groomed in a civilian way, dusky-skinned, neat beard; and finally, Tim Bennett, Davoud's deputy in MI5's Section G9C.

"Two decisions," said Gideon, clearing his throat. "One fairly straightforward, the other complex."

He glanced down at his iPad, then at his three companions, then at the laptop screen.

"The Facebook clip from the train, the murder of the old man. It has not been broadcast on national networks, but it's been shared and gone viral, as they say. Millions of people all over the world have seen it. Doubtless there will be more clips, God knows what of. Can we, should we ask, instruct Facebook to shut it down?"

Tim Bennett spoke from the screen: "Someone cannot be prevented from uploading to Facebook. All that's possible is to have the upload taken down. To do that, someone obviously has to see it and then alert Facebook."

"But won't Facebook now know the ID of the device that uploaded the clip?" asked Nicky, sounding much more confident in her understanding than she felt. She saw Julian smile to himself.

"Yes, they will," replied Tim. "But the terrorists could have any number of devices, use once and throw away. It's impossible to predict where an upload will come from."

"And," continued the PM, "it only needs one person to see it and share it and the thing is out of control. Is that right?"

Sir Bartholomew straightened up and leaned forward. "But even if we could, should we take the stuff down?"

Davoud almost flinched at that cut-glass accent.

"Explain," said the PM.

Sir Bartholomew, centre of attention, smoothed his tie. "Don't we want as many people as possible to see the horrors these so-called jihadists are capable of? The public will know the monsters we're up against and support us."

Tim Bennett shifted in his seat and, unsure whether to speak to his companions at Arnside or the faces on the screen, said, in a voice so quiet that everyone leaned forward a little, "But the public at the moment seem to be turning against us. The polls tell us that a huge number of people want us to negotiate, to free Suleiman and prevent any more murders on the train. Also, they're terrified of radiation."

Heads nodded.

"OK," said the PM. "So it's impossible to control Facebook. The clips will always be seen by someone and then shared. Even if they're later taken down, they're in the public domain. And the people will be even more suspicious of us, hiding the truth etc., patronising them. Agreed?"

There were nods all round.

"Davoud?"

"I agree."

"Which leads us to the major question. I need to confirm that we continue with our non-negotiation stance. Let's be clear why Suleiman should not be freed."

Davoud cleared his throat. "Let me be devil's advocate. If we don't free Suleiman, it makes no difference to Islamist atrocities. There will be – are – other Suleimans plotting attacks, training bomb-makers, persuading suicide bombers. So, keeping him in prison achieves nothing. And the risks on that train are huge: more murders and, of course, the nuclear fuel problem."

"But the answer to that," said Nicky, "is that freeing him will set a precedent. Kidnaps and hijackings will be seen to be successful and there will be more."

"Yes," continued Davoud, "but there are well-known stories – more than rumours – that ransoms have been paid and prisoners freed. People here will know more than I do about what goes on behind the scenes." He looked at Sir Bartholomew, who looked back at him, expressionless. "The terrorists will know that, too. They are already sometimes successful – often enough to keep at it."

"The issue is academic," said Chief Superintendent Mack. "This lot won't negotiate. Our negotiators are redundant. The jihadists know they hold all the cards."

Max Cox put his hand through his hair. "Assuming they're prepared to carry out their threat, and I assume they are, which is the greater price to pay: the freedom of Suleiman or another murder and the nuclear explosion? I'm sorry, but there's only one answer a sane person can give."

"The next step, I guess," said Julian, who had definitely decided he was no longer ambitious for the top post, "will be for them to threaten to kill one of the children. How does that change the scenario?"

"Imagine the video clip of that," said Nicky, genuinely appalled.

"And the public response," mused the PM. "All for the sake of a man they'd never heard of before, who's plotted stuff far away in the Middle East and Africa."

Including killing my mother and sister, thought Davoud, but said nothing.

"We need to talk with this Suleiman," said Gideon decisively. "He's at the centre of the situation. Davoud, you're the man. See if you can find out what he feels. Thin chance, I know, but he may be the solution as well as the problem. Get a helicopter to Belmarsh."

For a time, they could all relax. The pressure was on Davoud. He said nothing, recalling Suleiman's silence back in Jordan, his refusal to see him at Belmarsh.

Two hours later, while Davoud was flying south, the operations room, ministers in London and most of the world were glued to the TV screen. In Vancouver, the daughter of Keith Walters, the dead birdwatcher, was giving an interview to CBC News. In a sunny garden, she stood under a silver birch.

"He was coming to spend Christmas and the New Year with us," she said. "We wanted him to come and live out here, but he said he was too old for that; he would stay where he'd lived most of his life. Ever since my mum died he'd been lonely, but he'd begun to build a new life. And birdwatching was part of that. He was such a gentle man, wouldn't hurt a flea. A wonderful dad. I was an only child and he doted on me. And he died with such dignity, a strong man."

Her voice faltered, her lips quivered. "I'm proud of him. He lived by basic good principles and he died by them. But as for the man who killed him, and his companions, how could we feel anything but contempt? What kind of God is it that they imagine would want that kind of sacrifice – an innocent old man? Unbelievable."

★

Yusuf had summoned Shalima for a meeting. They stood outside, at the back of the train, leaning on the viaduct railing, looking towards the sea. Shalima needed the fresh air. They'd been in that claustrophobic train for almost a week: their unwashed bodies smelt, the kids were getting on her nerves. She knew that their mother was utterly exhausted and near to breaking point. The hostages had to spend the day and night sitting or lying on their seats, occasionally allowed to walk down the carriage aisle. Tensions were increasing. Nothing seemed to be happening. Except for the death of the birder. And that had apparently changed nothing. Yusuf seemed impervious, shut in his own world.

"We planned this together," Yusuf said to her. "We trained for it, then we went up into the mountains to convince them to support us, the Al-Qaeda leaders."

Shalima wondered where this was leading, why he felt the need to give her a pep talk.

"And now we are nearing crunch time. This is when we find out our own strengths and the strength of our faith."

"Are you questioning mine?"

He turned to look at her directly. "You must not weaken."

"I am not weakening. But I am angry."

Back in the Yemen, during the development and presentation of their plan, they had been equals. Not now: he had taken all power to himself. He had wanted a female leader only to establish his own uniqueness, as an extra means to persuade the Al-Qaeda leadership.

"You're the leader, yes, but you need to consult with me."

"About what?"

She looked directly at him, held his gaze. "Both of us decided not to join ISIS. For me, it was because they're too extreme and crude in their cruelty. And now you imitate ISIS by making a film of the old man's murder."

She was accusing him.

"But, Shalima, they must see we are serious."

"The death itself was sufficient for that." She looked across to Arnside. "Now the whole world, not just over there in their HQ, has seen that killing, and our glorying in it. They will hate us, and innocent Muslims will be threatened and harassed with hate crime."

"But that is good."

"Good?"

"You don't see the bigger picture. There are Muslims in almost all Western countries now. Because of us, tensions will, as you say, increase. Societies will split, there will be civil unrest. The West will weaken. But we will be hardened." His voice intensified. "There will be war between our faith and their apostasy, and we will win. In war there will always be innocent victims."

"Yes, Yusuf, I heard the lectures, too. I didn't come here with my eyes closed."

But she did close her eyes. She heard the river softly flowing beneath the viaduct, felt the warm sun on her face, heard the seabirds calling. There had been day after day of this still, warm brightness. This horror she was part of, in this peace.

Yusuf leaned back against the rail. "Izzy is getting too close to those kids. That's dangerous. Have a hard word with him."

His eyes were stony, glittering, that mantis again. She realised Yusuf would have no compunction in killing Izzy, or any of them, to keep discipline and unity. But that was it. If you were prepared to sacrifice your own life, you were certainly able to sacrifice others.

"They despise us," she said, "the hostages."

"Fear us is more accurate."

"No, despise."

"Perhaps, Shalima, co-leader, we need to remind ourselves why we are here: to free Suleiman, to put Al-Qaeda on the map again, and to glorify our faith."

Had Yusuf noticed she had not prayed once yesterday? Nor had Izzy.

"*He for whom Allah has not appointed light, for him there is no light.* We have the light."

"I don't need reminding," she said. "What is the next step? It will be impossible to confine those children for much longer. They will drive us all crazy."

"So we must speed up the process, put more pressure on." A pause. "The next victim must be one of the children."

He said it so matter-of-factly. She had been expecting it, but she was still horrified. The children were no different for Yusuf: they were just pawns he could move about the board and sacrifice. They hadn't abused Muslims or complied with government attacks on Muslims. There was a brutal nastiness to him that underlay all his principles.

"So, which will it be most heroic to kill: the four-year-old or the two-and-a-half-year-old? We didn't envisage children being on the train."

"No, but they are our strongest leverage now they are here." He had not picked up on her contempt, so fired was he by his zeal and obsession. "We will get the mother to make a tearful appeal on Facebook, another of Kal's film clips. With the whole world watching, do you think the government will not give in? The whole world watching as I shoot the child, live on Facebook."

It had been wrong to involve a woman. They were too soft. Other Muslim men understood this. Women were too compassionate or too predatory. Either way, they reduced a man.

"The whole world will hate us."

Yusuf smiled. "It is the price we pay for our faith: we

individuals will be hated but our God will be praised by the believers."

There was a vanity in his words, she heard it.

"But, Shalima, I will not kill the child." This time, a softer smile: he had been manipulating her. "We will offer to exchange them, the whole family. Because you're right, we need to get rid of them. They are creating unnecessary tension."

"Exchange them? Who for?"

"Somebody worthy, some celebrity hostage. The Prime Minister, Prince Harry, the Archbishop of Canterbury, Andy Murray, a top general, a VIP."

Was he serious? "Or Princess Kate, or Adele?" Shalima suggested.

"No women." Again, he had missed her sarcasm. "We offer the exchange and then we'll see how much they really love children. See who volunteers, like the old birder did. If there is no volunteer, there will be no alternative: I must shoot one of them. Then they must despise themselves as much as they despise us."

"And who will decide if the volunteer is acceptable to us?"

Yusuf was silent. "We do," he said eventually. "We do, you and I."

It was an unwilling concession, she thought. He still needed her. How proud he would be, how puffed up and vainglorious if the world witnessed him welcoming one of those high-ups into his parlour. How magnanimous he would feel, freeing the family.

Yes, she did not doubt his faith, but a different motivation had taken over: fame in this life, not a shortcut to Paradise.

Or was she seeing him through a shift in her own conviction? From a different angle?

37.

"Thin chance," the PM had said. *Very, very thin*, thought Davoud as he landed at the Vanguard Helipad on the Isle of Dogs and was sped direct to Belmarsh Prison in a police car with darkened windows. En route, he'd received a message that Suleiman would meet him this time. Davoud had only the one case to make.

A prison guard showed him into a small, windowless room, walls painted pale grey, grey vinyl floor, white ceiling with fluorescent light humming. In the middle of the room was a table with a metal chair at either side. All were bolted to the floor. Davoud sat down and the guard stood against the wall behind him. It was ten minutes before the door opened and another guard brought in Suleiman, his orange-and-brown Arab robes a splash of gracefully moving colour. Davoud stood to greet him, but Suleiman ignored him and sat on the other chair. Suleiman's guard retreated to another wall. Davoud sat down.

The Iranian Briton looked across and slightly upwards at the Arab's face: Davoud slightly built, neat beard trimmed, formal in his fawn suit; Suleiman tall and spare, luxuriant black beard, relaxed as he folded his robes around him. Davoud had checked that Suleiman, though kept in solitary confinement, had access to newspapers. His choice was *The Times*. So he would know what the situation was.

Davoud thought he saw humour in Suleiman's eyes as he waited for Davoud to start the conversation. This was a game for Suleiman. Like chess. But not like chess, because Davoud knew he had no complex moves to offer, just one. Suleiman would also know that Davoud saw him as the murderer of his mother and sister, and would be dispassionately curious about how Davoud was going to deal with this.

The light hummed, the guard shuffled his feet, somewhere a metal door clanged shut with a dull echo. Davoud felt the weight of so many lives on his shoulders.

"Do you," asked Davoud, "want to be the person to go down in history as the instigator of a nuclear catastrophe?"

Suleiman stared back at him, his eyes amused, just a slight curl of his lips. He would have been ready for the question. How ridiculous to imagine that such a man would have qualms.

"Suleiman al-Hariri," Davoud persisted, his voice quiet but clear, "the man so full of vanity that in his prison cell he could read about radiation horror – humans vaporised and burned to ash, babies born deformed – that he had caused, and feel fulfilled."

Again, no response.

That impassive face enraged Davoud. He was making no impression. He controlled his voice.

"I am asking you, begging, if you wish" – a slight nod from Suleiman, was there? – "to tell your friends to call off this operation. They will be flown to safety, I guarantee it, you have my word. You, however, must stay here."

The smile was slightly more visible.

"You are doing more than any other man not to glorify your faith but to defile it. Is that what you want your legacy to be?"

Davoud's anger and frustration were increasing proportionately to Suleiman's apparent nonchalance.

Suleiman stood up. The guards moved forward.

"By the way," said Davoud, "your extradition process is moving on. Remember Abu Hamza? He successfully fought in British courts for years, as you will know, but he was extradited to the USA, just as you will be. It only took a few months for the courts there to give him a life sentence."

He smiled up at Suleiman, and instantly regretted this petty gamesmanship.

Suleiman looked down at Davoud and spat on the table. He turned towards the door. Davoud nodded. The guards escorted Suleiman back to his cell. The door closed behind them. Davoud's eyes were fixed on the gob of spit.

Second interrogation of him less successful than the first. Lost my cool. His bloody arrogant certainty got to me. The man was unbending.

One of the ceiling lights in the Whitehall meeting room was still flickering when COBRA reconvened at 1630 that same day. The central heating had not been adjusted for the abnormally warm autumn day and Nicky Mason thought the room oppressive. Max Cox had put his jacket on the back of his chair and Sir Bartholomew was dabbing his forehead with his handkerchief. Julian looked impervious to such mundane issues, as usual. Gideon had his sleeves rolled up, tie loose. All five had opened their bottles of Highland still water, and Max was reaching for another bourbon biscuit.

"I do not envy us having to make this decision," said Gideon Camborne. "The final decision has to be mine personally, of course. The responsibility falls to me. But I want to hear your opinions. There have been three developments during the day."

He took a sip of water. "The first is a report from Davoud Nariman. He saw Suleiman in Belmarsh Prison and failed to elicit a single syllable from him. He remains implacable. The second is this which came through on Facebook an hour ago, and I am aware that the Home Secretary has already seen it."

Nicky nodded. She knew that all of them except Sir

Bartholomew had children; her own were at university. But Gideon's were younger, one at primary and one at secondary school.

Gideon tapped the remote and one of the TV screens at the end of the room came on. Nicky drew a deep breath.

The iPhone camera slowly pulled back from a view of the estuary, the sandbanks bright in the sunshine; panned across some empty carriage seats and then focused in on a youngish woman sitting by the window, one small child on her lap, the other, a little boy, sitting on the carriage table. Slowly the camera closed in on the woman's face. Her hair was straggly and unwashed, her eyes weary.

"My name," she said, "is Laura Dobson, and these are my children: Daisy, who is two and a half" – she held Daisy closer and smiled bravely (Nicky thought) down at her – "and this is my son Noah, who is four. He started nursery school last month."

Noah held his mouth close to the window, breathed on it and then made marks with his finger.

Laura's voice faltered. "There are another six people, as well as us, held on this train. One man has already died. Our guards have told us that someone else will die soon if their demands are not met. I beg the people who are in charge not to let this happen. We have been told about the nuclear fuel and the bomb attached to it. It must be hard for you to imagine how terrifying it is for us to be here. All I was doing was taking my children to see their Grandma. And now they are caught up in this. Please, please help us."

The last words could hardly be heard as her voice cracked. The camera stayed close on her face as tears rolled down. Noah hugged his mum, putting his little arms around her neck.

The screen faded. The four watchers sat in silence. Max shuffled in his seat, Gideon and Sir Bartholomew still stared at the blank screen, Julian looked down at the table.

Gideon cleared his throat. "Then there's this, which was posted on Facebook only half an hour ago. The man speaking is the leader, Yusuf Javeed, once Ryan Hudson."

He pressed the remote again and another screen came to life. It was a close-up of the hijacker's head and shoulders, his head nestling against and almost caressing the vertical steel barrel of his rifle. Round his neck was his red-checked keffiyeh.

"Allahu Akbar," he began. "Your British government has refused point-blank to negotiate with us on our demands for the freeing of Suleiman al-Hariri. That is why we had, regrettably, to kill the old man. They did not take us seriously. But still there has been no response. We do not want to explode the nuclear fuel; we are not stupid, we know the devastation that would be caused. We do not want to kill anyone else. But your government is stubborn. Even now they are killing Muslims in Syria. You have seen the plea from Laura Dobson. Her two British children are lovely. And that is why we are showing our goodwill. Listen carefully. We will exchange the mother and her two children in return for a high-profile hostage. By that we mean someone who bears some responsibility for the wars Britain is fighting and has recently been fighting against our brother Muslims: a senior politician or a military man, or someone from the Secret Services. Of course, the Archbishop of Canterbury might do."

Yusuf smiled. For maybe fifteen seconds the camera swung onto the faces of the two children, then back to Yusuf.

"You have thirty-six hours to find an exchange hostage, acceptable to us, to appear on the viaduct or…" – and here he paused for effect – "you will compel me to kill either Daisy or Noah. That death will be on your head. Allahu Akbar."

The Prime Minister switched off the screen.

The hum of the central heating and the faint crackling of the faulty ceiling light were deafening. The others watched the

PM pour himself a cup of coffee, heard the cup chink against the saucer.

"I'd like your opinions, first," he said, "on why we should accede to the terrorists' proposal."

Sir Bartholomew pursed his lips. Max was still staring at the table. Nicky Mason crossed her legs.

Julian said, "There's only one reason, isn't there? To save the children's lives."

The PM nodded.

"And," added Nicky, "to keep their deaths off our consciences."

"Imagine," said Max, barely audible, "if it was our kids on that train. My two sons. We have to imagine that and give our opinions as if that were the situation."

"No," said Sir Bartholomew. "We definitely don't do that. We have to keep personal emotion out of it."

Max looked at him, eyes suddenly fierce. "They are children. We must treat them as if they were our own. That is the only way we can make a humane decision."

"But, sadly, we are not trying to make a humane decision. We are trying to make a logical one. It has to be dispassionate logic."

"Why?" challenged Max. Nicky had never heard him so involved. "Are those two, Daisy and Noah, less important than my children, or yours, Prime Minister, or yours, Home Secretary? Maybe logic must dictate we have to sacrifice our own children for the greater good. Only if we would be prepared to sacrifice our own, can we sacrifice those over there in that bloody train."

"Easy to hypothesise on that," said Julian. "We can all say we would, knowing that the situation won't happen."

"Would any of us exchange our own children for Noah and Daisy?" asked Max.

There was silence.

"That mother's plea and the proposal for an exchange – what will the public want?" asked the PM.

"That's obvious," said Sir Bartholomew. "Any politician or military leader can be sacrificed to save those two kids. They despise us anyway."

"And they will say," added Nicky Mason, "that we are responsible for creating the situation by our political and military decisions, so we should take the consequences, not two innocent children."

They all knew it was true. Those in authority were widely despised, and partly because they never seemed to carry the can; left that to the foot soldiers, ordinary men and women.

"OK," said the PM. "Now, reasons why we should not accede."

"The obvious one," said Julian, "is that we must not set a precedent. If we accede, then it's a green light to kidnap, especially children and families. Our agreement will confirm they're the top bargaining counter."

"That's always been the argument for not negotiating with terrorists," said Nicky, "and it's hard to dispute."

"If we did agree to an exchange for the family, that still leaves the other hostages and the issue of the primed nuclear fuel," said Max. "The basic situation hasn't changed."

"So," the PM said, "let's assume we do not agree to an exchange. What if an individual, off their own bat, then decides to volunteer – say the Archbishop of Canterbury or Prince Harry, or a general with terminal cancer? Do we forbid them? Can we forbid them?"

"We have to," said Sir Bartholomew.

"But isn't that going against the freedom of the individual?" said Max. "Isn't that being totalitarian? Wouldn't we be playing by the same rules as the terrorists?"

The PM's mobile beeped. He read the text and immediately

switched the screen to Sky's rolling news channel. "This may complicate things."

"Over a thousand individuals," announced the reporter, "have already volunteered to exchange with the family held hostage on the train in Morecambe Bay. And that is within just two hours of the demand being made. It is not known if any significant public figures have put their names forward. An online petition has also been started, supporting an exchange. There is no news yet of what the government will do. Here is the mother's plea, as posted on Facebook."

The PM turned off the screen. "It's unbearable," he said.

He had his elbows on the table, his chin resting on his hands. He stroked his fingers across his lips.

"It's a question of the balance of risks," he said. "If we don't facilitate the exchange, one of those children will be shot and the film of it will go worldwide. Then very likely the second child will follow. If we don't free Suleiman, it is likely all the hostages will be killed and the nuclear fuel exploded. We still do not know if the skip of nuclear fuel will be breached by the explosion. It's likely, but not inevitable. The question is: can we take the risk – the risk of many deaths, of birth deformities, of radiation in the food and water chains?"

He paused. "If we do agree to the exchange and then the freeing of Suleiman, we could set our own conditions – about disabling the fuel explosives, for instance."

The rest waited. The final decision was his.

"I think Max is right," he said. "Can we sacrifice others if we will not sacrifice ourselves? In the old days, kings led their armies into battle. They faced the same swords and arrows their soldiers did. There was a nobility in that. Leaders don't do that any more, can't. Ways of fighting have changed. I can sit here and send a Trident missile to explode thousands of miles away. It is easier to start wars from armchairs and committee rooms. But we have to live with ourselves afterwards."

He stood up. "We'll reconvene at seven in the morning. I'll have the decision by then."

No one envied him.

38.

That evening Gideon Camborne cancelled his appearance at a party fundraising event, to the great disappointment of representatives of Google, GlaxoSmithKline and Amazon and their wives. Instead, back in Downing Street earlier than expected, he helped his daughter Amanda with her English homework and read a bedtime story with his young son Henry after a splashful bath time. He chopped onions for a simple bolognese supper with his wife Suzie in their kitchen. Afterwards, with his favourite album, *Dark Side of the Moon*, playing softly, she brought him up to date with their children's activities and anecdotes from school, with her day at work organising an excessively expensive party for Russian émigrés. Gideon had nodded occasionally but made no comment.

"You're quieter than usual, Gideon. It's the train situation, isn't it? I heard about the demand." She took his hand in hers.

He nodded. "Am I a politician or a human being? It seems I can't be both." He stroked her hand. "The whole world is watching to see which I am." He nestled his head into her shoulder. "When they're older, how will Amanda and Henry judge me on the decision I have to make? Will they despise me?"

She stroked his hair. "Gideon, of course they won't. You're their father. They'll trust you did your best, whatever you decide."

"I wish that were true, Suzie. But I doubt it."

"But no one outside the top circles knows all the implications; no one can make a judgement on you."

He stood up and walked over to the window. "Oh, that won't stop them. I don't mind political judgements, they are par for the course. But this will be a moral judgement: of me as a man, as a parent, not as a politician."

"But that's unfair. In the end, you were elected to do a job as a politician."

He turned round, brow furrowed. The clocks were ticking and chiming on the "Time" track. "Do right and wrong exist any more for a politician? Or is it all pragmatism, what's the best deal?"

"Whatever you decide, Gideon, it will be your judgement of what is best. I know that, and that is all you can do."

He leaned forward, elbows on his knees. "But I'm flawed. What if, over the years in all this political chicanery, I've lost my moral compass?"

"We're all flawed, darling, we're all human." She realised, even as she said it, how trite and corny this was.

"Yes, but no one else has to make this decision. At COBRA this morning, Max said we have to make decisions as if those children on the train were our own. Otherwise we're saying they're less important than our own. What if, God forbid, it was Amanda and Henry up there? Would it alter my judgement?"

"I know it's a cliché, but you can only do what you think is right."

"I know, and that's the problem." He kissed her on the forehead. "Sometimes, Suzie…"

He went upstairs to kiss his daughter goodnight and lingered longer than usual, seeing how she had made her room her own: the posters, Hedgerihog on her pillow, school blazer thrown into a corner, sports bag ready for tomorrow.

"You know the rules," he said, taking her mobile from her. "No technology in the bedroom. You need your sleep."

"Dad, you're so uncool." But she had learned it was useless to protest.

Not until you're a parent do you know what love really is, he thought, as he closed her bedroom door.

And he made his decision.

Davoud's helicopter clattered north through the twilight. He watched arterial road lights come on, villages and towns light up, isolated farmhouses. The lights decreased as they neared Arnside but on the viaduct the train was lit up, the sunset ending as an orange strip along the horizon.

From the field where the helicopter landed, a Land Rover ferried him to the community hall. He checked in the Raven operations room: everybody alert, but no change. No news from the government, no celebrity volunteers, the vast majority of the public wanting the children exchanged. The children, it seemed, were more important than the nuclear fuel. He felt in a limbo, waiting.

"I need some sleep," Davoud said and walked along the promenade to the Willowbank Guest House. In his room he stared out of the window across the bay. In the darkened glass he saw Suleiman's face, spitting. He stared at the trains and tried to envisage the children in the compartment. He heard again their mother's desperate plea. Davoud closed his eyes and thought of Sara safe at home. What happened next here was not his decision, but whatever was decided, he would have to implement it. Follow orders.

He had always been able to analyse things – codes, puzzles, situations, problems. See a logical way through. And he was still good at that. But now there was something else. He was reacting differently in a way, ironically, he could not analyse. It could only be that Jenny had changed him: brought him a sense of the vibrations, of the colour of ordinary life. What he had experienced only within himself, in his music, he now felt outside of him: as in the helicopter, sensing the individual lives far below him, the satisfaction of the mundane and the routine, the darkness gathering around need and love, the small acts of kindness or insensitivity.

On an impulse, he called Jenny on his mobile. He listened to the dialling tone.

I'm sorry I'm not able to take your call. Please leave a message after the tone.

It was not even her voice. He ended the call, leaving no message. And what would he have asked, and what might she have said? It was not fair to involve her, make her feel she was in some way responsible for what would happen later.

He rang Dunia instead.

"Hello." He heard the disapproval in her voice even before he said anything. She had caller ID.

"Can I have a word with Sara, please?"

"She's just going to bed. It will unsettle her."

"It's important, Dunia." He was tempted to add 'please', but refused.

He didn't know if Dunia knew what he was in charge of, or whether she just sensed something in his voice.

"All right, then, but be brief. I'll get her."

Davoud waited.

"Daddy!" Sara yelled down the phone, so enthusiastic. And his heart cracked a little further. "Where are you?"

"Looking out over a river, and missing you." Was that a mistake, he wondered, inducing a kind of fleeting guilt in her? "Tell me what you've been doing today." He longed to hug her tight and swing her round.

So she told him: about the English teacher she didn't like, about the hockey team she was in, about going to tea with her friend, about the long ears on her new pet rabbit. He listened, loving her excited voice prattling on, sensing her happiness.

"And on Saturday, we're going with Mummy's new friend, Antony, to the seaside. We're staying in a hotel."

Another fissure in his heart.

"Mummy says I've got to feed the rabbit its supper, Daddy. Bye."

And she was gone.

It could never be as before. He could never be Sara's proper dad. Somebody else would provide her with values, give her the experiences she needed. Give her dreams.

Davoud made his decision. And Jenny needed to know. He would phone her again.

All of them in the men's carriage were smelling. Finlay's clothes itched, his unshaven face itched. He felt dirty. He was tired, too: poor sleep, anxiety and, oddly for him, the lack of physical activity. He usually spent a lot of time lounging about. His legs ached. He took a drink of water from the bottle, splashed some over his eyes.

Bargo was the most restless, unable to sit still, walking up and down the carriage when he was on duty, obviously bored with the tedium, flashing fierce glances at the hostages. The latent violence in him frightened Finlay. But for the last two hours Bargo had been sitting at a table, busy on YouTube, scrolling and tapping his iPhone screen, chuckling and hitting the table with his fist occasionally.

He stood up. "Hey, Yusuf," he yelled. "Look at this."

Yusuf, never without his red-checked keffiyeh, strolled up. "Wondered what you'd been doing."

Bargo held up the phone in front of Yusuf. Finlay could hear only indistinct, tinny shouts and screams on the soundtrack. Bargo, smiling, eagerly watched Yusuf's face for his response.

But Yusuf merely handed the phone back, pondered for a moment, then said, "Shalima and Benny are on duty in the other carriage. Show it to them."

A little less confident now, Bargo walked through. Benny

was helping Noah with colouring in, playfully arguing with him about what colour the clown's trousers should be. When Bargo entered, Benny flicked him a defiant look and continued. Shalima was sitting with Muriel, watching over Ibra who seemed to be calmer, less fevered.

"Yusuf wants you to see this," said Bargo rather roughly. "It's a compilation I've made."

Shalima moved away from Muriel. Benny apologised to Noah and reluctantly got up to join them round another table. Together, the three of them watched the small screen, Bargo alert for their reactions.

The first excerpt was a BBC News report. On screen, men and women were rushing about, soldiers with rifles, stretchers being carried to an ambulance, bodies curled on the ground. The reporter, crouched by a mud wall, was saying, "Here in Damaturu in north-eastern Nigeria a ten-year-old girl blew herself up in this crowded market. Sixteen have been killed and at least fifty injured. Boko Haram, who have recently allied with ISIS, have claimed responsibility."

"Ten years old," muttered Shalima.

The second excerpt was from Pakistan's Dunya News channel. It showed children running through a school building, armed soldiers moving in. There was gunfire and screams. The voiceover of the reporter said, "Here at an Army School in Peshawar in north-western Pakistan, 132 children have been killed by terrorists. Gunmen burst into the school auditorium where children were listening to a lecture. Survivors have described being forced to watch their teachers murdered in a classroom. A spokesman for Tehrik-i-Taliban, who claimed responsibility, said, 'The army targets our families. We want them to feel our pain.'"

Benny glared at Bargo, scowled but said nothing. Bargo stared back, expressionless.

The third extract was from an ISIS video. There was no

soundtrack. In silence the camera slowly followed the gaze of armed ISIS fighters in their black-and-white keffiyehs and black balaclavas as they looked up, past fluttering black flags, at the bodies of four children, crucified on a rough wooden frame set up in a public square. The camera zoomed slowly in on the Arabic words on placards round their necks. Then the commentary, spoken in a flat voice: "We have had to execute seventy-four children who refused to fast during Ramadan, or who were Shias. The Qur'an is the word of Allah. Allahu Akbar."

Shalima turned away, sickened, and closed her eyes.

"Why are you fucking showing us this?" snarled Benny.

"Because we have to be strong. Because they must be afraid of the strength of our faith, the one true faith. We must close our hearts for a short time."

Shalima was glad Izzy was off duty and not seeing this. She could imagine his response. But they would show him later. She saw Benny's face set hard, holding himself in check. She wondered how the others would react: Ibra and Kal. The team.

"Just two more pieces," said Bargo.

The fourth extract was a piece of phone footage. It showed a line of children kneeling along a roadside in the desert, hands behind their backs, many with their hunched shoulders shaking. They were aged between about eight and fifteen, boys and girls. Fighters held black flags that flew in the breeze. Then other fighters, masked in black balaclavas, moved along the line and shot them in the head, their bodies falling forward into the dust and gravel. A BBC News commentary had been spliced on: "Two hundred refugee children, fleeing Syria, have been slaughtered by ISIS militants. The children are thought to be Kurdish, Christian, Yazidi and even Shia Muslims."

"Are you proud of this stuff, Bargo?" snapped Shalima.

He smiled. "Pride does not enter into it. How I feel as an individual does not matter. We must fight the kaffir until there is no more fitna."

"The end justifies the means, is that it?" said Shalima. But she saw the bloodlust in his eyes. Something very primitive in Bargo was excited by this slaughter, by the power, by the very ruthlessness. She had seen something like it in her father's eyes all those years ago as he beat her mother. She had seen it in the fighters in Somalia, in the middle of death-or-glory action. Had she herself had that same look in her eyes when she held her pistol to the temple of the old train driver?

"And now the future," said Bargo. "In this last section."

Benny abruptly walked away. Shalima saw him snatch off his Afghan cap and throw it onto the floor, underneath a table. He had worn that ivory-coloured *pakol* since day one.

It was another ISIS video. In a caged ring, a dozen boys, about eleven years old, dressed in black uniforms and balaclavas, were crawling on elbows and knees along the sandy ground. Men belaboured their shoulders with wooden sticks and others shot pistols near their heads.

"It's live ammunition," said Bargo. "The next generation of fighters."

Then the boys stood up and practised a choreographed series of karate-like moves, jabbing their arms, kicking their legs. Like a violent ballet.

"That's it," said Bargo, and switched off the phone.

Shalima said, "I deliberately chose not to go to Syria and fight for ISIS."

She left him and returned to Ibra and Muriel. Bargo stood there, feeling angry and betrayed. Benny was back playing with Noah and Daisy.

"I've done the clown's pants yellow," shouted Noah.

Benny made his decision. Shalima thought of Fiona with her boyfriend in the English Defence League, and that last text from her. Fiona had become a different person. Shalima realised that she had made her decision, too.

39.

Thursday 8th October, 0700

Promptly the Prime Minister opened the COBRA meeting. "Good morning. Thank you for the early start. I ordered croissants but I see they are not here. And that bloody light is still flickering."

He was not smiling. Nicky Mason, Home Secretary, saw the tension in his face. Max Cox, head of GW3, was already nibbling his third bourbon. Julian, the Defence Secretary, was sipping his black coffee. How neatly his nails were manicured! Sir Bartholomew Saunders from MI6 was as debonair as usual, but something about the way he lounged languidly – almost disrespectfully – in his chair, and the way he was not yet fully attentive, showed he had not fully discarded the sensuality of whatever exploits he had enjoyed during the night. Nicky, twenty-five years into a stable – that was probably the right word – marriage, couldn't decide whether what she imagined about Sir Bartholomew was exciting or sordid. Either way, she was curious, and felt guilty for being so. The sixth member of the group was Lieutenant Colonel Malcolm McPhail, who had flown down from Arnside. None of the TV screens were on.

"I have made my decision," said the PM. "It's been the hardest decision of my career. I decided to follow my gut instinct: to do what I feel is right, not necessarily what is politically the most adept. If I cannot live with a decision, it must be wrong."

Max nodded his head. Sir Bartholomew pursed his lips – not a muscle memory from last night, for once, Nicky was sure – but a sign of strong disapproval. The Lieutenant Colonel and Julian betrayed no reaction. Her own restless night had convinced Nicky that her ambition did not extend to making decisions like this.

"I know," continued the PM, "that many people will profoundly disagree with me. But that would also have been the case if I had made the opposite decision."

He took a drink of coffee and looked up.

"We will free Suleiman," he said.

Max immediately said, "You're right, Prime Minister. The only humane decision." His head bent a little lower. "You're a brave man."

"Thank you, Max. But it's not brave, and possibly not even humane. I've tried to assess the balance of risk."

This was, he knew, how he must sell his decision. It must have nothing to do with Amanda or Henry. Although that might come later, when it had all ended satisfactorily, if it ended satisfactorily. Yes, politically, that would go down well. But not yet. And even now, he hated himself for thinking like this, calculating.

"There must be conditions," said Sir Bartholomew.

"The weaponry on the train, the nuclear fuel," said the Lieutenant Colonel.

"Yes, indeed," replied the PM. "What do you propose?"

"Suleiman must not be released until the threat to the nuclear fuel is ended. That is essential."

"We are all agreed on that, I assume?" asked the PM.

Nods all round.

"Max?"

"Of course."

"But Suleiman must not know," said Sir Julian. "He must somehow be kept in isolation, no access to any social media."

Nicky wished she'd made the point. "Because he might refuse to be freed," she put in, rather hurriedly.

"Why might he do that?" asked Max.

"Because, in his extremist state of mind, he might prefer his fellow terrorists to lose their cool and blow the whole thing to smithereens. He might even order them to do so. Then he'd be the author of the apocalypse, feted across the jihadist world. A prisoner for life maybe, but a hero and a martyr." She became more convinced – impressed with herself – even as she uttered the words.

"The jihadists will counter with conditions of their own," said the Lieutenant Colonel. "They will demand a carefully choreographed and very public scenario. Like the exchange of spies with the Russians when Berlin was a divided city – at Checkpoint Charlie."

"Davoud is waiting for my decision," said the PM. "He will be in charge of all the details, liaising closely with you, Brigadier. All this, of course, is top secret. Not a whisper. No announcement or press conference until it's all over, one way or the other. We need this completed speedily. Back into your helicopter, Lieutenant Colonel. Thanks for coming down; I wanted to see you face-to-face, not on a video conference. I'll speak to Davoud now."

0900

The last traces of morning mist across the bay were dispersing as the sun rose higher. Only Emily noticed the beauty of it, seeking some relief from the horror in which she was trapped. Daisy had just torn her picture into pieces and hurled her crayons across the carriage, Noah was bawling because he had stomach ache. Their mother Laura, red-eyed, cuddling Noah, had a pounding headache. She could not stand much more of this. She was exhausted.

"Why can't we go to Grandma's, Mummy?" asked Noah.

"I want to see Daddy," said Daisy.

"Shh, shh, soon, soon."

Laura's looks to Shalima were either pleading or hateful. Joan was trying to pacify Daisy. Muriel had refused to minister to Ibra any more and now sat with the others, stony-faced. Izzy and Shalima were slumped in the furthest seats, Kal separate but watchful of them.

In the men's carriage, Finlay, Paul and Geoff tried hard to get involved in another game of dominoes. They had a league table, as they had with cards, and until now Finlay had been ludicrously determined to win. But now they were either fatalistically bored stiff or frantic to step out of the carriage and stretch their legs. Didn't they sing to keep their spirits up in lifeboats, thought Paul? But there were only three of them and it would be ridiculous even if it was allowed. Was singing un-Islamic? He'd sometimes been accused of over-cheerfulness, as if it was a crime. He thought of Mary and their quiet life: cats; their annual railway trip round the Highlands, steam train on the Mallaig line; the other annual event, their adventure to London to see a musical. It all seemed a long way away.

Geoff was thinking of his son Richard in London: how he had never apologised to him for not accepting the lad's homosexuality, never sought forgiveness for rejecting him. And now it was perhaps too late. His wife had left him over it. Divorced, he lived alone and spent many hours in his allotment, tending vegetables. It seemed now a mean existence, thin and cold.

Bargo, his Barrett M82 on the table, was half asleep. Benny, off guard, was slumped in his sleeping bag, earphones plugged in. Kal went out on the viaduct for a smoke.

Beyond him, Yusuf was finishing his *fajr* prayers. Should have been before dawn, he knew, but better late than never. Using his jacket as a prayer mat he knelt towards the east, facing the wooded fell above Arnside.

As he stood up, Izzy appeared in the doorway of the

women's carriage. He was angry. "These kids have got to play out. They need somewhere to run about. Can't you see that?"

Yusuf stayed calm. "Well," he said, "get off your arse and take them out, along the line a bit."

Izzy squared his shoulders. "Don't fucking talk to me like that. Just who the fuck do you think you are?" he blazed.

He began to step down from the carriage, but Shalima appeared behind him and held his arm.

"Stay calm," she said.

Izzy paused and drew in a deep breath.

"Who am I?" said Yusuf. "I'm your leader. Bargo will go with you."

"You don't trust me, do you?" said Izzy.

Yusuf smiled enigmatically.

Bargo climbed down from the train with his Barrett M82 and Izzy went back into the carriage. Moments later, Noah and Daisy appeared, chattering excitedly. Izzy helped them down. Then their mother stepped down too.

"Who said she could go?" Yusuf was angry now.

"I did," said Izzy. "She won't leave them. Can you not understand why?"

Yusuf caught Bargo's eye and nodded towards Izzy. "Keep close," he said. "Only a hundred metres along, no further."

The five of them moved away from the train's shadow and into the sunlight. At first Laura held her children's hands, but then they skipped away. She watched them and took a deep breath of fresh air, turned her face towards the sun. It would be much worse for Adam, she thought, her husband not knowing anything, imagining, helpless.

Izzy and Bargo leaned against the railings on opposite sides of the track. Izzy thought, *It's three hundred metres to safety for them, that's all.* The soldiers at the railwayman's hut would be watching them through their binoculars, on the alert, radioing to HQ, wondering if the family was being freed, after all.

The kids jumped from one sleeper to the next, then balanced on the rails and tried to walk along. Daisy fell on the gravel but got up laughing. Laura joined them, and they dropped pieces of gravel chippings into the river below the viaduct. "Can you see the splash?" she asked them.

Izzy looked back and saw Kal standing with Yusuf, both holding their rifles and staring at him, the sun flashing on Kal's silver bracelet. Izzy gave them the thumbs-up and laughed. If the kids and their mother made a run for it, they would be shot, he was sure of it.

After twenty minutes Yusuf shouted, "OK, that's enough, back in the train."

Reluctantly, cajoled by their mum, the kids returned, as slowly as possible. Benny was there, at the bottom of the steps. He lifted them up and Shalima received them. Benny offered a helping hand to Laura, but she refused it.

Shalima thought Yusuf must be aware of how the team were dividing – ever since watching Bargo's compilation of video clips. He must realise now how big a mistake that had been. Only Yusuf, Bargo and Kal were regularly at prayers. Yusuf had altered the make-up of the shifts so that Izzy and Benny were never together. Benny, as the only explosives expert, was key. Yusuf had to keep him onside.

Izzy looked at his watch. The deadline was less than thirty hours away. If he was told to take part in the cold-blooded murder of child, he would refuse. Yusuf could blow the fucking lot of them to Paradise and have done with it.

Yusuf was looking at him, a half-smile playing on his lips.

1130

Davoud sat at the table in the meeting room at Belmarsh Prison. The table and the metal chairs were the same as the last time he was here. But on the table, as he had requested, was a brass hornbill-spouted coffee pot, two small handleless cups and a plate of dates, mirroring his meeting with Suleiman back in the embassy in Jordan. As before, Suleiman was taking his time. It was part of the game he was playing. But Davoud was not impatient: he needed these ten minutes to ensure he was in control of himself.

He took a deep breath, eyes closed, and consciously relaxed himself, working his way up from his toes to his neck to rid himself of tension. The Prime Minister's decision was right (though Davoud had not told him that), and he was here to implement it. His job was to offer freedom to the man who had murdered his mother and sister. And here in the silence, the helicopter rotor blades from his rushed journey back from Arnside still clattered in his brain.

A key turned in a lock and the door opposite opened. Two uniformed guards brought in Suleiman and took him to the other chair. Then they left the two of them together. They would be outside the door, ready to rush in should the watchers at the one-way window give them the signal. Suleiman must have immediately smelled the aroma of strong Arabic coffee, but he too must have prepared his self-control. There was no surprise, no reaction at all on his face. He settled himself, his robes once again exotic and graceful in the square, grey, monochrome room.

"Coffee?" asked Davoud.

Suleiman just stared at him. So Davoud poured himself a coffee, selected a date and pushed the plate towards Suleiman. Davoud's game now. He took two sips of coffee and put the cup back on the table.

"The government has decided to free you," he said softly.

No response.

"Initially in exchange for the family on the train, the mother and her two young children. You will have read about them in the papers. Then, in return for the freeing of the other hostages, you will be flown to the Yemen with your fellow jihadists."

Not a flicker of expression in Suleiman's eyes. Davoud hated the man's inhuman self-control. Two minutes passed, the silence broken only by the occasional tick of the heating radiator.

"I need some time," said Suleiman, standing up.

It was the first time Davoud had heard his voice: thin, reedy, feeble. Almost laughable coming from that face with its fierce eyes and strong black beard, its mouth that issued ruthless orders.

"You have thirty minutes," said Davoud.

"I have as long as I like."

Suleiman was escorted back to his cell.

Davoud stayed in the interview room, sitting, pacing, standing. He wanted fresh air but couldn't face the clang of doors locking and unlocking; the tiled, windowless corridors. It was forty-five minutes before the meeting resumed, with a fresh supply of coffee.

Then Suleiman sat, leaned forward and delicately took a date. Davoud imagined the unaccustomed sweetness in Suleiman's mouth, the taste of back home. He waited a moment and then poured coffee into the second cup and nudged it towards Suleiman. Now, suddenly, he was desperate for Suleiman to agree, despite his loathing of him. He wanted rid of this man, wanted him far away.

Suleiman fastidiously took the date stone from his mouth, cleaned of all flesh, not a shred, and placed it at the edge of the plate. He took the coffee cup, sipped from it, and then held it, the fingers of both hands around the warmth.

He said, "You must come with me onto the train."

Now it was Davoud's turn to betray no reaction. The decision he had already made to volunteer to be exchanged for the family would have been an extra bargaining chip, now no longer necessary. He had no choice. So much for his grand humanitarian gesture.

He nodded his agreement.

"Secondly, the plane we fly in must be Russian, crewed by Russians. And you and the other hostages must come to the plane with us. Only when I and my friends are on the plane will you be freed."

"Can I ask, why Russian? That could be a problem."

"It will be no problem for the Russians. Vlaskov, the Russian President, will enjoy your defeat. He will be seen as the saviour of the hostages, the man who saved the world, or part of it, from a radioactive catastrophe. Something that you were powerless to accomplish. And it has to be Russian because even you and the Americans will not dare attack a Russian plane. They will fly us to the Yemen."

"How can you trust the Russians not to take you somewhere else, even one of their prisons?" asked Davoud.

Suleiman shook his head. "That would upset too many of their interests across the Middle East and, in any case, I will guarantee no Al-Qaeda attacks on Russian personnel and property."

Was Suleiman being naive? Probably not – the Russians were always looking to strengthen their alliances in the complex world of Middle Eastern politics.

"I will take your conditions back to the authorities," said Davoud. "They will decide."

"One important detail," added Suleiman. "Each hostage must be handcuffed to a jihadi until we reach the top of the aircraft steps."

"I see, but you understand we will have heavily armed military personnel overseeing the whole transfer?"

"Of course! I would expect no less."

Suleiman gave a patronising smile and selected another date.

1400

Davoud reported back to the Prime Minister in his Downing Street office.

"But we cannot allow you, the leader of the operation, to become a hostage on the train, Davoud. Nor is it necessary. We can renegotiate that with Suleiman."

"I had already decided to be the family exchange hostage before the decision was made to free Suleiman, before Suleiman set down his conditions. Those children have to be freed."

He must sound so sanctimonious. Hated it.

The PM looked at him for a long moment, then nodded.

"Unless I go with him," continued Davoud, "he will refuse to be released. We have to go ahead."

The PM smiled. "You're right, of course. You're a good man, Davoud."

Davoud listened as a personal call was put through to Vlaskov. It would be 1830 in Moscow. The call took less than ten minutes, even with interpreters.

"He was just about to tuck into his *pelmeni*, he said – beef dumplings according to the interpreter. Nevertheless, I could almost hear him gloating," said the PM. "What a PR victory he will make of it. But it's a price worth paying. No doubt the press and my political rivals will present it as a humiliation for me. This time, I don't mind. My conscience, for once, will be easy."

"Never a bad thing," said Davoud, "and usually a good sign."

"Get your chopper back north and sort it with those lunatics. Let's hope they don't create any problems. They've got what they want but that doesn't always end matters. They might get greedy."

They shook hands and Davoud left.

★

Sitting on a bench in St James's Park he phoned Jenny. She told him she'd been following the Arnside operation closely, like almost everybody else. Was he involved in that? He wasn't allowed to say. It was a massive responsibility for someone, she said. He wanted to tell her. His borders had started dissolving with Jenny and yet he could not share what at the moment was the central part of his life. It was a halting, lame conversation: not the fulfilling call he needed. He still didn't know what else she could have said to make him happier. He wanted her to approve his volunteering, but she must not know. So he lacked that warm reassurance.

So what else had he wanted? Some statement, clear and unambivalent, that when the operation was all over their commitment to each other would be even stronger. But that was his own insecurity; maybe she felt she didn't need to say it because it was implicit.

1800

The jihadists listened to the BBC News on their iPhones. The first item was a report of helicopter flights from Arnside to London, purpose unknown; rumours of meetings in London, again, purpose unknown. The jihadists looked at each other. Something was happening, but what?

An online petition demanding the freeing of Suleiman had been signed by eight hundred thousand people. This time the jihadists cheered. The third item was about the gathering of religious leaders in Lancaster, just outside the Arnside exclusion zone. Their spokesman said that at least two thousand people would circumvent the roadblocks and gather at 2pm the next day at the Grange end of the Kent Viaduct.

From there they would march along the railway line to within fifty yards of the trains. A military spokesman regretted the initiative and said that armed troops would prevent them from doing so, with force if necessary. He refused to confirm or deny that tasers and water cannon would be on hand. "This is a very dangerous and delicate situation," he said. "Our prime duty must be to keep people safe, even from the consequences of their own actions." The religious leaders reiterated that the march would take place, two hours before the ultimatum time.

"That could make things awkward for them," said Yusuf.

There were interviews with two people who were volunteering themselves for exchange with the train family: a sixty-year-old businessman who felt he'd enjoyed his fair share of life, and a beautiful young fashion model who had decided her world was vapid and meaningless. Finally, a farmer forcibly removed from the potential radiation area grumbled about how incompetently the authorities were transferring his cattle to safe land.

Yusuf noted the differing degrees of enthusiasm he saw in his team. They were more divided than ever. Their cheering had been ragged. It was disappointing: Shalima had not chosen the team wisely after all. But for now he could live with it; there could be retribution later. Whatever happened, the outcome would be a victory for him and Allah. The world was watching and waiting.

1900

Then Yusuf's phone rang. It was Davoud, insisting that he speak to him out of the earshot of the other jihadists, out on the railway line where he could be seen to be alone.

Yusuf stepped down from the train and leaned against the railing over the river.

"We have a proposal for you," said Davoud. "It comes from our Prime Minister and the government."

Yusuf smiled. He had reached the very top.

"But what I say to you now must be kept secret. If any of this agreement or any of the things you must do as a result of it is posted on social media, the whole proposal falls." Davoud gritted his teeth. "You have been successful; you will get exactly what you want."

Yusuf could hardly believe it. He knew he would be feted, a hero for his cause. "So what is this proposal?" he asked, keeping the excitement out of his voice.

"Tomorrow, Friday, your holy day, Suleiman al-Hariri will be freed to you."

Yusuf's heart leapt. The man he revered and hero-worshipped would be free – and he, Yusuf, would have brought it about. Allah be praised!

"This is how it will work. At noon exactly, Suleiman will walk out of Arnside Station along the railway line to you. He will be accompanied by two soldiers and the MI5 leader of the whole operation, a man called Davoud Nariman – me. I am your VIP. I am the high-level exchange you asked for in order to free the family."

Yusuf was only momentarily disappointed: Nariman was not a well-known name. But he was important, the government had put him in charge. He would be more manageable than kids, and he was bringing Suleiman with him.

"At the halfway point along the line, we will stop," continued Davoud. "Two of your team will bring the mother and her two children to the same point. When they meet, each party will continue: the family to the station, Suleiman and myself to you. Is that clear?"

To Yusuf it was very clear.

"After that, we follow Suleiman's demands. Each of the remaining hostages will be handcuffed to one of you jihadists.

Your driver will take the hostage train five miles north-west to Cark Station. There we will board two military vehicles which will take us to Cark airfield. On the tarmac, engines running, will be a Russian plane, crewed by Russians, to fly you all to the Yemen. This is what Suleiman has specified. Each handcuffed pair, ending with Suleiman and myself, will climb the aircraft steps and only at the top will the handcuffs be released, the jihadist going into the plane, the hostage returning down the steps. There will obviously be a military presence to ensure all goes well."

There must be a catch, thought Yusuf. What if Nariman was making it all up?

"I will now play you a recording of Suleiman saying what I have just said. Listen carefully."

It was difficult for Yusuf to recognise the voice, but it was him. He had heard Suleiman speak only twice, back in the Yemen, on training videos.

"But there are non-negotiable conditions," continued Davoud. "The first I have already stated: absolutely nothing on social media. Second, you have explosives attached to the spent nuclear fuel. These must be disarmed, and we must see them disarmed. Your phone videos must be sent to this phone only. We must have that evidence and it must be verified by our own experts before Suleiman and I step onto the rail track."

"How will I know you are coming?"

"I will send you photos, just as you will send me."

Yusuf needed time to assimilate this.

"I need your acceptance or refusal within an hour," said Davoud. "Many arrangements have to be made with the Russians, and clearance agreed with the Yemeni authorities – with whom we foresee no problems. But both take time. Is that clear?"

"Yes."

★

Five minutes later, Yusuf called a meeting with Shalima, Bargo and Benny, out on the viaduct. As twilight deepened around them, he explained the proposal and held nothing back. Bargo looked at him with hero-worship in his eyes. Yusuf could see that Shalima and Benny were excited, too: Suleiman would be welcomed, the children freed, the mission successful, no more killings. Perhaps they recognised what Yusuf had achieved, reluctant though they might be to do so. Back in the Yemen he would be free to plan another mission – although no other, he felt, could match this.

But Yusuf had one sticking point which only Benny, the explosives expert, could clarify. He sent Shalima and Bargo back in to tell Izzy, Ibra and Kal. Yusuf and Benny spoke for some time.

Thirty minutes later, he rang Davoud.

"It is all agreed," said Yusuf. "Except for one thing."

Davoud waited.

"You are asking us to make the nuclear fuel harmless before we have even seen Suleiman. This is too much to ask."

"But you have the hostages."

"Hostages are expendable, as you know."

Davoud waited again.

"We will not disarm the explosives until we can see you and Suleiman on Arnside Station. I have spoken with my explosives expert. It will take him one minute to disarm the explosives. We will film him so that your explosives experts can verify what has been done. When you receive that verification, both parties will begin to walk towards the meeting point. I think that is fair."

It was fair, thought Davoud, although that was a bizarre concept when talking to these extremists. And he knew that decisions could be made above his head about the expendability of hostages, which now included himself.

"Agreed," he said. In the end, what else could he do? All he had was Suleiman. What they had was a potential local Armageddon. He knew he could not trust Yusuf. But what he might be able to trust was Yusuf's need for victory and glory. When it came to it, would he throw that away for martyrdom – martyrdom that was becoming a daily occurrence, hardly reported on beyond where it happened? And Yusuf was a convert – somehow Davoud thought that at the critical point he would revert to the culture of individual achievement and pride in which he had grown up.

Yusuf, for his part, was glad of the social media secrecy. If this plan was publicised before it happened and something went wrong, not only would he have failed, he would be seen to have failed. He would be judged a fool. There would be plenty of time to celebrate on social media once the deed was done.

He had already collected all the phones on the train. Shalima had supported him, especially with the difficult Izzy. Only Benny had been exempted, allowed to keep the special phone that would detonate the explosives and the nuclear fuel. Yusuf of course kept his own phone, to photograph the disarming. How right he'd been to set up that final insurance policy. Just in case there was a double-cross.

1920

From his own phone, Yusuf sent his message to both Imran's phones: *Don't miss livestream from the viaduct at noon tomorrow.*

That would immediately go viral. The Morecambe Bay hostage situation was trending round the world. Rumours of negotiation were already rife, even the government's decision to free Suleiman. Yusuf hadn't needed to break his word. Rumour and human curiosity had done his work for him. The public would draw its own conclusions and make its own links.

2130

Davoud's phone rang. It was Tim Bennett up at Arnside.

"Davoud, you need to know this. The Prime Minister also knows and he's leaving the decision to you."

"What is it?"

"There's a post just gone up on a Facebook page called The Morecambe Bay Amphitheatre."

"The what?!"

"Yes, just that. The post says, *Don't miss livestream from the viaduct at noon tomorrow*. We're assuming the terrorists have set it up. We've checked the site and it's already got hundreds of thousands of hits. People have guessed what it's about."

"So they're going to film the exchange and live-stream it to Facebook?"

"That's what we believe."

"So the decision the Prime Minister has kindly left to me is what to do with the Facebook page."

"Exactly."

"Let me talk it through with you, Tim."

"No problem."

"At the moment we have a news blackout for tomorrow. We've been very strict with that; nothing live can be shown or reported. We don't want this to turn into a circus or a reality TV show. We could presumably order Facebook to shut down the page."

"We could, but they might not agree."

"We could make it very hard for them not to comply.

But if we did get it closed down, presumably the terrorists would just be able to switch the stream to YouTube or another Facebook page they've set up that we don't yet know about."

"It's possible."

"If it's going out anyway, maybe we should lift the official news blackout."

Davoud waited for a comment, but Tim didn't reply. It was his, Davoud's, decision.

"We must remember that what we're doing," Davoud continued, "is what the public want. We're freeing Suleiman in exchange for the young family, we're avoiding a nuclear nightmare. Why should we hide it? It should be a celebration."

He paused and then continued, "But we can't congratulate ourselves yet. Many a slip… No, we don't lift the official news blackout because that would mean we would be responsible for turning it into a spectacular. The Prime Minister wouldn't want that. But nor do we shut down the Facebook page. It's what the people want to see; they expect it now, from what you say about the number of hits. If all goes well, there will be a huge national celebration and the PM will get lots of brownie points. He'll appreciate that. He's taken some tough decisions."

"So, Davoud, the Facebook page remains, and the official news blackout remains in force?"

"That's it, Tim. That's my decision."

A silence.

"Hope to see you tomorrow then, Davoud."

"Don't order the champagne yet, counting chickens and all that."

"Good luck," said Tim.

"Goodbye."

It could all go so wrong, but he didn't know how. All he did know was that he could not trust Suleiman or any of those lunatic extremists.

40.
Friday 9th October, 0500

Just south of Sandside a frogman staggered across the mudflats and was found, sitting and shivering by the road to Arnside, by a military patrol. He was a freelance cameraman whose breathing apparatus had failed, or his nerve. His intention had been to float and swim down the River Kent and emerge under the viaduct.

"They'd have shot you straight off, you bloody fool," said the sergeant in command as they took him back to base for hot chocolate and a spell in custody.

With Davoud now committed to being with Suleiman, Tim Bennett had been placed in charge of the operations room at Arnside.

"It's essential you know exactly where all the jihadists are," Davoud had told him. "All day, but especially at the exchange. I don't trust them an inch."

They knew there were seven: one woman, originally reported by the train driver Charlie Hopwood, but verified by sightings on the viaduct; one who was ill with malaria; and their leader, Yusuf. Four other men had been seen at various times but so far they had not been identified, not even with the help of Interpol.

Tim had sent out reminders that all media helicopter activity was still banned around Morecambe Bay and its environs; similarly, all media personnel were still banished beyond the evacuation zone. These reminders themselves created a flurry of expectation and at least three cameramen with long lenses and binoculars were already hiding in Grubbins Wood, on Arnside Knott, and in the drainage channels of Meathop Marsh on the north side of the estuary.

In the meantime, press and TV were covering the influx of people for the interfaith peace march. Selfies were already being posted on social media – of hooded characters negotiating stone walls and fences, scurrying across lanes into the evacuated zone. Police and army reinforcements had been called up. First shown earlier in the week, interviews with relatives of the other hostages had been replayed through the night, as had a hurried documentary on Suleiman al-Hariri, detailing the atrocities he was thought to be responsible for. Two opinion polls showed this information had not altered attitudes: he must be exchanged for the mother and her two children. There were also reruns of interviews with friends and family of Ryan Hudson/Yusuf Javeed, all of them totally bewildered by how he had turned out.

A COBRA meeting was scheduled for nine o'clock. No other announcements had been made.

0546

Davoud slept fitfully in one of the small, single emergency overnight rooms in Thames House.

Suleiman, after saying his pre-dawn prayers, had returned to bed and slept soundly in his cell.

With differing motivations, the jihadists said their prayers separately out on the viaduct, facing east, their knees on the hard ballast, touching their foreheads to the gleaming rails, giving thanks to Allah, their voices thin against the gulls' shrieks. Even this early, the air was still and mild. Those not on duty guarding the hostages returned to their sleeping bags. But none slept except Benny who, thought Shalima, seemed curiously at ease with himself. Tonight they would be back in the Yemen, freed from this mission, feted as heroes, giving thanks to Allah. Izzy feared there might be recriminations from Yusuf.

Gideon Camborne awoke early. This was the day of reckoning: things might work out, or they might go horribly wrong. He had taken a mighty gamble. He turned to cuddle his sleeping wife, nuzzling his head into her back, feeling himself merge into her, needing to lose his isolation.

Across London, Jenny also woke. Had she said the right things to Davoud? Given him the reassurance he needed? Was he involved up there in the north, in that terrible situation?

0715

After his final phone call last night with Davoud, Yusuf had informed the jihadists of the situation and the plans. All were jubilant, but for varying reasons: Yusuf, Bargo and Kal because they were on the edge of success, mission accomplished; Shalima, Izzy and Benny for the same reason, but also because there had been no more cold-blooded murders. Far from the bloodlust of actual fighting, or the anonymity of long-distance planning, they had come to see the hostages as human beings. In the claustrophobia of the railway carriages, living in close quarters with them, this had been an unforeseen development. None of them, except Shalima and Yusuf, had envisaged being so close to people they were expected to murder.

Without any explanation, all the hostages were moved to the men's carriage. They sensed a greater relaxation among the jihadists, but they themselves were tenser. The movement signified something, but they didn't know what. Noah and Daisy were excited by the change and being with the men. Finlay thought Emily was fit, made more alluring by the headscarf. He thought of Roger McGough's poem about a bus full of passengers who hear the world is going to end at lunchtime and make love with each other. He could have done a lot worse. Fat chance here with those sharia law fanatics. She was obviously a Muslim. Surely they wouldn't kill her? If there was a final struggle, would he go down fighting, try to take one of the bastards with him?

The women, for something to do, set about tidying up the men's mess: collecting discarded food packets and empty cola cans into black plastic rubbish bags. Benny and Bargo threw the full bags over the rails and watched the tide slowly swirl around them, billowing but lodged in the sand. Gulls screamed, squabbled and jabbed at the bags. Sunlight was spreading across the bay.

0800

Davoud lay on his bed, fully awake, Radio 4 on but he wasn't listening, just a drone of voices. He had over an hour to kill before leaving Thames House. He could contact no one he really needed to talk to – Jenny, Sara Tim Bennett up in the operations room. He wasn't sure he wanted to talk to them, anyway. For the next six hours he had to live in a bubble until, at two o'clock, the Russian plane was due to fly out to the Yemen. If the plan worked, he would be watching it as it disappeared westwards over the Irish Sea. If the plan didn't work, he would either be a prisoner or dead. Once he was on the helicopter up to Arnside, whatever happened was out of his hands. But he was calm: what he had done was right, given the Prime Minister's political decision. And that decision was the correct one, the only one a human being could make; made more necessary because their enemies were not human beings.

He turned off the radio. Babble. Speculation. He would

shower, order coffee and pastries – he craved sweetness. Lying in bed, he had a fleeting nostalgia for the comfort of prayer, thought of his mother and sister, his father. Wondered why he had not yet given up on this crazy, cruel and beautiful world.

There was a knock on the door. It would be his freshly laundered clothes from yesterday.

"OK, just leave them," he called.

Why this need to be neat and clean? Because Suleiman would be resplendent in his robes, exotic on the shores of Morecambe Bay. Davoud himself would be a civil servant in a fawn suit.

On the train, breakfast was being eaten from yesterday's resupply of provisions. This was the best part of the day, thought Shalima. People were still hungry, and food still comforted. There was a busyness before the day spread, uncertainly and threateningly, ahead of them. This morning's prayers had been more fervent than usual, continuing the intensity of yesterday's, just after sunset and then in the pre-midnight darkness.

As they ate their Coco Pops the kids were relaxed. Joan was telling them about her own grandsons, how they liked football and fishing. Paul and Geoff had played with them since they'd woken up, teaching them *Here's the church and here's the steeple, open the doors and see the people* and *Pat-a-cake, pat-a-cake, baker's man*, the four of them playing slapsies. Now the adults drank tea or coffee and forced themselves to eat some marmalade sandwiches. Tense, they had little appetite. Most harmless subjects of conversation had been exhausted but today Shalima sensed them making an effort, keeping up their spirits. They knew something was in the offing – the jihadists were in a different mood, they were all together for the first time – but they didn't know what. If another death was planned, the jihadists' mood would be grimmer. The hostages were hopeful but dared not be confident, their eyes flicking towards Yusuf, seeking clues. Laura, Shalima saw, was still red-eyed with sleeplessness. It was far worse for her than for any of them, worse even than it had been for the old birder. The fear inherent in motherhood. Shalima thought of her own mother: a life lived wholly in fear, in fear of her husband and of what might happen to her daughter. What sort of mother was the White Widow? Shalima wondered for the first time if the White Widow was insane. Could she allow Noah and Daisy to be killed?

She looked across at Yusuf. He was locked into his victory, the triumph of it. But he was watchful, too, still the predator, the mantis with blazing eyes, his thin, oddly triangular face and his long limbs.

Things must not fail now, not at the last moment. Yet he knew his team, though they had prayed together, had been giving thanks for different things. Beneath their jokes and laughter, long pent up, he listened for notes of disagreement and looked for signs of antipathy. Izzy was the one to watch.

Suleiman drank his coffee but ate nothing. They had brought him pastries and olives on his final day here in the prison. They depended on his cooperation. He glanced towards his cell door. That fool Davoud thought it was all arranged. Suleiman could not stop himself from smiling.

Across Morecambe Bay, the tide was rising. Gently the water pushed in, seeping into and over the sand, filling channels, sheening the bay, pushing the birds back: plovers and oystercatchers and black-headed gulls taking off and landing again in a great caterwauling of complaint.

0910

In a limousine with dark-tinted windows, Davoud left Thames House to be sped towards the Isle of Dogs and the Vanguard Helipad. On the back seat, next to him, was a black holdall containing a dozen sets of silver steel handcuffs.

In an unmarked white van, Suleiman was driven away from Belmarsh Prison via the back exit. Two unmarked police cars preceded and followed him, each carrying four armed Special Branch officers.

The COBRA team assembled in their meeting room. They were subdued, tense, phones on the table in front of them. Coffee, tea, and full English breakfasts were available as well as croissants and pastries. A split screen showed eight different news channels but there was nothing new about the hijacked trains, only some coverage of the intended religious march. The news blackout had held. Instead, they watched more pictures of migrants landing from rubber boats on Greek islands.

A plane, a Legacy 650, droned in low over Morecambe Bay, silver in the sunlight. In the operations room in the community hall, heads turned to the window to watch it glide past.

"Look, Noah," said his mother, seizing on something new to interest him.

Yusuf and Shalima got down from the train carriage and watched from the viaduct as it came in low over Grange-over-Sands, to land beyond. There, at Cark airfield, the steps were lowered and a Russian attaché swiftly climbed up them. From the edge of the airfield a platoon of SAS watched.

0930

At the Arnside sailing club, two Zodiacs were being made ready. Each would carry half a dozen well-armed SAS and would take ninety seconds to race to the viaduct. Hurling grappling irons up to the railings, the soldiers would climb up.

At Sunnyside Farm on the north side of the bay, a second SAS squad waited, ready to sprint out onto the viaduct. A third squad waited, similarly prepared, in the Information Centre on Arnside Station.

A fourth SAS group was ready by the Wildcat Mk1 helicopter south of Arnside Knott, thirty seconds' flying time from the Kent Viaduct.

Because the passenger train was hidden from Arnside promenade behind the freight train, Tim Bennett had ordered that two snipers be placed upriver of the viaduct on each bank of the estuary: one on the embankment at the edge of Meathop Marsh, the other in the shelter of a rotting fishing boat on the marsh near Sandside. Six other snipers were also in position.

Coastline military and police patrols around the bay were picking up people trying to approach the planned start of the religious march. Rumours were rife – about the deployment of the SAS, about the whereabouts of the operations leader Davoud Nariman, about an unexpected plane landing at the almost disused airfield at Cark.

In the operations room information was being fed into the various laptops and iPads. Sky News was on the big screen with reports of clashes between religious leaders and the police in Lancaster, and of arrests out in the fields and along the shoreline. Tim Bennett waited for the phone call from Davoud, the fingers of his left hand drumming lightly on his desk between the phone and a half-empty cup of black coffee.

The phone vibrated and rang. Voices stopped in the middle of calls, fingers stopped tapping computer keys, necks tensed, ears strained, eyes did not register the advert on Sky News for discount furniture. Tim picked up the phone, looked at the screen, touched it and saw a photograph. It was a selfie: Davoud and Suleiman sitting next to each other but not smiling. A second photo: protruding from a loose orange-and-brown sleeve, a hand, the wrist handcuffed to that of another hand protruding from a fawn suit sleeve. Both hands dark-skinned. A third photo: this one, taken by someone else, showed the two men were strapped into seats in a helicopter. And then a text: *ETA 1130*.

"They're on their way," announced Tim. "Arrival time half eleven."

The information was instantly forwarded to the waiting troops. Tim stared for a moment at Davoud's face. What would he be feeling? Then he forwarded the photos to Yusuf's phone.

On the train, Yusuf was sitting alone at a table, the blank screen of the phone in front of him. He was staring at the container of nuclear fuel on the other train and stroking his beard. Text alert, vibrations on the tabletop. The carriage fell silent. Yusuf glanced down at the phone; a half-smile. Another beep, then picked it up and touched the screen. He swiped through the three photos. He closed his eyes, let his shoulders relax. Then he leapt up and punched the air.

"Allahu Akbar!" he yelled. "Yes!"

The jihadis jostled round to see the pictures, even Izzy. "We've done it!" shouted Bargo, high-fiving Kal. The carriage floor vibrated as they jumped with joy. Shalima hugged them all, including the still pale-faced Ibra, now recovering fast. Only Benny remained unmoved.

Daisy and Noah were frightened by the sudden shouting and leaned close to Joan and their mum. Daisy was frowning but Noah began to smile a little as the laughter continued. The adult hostages looked on, perplexed. This must be good news, but what was good news to their jailers?

Emily asked, "Can't you tell us what is going on?"

"Why not tell them?" asked Shalima.

But Yusuf said, "Not yet. There's many a slip still possible. Only when we see the helicopter land."

Shalima saw he was glorying in this last period of his power. But she also felt he was still calculating. There was a tautness about him.

Benny was unwrapping a Milky Way for Daisy; Izzy was play-fighting with Noah. Trembling and close to breakdown, Laura was gripping Joan's hand tightly. Joan wanted to tell her it could only be good news, but didn't dare. She wasn't that confident. Muriel was saying a silent prayer.

1130

The media must have been tipped off by someone at the Vanguard Helipad. On the big screen in the operations room a reporter was saying there were rumours of a helicopter en route to Arnside. Then there was a brief long shot of a helicopter – it could have been any helicopter anywhere – passing beyond the ridge of a hill. The reporter said no government spokesperson was available. Interviews in the streets of Lancaster showed a majority hoped that the rumours were true. The religious leaders had agreed to postpone a decision about their march until one o'clock.

The helicopter's clattering was heard in the operations room and on the train. In the operations room there'd been a final check that everyone knew the choreography of how the exchange would work. On the train, Ibra and Benny were detailed to stay with the hostages while the other jihadis rushed outside. The hostages crowded at the windows.

They all watched the helicopter descend and land on Arnside promenade. The rotor blades slowed and stopped, the doors opened and two men walked down the steps. A black holdall was passed down to the man wearing a fawn suit. The other man was in Arab robes, brown and orange in the bright sunshine. A minibus drove up. The two men got in, with two soldiers. Slowly the minibus drove down the promenade and turned out of sight in the direction of the station.

"Tell them," said Yusuf to Shalima. "Tell the family."

She hurried back into the train. All were watching Yusuf's iPad.

"Laura," she said. It was the first time she had used her name.

Laura looked up, her eyes wide with fear. She clung to Joan's arm even more fiercely.

"The man you've just seen in the suit is going to take the place of you, Noah and Daisy. In just thirty minutes you will be free."

Laura stared up, uncomprehending.

"What's the lady saying, Mummy?" asked Noah, trying to cuddle her, knowing something was wrong.

Laura could take no more. She collapsed and sobbed, her arm round Noah, grabbing for Daisy.

Joan and Muriel comforted her. "She's crying because she's happy," they explained to the children.

"In a little time you'll be going home," said Shalima. "Your daddy is waiting for you."

Slowly Laura stopped sobbing.

"Are you all right now?" asked Noah, stroking her tear-wet face.

Laura tried to smile. "Yes, I'm all right, love, I'm just being silly."

"Praise be to Allah," whispered Emily.

Yusuf came in. Immediately everyone tensed.

"If everything goes to plan," he said, "and it still might not…" – Laura gave a little yelp – "…in about twenty minutes' time, we will free the family. In return, Suleiman al-Hariri will be freed to us. He will come with Davoud Nariman, a top man in MI5 who has led the operation so far. As soon as they get into this carriage you will see they are handcuffed together. Each of you will then be handcuffed to one of us."

There was a sharp drawing of breath. Laura looked around the adults. Shalima saw a new fear in their faces.

"Kal, our driver, will then drive this train a few miles north to the station at Cark. We will then be transferred to the airfield there. You probably noticed a plane fly in there a couple of hours ago. It was Russian. That plane will fly us out, back to the Yemen."

"All of us?" croaked Geoff.

Yusuf smiled. "No. When each pair of us reaches the top of the plane steps, the handcuffs will be taken off and you will be free to walk back down and cross to British soldiers who will be waiting for you. It will be an honourable exchange."

The hostages looked at Yusuf and at each other. Could they believe him?

"And now we must make the final arrangements," ended Yusuf.

1200

Nothing was happening.

In the electrical department of Sainsbury's on Edgware Road, London, a bank of muted TVs were showing *Teletubbies*, *Ramsay's Kitchen Nightmares* and *A New Life in the Sun*.

But Jenny and about twenty other shoppers were bunched

around two particular TVs showing BBC News. The screen was split: on one half a still photograph of the Kent Viaduct, the river underneath it and the sands of Morecambe Bay; on the other half a close-up of the clock face of Big Ben. Across the bottom of the screen was the statement: *There is a news blackout on the hostage situation. We will go live as soon as the authorities permit.*

The big clock finger ticked up to noon. Jenny imagined the first sonorous, ominous stroke of the bell. She was aware of mutterings around her, felt her heart thudding. Davoud was up there; she was certain of it.

The eight snipers stationed on the edges of the bay heard the Arnside church bell faintly as they adjusted their elbows on the ground and focused their telescopic sights on the sloping ramp of the station's southbound platform, or on the train.

For Yusuf, standing on the railway track in front of the passenger train, the sound of the church bell was drowned out by the pulsating diesel engine which Kal had started up. Tense, he too stared at the end of the platform 150 metres away.

Inside the carriages the twelve strokes of the church bell were inaudible. Geoff and Paul were listening critically to the sound of the diesel engine; Muriel sat with her eyes closed, lips moving as she intoned a silent prayer. Joan was reading *Fireman Sam* to Daisy. Laura's fingers trembled as she put on smudged lip gloss and brushed her hair. Impatient, frightened, she wanted to look presentable, to look stronger than she felt as the world watched.

Finlay, sitting by the window, was building a Lego tower with Noah. He glanced along the curve of the viaduct which just allowed him to see the railway line enter the station. Emily was looking up at Shalima, trying to hold her gaze, trying to convince her with a look that she had turned their God into a merciless aberration.

On the promenade Chief Superintendent Steve Mack heard the bells and stood motionless, feet apart, his binos focused on the station platform.

In the operations room Tim Bennett, Lieutenant Colonel Malcolm McPhail and the rest of the team saw the same still photos as Jenny and the shoppers but heard the sound of Big Ben tolling. On another screen, on a feed from their own cameras they watched the empty southbound platform.

Inside St James' Parish Church on Church Hill, the Reverend Colin Smith and fifteen parishioners – twelve women and three men – heard the sound of the single church bell reverberate above them, bowed their heads and together spoke the Lord's Prayer.

Through their cross-hair sights the snipers saw a movement on the platform. Their minds concentrated, fingers and hands relaxed on their rifles. A group appeared, halted at the top of the southbound platform slope, then moved slowly down it. The snipers' telescopic sights followed Suleiman's brown-and-orange robes as the small group walked by the yellow strip and the *Mind the Step* warnings painted on the platform, past the sign: *Passengers must not cross the line*, and past the red signal lights. In the lead were Suleiman, tall and full-bearded, his robes billowing and wearing sandals, and Davoud, shorter, neat in his fawn suit and brown leather shoes. Handcuffed together, they appeared to be holding hands, an incongruous, exotic gay couple. Behind came two soldiers in full battle fatigues, carrying Bren guns, bulked out with body armour. Behind them came two paramedics, also wearing body armour. On their backs were rucksacks of medical equipment. In his left hand Davoud carried his black holdall.

Finlay looked up, his hand poised above the Lego tower, about to place a yellow brick. "They're here," he whispered softly.

"Wait," called one of the soldiers as they came to the sleepers and ballast of the railway track. He was plugged into an earphone and mike.

Standing by the train, Yusuf took an involuntary step forward, gripped his rifle tighter. He was only 150 metres away. He had imagined and dreamed of this moment: this victory. He grinned at Bargo standing next to him. It was Friday, the holy day, too: the best of omens. His heart was thumping. He wanted to fall to his knees, pray, give thanks to the great Allah. But not yet. First, the exchange. On his mobile, he spoke to Tim Bennett in the operations room.

"We can see Suleiman so, as agreed, we will now defuse the explosives. I will film it and stream it to you."

"We're watching," said Tim. This was the crucial moment. But how could he, anyone, trust the word of a murdering religious fanatic? But there was no alternative.

Yusuf called Benny into the women's carriage, empty since the transfer of all hostages to the men's.

"You have the special phone?" checked Yusuf.

"Of course."

Yusuf had his own phone to take the film.

"Benny, you know what you have to do now: deactivate the explosives. This I will carefully film for the operations room." He paused. "But, as you and me know, we still have the hidden insurance phone."

Benny frowned. "We do."

"That must stay activated."

"But…" began Benny. "We have agreed a deal."

Yusuf's right hand went to his holstered pistol. "Do exactly as I say, Benny. No buts. We cannot leave the faintest chance of failing now we have come so far. That insurance is in case they double-cross us."

Benny gave a nod of the head and a sardonic smile. "OK, chief."

The waiting group at the bottom of the platform watched Yusuf and Benny leave the passenger train, walk round and climb up onto the flatbed truck with the nuclear fuel. Chief Superintendent Mack turned and trained his binos on them. Snipers' rifles followed them. The ops room team watched their camera feed on the big screen. The sun was shining, and Yusuf shifted around to find the right angle for his filming.

"Ready?" asked Benny.

Yusuf nodded.

Benny said, "You need to pan the phone from this silver detonator, down the taped wires, then follow the wires across the foam to the phone. The watchers have to see that clearly. They have to be certain."

"I know that," said Yusuf. "I'm not a fool."

Benny hid the start of a smile. "Then I will cut the wires here, where they lie on the foam. Go ahead."

Yusuf held the phone so he could shade the LED screen. He panned along the wires and then zoomed back a little to take in Benny's hand with the cutters.

"Cut now," said Yusuf.

Benny did so, and held up the severed wire for the final shot.

Yusuf smiled, tapped the screen and sent the video half a mile across the bay to the operations room. He waited for confirmation of receipt.

In the operations room, Tim, the Lieutenant Colonel and an explosives expert called in from the bomb disposal squad studied the short video clip.

"That's sound," said the soldier. "No connection, rendered safe. But we don't know what happened when he stopped filming."

A sudden spasm of fear in the pit of Tim's stomach. "We can't do anything else. I don't trust those bastards, but presumably the jihadists and Suleiman will now all want to stay alive."

"Remember the virgins, the suicide bombers," said the Lieutenant Colonel.

"I know about the fucking virgins. Nevertheless, give the go-ahead."

Into the phone to Yusuf he said, "Fine, all set to go."

Yusuf climbed down from the flatbed truck and, fifteen seconds later, Benny followed him. But in that fifteen seconds Benny had tapped the phone icon on his special phone, then tapped the *Suleiman* entry, then tapped *Edit* and altered the last two digits of the number.

Yusuf stepped inside the railway carriage. The adults looked up at him. Joan stopped reading to Daisy. Laura's fingers stopped drumming on the table.

Noah said, "Come on, Finlay, put another brick on the tower."

Yusuf looked down at all their upturned faces. He saw lines of strain, lips tight with anxiety, eyes dulled with fear. He saw they did not dare to hope. He controlled them all. He looked at Laura: that ridiculous lipstick gashed across her pale face, her eyes beseeching him. She was trembling.

"Allah is merciful," said Yusuf and nodded his head towards the door. "You can go, with your children."

He watched her face collapse, her mouth babbling thank-yous, her eyes filled with tears. She scrambled up from her seat.

Joan kissed Daisy. "Go with your mum."

Daisy climbed over knees to join her mum standing in the aisle. Noah climbed over the table and Geoff helped him down.

"Are we really going, Mummy?"

Laura nodded her head, unable to speak.

"Your handbag," said Muriel, handing it over.

Laura's flustered face looked round at them all. She tried to say something, but no words came.

"Escort them, Shalima," said Yusuf.

She had been going to ask him if she could do this, take them to safety. Silently she thanked Allah. She needed to see his mercy made visible.

"You, too, Kal," said Yusuf. "Take them until you meet the other group, release the family and then escort Suleiman and Nariman back to us. But be on your toes. There may be trickery; there will be soldiers with their rifles trained on us. We may have to abort. Listen for my voice and obey my instructions immediately."

Shalima stepped down onto the track and helped Laura down. Kal handed down Noah and Daisy, then stepped down himself.

"We'll go in front," said Shalima.

"Pistols out," said Kal.

The Lieutenant Colonel spoke into his PPR headset. "We have six of the seven terrorists in sight here. Snipers, your sit-rep? Alpha 1?"

"Alpha 1 on target Skua."

"Couldn't miss that bastard in his robes. Alpha 2? With the family?"

"Alpha 2 on target Starling."

"That's the female. Alpha 3?"

"Alpha 3 on target Raven."

"Standing outside the train, three of them. Alpha 4?"

"Alpha 4 on target Rook."

"Alpha 5 on target Crow."

"Alpha 6 on target Chough."

"Now the one on his own, sitting inside the front carriage. Alpha 7?"

"Alpha 7, no shot."

"No shot? Jesus, he's the key man," said the Lieutenant Colonel.

"Maybe it's the sun dazzling the windows."

"Alpha 7 confirming that," said the sniper, after the Lieutenant Colonel repeated the explanation.

"That means the last one must be inside the train too, presumably in the other carriage guarding the rest of the hostages. Alpha 8?"

"Alpha 8, no sighting."

"Thank you, all."

The Lieutenant Colonel turned to his fellow officers. Tim Bennett stood with them.

"It's the guy that we can see sitting on the train that worries me. He's the one we saw on the video deactivating the bomb. He must be the explosives expert. The exchange is about to happen, so why the fuck is he waiting there?"

"He's done his job. It's up to the others now," suggested the major.

"But wouldn't he want to witness it?" the Lieutenant Colonel persisted. "It's the climax, what they've been working for. It's like the victory parade he's risked his life for." He scratched his head. "No, I think he's there because he might have another job to do. In case something goes wrong. And the only job he could do is press the bloody keys on that phone and blow the fucking lot up." He thumped the desk and yelled, "Christ, we've been had. It's a total fucking cock-up."

"Then we must kill them all now simultaneously," said the major.

"Alpha 7, sit-rep no change?"

"Alpha 7, still no shot."

The Lieutenant Colonel turned to his fellow officers. "So we can't take them all out. All that guy has to do is press some phone keys. He could do it wounded, especially knowing his reward is seventy-two fucking virgins."

"And there's the other guy, the hostage guard," said the major. "He might be wearing a suicide vest so at the first sign of trouble he can blow all the hostages up."

"A small price to pay, I'm afraid, if we've avoided a nuclear catastrophe," said the Lieutenant Colonel grimly. "But he might also be able to activate the bomb. These guys have planned well, they'll have thought about backup."

They stood in silence.

Tim Bennett felt his chest tighten and his stomach loosen as he made the biggest decision of his professional life. "Right, gentlemen, we hold fire. We cannot take the risk."

As he waited, Davoud's eyes were on the flowing water in the river's twisting channel, glittering in the sun.

Sara, sunlight bright in their living room in Jordan, fan whirring in the corner; Sara with her clipboard taking the register as they played school, bossing him about.

"Davoud?" she'd ask, and if he answered in a funny voice she'd get cross. "Do it properly," she'd say severely.

Those had been the best of times: her safe with him, just the two of them, holding her close, her cuddling, wriggling warmth, her words and ideas, being serious and joking.

She would grow to need him less. Must do, for her sake. If he came out of this alive he would keep faith with her, never break a promise.

Next to him Suleiman stood perfectly still: the man who had planned the murder of Davoud's mother and sister. Then Davoud must have shifted his body slightly. Their cuffed hands touched: the sudden accidental warmth of Suleiman's hand, the soft hair like an electric charge. Both of them flinched – the banal horror of the connection of their skins.

Davoud glanced up at Suleiman's impassive face, glaring down the track to the train. Did Suleiman love? Was he loved back? Davoud thought not, and for a moment pitied him. Suleiman did not share, nor was he a compromiser. Therefore compromise must be good: fudging, patching up, making do, making the best of things. Being English – the rejection of extremes, of ideologies.

Davoud looked down at his polished brown shoes, at Suleiman's sandals, the black holdall at his feet full of metal handcuffs, the railway sleepers, the dirty gravel ballast and gleaming rails stretching out over the viaduct. And he was suddenly certain that in the next few minutes something would go wrong. And Jenny was far, far away. Jenny – her smile, her optimism. Daren't think of that.

Suleiman gave a short grunt and Davoud looked up. He saw two children being handed down from the carriage. They and their mother and two jihadis formed into a small group, the mother between her children, the two jihadis in front. Davoud saw sunlight flash on their pistols; heard the crackle of the escorting soldier's radio, the brigadier's voice. "Go ahead. All systems go."

"Walk on," the soldier said to Suleiman and Davoud.

Davoud bent to pick up the holdall in his left hand, and tugged Suleiman's arm as he did so. Suleiman grunted impatiently.

They began to advance, in step, along the line. The soldiers and paramedics stayed at the end of the platform, as instructed by Yusuf.

"Move forward," ordered Yusuf.

"You mustn't run," said Laura, holding her children's hands tightly.

On the TV screens in Sainsbury's the same two shots were on the screen: the bay and Big Ben. Along the bottom of the screen was a new statement: *We understand that something is happening on the viaduct at this very moment. But we are not permitted to say more than that.*

A few others had joined Jenny.

She couldn't take her eyes off the unchanging screen. Holding herself still. Taut.

Back in Whitehall the Prime Minister and the COBRA group watched the same special feed as the operations group.

"It looks as if the family will be OK," said the PM.

"But what happens after that?" asked the Defence Minister. "Can we believe that they've really deactivated the bomb on the nuclear stuff? Will they free the other hostages when they get to the Russian plane?"

No replies, because no one knew.

Noah and Daisy tugged at their mother, wanting to stretch their legs and scamper. The breeze blew their hair. They were giddy. Laura too wanted to run, to escape as fast as possible. But Shalima and Kal set a steady pace.

Inside the carriage, Finlay said, "I can't see them now; the other carriage hides the curve of the track."

The others sat silent, staring out of the window at the bay or at their hands on the table, shuffling Lego bricks. Ibra sat at a table opposite them. He had been assigned this guard job – as if they would try anything. What could they do?

The smell of all their unwashed bodies and the stale air – gross.

Davoud and Suleiman led their group carefully onto the track. The sleepers were awkward distances apart so that he and Suleiman, without exchanging a word, had to synchronise their steps. Marching. Like comrades.

Yusuf watched from the front of the train, Kalashnikov over his shoulder, filming with his mobile phone. Next to him stood Bargo, tense and alert, rifle at the ready. Izzy stood behind them and slightly apart, leaning on the viaduct railing. The air was pungent with diesel fumes. Izzy looked up, hearing the whirring blades of a helicopter but it was out of sight. Below him, birds hustled and poked their beaks into the sand.

In Sainsbury's electrical department a larger group of shoppers had gathered now, bunched in front of the two silent TVs which showed the minute hand of Big Ben at two minutes past midday. At the front, her basket at her feet with two packets of bacon, a bag of pasta and a loaf of artisanal bread, stood Jenny.

Behind her, she heard a man's voice. "It's just like the terrorists announced, right on time. They're filming this on his phone."

Like most of the rest of the world, Jenny had known it was on. She didn't want to watch it – it was a kind of nasty voyeurism. Other people's misfortunes as a TV show.

She glanced round. Four phones were being held up, heads craning to see the screens more clearly.

"Look, there they go," said the same man's voice, "starting to walk towards the train."

Jenny thought of Davoud – was he in the control room somewhere, making split-second decisions in his quiet voice, directing this life-and-death operation? She gritted her teeth for him. What a huge responsibility if he was. *I know you'll do it right. Keep your head clear.*

★

Steadily the two small groups approached each other. The meeting point was about fifty metres from the train. Feet stepping on gravel, stubbing the sleepers, gulls screeching, the two children's high, excited voices.

"Two of them at the front: the Arab guy in his robes and the other guy must be the Secret Service guy. That's the rumour, anyway."
Secret Service?!
"They're bloody handcuffed together."
It must not be.
"In his Sunday-best suit by the look of it. He looks like an Arab, too. Brown skin, beard."
What?! A sudden rush of blood pounding behind Jenny's eyes. That image of Davoud at his desk splintered instantly. *Please, no!*
"He's small, isn't he, next to the big Al-Qaeda guy? With his specs looks like an office clerk versus a warrior."
A gag of nausea in her throat. Breathing fast. Ears straining, though she didn't want to know.
"Brave bloke. Must have volunteered to be exchanged for the family."
An image of the shot hostage, body bag on a stretcher. Her head dipped, hand at her neck, eyes closed, heart pounding against her ribs. A premonition. *Stay alive, Davoud, stay alive.*
The man with the phone was enjoying his role as commentator for people who couldn't see. Or, like Jenny, who daren't see. *I can't move away, can't stop listening. His life now chained to that murderous bomber.*
"Here come the kids and their mum, walking away from the train. They're letting them go."
"Thank God!" A woman's voice.
A little cheer went round the group.

Jenny couldn't pray; she didn't believe in God.

"There's two of the terrorists escorting them. See their pistols. One's a woman, for Christ's sake! She must be sick."

A growl of disgust among the group.

"The two groups are getting close now, the family and the Arabs. I think they're just going to walk past each other, on their separate railway tracks."

As they reached each other, the two groups paused. Laura's face was flowing with silent tears. She wanted to shake the hand of the man in the suit, their saviour. But in his left hand he was carrying a bag. When he held up his right hand in acknowledgment, the other Arab's arm lifted up and she saw with a shock the gleam of handcuffs. The man in the suit smiled at her. The other man's face was aloof, fierce, the key part of him focused on something else, certainly not them.

"No, the mother has turned her face towards the Secret Service guy, but we can only see the back of her head. The Secret Service guy has smiled at her and nodded."

Jenny could just hear the children's high-pitched voices.

Davoud, Davoud, you are such a special man.

Then they passed each other, the kids scampering, Laura running after them, shouting at them to stop, but exultant. One paramedic trotted after them. The other stayed with the soldiers, who looked forward at the backs of Suleiman and Davoud as they joined the two jihadists, one a woman.

"The two soldiers are returning with the family. They're safe."

A small cheer and some applause.

"And now the Arabs are approaching the train and the leader. The woman terrorist is leading them in with the other terrorist."

Shalima looked at Kal – he seemed dazed in the presence of the great man, Suleiman. Suleiman had totally ignored her. *Because I'm a woman*, she realised, and she felt a sudden rage. Suleiman quickened his stride, the shorter Davoud compelled to hurry. Yusuf, ahead of them in front of the train, was stepping forward to greet Suleiman, and at that exact moment Shalima knew with total certainty that somehow Yusuf had double-crossed them all.

Davoud, linked by the cuffs to Suleiman's urgent strides, also understood a sudden switch of power, an unforeseen change of plan. His heart plummeted into his stomach. He tried to hold Suleiman back, but with less than twenty metres between him and Yusuf, Suleiman suddenly yelled, "God is great! We blow up the nuclear fuel, we detonate it and blow ourselves to Paradise, all of us."

Davoud tried to pull him back. "No!" he screamed.

Shalima saw Suleiman's wild, insane eyes. Even Yusuf was taken aback. Kal roared a great, jubilant laugh.

Then, on Yusuf's face Shalima saw a new glow: the love of fame swiftly replaced by the ecstasy of a martyrdom shared with his hero.

"I am with you," shouted Suleiman. "I must be with you."

Jenny heard a deep-throated yell from the phone.

"What the fuck?!" exclaimed the man holding it. There was a gasp of horror among the watching group.

★

And that is when Shalima understood that the explosives must somehow still be live. She raised her pistol and, thirty centimetres in front of him, shot Suleiman in the forehead. A jet of his blood hit her in the face. He pitched forward, staggering, his left hand flailing. Davoud, dragged down, looked across at Kal's face. Kal stared, unbelieving, first at Suleiman stumbling and then at Shalima. Shalima just stood, stunned by what she had done. Kal raised his pistol and pointed it at her. Davoud turned his head towards Shalima and yelled something at her, simultaneously hurling himself at her, knocking her over, and dragging Suleiman with him so their bodies sprawled partially across Shalima's.

Kal aimed his pistol at both Davoud and Shalima. Their bodies jumped under the impact of the shots. Kal turned and raced back to the train.

Three pistol shots rang out.

Jenny jumped, heart thudding, head reeling, legs collapsing, grabbing the coat of a man next to her.

"What the fucking fuck?!" said the man with the phone.

"Oh my God!" groaned a woman.

"The film's stopped. Blank. Nothing."

"Jesus Christ!"

Still clinging to the coat of the man next to her, Jenny turned to the man with the phone. "Tell me, tell me what happened." Half-pleading, half-demanding, yelling.

"The family's safe. But there's three bodies on the track."

Jenny would have fallen if the man whose coat she was holding had not held her up.

Yusuf was already climbing the steps into the first carriage with only one purpose in mind, and Kal followed him. There, calmly waiting for him, the special phone lying on the tabletop in front of him, sat Benny.

"What happened?" asked Benny quietly. "I heard shots."

"Shalima killed Suleiman when he ordered us to blow up the nuclear fuel." The words snapped out, his voice trembling, a weird grin beneath wild eyes. "So that's what we do."

Yusuf grabbed the phone. "Allahu Akbar! We meet in Janna!" He looked out at the container which held the flask which contained the skip of nuclear fuel – and tapped in the key code.

Nothing happened.

The gull on the flatbed truck didn't move, just screamed again.

Benny raised his pistol from his lap and pointed it at Yusuf's face. The explosives were rendered safe, but he knew that Yusuf, in rage and frustration, would murder the hostages and him. The man was mad.

"It's all a lie," said Benny. "No good God could possibly want this for his creation, or you for his messenger."

He pulled the trigger. There was a deafening bang in the enclosed space. Yusuf fell back across the table and slithered to the floor, the phone sliding from his hand along the aisle, blood pouring from his shattered skull.

Bargo raced in, closely followed by Izzy and Kal. Ibra left the hostages, ran through and stood behind them.

Bargo looked down at Yusuf's body, half-slumped under the seat. Benny, his pistol on his lap, looked up calmly at the enraged Bargo. There was a smile on Benny's face.

Bargo jammed his pistol hard at Benny's temple, cupping his chin. "Where's the fucking phone, Benny?" he screamed.

Benny pointed to the floor. "Somewhere down there."

"Fucking get it for me." A menacing growl.

"It's over, Bargo," said Benny quietly, his eyes closed.

"Just fucking get it."

"OK." Benny opened his eyes and began to shift along the seat from the window to the aisle.

"Bargo," said Izzy, standing behind him. "I'll get it."

Bargo half-turned to Izzy, just too late to see Izzy's pistol swing down and smash into the side of his face. Bargo crumpled and fell onto Yusuf's dead body.

"What the fuck is happening?" yelled Kal. "What are you doing? You have betrayed Allah!"

But before Kal could do anything, Ibra, standing behind him, shot a bullet under his shoulder blade and into his heart. Kal collapsed to the floor.

Bargo, the side of his face smashed and bleeding, levered himself up onto one elbow. "Kill me, please," he pleaded.

"And send you to Paradise as a blessed martyr? Why should I do that? No, you pay, like us," said Izzy.

Bargo's head slumped.

Izzy, Benny and Ibra looked at each other.

Benny said, "The soldiers will be here very soon."

"No more killing," said Izzy.

Benny nodded. "There is no Paradise. Not this way. Not by killing innocent people."

"We free the hostages," said Ibra.

"And what after that?" asked Izzy. "We are taken prisoner and spend the rest of our lives in prison?"

"Or commit suicide," said Ibra.

"That is forbidden," said Izzy. "It is an affront to Allah. A suicide goes to Hell."

"Maybe not," said Ibra. "Allah decides."

"We must pay for our sins," said Izzy. A pause. "And I have children, I am a father. I must tell my children I was wrong."

"My wife and child were killed," said Ibra.

"Maybe," said Benny, "we can do some good. Make an anti-martyr video so people don't do what we have done."

Silence, except for a groan from Bargo.

"I'll tell them," said Ibra.

The six hostages, left on their own after Ibra raced out, had listened petrified to the gunfire and the yelling in the other carriage. The whole incident had lasted less than three minutes. Sitting stock-still, in shock, they looked up as Ibra entered. They expected to die.

"It is over," said Ibra. "You are safe. Free to leave." He stepped aside and smiled at them.

"Ladies first," said Geoff.

Saying nothing, with cramped limbs, not hurrying, they slid out from their tables and in an orderly line shuffled along to the door.

I'll make a mint out of this, thought Finlay suddenly: stories in the red tops, interviews on telly. He grinned. He fancied Emily more than ever: the passion of survivors.

At the door stood Benny and Izzy.

"Step down onto the line," said Izzy. "The soldiers will come to collect you." He handed his and Benny's pistols to Finlay and Geoff. "Our companions are dead."

Neither Finlay nor Geoff had ever handled a gun. They were surprisingly heavy.

The hostages stepped down onto the track, into the sunshine. Izzy and Benny followed, dragging the groaning Bargo with them. They lowered Bargo gently to the ground, then stood with their arms above their heads.

Benny said, "As you say, Izzy, now we begin to pay for our sins."

They heard a single shot from inside the hostage carriage.

"I could not do that," said Benny.

"Nor I," said Izzy. "A kind of bravery."

"Look!"

Everyone in the operations room now ignored the blanked Facebook screen and crowded round the screen which took the feed from the camera in the railwayman's hut at Arnside Station.

A procession formed in front of the train, to walk down the track towards the station: Izzy and Benny, holding Bargo, followed by Finlay and Emily self-consciously holding pistols. Then Joan and Muriel, Geoff and Paul.

The Lieutenant Colonel gave a sigh of relief. He clapped Tim on the shoulder. "Good call." His decisions had been right, by the grace of God. The whole ops room cheered and whooped.

In the COBRA meeting room in London there were handshakes, self-conscious clapping and vast relief.

"Over to you, Lieutenant Colonel," said Tim.

And the Lieutenant Colonel began to issue brisk instructions.

A squad of soldiers ran towards the waiting group from the station. They took charge of the terrorists. Emily and Finlay offered up their pistols.

Another squad ran from the Grange end of the viaduct and entered the train. Some paramedics escorted the hostages and others were already bent over the fallen figures of Suleiman, Shalima and Davoud on the track. Four explosives experts closely examined the flatbed truck with the flask of nuclear fuel. The two SAS Zodiacs roared up the narrow channel of the River Kent; the Wildcat Mk 1 helicopter was already hovering over the train.

In the ops room, the radio crackled. "There is another detonator connected to the flask. Now making safe. Three male terrorists dead on the train. On the track, the Al-Qaeda man is dead but the other two, our man and the female terrorist, are alive but with life-threatening bullet wounds. They need immediate, repeat immediate airlift to hospital together with the other injured terrorist."

"Davoud's alive!" shouted Tim, and the ops room cheered again. "But in a critical condition."

In a phone call to the Prime Minister, he conveyed all this information and it was agreed there would be a press conference at three o'clock, to be fronted by Tim and the Lieutenant Colonel. The bodies of Suleiman, Kal, Ibra and Yusuf were to be transported to the morgue in Lancaster.

Benny and Izzy were placed under close arrest pending transport to London. Bargo, Shalima and Davoud were flown by helicopter to the Royal Preston Hospital. The hostages were reunited with Laura, Noah and Daisy in the waiting room at Arnside Station. There were tears, laughter, tea and hot chocolate. Finlay took a chance and embraced Emily, who did not resist.

Jenny was neither jubilant nor relieved.

In the manager's office at Sainsbury's she sat holding a mug of hot tea, a plate of chocolate digestives untouched on the desk, her shopping in an orange Sainsbury's shopping bag. After the care and attention – "Can we phone anyone? Do you need a doctor? Can we get you a taxi?" – all she'd wanted was to be left alone for a few minutes.

She felt drained, numbed by the shock of it all. How close she and Davoud had come, how they had started to flourish together. The loss was terrible.

But she felt isolated in another way. She could not explain to anyone why she was so upset. She could not simply say, *He's my man, that man lying on the track up there*. It would lead to too many questions and complications.

But nor could she ask anyone what had happened. No one up there knew of her existence. She wouldn't have been vetted yet – Davoud would not have put her name forward: their relationship was too new. Could she go to a desk at MI5 headquarters – wherever that was – or the Home Office in Whitehall, say she was the girlfriend of Davoud Nariman and could they tell her what exactly had happened up there at Morecambe Bay? They would tell her nothing; she could be anyone.

She was disconnected, set apart.

What had the man with the phone said? Three bodies on the track – the Al-Qaeda man and two others? And Davoud was handcuffed to him?

Her eyes welled up with tears, but she gripped the chair arm, held herself in check.

The office door opened. "Are you all right?" the woman asked. "There's going to be a press conference at three o'clock. Thought you'd like to know."

Some information? Confirmation? Loss of hope?

"Thank you," Jenny managed to mutter.

"Stay as long as you like, no rush."

"Thank you again."

She looked at her watch: 1245. She had to get home, watch it at home, on her own. She would get a taxi; couldn't face the Tube.

1500

Two and a quarter hours later, Jenny sat at her kitchen table, hand wrapped round another warm mug of tea, watching the small TV on the cupboard top. Helpless, hopeless now. Dreading the neutral newsreader's voice speaking ordinary words which would confirm their sweet, promising love was over. His tentative smile, gentle hands, soft eyes.

The voiceover jerked her back to now. "And now we take you to the special news conference by Morecambe Bay."

Three men behind a desk packed with microphones – one in a military uniform, one in police uniform, and between them the other in a suit.

The civilian spoke: "We can confirm that all the remaining hostages are free and well. The nuclear fuel is safe. Three of the terrorists were found shot dead on the train. Two, uninjured, gave themselves up and are in custody. Two terrorists are in hospital: one, the female, is seriously wounded and in a life-threatening condition; the other has serious head wounds. The man, Davoud Nariman" – and here Jenny held her breath – "who volunteered himself to be exchanged for the family is in the Royal Preston Hospital. He is in a critical condition and is undergoing emergency surgery at this very moment. It does appear from our analysis of our video that he deliberately tried to save the life of the female terrorist after she killed Suleiman al-Hariri. We would like to thank all the emergency services and the public…"

But Jenny wasn't listening any more. Preston. She had to be there, with Davoud. There was hope. *He will live.* She would insist on it.

With extreme caution, the bomb disposal squad examined the explosives on the nuclear skip. They discovered the second phone wired to the detonator and hidden under the hardened foam. They disconnected the detonator. The two flatbed trucks and engines were searched for booby traps, but none were found and the train was declared safe. They searched the passenger train for further explosives but found none. They removed the rifles and pistols and declared that train safe, too.

A team of white-suited SOCOs carried out a forensic examination of the train once the medics had removed the bodies of Yusuf and Kal. Their bodies and that of Suleiman were taken by ambulance to the morgue in Lancaster.

A driver was brought in and the nuclear cargo train driven over the viaduct towards Sellafield. Soon afterwards the passenger train was driven away southwards. The viaduct was empty.

At the Arnside Educational Institute, surrounded by armed soldiers, the two surviving terrorists were isolated from each other, and the hostages debriefed. They wanted only to go home and be reunited with their families, to get showered and changed into clean clothes. Noah and Daisy relished being the centre of attention and ate all the ice creams they were given. Family members were given police escorts as they drove from the Furness peninsula to Arnside. Reporters, photographers and film crews were already flooding in past the redundant roadblocks.

The Home Secretary announced that residents were free to return. The PM, Home Secretary and Defence Secretary were relieved that the decision to free Suleiman had been vindicated, although not in the way they had planned. The PM ordered an enquiry into the safety and security arrangements of nuclear waste transport.

The men and women in the operations room also felt a huge wave of relief. They could not congratulate themselves for the success of the operation – no more hostage deaths, no nuclear catastrophe – because events had been taken out of their hands. Nevertheless, they were quietly satisfied with the arrangements they had made and with the cooperation between the services.

Jenny sat on the train north. Her mind was empty, not taking in the landscape or towns that rushed past the window. All her energy and willpower was focused on Davoud. She would help him live.

Hannah Walker had watched the events as they unfolded on her iPhone, in between carrying out her duties. She was thrilled at the small but vital part she had played.

41.
Two Days Later, Monday 11th October

The caretaker tore down the notice – *ALL ACTIVITIES CANCELLED UNTIL FURTHER NOTICE* – and now sat in his office grumbling to himself about the mess that had been left when the temporary chipboard flooring in the gym had been removed. He'd been given no extra help to put all the furniture back into its proper place. A Zumba class was due in this evening.

Jenny visited Davoud in Preston Hospital, holding his hand and waiting for the right time to ask him why he had wanted to save the female terrorist's life. When she opened the door of his private room, Davoud was embarrassed by the tears of happiness that filled his eyes. She kissed him, looked at his face, kissed him again and put her arms gently on his shoulders.

"My hero," she said, and Davoud couldn't tell if she was entirely serious. She had that half-smile. "When you get out of here, we're going on holiday together, just the two of us. Somewhere warm, with wine and a pool and good books to read, maybe a ramble or two."

Davoud squeezed her hand, and she kissed his fingers.

Dunia also visited and reassured him that Sara was fine and knew little of what her father had experienced. To Davoud's surprise, Dunia seemed genuinely concerned about him.

★

Finlay was the first to sell his story to the tabloids. The others followed, with the exception of Joan and Emily. Their stories were read avidly and no one begrudged them the good fees they earned. A TV documentary was planned, centring around the experiences of Laura, Noah and Daisy.

Bargo and Shalima remained on life-support machines in Preston Hospital. Izzy and Benny, now in Belmarsh Prison, were held in solitary confinement.

The Russian President Vlaskov announced how pleased he was that catastrophe had been averted, and that he and Russia were always ready to help fight terrorists across the globe.

Two Weeks Later

With the blessing of Network Rail, the Arnside Community Group made arrangements for a public walk across the viaduct. This had been a traditional New Year's Day activity until health and safety regulations had been used (as a pretext, they believed) to put a stop to it. The walk, on Sunday, would be a thanksgiving. All the ex-hostages agreed to attend, including Davoud Nariman (with a walking frame) and the daughter of Keith Walters, the murdered birdwatcher, specially flown in from Canada by the *Daily Mirror*.

Muriel and Joan discussed whether all the jihadists should be given the same sentence by the judge.

"Some saved our lives," said Muriel.

"But all were complicit in the murder of the birdwatcher," replied Joan.

The train driver hostage, Geoff Firth, and the ticket collector, Paul Robinson, were back on duty. Charlie Hopwood, the injured driver, was also back driving but had been excused any further involvement with nuclear waste trains.

The date of the trial of the taxi/delivery man and the others accused of grooming had been set. Hannah Walker had no doubts they would be found guilty and given long sentences.

In the kitchen of his father's London flat, Davoud spread greengage jam on two slices of toast for his father while, in the lounge, Jenny held his hand and turned the pages of his photograph album.

In Amman, Faysal Samara the baker finally gave in to his wife's pleas and retired, passing the business on to his son Latif. Feeling more melancholy than he felt he should be, he drank the mint tea his wife had made for him and slowly worked his way through a plate of dates.

Author's Note

Some of my family and friends will recognise ideas, observations and conversation which I have nicked from them. I am grateful.

In particular, I would like to thank Ian Plimmer who gave me great encouragement from the start; Tobias Neale for military information – any errors that remain are mine; my writing group – Mary, Muriel and Chris – who have been and still are critical friends.

And above all, my children – Alex, Joe and Kate – who have been my major motivators. I have this silly notion of trying to impress them!